IMPORTANT NOTE

As some of you may know, the first book in this duet, Haunting Adeline, was banned due to the warnings. But it is so necessary to have one. These are also available on my website.

This book contains very dark triggering situations such as graphic rape (these scenes are detailed, so please proceed with caution.) There is also graphic violence and gore, torture, sexual assault, kidnapping, psychological abuse, physical abuse, mental abuse, explicit sexual situations, human trafficking, slave trade, grooming, severe PTSD, and very particular kinks such as blood play, knife play, degradation, and somnophilia.

This book is significantly darker than the first. Please take these warnings seriously.
Your mental health matters.

AUTHOR'S NOTE:

If you are expecting a quick reunion, then this book isn't for you.

Don't worry, there's not any less spice.

Pinterest Board:

PLAYLIST

Story of the Year- Miracle

Sophie Simmons- Black Mirror

Klergy- No Rest for the Wicked

gavn!- Crazy

Bad Omens- The Death of Peace of Mind

A.A. Bondy- Skull & Bones

Echos- Saints

Jacqui Siu- Danger

Young Summer- Will It Ever Be The Same

MJ Cole & Freya Ridings- Waking Up

Skillet- Monster

Zero 9:36- Tragedy

Skylar Grey (feat. Eminem)- Kill for You

Aaron Camper- Hypnotizing

Gavin Haley- Sad Season

Glimmer of Blooms- Can't Get You Out of My Head

Ghostly Kisses- Spellbound

Echos- Guest Room

Red- Let It Burn

PART I

Let me go. Let me go. Let me go.
Pleasepleaseplease PLEASE

PLEASE PLEASE
PLEASE

FUCKING
LET ME
GO

Chapter One
The Diamond

S mell. The first of my senses to trickle in. I wish it were anything else because I'm instantly overwhelmed by the scent of body odor, spiced cologne, and what can only be described as the stench of evil incarnate.

And then my sixth sense seeps in, whispering notes of warning and urgency.

I'm in danger.

Those notes turn into a song full of screeching and loud noises, filling my body with heart-wrenching panic. Adrenaline spikes, and just barely do I have enough sense to remain as quiet as possible.

Slowly cracking open my crusted eyes, I'm greeted by complete darkness. It takes a second to process that there's a blindfold strapped around my head.

Then, the blissful numbness I awoke in crumbles, and I lose my breath when all-consuming pain filters in, engulfing my body in absolute agony.

God, is this what being alive feels like? It can't be death. I'd be at peace if it were. And I may have fallen for a stalker, but I'll be damned if I didn't land a spot within heaven's gates.

I fucking earned that shit.

Racking my brain, I try to think past the pain and remember what the fuck happened to me. Vaguely, I recall text messages from Daya asking me to come over. The urgency I felt when she wasn't answering my calls. Getting in my car, headlights, and panicking, being jerked forward, and then nothing.

And now I'm here… wherever that is. But not somewhere safe.

Christ, was that even Daya texting me? Did something happen to her too?

That possibility sends another wave of panic crashing through me. Scenarios curtail and evolve until I'm a mass of anxiety and desperation. She could be hurt or in serious trouble.

Fuck—*I'm* hurt and in serious trouble, and I've no idea how the fuck I'm going to get out of it.

My breathing is escalating further, and my heart is beating so heavily, it physically hurts as it slams against my chest. It takes what little strength I have left to keep silent.

Where the fuck am I?

Where's Zade?

Quiet, dull voices are next, muffled by the noise in my ears but steadily growing louder. I strain my ears, trying to hear over the beat of my heart and the pain swelling in my body like a water balloon.

Somehow the agony has a voice too, and it's fucking loud.

"Z will be looking for her," one man says quietly. "But we'll be fine once we get to Garrison's and chuck the van. We'll get her there quickly."

A particular memory knocks me over the head, flashes of being dragged out of my car and the residual pain of glass and metal biting through my skin. It explains why my back is on fire.

I've been fucking kidnapped—*obviously*. This had to have been the Society's doing. Zade had said they targeted me, and I know he had guards stationed outside of Parsons Manor. They must have used Daya to draw me out, which means there's a high chance she's been taken, too.

Fuck, I'm an idiot.

I didn't even stop to consider it could be a trap when Daya wasn't answering the phone. I was so intent on getting to her in case she was hurt or in trouble that it wasn't even a consideration to call Zade. Not only could it have saved me, but it also could have saved Daya, too.

I squeeze my eyes shut as a sob crawls up my throat. A tear slips through my lashes, and my chest shakes with exertion, trying not to break down. This was my own damn fault.

Zade warned me countless times they were after me, and the first trap they set, I walked right into.

You're such an idiot, Addie. Such a fucking idiot.

"You actually think we'll be able to hide her from him? It's fucking Z, man," another man responds, this one with a slight Hispanic accent.

"We're just giving the Society what they asked for. Which one are you more afraid of? Them or Z?"

Fuck, it *was* the goddamn Society. I knew it, but hearing it confirmed only sends a fresh dose of adrenaline into my system.

I don't know why I got tossed into this shit, but they need to take me out of this fucked-up salad of depravity; I don't belong here. I belong in a salad full of fruits and vegetables. Healthy things that don't run me off the road and enslave me.

The second man mutters, "I'd prefer not to fucking choose."

It sounds like a hand slapping someone's shoulder or back as if to reassure him. "Too bad you don't have a choice, Rio. Doesn't matter. This girl right here is worth millions. I mean, we got a fucking diamond here. Just imagine it, dude—Z's girl, the one and only, up on an auction stage. You know how many enemies he has? People will be frothing at the mouth to make his girl their little toy. I'll get my cut from Max, and the Society will compensate you, I'm sure. We'll be living fucking lavishly." He lets out a burst of hyena-like laughter. "I can buy my own goddamn private island after the money goes through!"

A shot of anger pumps into me at the man's callous words, speaking of me like I'm a house up for sale.

"Your idea of comfort must be different from mine. We'll have to go into hiding alongside her. At least while Z is still alive," the second man—Rio—responds. His name sounds familiar, and I think I faintly remember someone yelling his name after they ran me off the road.

"Don't worry, man. We'll get a head start with the ritual happening tonight, and I'm sure the Society will take out Z, one way or another. They'll protect us."

A derisive snort is the only response the first man gets.

Jesus Christ, I really am in deep trouble. Tears brim the corners of my eyes, and try as I might, no amount of trash talking keeps them from overflowing like rivers past the blindfold.

I barely manage to wrangle down the sob that's still threatening to spill, clawing its way up to the inside of my teeth.

Deep breaths, Addie. What did Zade teach you?

It takes several moments to collect my thoughts, but eventually, his voice filters in.

Leave evidence.

Gritting my teeth against the pain, I slowly grip strands of my hair and tug until they break free. The sharp pinpricks are inconsequential compared to the rest of my body.

I keep my movements minimal and slow. With the blindfold on, I've no idea if they can see me well. One movement out of the corner of their eye can alert them.

I wiggle my fingers until the strands loosen and fall away.

Just as I'm reaching for more hair, they hit a particular brutal bump in the road, and I can't keep the yelp from slipping free.

The pair hadn't been talking at that moment, but it felt like a crowded room just went deathly silent in a matter of seconds.

"Welcome to the land of the living, sweetheart," one of the men croons. It's the first guy who had referred to me as a diamond.

"Where are you taking me?" I ask, my voice raspy and hoarse.

"To your new home—well, temporary home," he corrects. "Whoever pays the most will provide you with your forever home." He chuckles as if I'm a dog about to be adopted into a loving family.

"Great," I croak. "Sounds like I've hit the jackpot."

One of them laughs humorlessly, but it sounds like Rio this time. "Hold on tight to that humor, baby girl. You're going to need it for where you're going."

Before I can open my mouth to respond, I feel a prick in my arm, followed by a burning sensation spreading throughout my veins.

I suck in a sharp breath. And it happens to be the last breath I take before darkness descends.

"Her vitals are unstable, and her blood pressure is dropping. We need to get her an IV."

I stir; the unfamiliar voice distorted beneath the ringing in my ears.

Agony blazes in every inch of my body, but it feels like I'm underwater, fighting to get to the surface yet kicking away from it because I just know the pain will only intensify. I'm encased in a shroud of fire, flames licking at my nerve endings, and the closer I get to consciousness, the brighter the flare.

There's a tiny prick in my arm, followed by muffled voices coming from different directions.

"Dislocated shoulder, head trauma, lacerations throughout her body." The man's voice fades out before cutting back in, a harsh shout that travels up my spine.

"Goddammit, Rio, this isn't a fucking hospital where I have the equipment I need. She could have internal bleeding right now, for all I know."

"Come on, man, she was fine just a bit ago," another answers, a note of concern in his tone. Rio's companion, I think.

"*Fine?* I have no way of knowing what kind of damage she took. It's evident she hit her head. She could be hemorrhaging and potentially die in seconds. You gonna find me a CT scanner?" When he's met with silence, a muttered, "Thought so," follows.

Darkness licks at the edge of my consciousness, threatening to drag me back under. I moan, and probing fingers pry my eyes open. A bright light flashes in them, but I hardly notice.

"Miss, can you tell me what hurts?"

An older man replaces the light, his face crowding over me. His image is blurry, but I can make out tufts of gray hair, a bushy mustache, and pale blue eyes.

I part my lips, but my tongue sticks to the roof of my mouth.

Jesus, what did they inject me with? Whatever it was, it's making me disoriented and dizzy.

"I know you're in a lot of pain right now, but I need you to tell me what hurts."

Everything. Everything fucking hurts.

"My… shoulder," I croak out finally. "My head."

"Anywhere else? Your chest or stomach?"

"Back," I gasp, remembering once more being dragged out of my car. My back feels as if it's been shredded with a cheese grater.

"That all?" he presses.

I nod my head, the incessant questions exhausting. A million other places hurt, too, but my energy is depleted, and I'm so very tired.

"I'm going to put you under anesthesia and get you fixed up, okay?"

Clarity surfaces over my surroundings, and the man's facial features sharpen. Along with another man standing behind him, who's shifting on his feet and watching us.

Time to go to sleep, princess.

Dark bottomless eyes and a wicked grin—Rio. He's the one who had dragged me out of the car. Flashes of that conversation elude me, but I know there was more to it. I can't think past the relentless pounding in my skull.

Just as my eyes were beginning to focus, my vision blurs once more, and my eyelids grow heavy. I can't fight the deep pull to just close my eyes.

I don't want to fight it. Not when it'll take me away from the pain.

Addie, baby, I need you to fight for me, okay? I need you to survive until I get to you.

"How badly is she damaged?"

The question stirs me out of the endless pit I've been drifting in, where only an illusion of Zade's voice lives. It's not real—his voice isn't actually there. But it feels so real. So soothing, that I fight to stay where I can hear him.

"How badly do you think? You ran her off the road."

Alongside the angry response is a swell of dull pain pulsing throughout my body. I hear a sigh, and then the older man continues.

"She'll have a few scars along her back from the glass. You're lucky they were fairly clean, so the scarring won't be too terrible."

"That'll decrease her value," a voice mutters, too low to discern who said it.

"Shut the fuck up, you're getting paid regardless. The fuck you care for?"

"Uh, maybe because your dumbass mistake is risking my *life?* Jesus, Rio, I knew she was banged up but not *this* bad."

Whatever Rio was going to say, it's cut off by the unfamiliar voice— the one who must be the doctor.

"She has thirty stitches between the two larger lacerations because she was dragged across sharp metal and glass. You couldn't have expected that not to cause permanent damage," he says, clearly taking Rio's companion's side.

"*Goddammit,* Rio. You do realize that might be coming out of my fucking pocket, right? I asked for your help, not for you to fuck it all up for me."

"How the fuck did you expect me to get her out, huh? Lift the car like I'm fucking Superman and roll it off so I can carry her out like some hero?" Rio spits.

My chest seizes. The roughness of his tone feels like scratching nails on a chalkboard. I've awoken to *that* damn voice too many times now. And each time is a stark reminder that I've been pulled down into a nightmare and haven't found my way out yet.

"If you hadn't hit the car so fucking hard, none of this would be happening, you piece of shit."

"If *you* hadn't been so fucking doped up and screaming in my ear, then you could've been the fucking driver like you were *supposed to be.*"

"Gentlemen, let's take a breather. She's awake. Her blood pressure is rising."

My breath stills, but I don't bother pretending. Slowly, I open my eyes to see three men surrounding me, staring at me as if I'm a lab rat in an experiment.

A very fucking horrible experiment.

My eyes clash with a dark pair first. Nearly black and lifeless from the lack of warmth. Tattoos cover his light brown skin, the laurel leaves on either side of his throat snagging my attention first. He's wearing a zipped-up leather jacket, but black ink swirls on his hands and up to each of his fingers, indicating he's most likely covered in them. He has sharp angular features, arched thick brows, along with a scar cutting through the side of his closely cropped black hair, completing his near-feral appearance. He'd be attractive if he didn't look like he'd rather see me dead.

My gaze moves to the man next to him; he's grungy-looking with scabs on his face from apparent drug use. A mop of greasy hair covered by a backward ball cap, a dirty wife-beater, and pants too big. I recognize him as the other man who kidnapped me.

Finally, I look over to the third man—who I assume to be a doctor. Gray hair, blue eyes, a bushy mustache, and wrinkles disturbing the otherwise smooth expression on his face. His stare is softer, matching the tenor in which he speaks. But something is off about him. A deep, penetrating vibe that I can't quite place.

I look away, a cold tremor settling deep in the marrow of my bones. The dull, throbbing pain is growing sharper but still not nearly as potent compared to when I awoke in that van. Whatever painkillers they pumped into my system must be fading, and I'm not above begging for more.

All of my muscles ache so profoundly that I feel as if a hard shell has molded around my bones. I'm incredibly stiff, and every movement twinges.

Breathing through the aches, I glance around. I'm in a darkened, white room. It's… sterile in here. Not clean like a hospital, which is where I expected to be, but we're not in a dungeon, either.

I'm not sure why I even expected that.

Dirty white walls, concrete flooring, and silver cabinets line nearly every wall in the room. Next to the hospital bed is a large metal table with a bowl and various instruments laid out on a bloody cloth.

Different sorts of machines are placed throughout the room. While I don't recognize most of them, the beeping device next to me monitoring my vitals is familiar, along with the IV that leads directly into my arm.

The doctor grabs a Styrofoam cup from the table next to my bed and hands it to me.

"Drink slowly," he instructs.

Shakily, I grab the cup and sip on it. The cold water feels like dumping ice on a burn. Painfully relieving.

Scratchy, white blankets cover me up to my waist, and when I look down, I notice I'm in nothing but a light blue gown.

Somehow, that's the worst part. They can see the evidence of just how cold it is in here.

Noticing where my eyes are trained, the doctor speaks up. "I do apologize for your clothing. I had to cut them off of you so I could properly treat you and assess the damage you've suffered."

"You can thank Rio for that," the grungy man mutters under his breath. Plenty loud enough for me to pick up on through the near-constant fear steadily swirling in my bloodstream.

"Shut the fuck up, Rick," Rio snaps back, his accent deepening with fury. "Or I will kill you myself, and unlike your precious diamond, no one will miss you."

This... this is a terror unlike anything I've ever felt before. It's nothing like the fear Zade invoked in me, and definitely not a cheap thrill I get from haunted houses and scary movies. This is what it feels like when you're well and truly fucked.

The monitor betrays my body, the beeping increasing until the doctor glances at it with concern.

I scarcely remember the events after they sent my car rolling. However, I do vaguely recall Rio's face hovering over me after he dragged me out of the car, his mouth moving but his words evading me. All except six.

Time to go to sleep, princess.

"Where am I?" I whisper and then cough, clearing some of the phlegm from my throat.

"At the fucking Ritz-Carlton, princess. Where do you think?" Rio snaps, his features still tight with anger.

Rick looks at him with an accusatory expression on his pock-marked face, but otherwise, he keeps his mouth shut, clearly taking Rio's threat seriously.

It's obvious Rio fucked up, and there's a part of me that hopes they kill him for it.

"My name is Dr. Garrison," the gray-haired man introduces, deliberately stepping in front of Rio. Swallowing, I stay silent. If the creep expects me to give him my name as if we're in a fucking interview, then he can shove the IV pole up his ass.

"How are you feeling?" he asks, taking a step closer. I bristle, and before I can tell him precisely what I'm feeling, he powers on, seeming to sense my incoming smart-ass response. "I imagine a headache. Any nausea?"

I tighten my lips. Probably for the best that he diverted the questioning. My mouth is only going to get me killed if I let it run wild.

I'm not going to get away with that like I did with Zade—though I'd still consider 'getting away with it' subjective. Even when he first made himself known and terrified the absolute shit out of me, there was always an odd sense of security in pushing his buttons, as if deep down, I knew Zade would never truly hurt me. Something that only makes sense now that he's managed to worm his way into my life.

The man is incredibly dangerous… to everyone else but me. Even when he had a loaded gun pointed in my direction and used it for more than just a weapon.

But these men? Not only would they hurt me, but they would kill me, too.

"Nausea," I clip, my voice still hoarse. Dr. Garrison begins fiddling with the IV, replacing the empty fluid bag with a new one. I hope it's morphine.

I drain the rest of the water in my cup, yet it does little to acquiesce the perpetual dryness in my throat. No matter how many times I lick my chapped lips, there's never enough moisture.

"You have a pretty nasty concussion. Which means we'll have to monitor you closely. I want to ensure you receive no further damage." He shoots the pair a nasty look, and I get the feeling this is something they already argued over.

My mouth moves on autopilot, opening and readying to tell him not to waste his time—the two other men will ensure that my body endures plenty of more damage.

Sensing my intent, Rio snips, "I dare you." His voice is stern and threatening, drawing my attention to him. "Your pussy will still work regardless, even if you've got brain damage."

My mouth snaps closed, and I avert my gaze back to Dr. Garrison. His lips flatten into a white line, seemingly not impressed with Rio's crude words.

Keep your mouth shut, Addie. We just went over this, dumbass.

"You've experienced extensive trauma, and despite what anyone says—" he gives Rio a nasty look— "we need you in tip-top shape."

They need me in shape so that I will be worth something. But I don't argue, not when it benefits me. Healing means gaining the energy to flee.

Licking my lips, I ask, "What day is it?"

"You really think that's important?" Rick barks. "You don't get to ask questions."

I struggle not to mouth back. My lips tremble with the urge to impart nasty, hateful words to spew past them. But I manage to refrain.

"It's Thursday," Dr. Garrison answers anyway, ignoring the filthy look from the grungy man.

Thursday…

It's been five days already since the car accident.

Zade would be looking for me by now. Most likely out of his mind and on a rampage… Jesus, he's probably going to kill a lot of people. No, he *definitely* is. And when a grin begins to form, I know that man has well and truly corrupted me.

"Something funny?" Rick asks. I squash the grin and shake my head, but all I can think is that even though I may die, so will all of them. And their end is going to be so much worse than mine.

As the fantasies take root in all the ways Zade will wreak havoc, my eyelids begin to grow heavy, and fatigue weighs down the little burst of adrenaline I was running on.

The three men watch me closely, and even in my concussed, broken state, I don't need a scientist to tell me that whatever he drugged me with, it's not morphine.

My eyes land on Rio, and my lids involuntarily close before I force them open. His lips quirk up at the sides, dry amusement swirling in those dark pits.

"Time to go to sleep, princess."

June 8th, 2008

What did I fucking do to deserve ~~this~~? I'm twenty years old. TWENTY YEARS OLD. And now I'm going to die. Jesus. And all I can think about is what will happen to my little sister. Mom couldn't take care of her if her life depended on it. Fucking ~~FUCK~~, my sister is going to die too.

Knowing that, that hurts so much more than what these men do to me. Than what Francesca does to me.

It's physical. They don't have the power to break me mentally when I'm already fucking broken.

Molly

Chapter Two
The Hunter

I t's not very often that people surprise me.

I expect the worst from everyone, even myself. *Especially* myself.

But when that voice registers through the fog of agony clouding my head, all I can feel is astonishment and the cold press of metal in the back of my skull.

"Glad you could figure that out, Jason Scott. Now let's see those hands, otherwise, this single bullet will find its way in both of your fucking heads."

The exact feeling is reflected on Jay's face as his features slacken and eyes widen, his voice saturated with utter bewilderment as he mouths, "*You?*"

"Yes. Me."

Mother… fucker.

My mind races, circulating through each encounter with her and trying to figure out how the fuck I missed this—missed her being a wolf in sheep's clothing.

She played her part pretty fucking well.

"This really hurts my feelings, you know," I say through clenched teeth, the muscle in my jaw pulsating.

"Why do I get the feeling that you'll get over it?"

A man's tortured scream rings out from someplace to my left, the heavy smoke concealing him.

A bomb went off somewhere, blasting me back into the stone altar they used for their sacrificial rituals. I've no idea what the fuck kind of damage I took, but if the increasing pain in my entire body is anything to go by, I need to get to a hospital.

And I don't need a fucking fortune teller to inform me that getting help is not in my near future.

The man-made underground cave we're in is still swarmed with chaos, wails of agony and terror bouncing off the stone walls, worsening the pounding in my skull.

This hellhole is where the Society sacrifices children. Some type of initiation in order to be welcomed into a club that provides them with an ample number of innocents to rape and murder.

Leaked videos surfaced on the dark web, the first one being nine months ago. Since then, I have worked day and night to get into this ritual.

And I finally did.

But evidently, the Society saw me coming and planned for my arrival.

Dan—the man who got me in—had mentioned they caught the culprit who was leaking the videos.

I was too distracted to realize the trap when another video popped up on the web afterward. A video that was intentionally uploaded, knowing that I'd see it and find my way into the club. They were drawing me in so they could take me out.

"You cost me a little girl, Z," the bitch says from behind me.

"Sounds like you knew that was a risk," I counter, a tad breathless. It hurts to even fucking breathe, and the pain is growing by the second.

The little girl who was offered up to me and three other men on the altar had been taken out of here, hopefully before the explosion. I entrusted her safety with one of my men, Michael, and I haven't heard from him yet.

"Both of you—up. You're coming with me."

"I may be a tad fucked up at the moment, but don't expect me not to kill you the first chance I get," I warn, nearly groaning when my back spasms. Fuck me, more than anything, I wish this shit were like in the movies where getting blasted by a bomb and proceeding to save the world directly after was possible.

"You're not going to do that, Z. You want to know why?"

I freeze, a sinking feeling already forming in the pit of my stomach. It's like the mouth of Jaws just opened up, and my heart is the unsuspecting swimmer about to get swallowed whole. She better not say what the fuck I think she's going to say, or I'm going to lose my shit.

My voice is deadly calm as I say, "I swear to everything that is holy, I will destroy you if you touched my girl."

Her answering silence speaks volumes, and everything goes black. My vision snuffs out, and a tsunami of rage crashes through me. I clench my fists, fighting to regain control of myself.

"Zade."

Urgency gnashes at my patience, screaming at me to get up and find my little mouse. I need to get to her now before they take her too far.

"*Zade.*"

Who knows how far they've taken her already? How badly they've hurt her.

My body locks tight from the thought, images flashing through my head of what they could be doing to her. If they touch her...

"Fuck, ZADE! Look at me, man."

Jay's voice finally registers, but I can't see him. I can't see *anything*.

The gun is pressed harder into my head as a warning. I don't remember moving, but I'm on my knees now, my spine straight as I stare ahead. Seeing nothing but a vision of ripping this bitch's body apart, limb by limb, with my fucking teeth.

"Stay down," she hisses from behind me.

"Let me... fuck, he's going to do something stupid," Jay rushes out, voice pitched in panic. Pain explodes on the side of my head from a fist flying into my temple. My sight comes rushing back in, my right-hand man's face appearing, his hazel eyes inches away.

"Get it fucking together," he barks through gritted teeth. The vein on his temple pulsates, sweat pouring down his red face.

My hand is wrapped around the barrel that's firmly digging into my head, seconds away from pulling it from her grip.

"Let it go," Jay orders sharply. "You're lucky you don't have a goddamn bullet in your head right now. You can't kill her yet."

"I'd like to see you try," she spits, nudging the gun. Setting my jaw, I release it and rest my hands on my knees. My muscles are vibrating so hard—so fast; my body appears to be still. But I can feel every tremor as she continues, "You may think you're powerful, but whatever scraps of power you have are insignificant to mine. I can make you disappear, and no one will ever have known you existed at all."

I snarl, on the precipice of demonstrating just how wrong she is, but keep my teeth glued together for the time being. Jay's right. She's holding a gun to the back of my head and can end my life in a matter of seconds. A bullet is faster than me, and I have no doubt she would make good on her threat and kill Jay next.

Closing my eyes, I inhale deeply and bring myself to a scary place I've rarely had to go in my lifetime. Numbness spreads, and tranquility replaces the white-hot rage. My mind goes silent, and when I reopen my eyes, Jay's spine snaps straight.

Whatever he sees unnerves him.

I need to get out of this situation in order to find Addie. Only then, will I be more than happy to show this cunt exactly what I'm capable of. This world will fucking smolder, and I will hold her face in the fire and watch her melt in my wrath.

"Did you take her?" I ask. I know she did, but I need to hear the confirmation from her mouth anyway.

I feel her hot breath fan across my ear, followed by her soft, mocking voice. "I did. I took her, and I'm going to sell her only to the ones with the sickest desires. And you can't do a thing about it."

One thing I've grown to loathe since forming Z—I have an incredibly vivid imagination. In this field of work, it's a curse. Every time I see a new video posted on the dark web or get intel on a new ring—the first thoughts that come to mind are all the depraved, sick things being done to these women and children.

My own mind tortures me with those images. And later, I'll be plagued by them, except it'll be my girl they're hurting.

But now? I'm fucking glad for it.

Because at this very moment, I am enjoying all of the ways I'm envisioning how I will kill Claire Williams.

"So," I start, grunting when a particularly painful twinge flares in my back. "Mark was never your abuser, was he?"

She titters. "Oh, he was. He just didn't know what it meant for him every time he laid his hands on me. Idiot never did figure out I was the one pulling all the strings. He was too stupid."

She circles Jay and me, the gun still pointed at my head while her red lips pull into a snarl. The color staining her mouth rivals her hair. Such a bright red that curls around her face and robed shoulders. During the ritual, she was the mystery person in the hood, offering me a knife that she knew damn well I would never use on that little girl. Instead, it went into another's throat.

"That's the best thing about the male species. You all are so far up your own asses, you never thought it could be a woman in charge. Never suspected the meek, abused wife because you all assumed I was *weak*."

I huff out a dry laugh. "Wrong. I didn't suspect the abused wife only because I couldn't imagine one victim actively victimizing other innocent women and children."

She smiles wickedly and bends at the waist, leveling her green eyes with mine.

"And I can't imagine a man that puts his life on the line to save these victims forcing an innocent woman into a relationship."

She assesses me closely while I stare at her, searching for any emotion. I only give her one—I tip my head back and laugh.

"Have you been stalking me, Claire?" I ask with mirth, meeting her glare once more.

Her lips tip up further. "We're all hypocrites, Z," she says, ignoring my taunt and straightening. "The only difference between you and me is that I chose to profit off of the pathetic men in this world. They're never going to stop abusing those they deem weaker. And they'll never stop raping and killing them. So, I decided that if that's the world we're going to live in, then I'll be damned if I don't gain something from it."

I smooth out my face, only clenching my teeth when the twinge in my back worsens.

Fuck. I really need a hospital.

But I need Addie more.

"You could do so much good in your position," Jay fumes, disgust twisting his features. "You have immense power. And you choose to feed into the patriarchy rather than *changing* it."

She snarls, whipping the gun to him and pressing it into his temple. Jay stiffens, but he doesn't cower. My muscles lock, the throbbing pain fading as I watch her finger dance over the trigger.

If she pulls that trigger... I will crush her throat beneath my boot before that bullet finishes passing through Jay's brain.

"You're wrong." She looks at me. "Let's say you did destroy all the rings, Z. Let's say you accomplished what you've set out to do. Do you honestly believe, for one second, it'll *stay* that way? Ha! The second the dust settles, evil will already be rebuilding their empire, this time stronger and better than before." She stares at Jay and me as if we're delusional.

"You'll *never* get rid of evil. Never."

She's not wrong, but that doesn't mean I can't put a massive dent in the cesspool of rotten souls and create a power vacuum. I'm not under any delusions that I'll be able to erase human trafficking in my lifetime completely. But that was never the fucking point. Saving these girls—these children—and giving as many of them a second chance at life as I can *is* the goddamn point.

My plan has always been to dismantle the government's shady control of the people and their hand in the skin trade. That alone will make a significant difference in the world.

It will be an ongoing battle long after I'm gone. The sun will explode, and the earth will deteriorate before a perfect world ever exists. Humans will kill themselves off before that can happen.

But Z? Z isn't going anywhere, even when I'm buried six feet under. I will raise a generation to take over, and they will do the same.

Claire looks over her shoulder then, and I notice a man approaching with a deep hood over his head. I can only tell his gender because he's built like an upside-down Eiffel Tower. Massive, broad shoulders stretching the robe, the seams nearly bursting, and then dramatically tapering down into chicken legs.

Dickhead skipped leg day so often that he can't even see them anymore because they're so skinny.

"Car is ready," he announces, his voice deeper than the Mariana Trench.

Claire faces me, lowering her gun as the man's raises, and flicks her pointer finger up and down.

"Up," she snaps, her tone sharp. "Now."

Blowing out a steady breath, I force myself to move, gritting my teeth from the aches in my body.

Grunting, I stand fully and train my glare on the red-headed snake before me. She's brave enough to meet my gaze head-on without an iota of fear. I'm sure she's used to men looking down on her, intimidating in nature. But Claire has never dealt with a man like me.

"What do you think you're going to do with me?" I challenge, staring at her with condescension like you would a small child who believes they can win an arm-wrestling match against you. "I'm a lot to handle, Claire."

Her lips tip up in a secretive smile, unconcerned as she draws near, a display to show me how unafraid she is.

"Patrick here will be taking you to our interrogation room. We're going to ask you some questions." She pats my cheek, returning the condescension. "You'll be useful and give us all the information we need. How your organization operates and the illegal technology you use, along with all the intel you've collected in your years as a terrorist. And then, I will make you watch your little girlfriend with her new master before I kill you myself."

I stretch my lips into a feral smile, baring my teeth as I lean in and show her exactly why she should be very fucking afraid.

"Better make sure those ropes are extra tight," I growl. Her eyes round at the corners, a hint of fear flashing as quick as lightning. Bitch may be ice fucking cold, but that doesn't make her immune to my fire.

"Lead the way," I encourage, gesturing before me. Claire looks me up and down, a scowl forming on her face at my superior tone. She's gotten used to people sniveling at her feet and bowing to her commands like metal beneath a torch.

She has yet to learn that I've never been just a man.

With a sniff, she turns and walks away, making a point to keep her back turned as if to prove a point. I've never needed to acquire fear in order to kill, but I don't mind teaching lessons. Addie can attest to that.

Jay's stare is searing into the side of my face, a panicked look radiating from his hazel eyes. He doesn't need to say the words; his expression says it all.

We're going to die.

Not if I have anything to fucking do with it. I have too much to lose that's worth far more than my own life.

Her chicken-legged companion, Patrick, allows us to pass before he falls into step behind us.

"Try not to stare at my ass," I drawl.

He growls and nudges me forward with a meaty hand, his gun poised in his other hand threateningly. Slowly, I twist my head to stare at him over my shoulder, eyes wild and a grin I can't feel on my face.

"Shut up and walk," he snaps, but his voice betrays him, wobbling at the last word. How hard it must be to feign bravery beneath the stare of a heinous monster with a malicious smile.

The smoke is beginning to thin. Bodies are strewn across the cave, an ocean of blood soaking into the rock. Following Claire, my foot knocks against a severed arm, the limb rolling directly into a decapitated head, the man's face frozen in terror.

The howls of pain are slowly fading as the mortalities grow, and I can't help but marvel at the fact that the Society sacrificed their own people's lives just to ensure that I would be caught. That speaks volumes.

Not only am I a threat, I am catastrophic.

Claire leads us to the door that she disappeared out of after handing me the knife. From the quick sweep of the room, I hadn't seen any of my own men, but that doesn't mean that they're not mixed in and possibly dead.

My chest tightens, hoping that's not the case. They understand the risks, but their deaths would be another responsibility to shoulder.

We follow her down a dimly lit hallway, an exact replica of the one I entered the cave through. Strips of LED lights line either side, giving off an ominous glow against the black walls and tiles.

This hallway steeply inclines upward now that we're coming from underground. It feels like climbing a mountain with the way my body aches.

Jay walks stiffly beside me, periodically glancing at me with fear and anxiety. It's clear that he's never been in a dangerous situation like this before. He's always behind the computer, never on the front lines. I don't know how to assure him. I've never been one to lie, and while I'm confident I'll get us out alive, I can't guarantee it.

In a matter of minutes, Claire is pushing open the door and leading us out into a dark alleyway, scarcely lit by the moonlight and a streetlamp at the end. The sweat gliding down the sides of my face is instantly cooled by the brittle, Seattle air.

Claire wastes no time leading us toward a nondescript black van waiting at the mouth of the lane, its tinted windows so dark that you couldn't see through it even if your face was smashed against the glass. Incredibly fucking illegal, but those license plates will prevent them from getting pulled over. They would only need to see Claire's name to look the other way.

The closer we get to the vehicle, the more Jay stiffens.

I lean closer to his ear. "Just think of Claire as your fairy godmother, and this is the pumpkin carriage that's going to whisk you away off to your princess."

"Or prince," Jay corrects through gritted teeth. He's sweating profusely and his eyes are dilated. "I wouldn't mind either."

I shrug. "As long as you still make me Uncle Z."

He scoffs, peering over at me as if I'm cracked. "You seriously think I'm going to have kids after seeing this shit every day?"

I shrug a shoulder again, pursing my lips. "Why not? Uncle Z will keep them safe. I can be their personal bodyguard. They may not like it, but I'll fucking do it."

He shakes his head, the tiniest of smiles tipping up his lips, understanding precisely what I'm doing.

I'm giving him a future. Painting a picture of him surviving and finding happiness, whether he decides to breed mini gremlins or not.

As we step off the curb and approach the black van, the back double doors open wide. Claire turns and nods her head towards the dark interior, indicating for us to get in.

Shooting her a wink, I make my way into the depths of the van with Jay close behind, her irritated huff following us in.

If this were anyone else, I'd tell them not to antagonize their kidnapper. In fact, knowing that Addie is in the same exact situation right now, I'd spank her ass if I knew she was being reckless. The smartest thing to do is keep your fucking mouth shut and listen to orders until you find a way out.

But putting Z in the back of a van will never be the same as putting an innocent civilian in it. For now, I can rely on the fact that they won't kill Addie. She's worth too much. And seeing my situation laid out in front of me, I am even more confident Claire isn't going to win this round.

She may be smart, but she wasn't smart enough to knock my ass out. That could've given her a solid chance.

I sit down on the cold metal bench, gritting my teeth against the pain, and train my feral gaze on Claire again. She stands right outside the doors, staring at me with a slight grin. Her tight red curls are glaring beneath the streetlamp, and for a moment, she appears innocent. She looks like a woman who has endured years of abuse in all forms and just wants to live a life in peace.

But the mirage shatters and all I see is a woman who became everything she hates.

She shoots a loaded look of warning my way, then slams the doors shut, triggering LED lights rimming either side of the floor to flicker on.

Jay settles on the bench across from me, immediately putting on the seatbelt attached to the van wall, while Patrick sits next to me. So close that he is practically sitting in my lap.

My eyes drift to him, a blank expression on my face. "You don't want to get in a swordfight with me, Patrick. I promise I'll win," I deadpan, glancing down between his legs.

Jay hisses at me to shut up, but I don't tear my gaze away from where I feel his eyes hiding within the deep hood.

"You don't know when to keep your mouth shut, do you?"

"What'd I say?" I ask, feigning innocence. "I thought that was your intent with the way you're sitting in my lap."

"It's going to be hard to get in a swordfight if you have no sword to speak of," he retorts, his tone dipped in malice.

I arch a brow, unimpressed with his threat. "Even with a chainsaw, it takes time to cut through a tree trunk. You'll be dead before you get that far."

"Keep talking," he snaps, daring me.

I smirk, but keep my mouth shut. If Jay weren't here, I would continue to antagonize him. It would be my goal for him to attack me and hopefully pull a weapon on me. Thus, presenting me with the perfect opportunity to disarm and kill him instead.

But it's possible he'd turn the gun on Jay, and I won't risk his life in place of my own, so I'll bide my time for now. Patrick is going to die. And very soon.

The engine rumbles to life, the metal vibrating beneath my ass. The vehicle surges forward, causing the three of us to sway heavily to the side, forcing Patrick further against me.

We look at each other, and slowly, he slides a few inches away.

That's what I fucking thought.

Now that the mouth breather has removed itself from my neck, I can actually think.

But it only takes seconds for my thoughts to nosedive, the deadened space I forced my mind into fading away, and that black rage resurfacing.

They took my little mouse.

I squeeze my eyes shut and bow my head, fighting to regain control over my temper. The fragile layer of resolve containing my anxiety and murderous rage is cracking. My panicked thoughts are too heavy, and just like a person standing on thin ice, it's eventually going to break beneath the pressure.

But I can't let it. Not yet.

I need to focus on getting us out, and it's hard enough with my body screaming at me.

There's the option of attacking and killing Patrick, but that won't stop the vehicle, especially if they hear me attempting to escape. The only alternative would be shooting the gun off until I hit the driver, which could send us careening into traffic and killing us all. Or Jay and I could attempt to drop and roll out of the back, except my body is too battered to withstand that.

Exhaling through my nose, I lift my head to find Jay already staring at me, brows knitted with concern. His black hair is matted to his forehead with sweat, and he's shaking like a leaf. He's definitely not fit for a mercenary life.

Fuck, that's it.

Jay's panic and my agony have made us both forget a very valuable tool. There are Bluetooth chips still in our ears. They're tiny and transparent, an illegal device that isn't noticeable unless you're really looking for it. So unnoticeable, that Claire hadn't even thought to check.

The device in our ears is activated by a tiny button or a voice command. But that means Jay or I have to use the word *call*.

I train my gaze on Patrick. "So, am I going to get my one call when we get there?"

He grunts. "Funny."

Silence.

Fuck, it probably got damaged by the explosion. Explains why my men haven't attempted to get a hold of me themselves. I cast a look to Jay, and he nods, a drop of sweat flinging off the tip of his nose.

"Come on, man, my grandma is sick. She's probably wondering where I am." I face Jay again. "Didn't you promise your brother that you'd take him to *Chuck E. Cheese* tonight?"

Jay works to keep his face neutral, but that's another reason he stays behind the screen. Kid can't act worth shit.

"Yeah, uh… I should probably uh, *call Baron* and tell him I can't make it."

Make it a little more obvious, Jay, dear lord.

Baron isn't actually Jay's brother, but another of my men that could help us.

A little satisfied smirk tilts Jay's lips, but he smothers it. The call must've been successful, which means Baron will be listening in and hopefully track us once he realizes something is wrong.

Jay continues after a few moments, "It's probably important he knows that we're being held *hostage*, right?"

Oh my God.

"I'd prefer he never know what happened to you and live the rest of his life wondering," Patrick retorts, oblivious to Jay's terrible acting.

Then, he turns to me. "You can keep playing your games, but you won't be laughing soon."

"How soon?" I counter.

I can't see his face, but I can feel the confusion radiating from the black hole in his hood.

"My grandma is waiting."

His fist clenching is my only warning before he sends it soaring into my cheek.

My head snaps to the side, and pain blooms across my entire skull. The punch would be tolerable on a typical day, but considering that I just suffered through an explosion, it feels like another bomb has been let off inside my head.

My instincts flare, and my fists clench with the need to hit him back. The beast inside my chest is thrashing and raging, and that precarious control slips a little more.

Addie. It's for Addie.

Just barely, I manage to refrain. I need to give our men time to get to us, though I know it won't take long.

"*Jesus*, a man can't call his fucking grandma? Asshole."

He shakes out his shoulders and turns away, and I scoot further down the bench. He can think it's because I'm scared, but in reality, I'm two seconds away from ending his life prematurely.

While we wait, I work to decompress, keeping the boiling anger in check. That lasts a whopping ten minutes before I'm getting thrown for the second time today.

Something heavy crashes into the van from behind, sending Patrick and me flying off the bench and into the wall that separates the front from the back.

Jay is jerked to the side, but the seatbelt keeps the lucky son of a bitch anchored.

I groan, pain flaring in several different parts of my body as I roll onto my back and try to breathe. I can't even tell which parts hurt anymore—fucking *everything* hurts.

Claire yells from the front seat, spitting demands at the driver to get the vehicle under control. The van continues to swerve side-to-side, the driver unable to regain control.

Another hit and the van lurches to the side and crashes into something solid. Patrick collides into me, colorful words spilling from my mouth as we slide towards Jay. My back slams into the wall as we come to a halt, the behemoth smashed up against me. My ears ring from the impact, and it takes several seconds to get my eyes to focus. Patrick may be disproportionate as hell, but he's still really fucking heavy.

"Jay, tell me it's who I think it is," I grit out, taking advantage of the chaos and wrapping my arm around Patrick's neck in a steel-tight grip. His hands fly to my arm, clawing at me as I gradually crush his windpipe. He struggles, and I clench my jaw as I fight to keep him still.

I'm weak, in an insurmountable amount of pain, and my muscles are loosening.

"Sure is," he pants, sweat pouring down his pale face.

"Good," I mutter before gripping Patrick's head and snapping it to the side, breaking his neck and killing him instantly. "That's for my grandma, dick."

"Bro, none of your grandparents are still alive."

June 10th, 2008

They drugged me. I only know the date because the pedos are coming on the 20th. And Francesca said I have 10 days to get my act together. Stop the unroolines or however you spell it. It's the last word I remember before they stuck a needle in my arm. If they thought that was going to keep me from escaping, well **GUESS WHAT FRANCESCA** I'm getting the fuck out of here.

Going back to get my sister.

And getting us the hell out of this stupid ass, pediphile state.

Fuck all of you.

Molly

Chapter Three
The Hunter

Claire is screaming from upfront to keep driving, but the engine stalls.

I kick Patrick's dead body off of me and stand, perspiration coating my skin. I'm point-two seconds away from passing the fuck out. My body is beginning to shut down from the physical trauma, but I can't allow it to just yet.

Jay quickly unbuckles and stands. "Come on, they're waiting for us," he urges, noting the state of duress I'm in.

"I need to take care of Claire," I say, but that notion dies the second we bust open the van doors. Other cars have already stopped on the side of the road, getting out of their vehicles to check on us.

Fuck.

I can't kill a woman in front of civilians, no matter how tempted I am.

Just as Jay and I crawl out, Claire emerges from the passenger side, a wild look on her face.

"Don't you *dare*," she hisses through her teeth. Red lipstick stains them, giving her a feral look.

"Or what?"

When she has no answer, I shoot her a wink just to get her asshole clenching from anger, and head towards the huge military-grade van waiting for me.

"Hey, man, you good?" a passerby asks.

"Yep, all good. Thanks for stopping," I say over my shoulder. The bright headlights from his car highlight the incredulous look on his face as he watches me climb into the open doors.

Michael's face greets me, and I nearly sigh in relief. If he's alive, that means the little girl we saved from the ritual is, too.

He leans forward and helps me in, assumingly noticing the agony painted on my face. I can feel my scars tightening, now incapable of concealing the misery. My poker face has cracked.

I'm ready to let Jesus take the wheel. The second I collapse on the bench, Michael pounds once on the wall, and we take off.

"We need to get him to a hospital," Jay says, glancing at me with concern. "A bomb went off, and Zade was within range of the blast."

"Why the fuck did they set off a bomb?" Michael asks.

"My guess is it was one of the self-destruct bombs, implanted specifically to destroy all evidence and anyone inside. They're commonly in places with top-secret information in case they're infiltrated or compromised."

I grunt. "We'll have to check in with who was impacted by the explosion and make sure none of ours were killed."

Jay nods, and I turn my attention to Michael. "You get the girl out safely?"

"Yep," he confirms. "With Ruby, and on her way to get treatment."

I nod, some of the pressure easing off my shoulders, but not nearly enough. It's like the Empire State Building is resting on them, and only a penny fell off.

They still have Addie, and the rage is steadily churning beneath the surface. I'm going to burn the entire fucking world down until I find her, and I don't care who gets burnt.

"Do we know anything about who was involved in her kidnapping?" I ask, voice tight with fury, clicking off the video on my laptop. I just finished watching the surveillance footage of Addie's car crash, caught by several streetlight cams. Watching her being dragged from her car, knocked out, then carried into the van has me shaking with rage.

Jay is already working on tracking it through street and security cams, but it doesn't feel like enough.

I've only been admitted in the hospital for a few hours, and I'm seconds away from leaving again.

Thankfully, I didn't suffer any serious damage. My entire back is black and blue from when I was propelled into the altar, but there wasn't any internal bleeding like I had feared.

I got lucky I didn't break my goddamn back, but I damn near came close to it.

"Her picture was posted to a forum on the dark web a day before she was taken. The poster was anonymous, of course, but the ad reads that if anyone brings Addie in alive, then they'd receive a fucking massive reward."

"How much?"

But I don't even need him to answer. I've already located the original ad, which has since been deleted, but nothing is ever truly erased from the internet. I click the ad, and Addie's face pops up. Beautiful unusually light brown eyes, cinnamon hair, and a light dusting of freckles peppering her nose and cheeks.

My heart clenches at her smiling face—the same picture used as her author photo outside the bookstore, and the very one that instantly drew me into her. It still has the same effect on me as it did then.

The price tag is listed right beneath it in bold, red letters.

Twelve million dollars.

Pocket change to those handing it out, but an incredible amount to the smaller fish in the pond. An amount that someone would have to work hard to spend in their lifetime.

"Fuck," I mutter, pinching the bridge of my nose between my fingers. A massive migraine is blooming, and restlessness invades my senses. I want to claw out of my own skin, if only it means Addie will be waiting for me on the other side.

Jay's lips are tense. "I know who answered the ad, and who was responsible for her kidnapping."

I drop my hand and pin a look to my right-hand man, waiting for him to drop the proverbial bomb. Dread washes over me, and I have a feeling this one might actually succeed in killing me.

"Max," he says quietly.

My eyes close, and my control finally shatters, slipping through my fingers like sand in an hourglass. It was only a matter of time, and the last grain has now fallen.

Inky-black darkness corrodes every cell in my body until there is no light left within me.

Red consumes my vision, and I snap into motion. My laptop is launched across the hospital room, the loud crash from it slamming through equipment and into the wall swallowed by the roar ripping from my throat.

I convulse violently from the force of the piercing wail falling past my lips, so long and sorrowful that it tapers off into a silent scream. Heaving in a breath again, another thunderous cry explodes out of me as I grab the bedside table and launch that next.

Without sight, the IV pole follows, whipping it towards a window and nearly shattering it from the force, the pinch from the needle being torn from my skin imperceptible.

My hearing goes after that as if I'm underwater and all sound is diluted. The tide batters into me, drawing me into its clutches and sending me spiraling down into the black pit of despair at the bottom.

My hands grab at more equipment, all of it crashing to the tile as anguish tears through my chest.

This is my fault.

All my fucking fault.

Just as I stand, muffled shouting arises, and I feel several sets of hands grab my body at once and shove me back down. I fight against their hold, continuing to roar, but my blindness works against me.

Straps circle around my wrists and chest, imprisoning me to the hospital bed.

But I'm too far gone.

Despite the frantic hands attempting to hold me down beneath the binds, my legs swing over the bed and I stand, straining against the weight threatening to take me back down.

"*Jesus,* Zade!"

My chest heaves and my vision becomes spotty, allowing me only snippets of my blurred surroundings. Four frightened nurses and Jay crowding me, eyes wide and faces pale as I stand before them with a nearly two-hundred-pound bed strapped to my back.

I am…

I am no longer a man—only a beast succumbing to primal instinct. I am annihilation.

"Sir, please calm down!" one of the nurses pleads shrilly, her green eyes nearly black with fear. I pant, my chest tight from lack of oxygen and the strap straining against my chest.

I can't, I can't. She's gone because of me.

How am I supposed to fucking *live* with that?

I shake my head, my energy depleting steadily. Words evade me and I stumble, struggling to right myself.

"Unstrap him," Jay demands sharply, already aiming for the one secured around my chest. He waits until one of the nurses unclips them from my hands before he releases the buckle. The bed falls to the ground with a deafening boom.

Security guards come barreling into the room, skidding across the cluttered tile when they see the absolute carnage.

Jay gets in my face and shouts, "Quit acting like a fucking lunatic and get it together! Trashing a hospital isn't going to save her."

My vision clears, and the wreckage becomes apparent.

Shit.

That potent fury is still present, spewing from my pores, but I manage to keep it in check. Enough that it just steams.

"What the hell…" a security guard says, his young face painted with utter disbelief.

"He's okay," a nurse huffs out. She's an older woman with short blonde hair and large wire-rimmed glasses that take up half her face.

She approaches me like one would a crocodile with its mouth wide open, her hand steady as she grabs my arm and lifts it.

A tiny trail of blood leaks down my arm from where the IV was ripped out, stemming from a tear in my skin no longer than half an inch.

"That… that is a nasty wound, sir. You better sit down so I can fix you up before you keel over and die where you stand," she orders, her voice stern as she points me towards the skewed bed.

It's just a scratch, and we both know that, but I sit anyway. I watch her as she grabs a bandage from a cupboard and begins to blot the blood.

A few of the guards question Jay and one of the nurses while the other two rush from the room, red and shaking. I can't manage to feel an ounce of guilt.

Not when there's a black hole in my chest where Addie once took up residence.

"Want to talk about it?" she asks quietly, dabbing up the blood with a piece of gauze.

"No," I mutter.

"Well," she titters, sticking a small Band-Aid on my arm next. It has dinosaurs on it, and all I can do is stare. If I didn't feel so empty, I'd laugh at how pathetic it looks.

"You can either tell me or tell the police. And I know you're a big, burly man—you've gone out of your way to prove that part—and police officers probably don't scare you, but I'd rather you spend the rest of your time in this hospital not handcuffed to a bed."

I pause. "I'll just stand up again and walk out with it."

She looks up at me, and then a chuckle slips past her pink lips. "That's fair. You have your heart broken?"

I raise a brow, and though she has to work to swallow, she doesn't relent. I soften my face and sigh. Right now, I appreciate her candor.

"You could say that." I sniff, rolling my arm to look at the Band-Aid again. They're green T-Rexes, mouths open in a roar. I imagine I didn't look much different not two minutes ago.

"She was taken. Kidnapped."

The nurse gasps, quiet and soft, but it feels like a shout when I'm so hollow.

"It's my fault. I didn't…" I trail off, deciding it's best not to tell her that I didn't kill a man who I should've, a long time ago. "I need to get her back."

She blows out a shaky breath and straightens. "I'll make sure no charges are pressed so you can save her." She points to the Band-Aid. "Maybe no more life-threatening injuries, yeah?"

I grace her with a strained smile, and assure, "I'll pay for the damages."

"That would be appreciated," she says.

I nod and turn my attention to the ground. The white tile blurs as I feel her presence leave, replaced with Jay's.

"I know where he is," he murmurs.

I look up at him, murder in my eyes. He tightens his lips, knowing I'm not going to settle down.

"Let your body heal, man. You'll be useless otherwise. We'll get him, and find where they took her the second you're not broken anymore. You may be able to move now, but the next few days are going to hit hard, especially now that you walked around with a big-ass bed on your back. Your *very* injured back, might I add."

"The longer I wait, the more likely she is to disappear. To suffer and have unimaginable things happen to her," I argue through clenched teeth. The muscle in my jaw is nearly ripping through my flesh from how hard I'm grinding them.

He bends down and puts his hands on my shoulders, dipping his chin until he catches my eyes. I glare at him, wanting to go back to not being able to hear or see anything.

Jay is stupidly brave and doesn't back down.

"I promise you, man, I will have the team looking for her. I will do everything in my power to get us closer to her." The intensity in his words and stare is easing my anxiety as much as it's capable, which is microscopic.

I'll never be able to relax, to not feel my insides twisting into knots and the panic gnawing at my heart until there's nothing left.

I know my body is going to give out on me, but nothing—and I mean, *nothing*—is going to keep me from finding her.

Clenching my fists, I nod. I have no plans to stay in this hospital. To stay still. But arguing right now isn't going to change anything at the moment.

I need rest. Lots of it. Because the second I open my eyes, I won't close them again until Max's head is in my hands.

"You can't just bust down the door all willy-nilly, Zade."

"The fuck I can't," I bark, glowering at Jay as he meticulously paints his nails eggplant purple from the seat next to my hospital bed.

It's the fifth day, and I'm green in the face with anxiety and frustration. I made five escape attempts within the first two days, but they kept knocking my ass out with drugs to the point where I completely lost time. I stopped escaping because I'd rather be semi-useful behind a computer than be dead to the world and not be doing anything at all.

The only other reason I gave in was that I was physically incapable of even squeezing my ass cheeks without my vision going black with pain. I may not have suffered any life-threatening injuries, but my body is sure acting like it did.

Jay curses softly under his breath when he gets a dot of nail polish on his skin, poking his tongue out as he carefully wipes the paint off.

My new computer is on my lap, the camera feed showing Max and the twins, Landon and Luke, lounging in his office, drinking expensive scotch and probably laughing over the big deposit that just came through to his bank account.

Twelve million dollars. The price for kidnapping Addie.

"You know he didn't do it himself," Jay reminds me, and then holds up his hands to marvel over his work.

I sigh, the veins in my hands popping as I clench them tight.

"I know," I seethe.

Max and the twins were at a club when Addie was kidnapped. Which means he knew where to find her and hired grunt men to do the work. And that means whoever he hired will most likely be receiving a cut from his reward. A job like that wouldn't come without a high price, and though Max has money, he doesn't have that much. Not until today, at least.

Now, we're waiting for him to transfer whatever sum of cash to the lackeys he promised it to. Then, we'll be able to trace the money trail and confirm their identities based on the account information.

If we're lucky, Max is as dumb as he looks and doesn't hide his tracks well enough.

Jay will handle that part while I take care of Max.

I could send in another mercenary to torture the information out of him, but this method will be much faster, and I refuse to let anyone else touch him except me.

Only I will show Max what pain truly feels like. Even then, he will only feel a fraction of what I feel without Addie.

I roll my neck, groaning as it cracks. When I look back down, an alert comes through.

Three million dollars has just been transferred to an offshore account. It takes me two seconds to find the name attached to it.

Rick Boreman.

Through the camera feed, Max is now setting down his phone and then cheers, clinking his whiskey glass with the twins.

I look up at Jay, rolling my eyes as he blows softly on his wet fingernails. He's going to chip the paint in two seconds with the amount of typing he does, which is why the colors change every couple of days. He's a nail biter, and the polish helps keep that habit at bay, though it's been virtually useless these past five days.

As much as he's trying to play it cool, Addie being gone has him crippled with anxiety. He's only seen her through a computer screen, but he doesn't need to know her in order to know that she doesn't deserve this, and if she were to die... the world would die with her.

For now, I will begin with Max.

June 11th, 2008

I want to die. The only thing keeping me alive is my sister. I haven't said her name. Not here and not out loud.

Layla

It hurts to even write it out. To look at her name and know that she's so far away from me. Suffering, as I am, just in a very different way. She's only one years old, you know? Still a baby. Mom doesn't take care of her. Feed her. Change her. Love her.

Layla <u>NEEDS</u> me. I'm getting out of here.

Molly

Chapter Four
The Diamond

"I can save you."

Something shakes me, sending fresh waves of pain spearing through my consciousness.

"Wake up, I can save you."

The voice penetrates the deep fog swirling in my brain. Blackness surrounds me, and it feels like I'm floating in a starless galaxy, but an icy chill is snaking throughout my body. Warning me of something dangerous.

A hand is on my arm, and it roughly jostles me again. "There's not much time left. I need you to wake up. I will help you."

A fissure of light cracks through the never-ending darkness. I focus on the light, and as someone continues to jolt my body, the crack widens until blinding light pierces my eyes.

I groan, clarity beginning to surface. The firm grip on my arm tightens, and the voice rousing me from sleep amplifies.

I'm shaken once more, and the harsh movement finally jerks me awake.

My eyes snap open, and for reasons I'm not sure of yet, my heart is beating out of my chest, pounding against my rib cage as violently as the person who had been shaking me.

An old, wrinkled face and dull blue eyes come into focus, only a few inches away from mine. I rear back, blinking at him with panic and confusion.

"What's going on?" I choke out.

Within seconds, reality comes crashing down, and I'm reminded why I'm here. Who I'm with.

I was in a car accident. Ran off the road. And then was kidnapped and brought to a doctor who clearly practices illegally.

Dr. Garrison.

The man who is currently in my face, staring at me with urgency.

"I'm going to help you. Please, get up."

The bone-chilling cold that penetrated the fog worsens as his hand grabs onto mine and pulls me forward.

I yelp in response, the aches in my body have increasingly gotten worse. It feels like a hot poker is being stabbed into every one of my nerve endings.

"I know it hurts, sweetheart, but we have to hurry before Rio comes back."

He gently tugs on me again, and it's then that I notice the IV has been removed from my arm.

I resist, and in an effort to stall, I ask, "H-how long have I been out?"

"Only for a night, sweetheart. Now get up, please."

Leaving me with no other choice, he helps me up, rushing me forward while attempting to handle me carefully.

"Where are we going?"

I'm nearly frantic, and confusion is muddling my thoughts. Mainly, I can't figure out why the hell he's helping me. Isn't he in on this, too?

It's then he looks at me, a crazed smile on his face.

"I'm going to take you somewhere safe. No one will ever find you, I promise."

A rock forms in my throat, and I work to swallow as my situation becomes more apparent.

No one will ever find you.

He may be saving me from Rio and Rick, but that doesn't mean I won't need saving from *him*, too.

"Why are you doing this?" I breathe, my eyes bouncing across the room, searching for a solution to get me out of this very big problem. There's only one exit that I can see, and he's leading me straight toward it.

For all I know, he's going to lock me in a box and feed me through a glory hole. The image disturbs me so profoundly that I think I'd rather take my chances with Rio and Rick.

"I became a doctor because I like taking care of people. But the hospitals never let me take care of my patients the way I wanted."

My heart drops, and he peers at me demurely like a little boy admitting his crush to the prettiest girl in grade school.

His smooth, cold hand slips into mine, holding it like he's about to drop to one knee and ask me to marry him. "I want to take care of you, sweetie. I-I'll treat you better than these people ever will. I promise I'll be good to you."

My mouth opens, but no sound escapes.

The fuck does he expect me to say to that?

Yes, please, whisk me away to your creepy lair. Nothing would make me happier.

I want him to let me go *home*. Not into the arms of another creep that will trap me for the rest of my life.

Taking a step back, I carefully pry my hand from his grip. His face drops, and hurt flashes in his pale blue eyes as he watches my fingers slip from his. He acts as if he did get down on one knee, and I've just rejected his proposal.

"I... I'm not sure that's a good idea. They'll know it was you," I say, attempting to reason with him.

I don't want to reject him flat out. His mental state seems unhinged at best, and I have no idea what this man is truly capable of.

He shakes his head, swoops my hand rather angrily, and tugs on me. I bite back another cry as he explains with impatience, "Not if we hurry. I have a plan; I just need you to come with me."

When he continues to drag me after him, my fight or flight instincts kick in. Pain be damned, I yank my hand out of his hold and scramble back.

"No, I don't want to go with you," I snap.

His face morphs into a snarling demon, and that coldness radiating from him crystalizes. This man is dead on the inside. He's no more than an icy, decaying tomb.

I feel the burst of pain lancing across my cheek before I register him moving. My head whips to the side, and fire erupts on the side of my face.

I gasp, my mouth popping open while I clutch my smarting cheek, feeling something wet coat my fingers. Pulling my hand away, I find several drops of blood staining my skin. He backhanded me with a fucking ring on. A *wedding* ring.

A cocktail of disgust and fury curdles in the pit of my stomach, but I keep my mouth shut. This is a very precarious situation, and I no longer have the luxury of doing or saying whatever the hell I want without severe consequences. And as much as I'm tempted to throw down with the old fart, I can hardly move.

Shit, Addie. Think.

He's breathing heavily, fury evident on his ruddy face. It's like staring into the eyes of a corpse, animated only by the evil inside him.

"I would treat you like a queen. You would want for *nothing*," he spits vehemently, slashing a hand through the air angrily with his last word.

I nod my head. "Okay," I placate gently. "But you're scaring me just as much as they do."

His spine straightens, and I watch the rage bleed from his stare like it just now dawned on him that he's acting like a goddamn lunatic. So quickly, his face transitions from hysteria to sheepish understanding.

"You're right, I'm sorry," he says, taking a step forward. "I'm just... if I'm going to get you out safely, we need to hurry, and you're not cooperating."

I tense but refrain from retreating as he grabs my hands in an apologetic manner.

"I'm sorry I slapped you, sweetheart. I'm just trying to help you. Please, come with me. I promise you'll be happy with me."

The panic and adrenaline heighten to dangerous levels, causing my heart to thump painfully against my chest. It's hard to fucking think when he's staring at me so eagerly, and my entire body feels like it's been pushed through a fucking meat grinder.

But this could be the perfect opportunity to escape if I play my cards right. I need to get out with as minimal noise as possible, so I don't alert the terror twins, which leaves me with two options. Hit this clown over the head and run or let him take me away and find a different way out. Regardless, I'm not staying here.

"Okay," I whisper, wheezing in a breath through my tight lungs.

When he sees me visibly relax, he quickly follows suit, victory sparking in his icy pools. Grabbing my hand again, he urges me toward the door with a flickering red exit sign above.

I glance around, shivering from the cold, dankness of the room. Everything in here is gray and diluted, and the light fixtures whirring above are corroded with dust and bug carcasses. There isn't anything here that gives this place... life.

Jesus, how does he operate in here? It looks like we're in a morgue rather than a hospital room. I'd hate to die here, though it seems like many have.

It reeks of sterile death.

We pass by the table littered with instruments, several of them sharp. If I stab him in the jugular, he won't be able to scream and will be dead within minutes. Then, I can make a run for it. I've no idea what the fuck I'm going to do once I get out of here, but there will hopefully be somewhere I can find help.

With one quick glance, I note that his focus is straight ahead, intent on his mission to take me for his own. I snatch the scalpel from the metal table, but he hears me coming and turns right as I go to plunge the knife into his neck, slicing his nape instead.

Blood spurts onto my face, and I turn away in an attempt to avoid getting any in my eyes.

He screams loudly, turning and backhanding me once more, sending me crashing into the unforgiving ground.

I land awkwardly on my tailbone, and I yelp from the impact. Agony shoots up my spine, taking my breath away, and he's on me before I can think of what to do next, let alone breathe.

"You bitch!" he shouts, his hands circling around my neck and roughly banging my head into the concrete.

Stars explode in my eyes, preventing me from seeing anything for several seconds. It feels as if the back of my head has been cracked open, but the hands constricting my windpipe bring me out of the pit of agony.

Panic takes over, so intense it feels like poison in my veins. I claw at his hands, leaving bloody scratches in their wake, but they don't deter him. Dr. Garrison's face is contorted into pure rage, his pupils dilated until they're nearly black, and his teeth bared, every single yellow, crooked tooth on display.

I thrash and fight, but his hold doesn't lessen. And it's then that my life flashes before my eyes like an old movie reel.

My mother, gracing me with one of her rare smiles when I say something ridiculous. My father, lounging on his chair and yelling at football players on the TV—the most excitement he's ever shown in his entire life.

Daya, with her head tipped back and laughing loudly at something I said or did, displaying the tiny gap between her front teeth. Something she's always hated, and I've always loved.

And then Zade. The fucking wrecking ball of a man who has brought out such a burning fire within me that I crumble like ash beneath him. Yet, he made me feel so strong. So brave.

He made me feel *so* damn loved and treasured.

Just like a diamond.

Although, Zade would never call me something as trivial and common as a diamond. He'd call me the rarest jewel on earth.

I should've told him that I…

Just as darkness overwhelms my vision, only a pinpoint of light remains, his hands loosen and something wet and warm floods over my face. Instinctively, I open my mouth, gasping desperately for oxygen as my lungs expand.

The taste of copper invades my tongue, and I suck in so deeply that my eyes bug from my head. It takes a few moments to process that only half of Dr. Garrison's head is suspended over me, a mere second before his body topples onto mine.

A mixture of coughing and a gurgled scream fights for dominance over my throat. My eyes widen impossibly further as the mangled mess of the doctor's head rests on my shoulder, the pool of crimson seeping into my gown. I nearly convulse from the coughing fit still seizing my throat, and the swirl of emotions of being trapped under a corpse with blood dripping in my mouth.

More of his brain matter is on me, than in his head. Or what's left of it.

"Stop freaking out, you're *fine*." Rio appears above me, staring down at me with annoyance and a tinge of anger.

"Get used to the sight of dead bodies, princess. You're going to see a lot of them where you're going."

Grabbing the scruff of Dr. Garrison's collar, he lifts him up and suspends him over my face again. Immediately, I'm drenched in even more bodily fluids and brain matter. Barely closing my eyes in just enough time, I cover my face as Rio laughs and wrenches the body off of me, dragging him to the corner of the room.

Finally, the pressure eases, and I am able to breathe without coughing, but then a low whimper leaks past my lips.

My body curls in until I'm a tight ball, trying not to think about how blood is in my mouth yet thinking of nothing else.

I gag, my stomach revolting from the thought.

H. D. CARLTON

Something hard nudges my shoulder harshly, halting my retching. I lift my head enough to see Rio's boot, and then proceed to spit on it, pure red splashing on the black leather.

Two birds with one stone—a *fuck you* and an attempt to rid my mouth of Dr. Garrison's blood.

Rio doesn't appear bothered by it, though.

"You're going to be fine. The dude was trying to kidnap you."

"Just as you did. So, you're saying you deserve the same fate, right?" I hiss, my body beginning to go into shock. I'm trembling violently, and there's a numbness crawling up my arms and legs.

Stay calm, Addie.

Breathe.

Just breathe.

Rio laughs while I close my eyes and work not to freak the fuck out.

His presence closes in on me. I know that he's crouched down, and hovering above me. Warm breath fans across my ear as he continues to chuckle.

"You have a smart mouth on you, but in this world, it's not so smart. My advice? Dumb it down until the only words you're capable of speaking is *yes, sir.* You'll last much longer that way."

A tear drips from my eye and I feel the beginnings of a sob forming at the base of my throat.

"Isn't that what I'd want? To not last long? Better than suffering forever, right?"

He sighs wistfully. "You're right. You're going to die here anyway. I guess it's not a matter of how long you last, but rather, how bad it hurts when it's over."

My lip quivers. He sighs again, and the frustration has seeped back into his tone.

"Come on, get up. We need to get moving." He stands and walks a few feet away, looking back down at me. Waiting for me to follow.

Dazed, I manage to sit up. The pain is starting to settle back in my bones, making itself known once again.

"Can I at least shower first?"

Rio's eyes sweep my crimson-stained body, and he grins at me. "Sure, princess. You can shower. But you can't get those stitches wet on your back, so it looks like you'll need my help."

Shit.

Eyes boring into my ass were more tolerable than being covered in the entrails of a dead man. I kept my back to him while rivulets of blood washed from my skin. I nearly puked when I saw chunks and fragments of bone swirling toward the drain, too.

I mainly stayed out of the water and used a fresh rag and bar soap to clean up. Rio directed me on areas to avoid on my back, but didn't touch me, and for that, I thanked the She-Devil above.

The hardest part was washing and rinsing my hair without bending too far over and giving him a view of what he called the "money maker."

Fucking asshole.

The shower was in a quaint little apartment on a higher level in the building, much nicer than the makeshift hospital room below, but still no better than a cheap apartment in New York City.

I assume it's where Dr. Garrison slept when he wasn't operating on people brought in from human traffickers. He wore a wedding ring, though I saw no evidence indicating that a woman lived there with him.

Dear God, I hope she's not chained up somewhere.

Now, I'm in the backseat of a van again with a dark sack over my head, sopping wet, and shivering in my bonds like an old engine. The bastard failed to mention that there were no clean towels and got a kick out of watching me use a hospital gown to dry off. Even more so when I attempted to wrap one around my hair.

He wouldn't let me wear it, stating my hair is too pretty to bundle up in an ugly blue gown, but really, I think he just enjoys being a dick.

The clicking from my chattering teeth is swallowed by the hard rock music pouring from the speakers. My thick hair is still soaked, and the heat is on low—not nearly enough to keep me warm. If it weren't for the lack of body contortion and levitation, it'd look like I'm in the middle of an exorcism from how hard I'm shivering.

It *feels* like I am. Everything hurts so goddamn bad, and with every tremble, the pain intensifies.

I've never been more miserable in my fucking life.

"Don't worry, diamond. We're almost to your new home," Rick croons, the sound grinding against my already frayed nerves. "Francesca is going to *love* you."

The ominous tone in his voice tenses my body further. Something about the way he said it makes me feel like I have more to fear from her than any man who comes my way.

"W-who is she?"

He's quiet for a moment, but it's not Rick who answers. "The one person you want to impress the most," Rio says, his voice grave.

"Why?"

"Because she will determine just how miserable your life will be until you're sold."

My head drops and I squeeze my eyes shut. It's only been six days, and I feel defeated already. I've been gone for such an insignificant amount of time, and my spirit is already fissuring.

I take a deep breath and blow it out, slow and steady.

I'm not going to give up. I know with every fiber of my being that Zade is going to do everything in his power to find me. But I'm not going to sit around and wait either. I'll meet him halfway if I can.

So, if winning over Francesca is what I need to do, then I'll do it.

I've always been stupidly brave—to the point where I've been more stupid than brave. I'm not going to stop now.

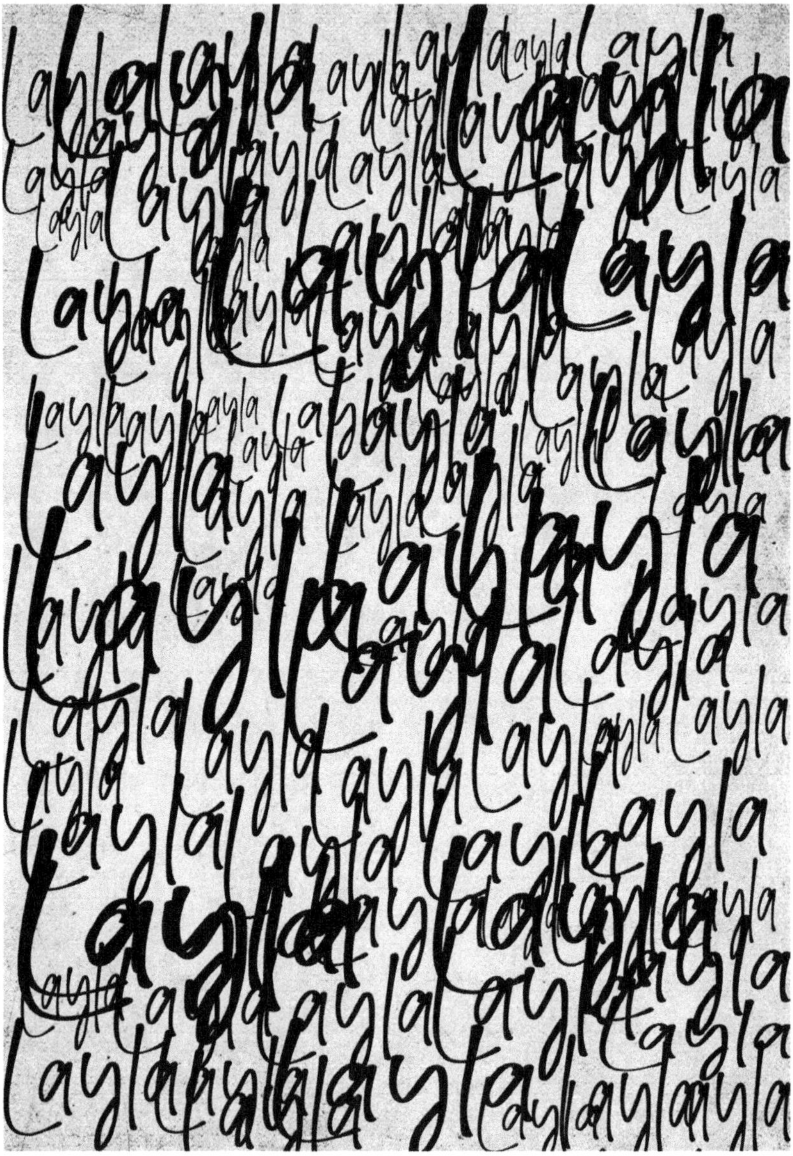
Layla

Chapter Five
The Diamond

At one point in our lives, we're all afraid to die. For some, it happens the first moment we fully understand what death means—before depression, anxiety, and other mental health issues arise.

For others, it's before they've found something to believe in—whether it's God or something else that's spiritual.

And there are those who flounder through life, terrified of the day they take their last breath. I think for some, they aren't so much scared of death itself, but rather, how they're going to die.

So, how am *I* going to die?

Will it be painful? Will I suffer? Will I be terrified?

Gigi felt all those things when she was murdered by a man she trusted, and likely cared deeply for.

When she started having an affair with her stalker, Ronaldo, it not only destroyed her marriage, but it took her life. Only not by her stalker or husband like one would expect, but by her husband's best friend, Frank Williams.

For so long, I was convinced I'd have a similar demise at the hands of my own stalker. Instead, I gave in to his dark perusals, and found myself loving him instead.

I tried so hard to run from him, and now all I want to do is run *to* him.

During the rest of the car ride, I stayed silent. At least, verbally—my teeth chattered the entire way and eventually, one of the men got annoyed and turned up the heat.

An imperceptible amount of time passes before we come to a stop, dread settling deeply in my gut. I steel my spine and wait as both men exit the van, the doors slamming in tandem.

Then, the door to my left slides open, inviting an icy breeze in. A rough, calloused hand wraps around my arm and tugs. It feels like the Grim Reaper is holding on to me, escorting me to my death.

"Ow," I cry out, on the verge of screaming from how bad it hurts to move. He ignores me and barks, "Let's go."

That's Rick's voice.

His grip on my arm is unnecessarily tight as he drags me out of the vehicle. As if a woman who was just in a bad car accident and riddled with injuries is going to overpower him and get away.

I don't even know where the fuck we are.

A gust of freezing wind blows, sending another wave of goosebumps across my body. My teeth start chattering again, the cold becoming nearly unbearable.

The black sack is ripped off my head, and I flinch from the harsh

---

light. It's dreary outside, but since I haven't seen daylight in quite a while it has made my eyes sensitive.

Squinting, my gaze immediately jumps to the monstrosity towering before me.

Rick splays his arm out towards the two-story colonial home, presenting the house to me as if I'm at a five-star restaurant, and he's pulling the lid off my tray to reveal the best meal I'll ever have. I've never been anywhere so fancy, but from the videos I've seen on the internet, it looks like a bunch of baby portions of foam and sticks wrapped in meat.

So—not appealing.

The house isn't as run-down as I would have thought, but still not in the best shape. Vines of moss are running up the cracked white paneling, reminding me a little of Parsons Manor. Just not as… pretty. It's discolored with boarded windows, a sagging porch and—*is that duct tape?*

"Looks… inviting," I murmur.

Glancing around, I note that we're out in the middle of nowhere, surrounded by dense woods. It looks like they just plopped a random house in the middle of a forest. A dirt driveway trails off through a thicket of trees, and I suspect that's the only way in or out. Unless I want to take my chances out in the wild.

"Let's go, it's fucking freezing," Rick orders, dragging me after him. Rio walks ahead of us, shooting an indecipherable look over his shoulder before he leads me into the house straight out of *Courage the Cowardly Dog*. Only double the size.

But I imagine the shit that happens in this house is full of horrors much worse than that purple dog ever experienced.

Adrenaline and fear swirl in my stomach, and although there is a heavy weight low in my gut, it's not the warm heady feeling I'm used to.

This is dread.

It spikes higher when Rick hauls me through the entryway and pushes me forward. While the air is stale and musty, it doesn't resemble a meth lab as I had expected.

This home looks like it comes straight from the 1800s, with an abundance of woodwork, outdated wallpaper, and odd nooks and crannies that make zero sense. I'm standing in a massive living room with brown, cracked leather couches, threadbare floral rugs, and crooked paintings on the walls. The TV is shoved into a corner, *Tom & Jerry* playing on low and a drooping cobweb hanging above it.

Grime is caked into the cracks, and every surface is coated in dust. The deep brown hardwood floor is wonky and uneven and creaks from the slightest shift of weight. I imagine if this place was haunted like Parsons Manor, no ghost could walk by undetected.

To the left is a dining area, paraphernalia everywhere. Crushed beer cans, needles, and crack pipes litter the table, along with a circular mirror, a small mound of cocaine on it.

Hesitantly, I walk farther into the house, the pit of dread growing wider and wider, like a shark's mouth right before it ravages its prey.

It's hard to breathe in here. It smells faintly of mildew and the entire house is wrapped in bad juju like a scratchy wool coat. It's thick, uncomfortable, and suffocating.

"Welcome to your new home," Rio declares mockingly. He's been watching me take in the house, and even though it's only been seconds, I've long since grown uneasy beneath the weight of his stare.

Before I can open my mouth, three men walk in from a doorway straight ahead. It seems to lead to the kitchen, based on the glimpse of a refrigerator from my standpoint. The raucous men were mid-laughter, but the second they noticed me, they quieted. Their movements are slow as they approach the kitchen table, more intent on picking me apart than watching where they're going.

"This the diamond?" one of the men calls out, his teeth so black, it looks like bugs have infested his mouth.

Rick saunters towards the table and takes a dramatic seat, pride radiating from his face.

Smiling wide, he says, "You fucking know it is! Max already deposited the check so we can do whatever the fuck we want, boys."

Their cheers arise, and the look on Rio's face is near murderous.

"Fucking idiots," he mutters under his breath. Then louder, he reminds him, "No, you *can't* do whatever you want, *estúpido*, because you have a big fucking target on your head in the shape of a Z."

Rick waves a hand, unconcerned. "Don't worry, Rio. We'll hide out until the fucker is dead, and *then*, we can do whatever we want. This payday is fucking massive, and not only that—we'll get a taste of her, too."

I shrink beneath their lewd gazes. Instinctively, my arms wrap tighter around myself, but that only elicits a few grunts of amusement.

"Aw, don't be shy, baby girl. I promise I'll make you feel good," one of them croons, his black hair sticking up in several directions from the copious amount of grease in it. I swallow, a lump forming in my throat as my gaze fixates on a dark red puddle on the table I hadn't noticed before.

I can't even begin to imagine what that could possibly be from.

"What, princess, we ain't good enough for you?" Rio asks. I glance at him and note the smirk on his face. But he's tense, his grin strained.

I don't even acknowledge him; my eyes trained back on the pool of blood. Tracking my line of sight, Rio turns to see what I'm staring at. He barks out a laugh when he sees it.

H. D. CARLTON

"Want to place a bet on what it's from?" My face contorts in revulsion as I shoot a glare at him.

"My bet is that some bitch lost her virginity right there," Rick chimes in, lighting a cigarette with a grin.

I bristle, and anger rises in my chest. "You're sick," I spit, my voice watery and full of so much hate. Rick only laughs and goes back to the conversation between his friends. I'm watching one of them inject himself with a needle when I feel someone charging in the house behind me. I startle and turn to find another man, and nearly lose my shit.

There's a girl slung over his shoulder.

My mouth pops open, and his brown eyes settle on me.

"You got a problem?" he barks.

I flinch, panic rising as the girl's lifeless limbs sway behind him. I've no idea if she's dead or alive. I'd hope this man wouldn't be carrying a fucking dead girl *inside* the house, but then again, these assholes would be the type to do something like that.

I shake my head, speechless as he walks toward me. He reeks of body odor, but that's to be expected when he looks like he bathes in motor oil.

I've never been good at controlling my mouth, but in a house full of rabid men, the last thing I want to do is test my luck. So, I keep silent even as he leers at me.

"You keep your mouth open like that, don't be surprised when someone sticks their cock in it."

My eyes round and my teeth snap shut. The man chuckles from the audible click.

My heart picks up speed, and I take a few steps back. The fear pumps through my veins, settling low in my stomach and eating at my insides like acid.

64

"Jerry, her room is ready. Extra fucking chains this time," one of the men calls from the table, pointing towards the girl.

My eyes widen impossibly further. Did she escape or something? I have so many questions but know better than to ask any of them. I'm relieved to hear that she's not dead, at least. Otherwise, chaining up a corpse would be... I shudder from the thought.

The man—or Jerry—shifts the girl on his shoulder and walks off without another word, aiming one last scathing look my way.

Sucking my bottom lip between my teeth, I bite hard as I watch him head towards the kitchen. He's lucky I don't bark at him like a dog as I'm tempted to. Anything to make the dickhead think twice about looking at me like that. But that would be stupid, and I *cannot* be stupid in this place.

The last thing I see right before he disappears is the girl's head lifting. Dark brown eyes meet mine through tangled tresses of blonde hair, filled with both fire and ice. The look on her face stops my heart cold, but the creepy smile on her face is what sends it sinking down to the pits of my stomach.

Christ, the look on her face is straight out of a nightmare.

My mouth parts again, but they're gone before I can register what just happened. I'm equal parts scared for and *of* her.

"Don't worry. If you're a good little girl and do as you're told, we'll keep you conscious from here on out," Rio says, pulling my attention back to him.

I'm not sure I *want* to be conscious.

Furthermore, I'm two seconds away from telling him that the girl needs to be admitted to the nuthouse.

But I don't say that out loud, considering we *are* in a fucking nuthouse.

He nods his head towards the direction Jerry and the girl disappeared off into.

"Let's go. Francesca and Rocco should be back in a few hours, and she'll come to meet you. But until then, I've been ordered to show you to your new room."

I glance behind me, staring out the still wide-open door and at the shiny black van. My brows furrow, expecting it to be damaged from when they ran me off the road. Instead, this one is brand new, not a scratch in sight. They must've switched it out at Dr. Garrison's, and that makes my stomach roil.

I know enough about tracking that they would've made it incredibly easy for Zade to find them in a vehicle with a crushed fender.

But then a smile forms on my face with the reminder that Zade is coming, and he is more than capable of finding me, whether they're transporting me in a fucking Ferrari or a Volkswagen from the 1980s that farts pollution every time they hit the gas. He'll find me.

It's right then, a memory sidelines me, and my smile falls to a dramatic death as horror takes over.

Just get her in the van, Rio. Max is already going to be pissed we fucked up his van…

My eyes blow wide, and when I whip back around, Rio is staring at me with dark eyes, tense and ready to charge at me. My gaze flickers down, noting the gun in his hand.

He probably assumed I was about to make a run for it.

And I can't say I didn't briefly consider it, but I'm not dense enough to think I'd make it more than five feet without one of them catching up to me. Or one of their bullets.

I'm injured and can barely stand upright, and I've no idea where the keys are. Running right now wouldn't be wise. And if Zade were here, he'd tell me to bide my time until the right moment.

Don't act irrationally.

I can't let my panic and desperation rule my decisions. Not if I want to get out of this alive.

Licking my lips, I take a step forward, indicating that I won't be running. "Max sent you?"

"You heard that?" He relaxes, unconcerned with my questioning, and jerks his head towards the kitchen, signaling for me to follow. That kind of makes me want to cry.

Clearing my throat, I force out, "Sure did."

I fall in step behind him, the urge to cry deepening as I make my way farther into the belly of the beast. It feels like a bungee cord is strapped around my waist, pulling me back towards the exit, and the longer I walk, the stronger it becomes.

He shoots a look over his shoulder. "Baby girl, I don't know what you did to piss that man off, but he has a vendetta against you. You're plastered all over the dark web with a fat price on your head. Max hired Rick to bring you in, and since the guy is a complete *idiota*, he asked me to help. If it weren't for the fact that he knew where you lived, we wouldn't have gotten a head start and might've had to fight some competition to get to you."

Any moisture in my mouth dries. There's a price on my head? What the fuck for?

I guess I shouldn't be surprised because… well, why the fuck else would I be here?

The new information distracts me enough to take in my surroundings through blurred eyeglasses. I cling onto all the insignificant details, like the sagging cabinetry, purring yellow refrigerator, and the endless ocean of brown wood and ugly wallpaper. Now, he's leading me toward steep wooden steps that creak beneath our weight.

"Does Rick work for the Society?"

Rio glances over his shoulder at me, his brow cocked, seemingly surprised that I know of them.

"No, he's Rocco's friend, who is Francesca's brother. She works for the Society, and Rocco and his friends reap the benefits."

"Do you work for them?"

"I do, though I answer to Francesca right now."

I lick my dry lips, then ask, "So who put the price on my head?"

"It doesn't matter who. Only why. Now hurry up, I have to take a leak, and if you don't move faster, I'll unzip and paint a picture on that pretty face of yours."

The disgusting threat does the trick and snaps me out of my daze. Shooting him a nasty look, I quicken my pace, despite the way my muscles groan in response.

Ending the conversation is best anyway. I need to concentrate on every detail in this house. Starting with how quiet it is.

As he leads me down a long hallway, several doors on either side, I realize it's not the type of silence deriving from vacancy, but the kind when someone is holding their breath, praying for the footsteps to keep on walking by.

Swallowing nervously, my eyes bounce around, trying to pinpoint any glaring details, but the heart-pounding dread is making everything fuzzy.

How the fuck am I supposed to stay calm and play it smart so I can get out of here when a million alarms are going off in my head, warning me that there *is* no way out?

There's always a way out, little mouse. You just have to find it.

June 14th, 2008

The Culling is today. Francesca has not only been preparing us to become goddamn sex slaves. Obedient little whores for the rapists. She's also been preparing us for today. Where we get hunted like little birds. Flying away just to be shot down. **BOOM** Just like that. Best fucking part? **WE** get punished for it. This whole fucking thing is designed for failure.

Be a goood little girl. Open wide, baby. Spread those legs. How flexible is she? Let's see if you can touch your toes. Fucking sick assholes. **All** of them. I hope they fuck up and accidentally kill me when they hit me.

I'll be glad for it.

Molly

Chapter Six
The Hunter

R*age.*

It's not appreciated enough. Not *studied* enough.

The capabilities of the human body are no longer limited to the laws of physics. The absolute destruction that resides in my fingertips could burn down entire cities—reduce them to ashes and embers. A simple stroke of a match, or a flick of my wrist, and as far as my eyes can see would be consumed in the same black fire that rages inside me.

For now, I turn the destruction on myself. My reflection seethes, overcome with a violence only seen through telescopes. Our universe was forged in brutality, and now the cosmos resides in not one, but two black eyes glaring back at me.

Your fucking fault.

My fist flies into the mirror, nearly shattering it entirely with one hit. Tiny shards explode from the impact, raining down in the sink and across the floor. It imitates exactly what my soul feels like. Fucking shattered.

I've only just gotten home from the hospital, and already I'm adding to the list of injuries. But I'm too lost to care.

Snarling, I pull back and drive my fist into the mirror again. Over and over until only a few crooked pieces remain.

Fuming, I spin, searching for the biggest shard I can find, and snatch it from the floor, ignoring the jagged edges slicing into my skin. And then I grab a smaller one with a sharp point before straightening again.

Holding out the large chunk before me, I position it until it's angled just right, serving as my new mirror. Using the smaller piece, I dig the tip into my skin and start carving.

I go slow, my movements shaky from the tremors racking my body. The glass slips in my hold from both the blood pouring out of my knuckles and from where the edges are biting into my skin, and I continuously have to readjust, creating more cuts.

But the pain barely registers when it's so fucking loud inside my head. It's clouded with fury, and every goddamn organ in my body feels as if they're in a blender.

My little mouse is gone.

She's been stolen from me.

And the man behind it is the same man that I knew had a vendetta against her.

And I left him alive.

I fucking let him go on living, stewing in the anger that I caused.

Chest pumping, I dig harder, bright red bubbling from where the glass slices into my skin.

When I'm done, I drop the shard, my entire body vibrating.

I failed Addie.

And I'll never let myself forget it.

Not with the rose now carved over my heart.

Blood coats the bottom of my boots, leaving a scarlet foot trail behind me as I approach Max's house.

He finally hired guards.

Little good they did when now, all six of their bodies litter the ground. With bullet holes between their eyes that are staring sightlessly up at the stars, they were snuffed out because they protected the wrong person.

I don't care how loved they were. I don't give a shit if they had families and if they had wives and little kids at home, eagerly awaiting their arrival. Daddy's gone, kids.

I kick open the front door, and loud chatter cuts into different versions of *what the fuck*.

Max's house is nearly all open concept, washed in black and gold with medieval décor. He's a rich man but no amount of money could protect him from me.

On either side, two large staircases lead up to a balcony that circles the house in a half-moon. The man of the hour appears over the balcony, a wild look in his eyes as two more guards rush up behind him.

His white-blond hair is mussed, the strands standing on end, and when he spots me, that look turns feral, his eyes rounding with hysteria.

I cock a brow. "Did you rub a balloon on your head?"

He blinks, and before any of them can process my presence, I lift my gun and shoot off two bullets—one for each guard.

Too easy.

Apparently, his money couldn't even buy guards that are good enough to entertain me. If they were anything like me, I would've been shot dead before a syllable could even leave my mouth.

Max's eyes pop open wide as his men fall to the ground, blood quickly draining past the rails and onto the pristine tile on the ground floor. He turns to run, but my voice stops him cold.

"Come here, Max."

Slowly, he looks back at me, terror radiating from his eyes. There's a particular stink to men who are faced with the consequences of their actions.

They're fucking petrified, but only because they know they're going to die. And no matter what they believe in, they know damn well there isn't any chance they'll be led to those pearly gates.

"Whatever you think I—"

"Don't insult me further by questioning my knowledge," I cut in, my voice deadly calm. "You know better than that, Maximilian."

His lips tighten into a white line, but he has enough sense to turn and make his way down the steps, straightening out his rumpled blazer to reestablish his fragile façade of confidence. He's struggling to maintain a calm expression, with his fists clenched and shaking, and sweat lining his hairline.

He pauses at the last step, standing before me with his nose in the air. He wants to die with his head held high.

How naïve.

He will bow at my feet, begging for forgiveness and lips pressed so far into my boots that his teeth leave imprints behind.

"Where is she?" I ask, my voice cold and devoid of emotion.

He stares at me, his throat bobbing as he works to swallow. "I wasn't told the location."

"But you're in contact with the men who have her," I counter. He blinks, licking his lips to stall while he finds the proper response.

"It's been fulfilled. I transferred Rick's percentage, and we cut ties."

Max transferred money to one account, so I figure only Rick Boreman got a cut, though I'm not entirely sure why yet. On the surveillance cam of Addie's car crash, there were two men, and Rick was not the one to drag her out of her overturned vehicle.

I purse my lips, the scars on my face crinkling, nod my head, and walk toward him slowly, like a cheetah stalking its prey. A trickle of satisfaction drips into my bloodstream when he tenses, solidifying beneath my eyes.

"And you're telling me that you have no way to contact either of them?"

He swallows and shakes his head. "Rick disconnected his phone after the transfer went through. Probably to hide from you."

I hum, dragging my eyes up and down his form, noting the awkward stance and the way his feet are angled inward. He's seconds away from pissing himself.

There's no self-assurance of being in a public place, knowing the worst of your sins were intimidating a couple of women in a restaurant.

He's been a very bad boy this time.

"So, why'd you do it, Max?"

"You killed my father, so the deal was off," he spits, fury flashing in his irises. Stilling, I can only stare at him as I process his words.

After I killed Archie Talaverra, I cut off his hands and set them on Addie's doorstep as a reminder that she's mine, and no one else is ever to touch her. Max found out and started placing blame on her for Archie's death, so I made him a deal. I wouldn't kill his father, and he wouldn't touch Addie. It took kidnapping and recording a video to drive home the point, but he kept to his word. Until recently.

Funny thing is, I never killed his father.

"Excuse me?"

He blinks, his face gradually turning red.

"You kill—"

"I heard what you fucking said," I bark. "What made you think it was me?"

His face contorts. "Because you fucking *said* it was," he bellows, taking a threatening step towards me. I do better and lunge in his face, causing him to recoil and lose his footing.

I catch him by the collar of his shirt and jerk him close. "Explain, Max," I snarl. "Because I didn't fucking kill your father. If I had, I would've killed both of you. We made a fucking deal, and *I* kept my word."

He shakes his head, breathing fire. "You sent me the video of you decapitating my father on Friday. On the video, you said, 'This is for Adeline Reilly.'"

Fire fills my veins, every single one in my body protruding.

"Was it my voice?"

"Wha—I don't know, man! I don't have a goddamn recording of your voice to compare it to. It was deep like yours, that's all I know."

I nod my head, letting him see in my eyes just how much he fucked up. It doesn't take a genius to figure out who actually killed his father.

"Did you bother confirming if it was me?"

"Oh, my bad, bro, I'll call you up next time," he retorts.

I grin savagely. "Are you telling me you're not resourceful, Maximilian? Because I am, and I have many resources to make you suffer. If you're going to get revenge for a murder, then you better be sure about who actually fucking did it."

He flounders, his mouth flopping as he realizes that he acted without thought. He saw his father die a brutal death, decided who it was based on a single sentence, and sent Addie to the slaughterhouse.

Red is seeping into my vision, and it takes all of my control to keep it at bay. To see clearly—because I want to witness every fucking second of Max's death.

"You want to know who killed your father, jackass? The very people you sold Addie off to. The Society killed him so you would betray me, and then target Addie. You fell right into their fucking trap and did all the dirty work for them."

He shakes his head. "How would they know about our deal and what you did to my father?"

"I don't know, Max, did your father open his fat fucking mouth and flap it to anyone who would listen? Did *you*? Whining about how I kidnapped him and threatened him if you so much as touched Addie and Daya. You tellin' me neither of you didn't go around bitching about it to anyone that possesses ears?"

His teeth click, confirming my presumption. "It's not hard to find out about our rivalry when you don't shut the fuck up about it," I hiss.

He grunts as I haul him towards the front door, his feet dragging on the tile and nails clawing at my hand in panic. I plan on taking this very slow with him. Getting as much information as I can before I send him down below.

"Wait, wait, it was a mistake. Let's work something out," he sputters as I drag him down the porch stairs and towards my car. "I'll get her back!"

I flash him a ferocious smile. "Don't worry, Max, I plan on working out a lot of things with you. Or rather, working them out *of* you."

The bloody scalpel clatters against the metal tray, and Max's groans fill the air. He didn't find it humorous when I started playing "Bodies" by Drowning Pool to drown out his incessant screaming.

I laughed the entire song, even though I can't feel anything right now but burning flames in my hollow chest.

Wires are attached to Max's chest, leading to a machine designed specifically to restart a heart the second it stops. I built it when I first started in this business, though it's rarely used anymore. In the beginning, my rage towards sex traffickers went unchecked. But over the years, I found the faster they die, the more I can kill.

I've killed Max via asphyxiation twice now. The second his heart stops beating, my machine brings him back to life via electricity, where I proceed to torture him slowly, and then kill him again. Rinse, repeat.

I hadn't even started asking questions yet, too angry to speak.

He's gone mad now. So close to death just to awake to my smiling face, over and over. Yet, I still feel nothing.

"Rick Boreman is who you transferred the money to. Who was his partner?"

"R-Rio," he answers. "Dunno his last name."

His speech is choppy from the toll his body has endured.

"How do you know them?"

"I don't re… real-ly. C-Connor and Rick were friends. I knew Rick had connections, so I got his number from Connor's old phone."

"And how did you know what Rick's involved in?"

"Connor talked about the Tala-la-verras pos-ssibly sticking their hands in the trade, and he men-mentioned he had connections to do so through Rick. They never ended up getting in-involved, so nothing more was ever said about Rick than… than that."

I cock a brow. The Talaverras getting involved in human trafficking would've been a fucking disaster. Especially with Archie involved and his playboy status—he would've condemned a lot of girls to that fate. Suppose I did more good than I initially thought by killing them all.

"Who do Rio and Rick work for?"

Max shakes his head, his mouth curling into a smile. "Rick doesn't work for nobody. H-he's just friends with the right people. I knew where y-your girlfriend lived, and he knew how to get her in the right hands. It was mutually ben-beneficial."

He looks like he's fading, so I roughly slap his cheeks a few times. He grunts at me but keeps his eyes open.

"And Rio?"

Another grin. "Who else? The Soc—"

"Don't be obtuse, Max," I cut in, picking up a pair of scissors and dragging the tip against the web of skin between his two fingers. When he doesn't come up with a new answer, I spread the scissors and snip the delicate flesh. He screams, but the sound isn't quite anguished enough.

Not yet.

"I want the names. The people they directly report to, and who they took her to."

He works to swallow; his face pinched in pain as he struggles to answer.

"I-I don't know, Z. I told you, I ha-hardly knew them! Only what C-Connor told us about Rick, which wasn't anything at all other than he was friends with a trafficker. When I saw the ad, I-I asked for his help, and that was the end of it!"

"How did they know how to take her?"

He licks his lips, his eyes drifting again from exhaustion.

"I knew her place was sur-surrounded, so we drew her out. Luke knows where Daya lives, so… so he paid her a visit. Broke in and tied her up and used her phone to lu-lure Addie out. Rick and-and Rio waited outside of her driveway and followed her."

I still, going nearly blind with fury at the knowledge that Daya might've been taken, too. No one fucks with my girl, and that includes her friends and family.

Addie's been gone for seven days now, and in that time, all I've thought about was getting to Max. It didn't even cross my mind that Daya hadn't reached out yet, looking for her best friend.

If I'm being honest, I can hardly think straight with every organ in my body seized by the constant agony with her being gone.

"Where is Daya?"

Max laughs, the sound wet and humorless. "Last I heard, bro, Luke still has her. Reliving his-his favorite memory with her probably."

Fuck. Looks like Max is going to have to wait to die for good. I need to go murder his friend first and get Daya the fuck out of there.

"Hm." I clip the skin between his pinky and ring finger. He clenches his teeth, but it doesn't prevent the scream from slipping through the cracks of his teeth.

"God fucking dammit!" he bursts, panting through the pain.

I'll keep him alive long enough to get Daya. Then, I'll come back and finish off the job—permanently. I don't have any more time to waste on him.

"Who was the person you spoke to when you answered the ad?" I push.

"They were anon-ymous. You-you think they introduce themselves when they answer the phone?" he snaps. "I told them I knew where she was and who was helping me. They told me they'd transfer the money when Addie was in their possession. Th-that's it!"

I grab his other hand and clip the skin between his pointer and middle finger, purely because I don't appreciate his attitude.

"Do you know how many men laid in this very chair before you?" I ask casually, glancing at his shredded face.

"N-no," he cries, dragging the note out in a sorrowful wail.

"Me neither," I shrug. "Lost count. But what I do remember is that I broke every single one of them."

Max squeezes his eyes shut when I lean forward, not brave enough to face his tormentor. "But you're the first one to have broken me first, Max. I can admit that. You broke me into tiny little pieces when you took Addie from me. Because of you, I'm no longer a man."

I straighten my spine. "Do you know what that means for you? It means I have no humanity left in me. No empathy. No guilt. Nothing. I could do this all fucking day, and even when your body gives out, I'd just bring it back again."

Tears spill from the corners of his eyes, but they have no effect on me.

"I'm s-sorry, man. It was an honest mistake," he groans. "I only did it 'cause of my f-father."

"You only got a girl kidnapped and sold into the skin trade, you mean? You only condemned an innocent woman to torture, trauma, and rape because your daddy died?" My voice begins to crack by the end, and I clench my jaw, struggling to hold on to what little sanity I have left. I'm falling apart at the seams, tears building in my vision.

He shakes his head and blubbers, "I don't know what you want me to say."

Breathing in and out, slowly I regain control. I nod, accepting that response for what it is. We both know there is absolutely nothing he can say to atone for what he's done.

"All it would've taken was a little research, my guy. Even if you were hotheaded enough to threaten me directly—that actually would've saved your life."

And my soul.

He snivels, having nothing to say. So, I pick up the mini saw and flip it on. His nearly black eyes blow wide, dilated with terror.

I've sliced up his face pretty good, but I find there's a much better use for it.

"Do you know what's possibly being done to Addie as we speak?" I question, the buckle of his belt clanging beneath the soft whirring of the blade.

He squeezes his eyes shut again as I unfasten his pants and yank them down. I wrinkle my nose. He pissed himself.

"P-please, man," he cries, sobs racking his throat. Snot leaks from his nose and into his mouth, and all I see is a man who's only sorry he got caught. A man who was too arrogant and too stupid to think he wouldn't suffer the consequences for his actions. "Don't do this."

The cavern in my chest widens, devouring what was left of my conscience.

My soul has no place inside a monster.

So, I got rid of it.

"She's being raped," I tell him, my voice deepening with unbridled fury. Those images *haunt* me. "Can you imagine by how many men?"

He shakes his head, his legs trembling as I yank down his boxers, glad that I'm wearing thick nylon gloves.

"It's all I can think about," I choke out on a whisper. "I'm plagued by the torture she must be suffering through. The pain and how she probably wants to die."

And how I want to die.

I grab him between the legs, seeing nothing but a slideshow of Addie's torment on repeat. I could saw off my own fingers, and I'd hardly notice.

They're hurting her. Scaring her. Making her cry.

The blade cuts through skin and muscle, eliciting a scream that horror movies can't imitate. That sound can only be born from the type of horror very few humans actually experience.

It sounds like music.

Is it the same sound Addie is making?

Blood spurts, painting Max and me in crimson. He sucks in a deep breath, preparing to let loose another scream no one else will ever hear, but then he passes out.

Pussy.

Quite literally now.

I switch the blade off, curl my fingers in his bottom teeth and yank it down, and drop the now detached piece of skin down his throat. Then I work to cauterize the wound, preventing him from bleeding out while I'm gone.

I'm not quite done with him yet.

It wasn't hard to track down where Luke lives. The imbecile posts his entire life on social media anyway. Except for the fact that he's keeping a girl hostage in his house. They always seem to forget those details.

Indiscernible screaming can be heard through the doors of his home. A loud crash follows, and I smile, already knowing I'm going to walk in on Daya giving this guy hell.

I slide my pin into the keyhole and jam it, breaking the lock. And then I walk into his house as if I'm walking into my favorite burger joint.

"Why do you always have to *move*?" Luke shouts from down the hallway. I slide out my gun and start spinning the silencer on as I make my way towards the ruckus. "I'm trying to take care of you!"

When I round the corner, I stop short.

Daya is tied to a chair, tipped over on the side, with her arms trapped uncomfortably beneath her weight. She's screaming through the tape stuck to her mouth, death radiating in her glare. When she spots me, her eyes widen, and then she starts wriggling fiercely as if she's trying to make her presence known.

Can't really see her any clearer when she's right in my face.

Noticing Daya's reaction, Luke turns his head, and his own eyes pop open before he scrambles for his gun. I shoot the back of his knee before he makes it a step, feeling nothing even as he falls to the ground with an agonized shout.

"Simmer down, Daya," I say, walking over to her. "I can see you. Wiggling like a worm on a hook is only going to rub your skin even rawer."

She huffs, impatiently waiting as I lift both her and the chair up as one, untie her from the ropes, and help her up. She takes one look at me, noting the dark circles under my eyes and the hollowness in my gaze, and wraps herself around me.

I blink, freezing for a moment before I sling an arm around her. Immediately, she breaks out into a fit of tears, her sobs vibrating my chest. I place a hand on the back of her neck and squeeze reassuringly. It's the only thing I can think to do to let her know that I'm here and that she's safe.

My throat is too tight to speak because as relieved as I am that Daya is okay, I'm incapable of actually feeling it.

"Please tell me you know where she is," she begs, clenching my hoodie in her grip.

I sigh, grab her by the arms, and gently pull her away. She looks no better than I do. Her sage green eyes are bloodshot from crying, black, straight hair disheveled, and bruises mar her deep brown skin.

"Not yet," I whisper, unable to speak the disappointing words any louder. Her eyes close in defeat, but she nods her head.

"We'll find her. We will."

"What did he do to you?" I ask, bringing the conversation back to the parasite dragging himself on the floor towards his gun. It's resting on a coffee table ten feet away from him. I turn and shoot the gun, sending it skidding across the floor and under his white couch.

I bet not a single ass has ever sat on that thing.

"Nothing that I haven't let him do before," she mumbles.

I cock my head. "We both know this time around wasn't consensual."

She looks away, appearing embarrassed.

"You know you didn't ask for any of this, right?" I remind her, shaking her just enough to emphasize my point. She nods her head, though she doesn't look entirely convinced.

"Max is at my place. Let's take care of Luke here. You can even release some pent-up anger if you want."

I go to turn, but she stops me, her hand wrapped tightly around my wrist.

"Don't lose your humanity yet, Zade. Addie is strong, and she will survive this."

I stare at her, and I wonder if she can see something inside me that I can't.

"It's already gone."

I pound harder. Fuck, I need to do it harder.

The answering moans send a shot of pleasure down my spine.

And every time I hear it, all I can think about is Addie. I can never stop thinking about her, even as the begging follows the screams. *Harder.*

"Please." The plea is breathless. But it's not good enough.

"Please, what?" I demand through gritted teeth, sweat dripping down my temple from exerting myself.

It's still *not enough.*

It never will be. Not until I have Addie again.

"Zade," Daya calls. "Please."

I look over to her, my mallet suspended over the massive nail lodged into Luke's leg. She looks a little nauseous, but I can't find it in myself to care right now.

I've been pounding the nail into his forearm for the past few minutes, and I've gotten it down far enough that it's all the way through and embedding into the wooden table, but it's a huge nail, and there's still some length to go.

Luke's moans are full of agony, and his desperate pleas make me feel as good as I'm capable of feeling.

Not fucking enough.

I want him to scream so loud until his cries give out and his voice box shatters completely.

Daya's hand is resting on my arm, her own plea cutting through the noise in my head.

"He hurt you," I say flatly.

She nods. "He did. And I'm ready to take over now."

I release the mallet, the heavy rubber dropping painfully onto his arm before clattering to the table. His answering scream vibrates through his house.

Not. Enough.

I swipe at my nose and turn away, my hands shaking with the need to keep pounding down the nail until the head connects with his flesh.

It's been over an hour since I dragged Luke onto his dining room table and started conducting my torture. I found some tools in his garage and decided to make good use of them since he'll never get the chance.

Daya clears her throat. "Luke? Stay awake, buddy boy." I hear skin slapping and glance back to see her roughly smacking his cheek. His head lolls, more groans releasing from his throat.

"Please," he whispers, his voice hoarse. It needs to be depleted. Even then, I won't be satisfied.

"You know, I've been saying the same thing to you for a week," Daya says, her voice breaking. Her eyes fill with tears, and it only stokes the flames in my chest.

She and Addie love each other fiercely. And because Addie is my family, that makes Daya my family, too.

It's best I make an example of him so others will know to never fuck with them again.

Doesn't help that he played a massive role in getting my girl kidnapped.

And that... that is just unforgivable. Un-survivable.

Luke swallows, yet words fail him for several moments. "It wasn't personal," he croaks. "I was only doing what Max told me to."

"Max told you to stick your dick inside me?" Daya counters, her tiny fist curling in a tight ball.

I hope she fucking uses them. I would only stop her so I could deliver a few of my own punches before I let her end his miserable life.

"No, Daya, I just... I've missed you so much."

Daya closes her eyes, a tear leaking past her eyelashes. I've no idea if these two had much of a relationship past one night together, nor is it my business. But it doesn't matter because whatever Luke stole from Daya, she plans on taking it back.

"I didn't miss you, Luke, you know that, right?" she retorts, her pale eyes blazing. His mouth opens, but she keeps going. "Anytime I thought of you, it was out of disgust. I should've known you'd find a way to surprise me and turn out to be so much worse than I thought."

"L-look, I'm sorry for the role I played, but you have to understand that Max is crazy." When I step closer, not a shroud of understanding reflected back at him, he becomes more desperate. "Seriously, man! If I didn't do what he said, he'd have me killed!"

"Did he tell you to abuse Daya? Rape her?"

He flounders, his mouth opening and closing as he searches for the right answer. Or rather, the right lie.

Daya's eyes cling to him as she holds her hand out to me expectantly. I don't look away from Luke as I grab a knife from the table next to me and hand it to her, knowing what she's asking for.

She doesn't waste time. Doesn't hesitate for a second. She just grips the black handle in a tight fist, the metal glinting off the dining room lights as she rises it above him and plunges it down into his throat. Sharp metal cuts through flesh and bone, silencing his pleas.

Luke's eyes widen into round discs, staring at his reaper with disbelief. It's always disbelief. As if they didn't see it coming. Or maybe, they just can't accept the fact that they're actually dying.

Men like this, who have lived their lives so selfishly and with no regard for others' lives, are always the most desperate to live forever.

But they never understood that's what makes them so goddamn weak. It's the people who have no regard for their own life—people like me. *We* are the ones that are the deadliest.

What's stopping me from taking people down with me when I die?

Nothing.

Not a goddamn thing.

June 16th, 2008

I found a way out. I fucking FOUND IT!!! But shh. I can't say. No one will ever find this journal, but writing it down feels like jinxing it. I'm shaking I'm so excited. They didn't get me at the Culling. Those assholes were boohooing because they didn't get a taste of me. They think they'll get their chance when they try to buy me. **But they'll never get the chance.**

I drew a little picture of me and Layla. We'll be reunited soon. And then we'll disappear. Forever.

Molly

Chapter Seven
The Diamond

"You bring product into my house looking like *this*?" a woman hisses sharply, drawing my eyes up. I'm standing with my back turned to a dirty full-length mirror, head cocked over my shoulder, and my shirt raised up as I observe the stitches on my back. Massive bruises mottle my skin, turning it into an ugly color.

Clearing my throat, I let my oversized, dingy shirt drop and turn to meet her gaze head-on.

In front of me is a beautiful woman, her face caked in make-up and skin doused in citrus perfume. A tight dress clings to her curves, and a pair of strappy heels give her Amazonian height.

Her outfit is not fit for this weather, but she looks as if she could walk through a blizzard barefoot and not bat an eye. She only appears to be in her mid-thirties, and while she's beautiful, she looks tired—weathered.

Walking alongside the devil will do that to you.

This must be Francesca.

And right now, she's glaring at me, shooting daggers from her golden-brown eyes.

Shit. Here we go.

Rio shifts uncomfortably but doesn't respond to her outraged question. And that small action tells me a lot. If you don't have a valid reason for your mistake, keep your mouth shut. Maybe even if you do, still keep it shut.

Her eyes narrow and trail down my body as she walks towards me, checking me out. Determining how much money I could make her, most likely.

I'm grateful Rio found some clothes from another girl's room, and that I'm not wearing the hospital gown anymore. I imagine her reaction would be far worse than it is now.

She stands before me, her strong perfume tickling my nose. I keep silent, watching her pinch the dirty, white shirt and lift it up. Her stare sharpens as she spots the ugly bruises coloring my torso. They're everywhere, and I have a sickening feeling she's going to make it her mission to find every single one.

She then circles me, a sharp gasp piercing the still air when she spots the two large gashes on my back.

"What did you do to her?" she snarls.

Rio keeps his eyes down on his black boots, specks of dried blood still on them.

"Car accident," he answers shortly.

"*Stupid.* This is going to take weeks to heal. When can the stitches come out?"

He finally looks up, his dark brown eyes swirling with hate yet an apologetic expression on his face. It's manufactured just for Francesca. He's not fucking sorry at all.

"Dr. Garrison said four to six weeks."

She hisses and lets the shirt drop, circling back around to face me.

"Is she on birth control?"

My brows furrow and I frown, wondering why she's asking *him* and how the hell Rio would even know that.

"Garrison said she has the IUD."

Tears begin to build, and it takes effort to keep them at bay. It makes me want to vomit that I was violated like that. I had no idea he checked, which means he did it while I was unconscious.

She hums, pleased by that, and finally address me directly. "Do you know who I am?"

It takes a few seconds to rein my emotions in, but I manage to swallow them down enough to answer her.

"Francesca," I say confidently, inserting as much volume in my voice as possible. She doesn't present herself as the type of person who'd appreciate mumbling.

That's the good thing about being a writer, I suppose. I've built and crafted so many imaginary personalities that it doesn't take much to figure out the ones in real life.

Francesca, here, has no patience and doesn't tolerate insolence, laziness, or weakness. She exudes strength, and that's what she expects in return. Not to be confused with defiance, of course.

She pops a manicured eyebrow up her forehead. "Yes," she says. "That's my name. But that's not what I asked you."

Frowning, my brows knit, unsure how to respond. Before I can figure it out, her long acrylic nails pinch my cheeks. I inhale sharply, the talons digging into my skin as she pulls my face into hers, a calm but menacing expression on her face.

"I am your madam. You will not speak, act or even *think* without my permission first, you understand me?"

"Yes," I whisper, though the sound comes out garbled between my pinched lips. She pushes my face away harshly, causing me to lose my footing and land on my ass. A puff of air escapes me from the impact, followed by a whimper, and I screw my eyes shut as pain rackets up my spine.

These assholes don't want the product bruised and bloody yet can't keep their goddamn hands off me. Makes a whole lot of fucking sense.

I don't need to be an expert in the skin trade to know that no one wants to eat a bruised apple. They want nice, shiny apples to sink their teeth into and rip apart themselves, piece by piece.

Francesca sniffs, peering down at me with disdain. Blowing out a slow breath, I meet her stare, working hard to keep even a hint of anger out of my eyes.

"Obedience is the number one thing I ask of you. I personally don't like to administer drugs to keep the girls compliant. I like my girls lucid and in control as it makes for a better experience for our buyers. No one wants a drug-addicted whore who can barely keep her eyes straight and fist a cock properly. That means if you disobey me or fail to do as I instruct, you will be punished. Understood?"

I drop my eyes before she can see the emotion spit from them like grease in a hot skillet. Swallowing down the rock in my throat, I choke out, "Yes, ma'am."

She makes a sound of aversion. "Never call me that. Reminds me of my mother," she snaps, muttering the last part.

"How would you like me to address you?" I ask, finding the courage to look up and meet her eyes once more.

I know what I'd *like* to fucking call the evil bitch.

Rio chortles from the doorway but sobers when Francesca shoots a pointed look over her shoulder.

She trains her narrowed gaze on me, seeming to contemplate something.

"Just call me Francesca," she responds. "Rio here is going to implant a tracking device and tattoo your Slave ID. Everyone gets one, and they will only be covered once you have your master."

My heart shrivels and dies the moment she mentions a tracking device. I'm not sure why I'm surprised, but it sends a fresh dose of panic into my bloodstream, twisting my gut painfully. Tears begin to burn the backs of my eyes, the hopelessness deepening.

"Yes, Francesca," I force out, my back hunching from the emotions circulating throughout my body, so potent that they nearly disintegrate my spine and send me crumbling to the floor at her feet.

As temporary as it is, she appears pleased and heads for the door, pausing to look Rio in the eyes and order, "Keep her sedated. We'll let her heal for a week before she's required to acclimate in the house and begin her lessons. You broke her, you fix her, so she will be your responsibility until further notice."

His lips tighten, but he nods. Despite the fact that I was just told I'm going to be tagged like cattle, there's a pinch of relief circulating throughout my body. The second she disappears, firmly shutting the door behind her, I get up as quickly as my broken body can handle and shuffle towards the bed, flopping down on it.

An angel and a devil rest on my shoulders; the soft one coaxing me to curl in a ball so I can shatter into tiny pieces, while the other yells at me to keep fighting—to not break down like all hope is lost.

Keep it together, little mouse. You'll survive this. You will.

Steeling my spine, I force the tears back. I have at least a week before I'm thrust into the thick of what it truly means to be human trafficked. A week to be ignorant of the horrid things they do to girls here.

Rio grabs a black bag from atop the dresser next to me. I had noticed it when I first entered the room, and since then, I've treated it like a bag full of snakes. Seems I wasn't far off in thinking so. The bite of a python would feel no different than being permanently branded.

Holding my breath, I eye him closely as he approaches me, his weight compressing the edge of the lumpy mattress. Slowly, he unzips it, the sound tearing through my nerves as it does the bag. Next, he pulls out a small tattoo gun, ink, and what looks similar to a piercing gun but... not.

"Tracker first," he announces, holding up the torture device. He grabs a tiny microchip from the bag, inserts it into the gun, and then twirls his finger, signaling for me to turn.

Apprehensively, I face away from him, shivering when I feel his fingers brush across the nape of my neck as he gathers my hair to the side.

"It'll hurt," he warns a second before a sharp stabbing pain pierces my neck. I yelp, wincing, two seconds away from whirling around and slapping the shit out of him. My vision blurs with tears, but I can't tell if it's from the pain or because I have a tracking device inside my body.

I turn back around, shooting him a nasty look to cover up the fact that I'm on the verge of crying. He ignores it, opening a new needle and preparing for the tattoo.

"Where's this one going?"

"On the wrist."

I rear back when he lifts his hands towards my arm, attempting to stall. "Do you do this often?"

"Yes. Now how about you make this as painless as possible for both of us and let me see that pretty little hand."

Tightening my lips, I don't resist when he grasps my wrist in a surprisingly gentle hold, coaxing me to lie my arm on his jean-clad thigh. Tears settle in along the ridge of my lids as the buzz of the tattoo gun vibrates against my flesh, followed by the bite of the needle.

"Did you do your own tattoos?" I ask, though I don't really care. I'm searching for anything to distract me from what he's doing.

"No," he answers shortly.

"How many do you have?"

He glances at me. "A lot."

"This is my first one," I whisper. "Do any of yours mean anything?"

Another glance, this one saturated with a little more irritation.

"Some do," he concedes.

I stay quiet for a beat. "But none of them are brands, are they?"

This time when he looks at me, the emotion in his gaze is indecipherable. He doesn't respond, and I take that for an answer in itself.

The tattoo only takes a few minutes, though I'm sure his lines are uneven from my trembling.

When he finishes, the first tear falls, and I quickly swat it away. If he notices, he doesn't make it known.

Packing up his tools, he straightens and stares down at me. I can't read the emotion in his eyes, but I don't think I care to, anyway.

"How are you going to sedate me?" I ask, picking at a loose thread on the army green blanket. My neck and wrist burn, and all I want to do is fade away.

Is that weak? Would Zade be disappointed if he knew I was eager to fall into a pit of unconsciousness instead of clawing my way out of here?

You need to be at full strength, I soothe myself. I'm sure there is plenty I should be doing regardless of my physical state. Learning patterns, listening for anything that could help me, but I'm too fucking tired, and my body is steadily shutting down anyway.

He shrugs, a strange glimmer sparkling in his dark eyes. "Pills. But that's not what you should be concerned about."

Rio steps toward me again, his boots echoing on the floor until his knees brush the white sheet. He bends at the waist, his lips scarcely brushing across my cheek while hot breath fans against the shell of my ear.

"Better hope the men here don't come in for an easy meal," he whispers, eliciting a cold chill.

My throat dries and clogs with a pool of emotions. Mainly disgust and anger, but also terror. The thought of men taking advantage of my body while I'm out cold is sickening. My stomach twists in response, and it takes all of my self-control to hold back the hot tears in my eyes.

"Francesca would let that happen?" I force out, my voice hoarse and strained. He retreats an inch, watching my expression closely. I stare straight ahead, refusing to meet his soulless gaze.

"She wouldn't know." He pauses, a vicious grin tipping up the corners of his lips. "And neither would you."

I hold tightly onto my composure, body shaking as my control threatens to slip. Another tear slips loose as his thumb brushes my bottom lip, prying it open and placing a white pill on my tongue.

"Swallow," he orders quietly. I do, only if it means I won't remember any of this.

"Good girl," he praises. *Fuck you.*

Then, he brushes a finger down my spine lightly, leaving chills in his wake.

"Don't worry, princess, maybe I'll be taking good care of these stitches when they come sniffing," he murmurs, offering a shred of hope I refuse to cling to.

I snarl, and glare at him through blurred vision.

"And you'd be any better?" I hiss, challenging his morals. They're as obscure as frosted glass.

Slowly, he straightens his spine and shoots me a cryptic grin. "I guess you'll never really know, will you?"

Turning, he walks out of the room. The second the door clicks shut, several more tears escape. And once those are set loose, a flood follows. I curl into a ball and slap a hand over my mouth right as a sob breaks free.

For an indiscernible amount of time, I crumble, weeping until my eyes swell and I have nothing left to give. And then slowly, I suck in deep breaths until I've pieced myself back together again. It's messy, and some parts of me have been rearranged, but I'm no longer in ruins, and that's the best I can do for now.

Wiping my eyes, I blow out a shaky breath and take inventory of my new room. The pill is beginning to set in, and coupled with my pity party, it's hard to stay awake, but I haven't gotten a second to take it in without someone breathing down my neck.

They assigned me a room at the back of the house, though a decent size. It's sparse, the cramped space occupied by a mirror, a lumpy bed with a deflated pillow and scratchy blanket, a nightstand, and a dresser.

Just like the rest of the house, the wood creaks with every step, and I have a feeling I'm going to learn the exact spots that don't make any noise.

On the bright side, there's a nailed-shut window that provides a perfect view of the driveway, allowing me to see who comes in and out, and I don't have to share a room with anyone.

Before Francesca showed up, Rio had informed me that five other girls are being groomed for auction. Francesca's job is to mold us into proper sex slaves. Teach us how to act, how to look, and what not to do.

But what she really does is teach us how to survive.

I don't see the fucking point in any of it.

The more compliant, obedient, and pleasant we are, the less likely we are to be needlessly abused, Rio claims. But there's no doubt that the buyers will have a brutal, sadistic side, nor is there any doubt we'll be on the receiving end of it, regardless of what perfect little pocket pussies we are.

They want us to feel as if there is no escape, so we might as well act right and take the good days with the bad. But that's not surviving; that's conforming.

It's accepting that we will die here one day. Never to see our family or loved ones again. Never to experience freedom, laughter, and independence for the rest of our miserable lives. To never truly love and be loved.

But I won't fucking accept it.

I'm going home—to Parsons Manor.

And to Zade.

A creak from beside my bed rouses me from a deep slumber I've been wading in for what feels like years. I startle awake in a cold sweat, disoriented, and confused when there's nothing but blackness, and the soft white glow of the moonlight peeking through the window, the strands weak beneath the shadows.

Only a whisper of my escalated breath can be heard over the pounding in my chest.

It takes several seconds to remember where I am. And the moment it registers, the hairs on the back of my neck rise.

Someone's watching me.

Slowly, I sit up, my eyes adjusting to the darkness that's pressing in around me. I turn my head to look out of the window, light rain pattering against it.

Lightning washes the old room in a flash of bright light, and I take the brief moment to get a good look around.

No one is in here—at least not that I can see.

But I feel the weight of eyes on me, searing the side of my face like a hot iron left on a silk dress.

"Who's there?" I whisper. The words barely make it out, my throat underused and dry.

When no one answers, I look toward the nightstand and search for the markings on the side of the table. There are six tally marks, but with it being so dark outside, it has to be after midnight. I'm on day seven now.

Before I let the pill take ahold of me on my first day here, I scratched a line into the cheap, soft wood to mark the days, vowing to keep track any moment I awoke from my drugged slumber.

Rio's always there when I wake up, ready to escort me to the restroom and shove soup and water down my throat before I'm knocked out again. He's been putting the drugs in my food, and I know that I could refuse, but what's the point? I'm not getting out of here if I'm starving and dehydrated. And I've found I don't mind drinking the poison.

Too drugged to care, he watched me scratch a line in the wood on the second night, and for some unfathomable reason, he started tallying them for me when I told him the days are blurring.

He doesn't say much, nor has he mentioned any men attempting to take advantage of me. If they tried, they certainly didn't succeed considering I'd feel the evidence of it. I doubt any of them would bother with a bottle of lube.

So, whether it's because he doesn't care to inform me of his good deed or because no one has attempted it—I don't know.

There's another soft creak from my left. My eyes snap in the direction of the disturbance, right in the corner of my room.

"Who are you?" I ask, though the words don't come out any better than the first time.

I hold my breath, waiting for a response. Several stilted seconds pass, and then just barely, I hear another low creak, as if someone shifted their weight from one foot to the other.

Something I noticed sometime after my arrival was that part of the plaster had been chipped away, revealing wooden bones beneath. Two planks are exposed, with a large enough gap between them to allow all kinds of bugs to creep in.

It made my skin crawl the moment I noticed it, but it was quickly forgotten when Rio came in with steaming soup in his hand.

"What do you want?" I call out.

Another flash of lightning, so quick that I barely have time to process what my eyes are seeing.

There—between the two wooden planks—is an eyeball. Wide and staring at me intently. Just as sudden as it came, the light flickers out, and the room is cloaked in shadows once more.

Jolting violently, I fall backward off the bed, landing painfully on my tailbone. I hardly feel it when panic has taken over. I'm not even capable of screaming for help, too lost in terror to do anything but desperately kick my feet, scrambling back toward the wall and away from the eye.

I plaster myself against it, chest heaving and heart racing. The rain outside grows stronger, droplets slamming into the window with a ferocity that rivals the beat of my heart.

My nails dig into the wood as another low creak breaks through the pounding in my ears.

Someone is in there. Can they see me now, tucked into the corner of the room?

Sucking in a deep breath, I hold it, waiting for something to happen. It feels as if my head is shoved into a guillotine, trapped in that heart-stopping moment of anticipation for when the blade drops.

I'm expecting a figure to break through the planks, a terrifying demon straight from a horror film, bent backwards on its hands and feet and crawling toward me at an unnatural speed.

Something I'd enjoy watching from behind a screen—safe and sound.

But I'm anything but safe in this place.

Another flash of lightning, followed by a loud crack of thunder.

I flinch, expecting to see the eye still staring at me from between the wood, but nothing is there.

A noise slips free from my throat, something between a wheeze and a laugh.

I'm going insane. I have to be.

Shakily, I climb to my feet, my knees nearly clacking together from my fried nerves. It's enough to momentarily distract me from the lingering pain in my body.

I'm an idiot. Someone hiding in the walls is just preposterous. But then my smile slips with one sobering thought.

That girl from Satan's Affair used to watch people from within the walls of the haunted houses before she killed them. But it can't be her. Last I heard, she was still locked up.

There's no one in the walls, Addie. You're being crazy.

Right. I'm being crazy.

Determined to prove it to myself, I decide the only way to know for certain is to look. Tiptoeing to that spot in the corner, loud creaks emphasize each step. I haven't learned any of the quiet spots yet—haven't had a chance to.

It'd be less terrifying if I could flip on the light, but it's too risky. I'm not willing to attract their attention and would rather take my chances with the lurker. That's another sobering thought—realizing that I feel safer with the monster in the wall than I do with the ones that run this household.

But if I'm ever going to sleep again, drugs or not, then I need to be sure there's no one hiding in there watching me sleep.

Another flash and I rush forward to investigate the depths behind the wooden boards.

Nothing is there, at least not that I can see. I'm not brave enough to put my eye right against the planks, but it's enough to satisfy me right before I'm plunged back into darkness.

Slapping a hand on my chest, I breathe out another laugh, choppy and uneven.

As I'm making my way back to the bed, I step on an uneven spot, the wood shifting beneath me. I freeze and look down. Wiggling my foot, the wood shifts again, groaning in protest.

My curiosity piques, along with a spark of excitement. I crouch down as quickly as my body will allow me to, which is admittedly very fucking slow. While I'm healing from the car accident, I'm still just as achy from the lack of movement.

Planting my hands on the plank, I slide it as far down as it will go until there's a gap.

I pick at the edge of the wood, hissing when my nail bends backward painfully, nearly tearing from my finger. Blood sprouts, but I ignore it, determined to see if anything is hiding in the floorboard.

Finally, I find purchase and manage to lift it high enough to lodge my finger beneath it. Carefully, I pop the wood out and stare down into a black abyss.

Blowing out a breath, I plunge my hand into the hole and feel around, cringing when my fingers brush across bug carcasses, and lord knows what else, but my disgust morphs into excitement when I bump into something solid.

I snatch it up and almost squeal when I see that it's a journal.

No fucking way.

I just stare.

Finding Gigi's journal inside a wall in Parsons Manor was unbelievable. Something that only happens in movies.

But finding another journal inside the floor?

Impossible. Fucking impossible.

But the evidence is in my hands. A cheap leather notebook, nowhere near as fancy as Gigi's. The material is cracking and completely missing in some areas, yet it's the most beautiful thing I've ever seen.

Eyes wide, I open the journal and almost yip when I find several written entries inside.

I glance around the room, almost like I'm searching out for someone else to confirm that I'm staring at what I think I am.

It's too dark to see anything now, so I stuff it back in and replace the wood, promising myself to read it later when I can see clearly. Then I stand, too excited to whine over the pain, and slip back into bed.

My heart is racing, partly from the euphoria of finding another journal and partly from disbelief.

She-Devil? If you did this… thank you.

I lie down, feeling slightly comforted that I now have something to cling onto while facing whatever is coming for me.

The storm raging outside lulls me back to sleep, and just as I'm slipping into consciousness, footsteps creak from within the wall, slowly retreating.

June 18th, 2008

TODAY'S THE DAY! Today, I will finally escape this fucking **HELLHOLE**.. Two days before doom. Whatever doom is, I don't think Francesca ever did say what was happening on the 20th. But preparations have all been for this day.

Am I getting sold off? Who fucking knows. Meeting my wannabe master who probably wants me to kneel on the floor and call him daddy.

I won't be here to fulfill anymore sick fantasies for these deranged fucking people.

Where should I go next with Layla?

The mountains? Somewhere cold and beautiful like Alaska maybe. Who's going to get me in Alaska? No one but the bears.

Molly

Chapter Eight
The Diamond

"You have such pretty hair," a soft, whimsical voice says from behind me.

Inhaling sharply, I whip around, startled from the unexpected intrusion.

It's her.

The girl Jerry was carrying in over his shoulder when I first arrived. The girl with fire and ice in her gaze, and the same creepy smile tipping up her lips that she's currently wearing.

Long blonde hair curls around her waist, and deep brown eyes stare at me from the doorway. She's slightly hunched and terribly skinny.

I'm standing at the full-length mirror, attempting to French braid my hair. Rio rudely awoke me this morning by storming in, throwing a soft pair of joggers and a t-shirt at me, and demanding I get ready before slamming the door behind him on his way out. For what, I'm afraid to ask.

My seven days of purgatory are over, and just the thought of being awake makes me nauseous.

I've been waiting around for further directions, so to give myself something to do, I'm trying to fix my hair away from my face.

"Uh, hi," I say, trying to regain my bearings.

I'm instantly on edge, tense beneath her probing gaze. There's something entirely unnerving about her presence.

She straightens and walks farther into the room, standing several inches above me.

"Do you want my help?"

My instinct is to say no. I very much want to kick her out so that I can breathe again. But it would be wise to make friends with the creepy girl rather than enemies.

So, I nod my head, keeping a close eye on her as she approaches me. She's wearing a long white gown that is nearly see-through—the curves of her body and her dark nipples apparent. I keep my eyes averted, trying to give her some semblance of respect that I'm sure she's missing from the men in this house.

Hesitantly, I turn my back to her and watch her closely through the mirror. She smiles wider, displaying crooked teeth as she reaches for my hair. She presses her entire front into my back, and a sick feeling curdles in my stomach when I feel her nipples brushing against me.

Furrowing my brows, I step away, feeling all kinds of weird. She snickers but doesn't come any closer.

Instead of gathering my hair together, she pets me. Brushing her fingertips against my cinnamon strands, almost seeming to relish in the feel.

My discomfort worsens, even when she finally gathers all my hair together. She's gentle with me, though, her eyes glued to her task.

"What's your name?" she asks, running her hand through my hair to clear out the knots.

"Addie," I say. "Yours?"

"How did you get your hair so soft?" she asks in place of an answer. I thin my eyes, not liking her avoidance.

"I don't really do much with it. No heat and no dye."

She hums, and I arch a brow. "Your name," I insist. She pauses and holds out a pale hand, and it takes a second to realize she's asking for the ponytail holder. Blowing out a breath through my nose, I slip the band off my wrist and drop it in her palm.

A few more moments of silence pass, and I don't soften my gaze, boring holes into her face through the mirror, still waiting for an answer.

"Sydney," she responds finally, her voice pleasant as she begins to braid.

Part of me gets the feeling she made me wait on purpose, like a power move. Nothing she's doing is outwardly vindictive or cruel—in fact, she's being incredibly gentle as she twists my hair—but that feeling triggers my sixth sense anyway.

Like when someone laughs at something you said, but you just know they're laughing *at* you, and not with you.

"Francesca wants us to meet her in the pretty room."

I've no fucking idea what the pretty room is. So, when Sydney finishes with my hair and motions for me to follow her, I do so without question.

She leads me down the hallway, a line of girls walking opposite us and towards a room a few doors down from mine.

We file into what looks like a beauty room, Sydney's nickname for it making sense now. She's not calling the room pretty, but rather where we go to *get* pretty.

A long clothing rack lines one wall, with an array of colorful lingerie hanging from it. Three vanities are set up on the opposite side, covered in makeup and brushes. There are a couple of full-length mirrors leaning against another wall and several shoe racks with an assortment of heels lined on each row.

Swallowing thickly, I follow the girls' lead and stand with them in a straight line facing the door. I assume we're waiting for Francesca.

"What are—" I start.

"Shh." A girl cuts off my question, the command short and harsh. Sydney giggles from the other side of me, and I snap my mouth shut, glancing at the one who either is just being a bitch, or has just saved me from getting hurt. Either way, I'll take my chances and listen.

She has long, brown hair, the tips reaching her butt, and hazel eyes. Her face is stony as she stares straight ahead, but I don't study her long enough to decipher the emotion swirling in her irises.

She's tense, that much I can tell. And I'm not sure if it's for what will happen when Francesca arrives, or because of something else.

Or maybe it's because she's been abducted and sold into human trafficking, and no matter what's happening, it's all fucking bad.

Moments later, heels echo loudly on the wood as Francesca makes her way up the stairs and down the hallway toward us. I guess that's one comfort in this house—I'll always know where Francesca is and if she's coming. She's definitely no Casper the fucking ghost with those monstrosities on her feet.

How many blisters did she have to suffer through before her feet were calloused enough to wear those all day, every day?

Twenty? Thirty? Maybe a weird number like forty-two.

When she walks in, her gaze immediately finds mine. I look away instantly, unsure if she'd consider it a challenge if I met her stare.

She walks past me, her fruity perfume lingering as she eyes each of us.

"You all look like shit," she comments snidely, and I can feel the weight of her glare spearing into the side of my head particularly.

Yeah, 'cause it was my fucking fault I had been ran off the road and dragged out of a wrecked car. Bitch.

She pauses in front of a girl with fiery hair, lifts a burnt orange lock, and looks at the split ends in disgust.

"I told you to trim these, don't make me ask again or Jerry gets another night with you," she comments, dropping the strand and moving on. The girl blinks, a flash of pain there and gone, but Francesca has her eagle eyes focused on her next victim.

A girl with dirty blonde hair and beauty marks splattered on her face and down her neck. Francesca observes them closely.

"We've spoken about this, Bethany. Beauty marks are one thing, but moles are unacceptable." My brows furrow, wondering how one would have any control over that.

"You were told to upkeep on the hair sprouting from these ugly things every day. Why do I see hair?"

The girl—Bethany—shifts uncomfortably. "I'm sorry, Francesca. When I had the flu—"

A sharp slap cuts off her words, the sound ringing in my ears. Bethany is holding her reddened cheek, mouth parted in shock.

"Do you *still* have the flu?" Francesca snarls.

Bethany shakes her head slowly. "No, ma'am. I broke the fever last night."

My eyes nearly bulge, but I work to smooth out my expression. This is probably the first day she feels somewhat human again.

"Rocco!" Francesca calls out loudly, causing the six of us to startle.

We all seem to straighten our spines at once.

Rio has told me about him, but I haven't had the displeasure of meeting him yet. If the palpable tension in the air is anything to go by, he's someone to be feared. They all are, really, but for the first time since meeting these girls, I can taste it.

All except Sydney, apparently. She's hiding her giggles behind a hand, staring at the door with glee. I shoot her a nasty look, but she's not paying a lick of attention to me.

Heavy footsteps ascend the steps, each thud rocketing the tension higher. By the time he enters, we're all made of stone, and Sydney is vibrating with excitement.

His presence is pure evil, and I just know that when this man dies, he won't go to Hell. He'll stay in the fourth dimension, where he'll continue to haunt and terrorize the living.

Rocco is a large man with an even larger gut. Sweat coats his skin as he scans the six of us. He definitely looks like Francesca's brother, both with hooked noses, tanned skin, and golden-brown eyes.

Though they look related, Francesca is beautiful, whereas Rocco is… not.

The only beauty that has ever touched this man has been at the hands of a woman. Touches that were stolen and came with a steep price that only she paid for.

Francesca nods at Bethany, "She hasn't been up-keeping the ugly growths on her face."

Rocco's eyes snap to the trembling girl, and though he's not looking at me, the power behind his stare sends a shot of terror through my system. Bethany attempts to keep her face blank, but her entire body is rattling so hard, I can hear her bones knocking together.

Silence descends on the room, so when he opens a switchblade, the sharp metallic ring sounds like a strike of lightning.

Bethany jumps, and I'm not the only other girl that shifts uncomfortably.

"P-please, Roc—"

"Don't speak," he snaps, his rusty voice sending shivers down my spine. I've no idea what he's going to do, but I am sure of one thing; that voice is going to haunt my nightmares for the rest of my days.

"You're worthless to us if you're ugly," he scolds, walking over to her and clutching her face in his meaty palm. She whimpers as he squeezes her cheeks roughly and jerks her head to the side so he can get a better view of her moles.

She bristles, but somehow forces herself not to fight his hold like a rabid dog. He points the tip of the blade to her skin and slowly starts cutting.

I gasp and go to step forward, but next to me, the brown-haired girl's hand snaps out and grabs ahold of mine, clenching so hard it's painful.

And from my other side, Sydney *ohhh*s like an older sibling who's watching the younger child get in trouble. I whip my head towards her, fury radiating from every pore in my body.

"What is wrong with you?" I hiss, keeping my voice low.

Sydney's dark eyes meet mine, and I realize they're not much different from Rocco's. Dead and cold.

"A lot," she answers blandly.

Bethany screams as Rocco continues carving into her face, and I physically cannot hold myself back.

"Aren't you making her uglier?" I snap. Bethany is by no means ugly, but their logic is backwards. If a mole with a few hairs is such a big deal, how is cutting up her face *solving* the problem?

They're scarring her face, for fuck's sake.

Rocco freezes, and Francesca's head turns towards me, rage evident through her caked makeup. But something in her expression is what causes instant regret. Not because she's angry with me for speaking out, no.

Because she won't be able to save me.

Sydney snickers loudly from beside me and takes a giant step away. Clearly not wanting to be associated with my bad behavior, though the way she's been acting is repulsive.

I bite my lip, my eyes dropping along with my heart. It begins to thud violently as fear fills my veins and adrenaline circulates deeply throughout my body, making me feel nauseous.

I close my eyes in resignation, hating myself for my lack of self-control. This isn't like confronting a psychotic stalker. He's not enigmatic, nor will he toe the line between pain and pleasure. There's no sick thrill when a disgusting man is staring me down, probably imagining all the worst ways he could defile or murder me.

He isn't Zade.

Rocco releases Bethany, blood dripping down her face and staining his fingertips. She's trembling, her face contorted with pain, whimpers leaking past her lips as she reels from having her face cut open.

"What did you say, diamond?" Rocco drawls, his voice dipped in venom. I tighten my lips, hating that Rick's nickname is beginning to stick.

Thousands of thoughts race through my head in a matter of seconds. Different scenarios on how I can get out of this unscathed. What I could say or do to calm the violent tornado coming my way, if only it prevents my world from completely crashing down around me. But in the end, I come up blank.

I glance at the brown-haired girl beside me, and she's staring at me like I'm an idiot. I *am* an idiot. But fuck, I couldn't watch a girl get mutilated for having a fucking mole on her face and stand by in silence.

Watch your own back, little mouse. No one else will.

My mouth has dried, and I fear my tongue will shrivel up and crumble from lack of moisture. It's all been rerouted to my eyes, yet I don't dare let the tears fall. I lick my lips, wetting them enough so I can push out words, useless as they'll be.

"Nothing, I'm sorry," I choke out, keeping my voice small and pleasant. Attitude will undoubtedly result in even worse repercussions, and while I'm successful in that endeavor, I'm unsuccessful in keeping the tremors out of my tone. The fear.

"Stupid girl," Francesca hisses, her eyes thin and heated. Rocco walks towards me, his candor slow and purposeful as he opens and closes the switchblade. Over and over, each metallic ring pumping dread into my system.

He stops mere inches from me, his beer gut brushing against my stomach and his rank breath burning my nostrils. Jesus, he smells like body odor and week-old cheese that's been left out in the sun. The little self-control I possess is put towards not cringing from the smell.

"Look at me," he whispers.

I do, lifting my eyes to meet his cold, deadened stare. A piercing shrill in my ears develops as we glower at each other. It forms deep in the recess of my mind and builds to a crescendo until I can hardly hear a sound outside of it.

It's a warning. My own body is sounding an alarm, alerting me of the serious damage coming my way. Just like a tornado alarm, right before the deadly twister rips lives to shreds.

His thick palm seizes my throat, his lips curling as he lifts me up to his height, suspending me on the tips of my toes. Instinctively, I claw at his hand, and I assure myself that if I die here and now and Zade finds my body, he'll know exactly who was responsible based on the skin caked beneath my nails.

Rocco doesn't flinch, despite how deeply my nails bite into his skin. The edges of my vision darken as my body depletes of oxygen, steadily emptying from my lungs while stars burst across my eyes.

"Don't kill her. She's valuable," Francesca snaps, though her voice sounds far away, like I'm trapped in a vortex.

Snarling, he swings me around and tosses me to the floor like a wadded-up gum wrapper.

I grunt from the impact, landing awkwardly on my right wrist, but before I can lift myself up, he's climbing on me, his weight suffocating.

Survival instincts immediately kick in, and my fight or flight activates—namely my fight. I twist beneath him and swing my elbows towards his head. But I miss, a weak attempt at knocking out a two-hundred-pound-plus man from on top of me.

"Get off me!" I screech, bucking my hips, desperate to dislodge him. So desperate that I've become rabid. I will tear the flesh from my bones with my teeth if it means getting out from beneath him. I will do anything—absolutely anything—to escape.

"Rocco," Francesca warns, cutting through the sheer panic that has consumed my mind. "She needs to heal."

"She needs to learn her place. It doesn't have to hurt," he argues, breathless from wrangling my struggling body into compliance. He's failing—but so am I. I'm weak and still in pain, and he's so much stronger.

He's going to win.

"Right, diamond? This could be quick and painless. A little lesson to teach you to keep your fucking mouth shut."

He bashes my face into the wooden floor, dirt and dust grinding into my face as he rips at my joggers. The fabric tears, the loud ripping noise sending another shot of horror into my system as his excited breathing escalates.

"No!" I shout as he tears at my underwear next. He ignores me and unfastens his jeans, the bite of his zipper coming undone his only response. Rivulets of tears stream down my cheeks as I feel his flesh against my backside.

I try to twist again, but one punch to the back of my head deters me, my world exploding. Pain has been a constant companion this last week, but it's nowhere to be found now. My mind feels as if I could run a mile, yet my body physically cannot stop this man from defiling me.

"Don't hit her!" Francesca snaps, more worried about him bruising the apple. But how can that be when I'm going to be fucking rotten by the time he's done?

In one thrust, he buries himself inside me, and I scream. Loud and piercing, the pitch matching the shrill ringing in my head.

"Goddammit, Rocco, you're not wearing a condom," Francesca shouts, and there's a soft whisper in my head, wondering how she can stand to watch this. Just stand there, angry that her brother isn't wearing a condom as he rapes a girl.

He grunts and then laughs as he repeatedly drives himself inside me. "Feels fucking incredible, too."

There's nothing I can do to stop him, and the defeat that coats my skin like hot oil fucking burns.

I try to crawl away from him, my nails digging into the wood and anchoring me as I try to pull myself out from beneath him. They bend and break from the pressure, tearing from my skin as he drags me back down, scratches gouging the floor.

He slams into me once, twice more before pulling out and finishing on me. Ribbons of his seed spurt across my back, and I can't help but gag. He growls, his palm crashing into the side of my face.

"Rocco!" A heel stomps into the wood in a fit of rage, the vibrations traveling to my bleeding hands.

"Fucking bitch," he mutters, ignoring her. I gag again, the feel of his essence seeping into my flesh nauseating.

Francesca sighs, rushes over to me, and grabs me roughly by the arm.

"Get up," she spits, hauling me to my feet. I'm so angry, so distraught from what he just did that I react. As soon as I'm on my feet, I twist at the waist and send my fist flying into his nose. He howls in response, gearing up to charge at me, but Francesca steps between us and blocks him.

"Stay down! You've done enough," she snarls, then drags me out of the room. I'm still naked from the waist down, with blood smudged between my thighs. My body was unaccepting of what he was doing, making the intrusion raw and extremely painful.

She pushes me into my room and slaps me across the face, causing me to stumble. The door slams, and then, "Why did you do that, stupid, *stupid* girl?"

She slaps me again, and my ears ring from the pain. I grab my cheek, continuing to scramble away from her as she backs me against the wall.

You're bruising the apple, Francesca.

Her hands grip either side of my face, and her manicured talons dig into my reddened cheeks.

Putting her face in mine, she snarls lowly, "You keep your mouth shut, do you hear me? The men in this house will do everything to make your life hell until you've been paid for. And you sure as fuck don't *hit* them!"

She shakes me, "Tell me you understand," she whisper-shouts, keeping her voice quiet.

"I understand," I cry, my cheeks hot and wet from the constant tears.

Francesca releases me angrily, tearing herself away and shooting a heated glare over her shoulder as she paces the room. I slide down the wall, no longer capable of holding myself up as sobs rack my body. A streak of blood follows me down, and I realize Rocco ripped open the stitches on my back. Spearing my hands through my hair, I grip the strands tight, willing myself to calm.

Deep breaths, Addie. Deep breaths.

Just breathe.

Breathe, little mouse…

Chapter Nine
The Diamond

It seems when my life turns upside down, I always have a diary to offer me escape.

I'm not sure how she managed to get a hold of a journal, but I find comfort in Molly's angry words. A young girl that was stolen from her life just as I was. And groomed by Francesca, no less.

My mouth dropped when I read that Francesca has been doing this for at least thirteen years now. How many girls has she watched be raped, tortured, and sold off to demented people? How many did she hurt herself?

My stomach rolls, and my throat thickens with disgust as I take in the words of a broken girl. She was full of life in a world that was determined to take it from her, and through each entry, I fall more in love with her. I feel her in every stroke of the pen, so I brush my trembling fingers across them and mold myself into her harsh lines.

She's everything I want to be.

When I come to the last page, my heart breaks, and millions of questions arise. As quickly as I had found some form of comfort, I'm now left desolate and empty once more.

Tears line the edges of my lids as I tear through pages, frantic and in need of more of her words. But I find nothing but blank pages.

Did she ever make it out? Did she make it back to Layla and take her away to find a new life? A better life?

I exhaust myself with questions that I'll never get the answers to. At least not while I'm stuck in here.

Defeated, I snap the journal shut, and manage to scrounge up enough energy to roll off the bed and crawl to the open slot. Hot tears spill over as I replace the journal back into its hiding spot. And as I seal the wooden plank back down, everything I tried to not think about rushes back to me.

Nearly falling in my rush back to the bed, I curl up in a ball, clenching my fists, my broken nails screaming. My entire body quakes from the memories slaughtering any semblance of peace I found with Molly. With everything I have, I hold on tightly to the sobs shredding my throat in an attempt to escape.

I won't let them.

It couldn't have been more than a half-hour since Francesca stormed out of my room, and went to calm Rocco down, who, from the sound of it, went on a rampage and started destroying the house. I immediately tore off my soiled clothing, and dressed in a fresh pair, but it did nothing to soothe me while chaos ensued below my room. That's when I remembered the journal in the floorboards and found solace in Molly.

For an indescribable amount of time, I stare at the wall. If my eyes even stray towards the dusty wooden floor, all I can see is an image of myself lying on the ground with Rocco mounted over me. I watch the desecration of my soul, like an out-of-body experience. Standing over the apparitions, unable to stop it from happening.

Desperately, I attempt to train my thoughts on anything else—Zade or Daya—but the train derails every time, leading me back towards the beauty room. They're merely ghosts haunting the hallways of my brain, and anytime I reach out to them, they only fade away.

I squeeze my eyes shut, frustration mounting.

I should've listened. Yeah, that's what I should've done. Allow a girl to be mutilated to save myself.

Shaking my head, I thump the heel of my palm on my forehead. How am I supposed to live with that? If I ever get out of here, how am I supposed to be okay knowing that I stood by while awful things happened to other girls, purely to save myself?

They stood by while you were raped.

They did. Do I hate them for it?

I don't know. Kind of. There's a morsel of inky blackness unfurling inside of me, and I kind of want to kill them, too.

"No," I whisper. I can't expect everyone to be so sacrificial. I can't expect a girl who's being abused just as I am to try and save someone else. *Try to.*

Because that's the fucking problem. There *is* no saving them. Bethany is still going to have that mole cut out of her skin. All of those girls in there—they're still going to be raped and tortured, no matter how many times I step in.

We're all just lambs waiting to be slaughtered, and getting myself killed isn't going to stop the wolves from feasting.

So, what the fuck am I supposed to do?

Zade's voice whispers in my mind, and my heart clenches painfully.

Pick your battles. Be smart.

Easier said than fucking done.

I startle when my bedroom door slams open about ten minutes later, the doorknob knocking into a perfectly round dent in the wall. There's obviously a long history of this door being kicked in.

Breathing heavily, I watch Rio enter the room, carrying a first aid kit and appearing calm as ever despite him kicking down the door.

"Already causing trouble, princess?" he asks casually.

I refuse to answer, tightening my lips and glaring at him through swollen eyes. He raises his brows when he catches sight of my face, causing my cheeks to burn hot from anger. For a moment, he looks furious, though I can't tell who with.

He twirls his finger in the air, indicating that I turn over.

"I have to clean up the mess you made," he tells me, his face smoothing into an unreadable expression. "You're getting blood everywhere."

Huffing, I roll onto my stomach, tensing when I feel his fingers brush my t-shirt up my back.

"It's not my fau—"

"Everything is your fault here," he interrupts, his voice deepening with severity. "Don't ever forget that."

He rustles through the supplies, sighing like this is a huge inconvenience for *him.*

"I'm terribly sorry to interrupt your day of trafficking women," I mutter, stewing in my fury. His response is to place an alcohol-soaked pad on my ripped stitches. The burn is startling, and I hiss through my teeth, curses building on the tip of my tongue.

Fucking *asshole.*

"Your mouth is going to get you in worse situations than this," he informs me. "What's it going to take for you to learn your lesson? Getting a girl killed?"

Swallowing, I choke out, "I'm sorry."

A loud, booming laugh bursts from his throat. I snap my head to him, enraged as his shoulders shake with mirth. His dark eyes are twinkling with the first real emotion I've seen thus far. It's almost as terrifying as him being angry.

"You're laughing at me," I say with disbelief.

"Baby girl, I'm not the one you need to be afraid of. I much prefer that mouth of yours."

"You just said—"

"You mouth off without thinking it through, and that's what you need to learn to control," he cuts in, his smile dimming, but his eyes still alight with amusement. "As sexy as your fire is, princess, that's the last thing you want in this place."

I curl my lip in disgust, thumping my head back on the bed while he resumes cleaning up my back.

"Don't call me sexy," I snap, only because he's right, and I have nothing better to say.

"Z gonna kill me for it?" he challenges airily, feigning indifference. Although, that's not how he sounded when I awoke in that van and overheard Rick and him discussing if the Society will offer them protection from Zade's wrath.

I shrug. "He's going to kill you anyway, so I guess it doesn't matter."

He's quiet, and just when I'm convinced that he's not going to say anything at all, I hear him whisper under his breath, "I know."

As Rio is leaving, Francesca comes barreling down the hallway, her heels resounding on the floor. Her hand wraps around Rio's arm, stopping him at the door.

"Is her back worse?"

He shakes his head. "Nah, they're superficial. She'll be fine," he answers, though his last words sound like they have a double meaning. When she turns away from him, he casts a wink over his shoulder before walking off, leaving me confused.

He's so fucking hot and cold.

Francesca storms into the room, appearing frazzled with her wild hair and eyes. Her dress is ripped at the collar, and I wonder just what kind of tantrum Rocco was throwing.

"Get in the beauty room. Now."

Her abrasive footsteps carry her right back out of the room. I scramble from the bed, rubbing my dry eyes while I hurry after her. Rio clipped my broken nails and cleaned them up for me, but I still feel broken. Every step is a reminder of what happened in that room, and my stomach turns as I draw closer. It takes all my strength to focus on the lineup of girls and not the spot where I lost my mind.

None of them catch my eye. Except for Sydney.

Her bottom lip is fitted snugly beneath her crooked front teeth as she bites back a grin. She finds this funny, and I decide that Sydney—I *do* hate.

Ignoring the psycho bitch, I search out Bethany, and a lump forms in my throat when I spot a bloody open wound where her mole used to be. My chest tightens, the confirmation feeling like sharp knives grazing my nerve endings.

I was raped for nothing.

Fuck, I knew that. But it still feels like getting fucked all over again.

Clearing my throat, I stand straighter, embarrassment and shame burning my cheeks. I don't know why. It's not like being raped is something *I* should be ashamed of. Maybe because I feel so fucking stupid.

"Today was supposed to be prepping for the Culling, but you had to go and cause a distraction," Francesca snipes at me.

My heart sinks like a stone in water, too preoccupied with her words to feel embarrassed. Molly mentioned the Culling in her entries, but she didn't go into detail about what it was—only implied that she was being hunted.

Licking my cracked lips, I ask, "What's the Culling?"

Francesca smirks. "It means to hunt animals. The men will hunt, and you, my dear, are the prey."

My chest tightens, but deep down, I knew that answer already. I just didn't want to believe it. I suppose I shouldn't be surprised that they actually fucking hunt women like we're game that will be shot and mounted above a fireplace.

This is purely for sport. To laugh and get their rocks off while a bunch of girls run for their lives and what—try to avoid being hit with a fucking bullet or something?

I have to fight to keep down the urge to vomit. I don't want to be hunted. And it seems that's all my life has been for the past several months.

Francesca casts her gaze down the line.

"The event will take place later this week, and I have an important client visiting—Xavier Delano. He is one of the top buyers in the market, and if you're lucky, you'll be selected for auction. But you will *only* be selected if you are deemed worthy after the Culling."

Her glacial eyes find me, an abhorrent expression twisting her features. "Except you. You look repulsive."

I swallow the retort sitting on my tongue and nod my head in acceptance, like a good little captive. Not like I fucking want to be selected anyway. Guess I should be glad I'm covered head to toe in bruises.

She clicks her tongue, as if she finds me stupid. "You will still be expected to participate in the Culling."

Of fucking course I am. What's another injury?

"Alongside Xavier, we have several other potential buyers coming here as well. You want to make the best impression on these men. I won't tolerate any insolence, you understand?" Mid-speech, her eyes drift to the other girls, but by the time she ends her sentence, her gaze has locked back onto me.

I flatten my lips into a hard line and nod once. The other girls also acknowledge her order with a dip of their chins.

"The less interest they have in you, the less likely you are to leave my house. And you know what that means? That means that I don't produce the best girls, and I will get very fucking angry if that ever becomes the case."

How aren't her teeth rotten from the vile things she spews all day?

It takes tremendous effort to keep my face blank with the turmoil rolling through me.

She approaches me slowly. "Let's run some scenarios. What do you do when a man asks you to get on your knees for him?"

"Get on my knees," I answer, my voice hoarse.

"And when he tells you to unfasten his pants and take out his cock?"

"Do as he says."

She nods, studying me closely.

"And then what?"

Bite his dick off.

I know what the obvious answer is. Nevertheless, I also know what controlling men truly get off on.

Power.

"Wait for him to give me permission."

Surprise flickers across her irises, and I hate the reaction that look pulls out of me. The last thing I want to do is make a sex trafficker proud, but in all honesty, it's precisely what I need to do. I just don't want to *feel* it.

During our training lessons, Zade had taught me a lot about human trafficking and how I could escape it, should the Society ever come for me.

Get them to trust you. Make them see you as a human being, not an object to be sold.

Would it even matter if they did see me as a person? People like this—they don't have any compassion for humanity. Not when they're hardly human themselves.

She sniffs. "Good."

And then she moves on to the next girl, the one with hazel eyes and who had kept warning me to keep my mouth shut.

"Jillian, how do you address them?"

"Yes, sir," she replies instantly, her eyes unfocused as Francesca stares her down. Our captor nods once and moves on to the girl with fiery orange hair.

"Phoebe? When they address you, do you look them in the eye?"

"No," she responds confidently.

"Why?" Francesca tests.

"Because it's disrespectful."

Fuckers. They want us meek and cowering. Sad, little girls who should have no other thoughts, apart from how to please their master.

Fucking disgusting, is what it is.

Bethany is next, but she's not as composed as the other two girls—Jillian and Phoebe. She was obviously mutilated after I was dragged out of the room, but who's to say more wasn't done to her?

Maybe in the midst of his tantrum, Rocco raped her, too.

I clench my fists but keep my feet glued to the floor and my spine locked and unbending.

"When the men don't like something on your body, like say, a hairy mole, what do you do, Bethany?"

Her lip trembles and I can see the battle in her body language not to break down. It takes her a moment to compose herself before she answers, "Make sure there's no hair."

Francesca nods slowly. "Good." She glances at the wound where her mole used to be. "I hope to God you don't have any more of those in places I can't see. Because if you do, and I find out they're unkempt, those will be cut out as well."

Then she turns her eyes to the last girl in line. She's meeker than the others, mousier. Short brown, curly hair, wire-rimmed glasses, and pretty doe eyes.

She keeps her eyes down, even as Francesca addresses her.

"And when you go into the Culling, Gloria, what is the one and only rule?"

She licks her lips, glancing up at Francesca before quickly dropping them again.

"D-don't get hit," she whispers, her voice high-pitched and small.

My brow furrows.

"And what happens if you do?"

She swallows audibly as she begins to shake violently. "W-we will—" She stops, gathers her wits, and forces out the rest of her sentence. The words are spoken so quickly, they nearly merge together. "We will be punished."

"Good," she clips, and then she heads for the door, stepping out to grab something just outside of the entrance. My heart drops when she walks back in with a crossbow.

"I want you out of my house, Sydney, so you will participate, but if you try to escape one more time, I will personally kill you myself. You're no longer worth the hassle."

Sydney gasps, as if this is the first time that she's hearing this, but I have a feeling this has been a conversation for however long she's been in this house.

She crows, "I only run because I want to stay with you."

"Well, you can't," she snaps back. "This isn't a fucking Holiday Inn. Now that I have the diamond in my possession, I can no longer allow you to embarrass me. You *will* be sold."

"What does she have to do with me?" Sydney argues.

"Because she is my most valued girl, and if it is noticed that I have a goddamn leech attached to me that is incapable of being sold, they could deem me unworthy and remove her from my household!"

Rage flashes across the unhinged girl's eyes, and it looks like she's rapidly descending into a pit of hysteria. When she catches my stare, she snarls at me, as if it's my fault Francesca isn't allowing her to stay.

Francesca gathers herself, her eyes tight with lingering anger.

"Tomorrow, we're going to practice," she orders, pulling my attention away from the seething girl. Her eyes flicker to me accusingly. "And I don't care how special you are, I won't tolerate failure."

How do volcano eruptions begin? Pressure. And it's brewing inside of me. The fiery magma is rising, thickening with hatred, growing denser with bloodlust.

Eventually, I'm going to fucking explode, and I promise I will burn this entire goddamn house down with me.

November 2021

I wasn't going to do this at first. But I decided that if Molly couldn't ~~contu~~ continue to write her story, then I would write mine.

It feels weird, but also right. And part of me feels like Gigi led me to this journal. Something to help me hold onto my sanity. So I stole a tube of lipstick to honor her.

I have a strong feeling I'm going to lose my sanity here anyway. Or come very close.

The only thing I know for certain is that I need to get out of here. But I need to heal first, and there's a good chance this Culling will make it worse. I still have stitches in my back, and the pain has only lessened a fraction.

But I can't do this for long. I can already feel myself fraying at the edges. The weight of Rocco on top of me forever presses down on me. As if I'm walking around with him on my shoulders.

But I need to hold on. The only thing I can do is bide my time. And wait. I'm sure Zade is looking for me by now. And that makes me feel a little better, even if I die here.

Chapter Ten
The Hunter

"I've got a location on the van," Jay says, turning in his chair. I've only just stepped into his office, having just got back from Daya's house.

A week has passed since I got her out of Luke's clutches, and since then, she's been helping out. I put her in charge of researching Rio and Rick while Jay has been focused on tracking down the van. We hit a dead end in Oregon. The vehicle disappeared from cams without a trace, and I've been losing my mind since.

She's been gone for twelve days now, and I've felt every fucking second of it.

"How'd you find it?"

"Finally got a hit on a satellite image taken yesterday."

"Walk and talk," I order, pivoting and walking right back out. "What's the address?"

He rattles off the address while he scrambles from his chair, followed by a muttered curse, a loud thump, and another colorful word or two.

I glance back to see him struggling to put on a second shoe, hopping on one foot and nearly face-planting into the wall.

Shaking my head, I make my way down the stairs, leaving him to figure out how to be a functioning human again.

By the time I swing open the door to my Mustang, Jay is locking his front door behind him and hurrying to the car.

He lives in a modest home with his younger brother, Cameron, though I'd never know if it wasn't for the occasional screeches when he yells at whatever game he's playing. Or whoever he's playing with.

Jay and Cameron's parents were drug addicts and skipped out when Jay was sixteen and Cameron seven. Luckily, Jay is an actual genius and managed to keep it a well-kept secret from the state. He's worked numerous jobs to keep the bills paid and his brother in good health.

Six years later, Jay has legal guardianship of Cameron, and they're living lavishly. Cameron isn't aware of what his brother does for work, and right now, he's too young to care. I think he's more concerned with not dying in *Call of Duty* to notice, and Jay is happy to keep it that way.

"I need to call Michael to babysit," he says, dropping into the passenger seat with a huff. His phone is already out, his thumb flying across the keyboard.

"Dude, he's thirteen."

Jay pauses to look at me, a dry look on his face. "Exactly, which means he's going to be up until six o'clock in the morning with a bag of Doritos in one hand and his dick in the other, running up my credit card with porn." I tip my head side to side, conceding. "Plus, I don't feel comfortable leaving him alone," he finishes quietly.

My gaze flickers to him while I speed out of his driveway. Claire is determined to hurt me, which puts the lives of my employees and their families at risk, too. I make a lot of enemies, and by association, so do my employees. No one goes into this job without knowing this, which is why most of them choose not to have a wife and kids. Obviously, not everyone can or will isolate themselves from loved ones, so providing protection for anyone directly impacted by the organization is essential.

"I get it. I'll call in a few extra men, too. Nothing will happen to your brother."

Jay nods, his shoulders relaxing an inch. It's the same thing I said to Addie, and I failed her.

I slide out a cigarette from my pack and pop it in my mouth.

I won't fail again.

"This is the location?" I ask, my voice tight. "You're sure?"

We're in an awfully shitty part of town in Portland, Oregon. The address Jay directed me to is a three-story brick building that looks like it was built in the 1800s and abandoned before the century turned.

The building is slightly lopsided, the windows are crusty and blackened with grime, and the interior looks to be completely dark.

"This is it," Jay says quietly. "The van is around the corner still."

"Fuck," I curse, briefly squeezing the steering wheel until the leather groans.

"Doesn't look like they're still here," I bite out, swinging open the door and stepping out. "We'll check out the van after."

I slip out my gun from the back of my jeans and approach the door quickly and quietly, keeping my eyes on my surroundings at all times.

"Jay, stay behind me," I order. He listens without argument, his breathing escalating as I approach the glass door. He doesn't have any weapons on him, only his laptop. I'm tempted to hand him one, but I'm pretty confident he'd do more damage hitting someone upside the head with his computer rather than firing off a gun he has no idea how to use.

I peer through it, a crease forming between my brows when I see the upheaval. It appears like it was once an administrative office. Cluttered desks fill the space, with random items scattered across the surfaces; toppled over picture frames, pens, and flyaway papers.

My eyes scan the area as well as I can, watching for any movement and listening for any sounds.

When I hear and see nothing, I grab the handle and tug on the door, setting my jaw when I find that it's open.

Addie isn't here, but I knew that already. Just as well as I know that something bad happened here.

Quietly, I creep into the building, Jay sticking close behind me. The energy here is stale and heavy, filled with dust and decay.

"What the fuck were they doing taking her here?" Jay whispers, sweeping the room.

I shake my head, incapable of verbally answering when my heart is beating in my throat. But that's exactly what I'm about to find out.

Not wasting any more time, I rush through the space, checking a few rooms, only to find them empty. In the back is a stairway with a dim light shining from beyond the steps, the only sound a quiet whirring from the light bulb.

Glancing back at Jay, I put my finger to my lips before carefully making my way up the stairs. From the sound of it, there doesn't appear to be any activity, but if lights are on, I won't take any risks.

The whirring grows louder as I near the top, and with it comes a wretched smell that burns at my nostrils.

I nearly choke on how rancid it is, and I hear Jay cough from behind me.

Well, fuck. That's a smell I'm very well acquainted with.

Someone died up here, and I will gladly place a bet that the body is rotting in the same place where they fell.

The landing opens up to a small, dark area with a hallway branching off from it, strands of light stretching from the back of it and toward us. Straight ahead appears to be a second stairwell, leading to the final floor.

Planting myself against the wall, I motion for Jay to follow my lead, then peer around the corner and down the hallway, eyes narrowing when I glimpse an open room with what looks like an IV pole standing in the corner.

I can't see much else from my vantage point, however, I'm positive there isn't anyone up here. Not anyone *alive*, anyway.

"Let's go," I whisper, making my way towards the room, gritting my teeth as the smell worsens.

As soon as I breach the entrance, I stop short, causing Jay to collide into my back.

On the floor is a massive pool of dried blood, a dead man lying directly in the middle of it. He's bloated, well into the process of decomposition.

"Jesus, fuck," Jay mutters, as we both stare down at the stranger, disgust curling our faces. Dead bodies don't bother me, but their rot will curdle the strongest stomach.

Immediately, I notice dry bloody footprints leading from the corpse and toward the doorway we're standing in. Grabbing my phone, I click on the light and follow the footprints down the hallway and toward the second staircase.

"Female," he says, confirming my thoughts. I get closer, taking care not to step in the blood. "You think they're Addie's?"

"Most likely," I murmur. The prints are tiny and barefoot. Unless they took other females alongside Addie, I doubt they're anyone else's.

I sweep the corners of the room, locating several cameras pointing in different directions.

"Cameras," I call out, stepping around the blood and farther into the room. Those will confirm whose prints they belong to.

My heart pounds as I take in Frankenstein's lair. Several machines are set up, a long metal table with a copious amount of instruments, and a bed with a blanket laid haphazardly across it.

"He's been dead for several days," Jay observes. "Shot in the head. From the back."

I listen to him prattle on about his death as I scan every inch of the room.

"Let's follow the footprints," I mumble, my brow pinched as I try to piece together what could've happened.

Following close behind, Jay and I make our way back down the hallway and up the second stairwell. The landing opens directly into a studio apartment. Straight ahead, the entire wall is all glass, giving the room incredible natural light. A massive bed is in the middle of the area to my left with a small kitchenette to the right, dishes still in the sink and now attracting flies.

In the back corner of the apartment is a white tiled partition with a shower stall behind it.

The footprints lead all the way to it, and in the corner is a bloody hospital gown, dried and wrinkled now.

I stare, trying to process what the hell happened.

"Somehow… she was involved with that man's death. And then it looks like she walked up here and showered," Jay concludes.

I shake my head, coming to the same conclusion. Fury is seeping into my vision, casting everything in red.

"Either she or someone else shot him from behind," I surmise. "Most likely someone else if she was covered in his blood and then had to shower it off."

"You think she was in front of him?" Jay questions curiously.

"Or under him," I grunt, hands beginning to shake as images of Addie being attacked by the man downstairs flood my head. Whatever he was attempting to do to her, it was bad enough that a human trafficker had to step in and kill him for it.

My hand goes flying into the nearest wall, breaking straight through it. Like a malfunctioning robot, I cock it back and drive it through a second time. And a third, a fourth, a fifth, before Jay's hands wrap around my arm and using my momentum, yanks me backward. I stumble, and we both come close to falling from the force.

"Snap out of it, dude," he barks, sweat gathered across his hairline.

I growl and roughly shake my head, like a lion shaking off a hit to the head. My knuckles are split, droplets of blood dribbling on the cement floor.

"We'll have to clean up any traces of your blood," he mutters.

"She could've been hurt," I clip, ignoring him. I'm ready to storm back downstairs and beat the shit out of a dead man. Torture him in the worst imaginable ways, despite him not being able to feel a damn thing.

Fuck. So badly, I want to tear through whatever veil separates the dead from the living, reach in, snatch his soul back out, and make him wish he never had one.

Every muscle in my body is locked tight and brimming with tension.

"We're going to find her."

"Hack the cameras," I snap, charging up to the massive window and looking out at the back end of the building. Jay sits on the edge of the bed, briefly looking at it like he's sitting in a cesspool of DNA, then cracks open his laptop and gets to work.

I peer through the grime and find the black van sitting right at the parking lot exit, abandoned. My fists clench, noting the bashed-in fender and damage to the driver's side of the vehicle.

I'm two seconds away from losing my shit again and punching the window, so I work to decompress, closing my eyes and cracking my neck.

Keep it together, I chant to myself. Over and over and until I regain control. I've seen some fucked-up shit in my life, more than most could handle, yet Addie's abduction is the worst thing I've ever experienced. There is no control anymore. Though with her, there never really fucking was.

I will gladly pour gasoline on everything in my path and set it aflame, if only it leads me back to my mouse.

"Zade, you're not going to want to see this… but you need to."

Chapter Eleven
The Hunter

Baby, what have I told you about lashing out when you're angry?

Why is it now, the remnants of my mother's voice plague me? Destruction is right beyond my fingertips, just waiting to be set free. It would be as simple as flicking a lighter, igniting a small flame that would lead to obliteration.

"Zade?" Jay's voice cuts through my mother's whispers, fading like wisps of cigarette smoke.

Speaking of, I shove my hand in my hoodie pocket, snatch one out of the packet, and light up.

Jay's mouth opens, poised over words I honestly don't want to hear right now.

"Don't tell me not to smoke, and don't ask me if I'm okay," I cut in, voice hoarse with rage.

His mouth clicks shut, and he nods, looking back at the video of Addie fighting for her life, time-stamped seven days ago. The cameras don't have audio, so while I'm unaware of the reasoning for the doctor trying to kidnap her, it doesn't change the fact that he tried. Made clear by him quickly urging her out of bed, and her resistance the entire way.

She ambushed him with a scalpel of some sort, and he attacked her in retaliation. Only for the back of his head to be blown off while on top of her.

And while that is incredibly traumatizing, that's not the part that has me boiling with rage. It's the asshole that killed the doctor, then followed her up the stairs and watched her fucking shower.

Rio.

Daya has done her research, and while there was plenty to find on Rick Boreman—there's almost nothing on Rio, outside of being born and raised in Puerto Rico, his school records, then migrating to the United States when he was eighteen. From there, she could find almost nothing on him. Only the apartment he rents, and two speeding tickets.

I call bullshit on that.

"Kind of weird this guy has cameras in his room only facing his shower and bed," Jay mumbles, more to himself. I'm too busy inhaling a cigarette like it's giving me life rather than taking it. If I watch that video again, I'll be liable to whip out my gun and shoot the monitor until it's nothing but shards of plastic and metal.

Jay's fingers fly across the keyboard so quickly, I think I see flakes of his purple nail polish flying off. The video feed from when Addie was here disappears, and in its place are archived recordings that span back several years.

Whoever this guy is, he's been illegally practicing for decades. Several times a month, injured people are brought to him—people that look like they're up to no good.

I flick my cigarette to the ground and crush it beneath my boot, blowing out smoke as I watch Jay skip through several recordings. Just as I lift my boot to kick away the butt, I freeze and clench my jaw, hearing Addie's smart mouth even now.

Stop littering.

This place will be ashes by the time I'm done, but I said I would stop, so I will.

I pick up the butt, stuff it in my pocket, and force myself to refocus on the screen.

Several clips of women showering display on the screen, and with each passing video, my teeth clench harder and harder until every bone in my face threatens to crack.

They are all dressed in hospital gowns before and after their shower, and plenty are covered in bandages or have casts. They were patients, and they were unknowingly being recorded for the doctor's viewing pleasure.

Jay's face is tightened into a scowl, hundreds of videos on the screen. But then he pauses, hesitation permeating the air.

"What?" I ask, scanning my eyes over the screen to find what he's seeing. It takes two seconds, and my heart stops. "Play the videos."

Jay shakes his head and croaks, "You know what happens in them, Z. You don't have—"

"Dammit, Jay, I do have to watch them. You know I fucking do."

He sighs, acquiescing with a slump of his shoulders, and clicks the video. It's just like the rituals—I wasn't there to save them at the moment, but I'll be damned if I turn my head away from their pain now.

On the screen, the doctor is carrying an unconscious woman to his bed, having just come from the second floor where she was probably treated for wounds.

He lays her down, removes her hospital gown, and then his own clothes. And for the next several minutes, he defiles her unconscious body. Disgust swirls in my stomach, growing stronger alongside a whirlpool of anger and the deepening desire to resurrect him so I can kill him myself.

As Jay continues to flip through videos, we realize that woman was one of probably hundreds of patients that were taken advantage of while they were unconscious.

Patients that were also children.

"I think we've seen enough. I don't want to keep looking at this shit anymore," Jay says, voice tight and uneven.

Clenching my fists, I nod, "Look up who this guy is real quick."

He does as I ask, and I turn away, fiending for another cigarette already.

"Dr. Jim Garrison," he announces fifteen minutes later. "Previously married to Wilma Garrison. She died of a heart attack in 2004. There are reports from her two daughters from a previous marriage citing foul play, but he had Wilma cremated before an autopsy could be done, and nothing ever came of it. In 2000, he was fired from a hospital for malpractice, and he bought this building only a few months later. There were a few lawsuits against him, but he must've had a good lawyer because he got away with those due to lack of evidence. Seems to have been operating here since."

Sounds like he is a sick fuck who was doing something evil to his patients, got fired for it, and created his own business to carry out all his dark desires. Most likely killed his wife—maybe she found out about what he was doing or perhaps he simply got tired of her.

"Go back to the videos when the patients are brought in. I want to see if I recognize anyone."

He gratefully flips back to the camera on the second floor, hundreds of different faces bringing in injured people of different ages. Most of the time, they're women and children, but a few men are mixed in there, too. My guess is from shoot-outs gone wrong.

He comes across a clip of the doctor treating what looks like a five-year-old girl with a bullet wound in her thigh. A mammoth of a man with light brown hair tied up in a bun and tattoos crawling up his arms and neck stands at the foot of the bed, watching the doctor work with an intense look on his face.

Jay poises his finger over a key, ready to flip to the next video, but I put a hand on his shoulder, stopping him. "Wait, I want to watch this one."

Swirling in my gut is an inexplicable feeling that I need to see this.

I lean closer to the screen, zoning in on the tattooed man and the little girl he brought in. He could be a trafficker in this area, and if little girls are getting shot, I can only imagine the situations the children are being put in.

The doctor is frantic as he works to stabilize the child, administers what I assume is anesthesia, and then quickly performs surgery, blood spilling from the girl's leg as he extracts the bullet. It seems as if the doctor is shouting, but after fast-forwarding, we watch him finish up with the girl and then leave the room. The entire time, the man stood as still as a statue, hardly moving an inch.

I frown, focusing on the screen as the man rounds the bed, lifts his hand, and gently swipes the girl's hair from her face. She's still knocked out from the anesthesia, so it's impossible to tell how she feels toward him.

Setting my jaw, I stare hard, trying to interpret his tenderness. Is it coming from a man who is fetishizing her or from someone who saved her? And how the fuck did the little girl end up with a bullet in her leg?

I'm not entirely sure what it is, but something about this video feels… important.

"Send all of these files to me, and then let's get into the security cameras and see if we can get a view on the vehicle that they left in."

I slap Jay's back before turning back to the grimy windows, a silent thank you.

He's been handling my attitude like a champ, and even in the throes of grief and fury, I can still recognize that I'm being an intolerable shithead.

"Shit," Jay mutters, the sound of his fingers clacking on the keyboard growing louder and more intense. I grind my teeth, already suspecting the answer before it comes out of his mouth.

"No cameras back there. No cameras angled toward the parking lot from other buildings, either. I'm sorry, man. I got nothing."

I tip my head back, breathing in deeply through my nose as black fire licks at my nerves. Addie left here only a week ago, but that's an incredible amount of time in the human trafficking world.

"You sent the files?" I ask. I don't even recognize my own voice.

"Yes," Jay confirms. I hear rustling as he packs up his belongings, sensing the obliteration on the horizon.

"Get out of here, Jay."

"Yep, consider me gone."

"And Jay?"

He pauses. "Yeah?"

"Set up cameras that point toward these windows. Just wait until after I break through it," I order.

He hesitates but ultimately agrees and shuffles out.

I give him two minutes to leave. Two minutes of warfare raging in my head, bubbling to the surface, and bleeding out onto the floor where I stand, just like the bloated dead man below.

My body moves on autopilot. I head down to the hospital room and rifle through a cabinet, collecting drapes, clothing, and anything else that's flammable, then scatter them throughout the entire building. Next, I grab alcohol-based liquids, and saturate the littered floor with them. Fires are more common in hospitals than most realize, and it's fucking perfect for the destruction I'm intent on causing.

After that, I take every bedsheet I can find in his studio and tie them together into an extensive rope, then set it aside.

Breathing heavily, I aim for a heavy cabinet in his kitchen and empty out the contents. Dragging it to the massive window, I lean it snugly against it and then take a step back.

I inhale deeply, gather every ounce of wrath, use it as fuel, and kick out my leg with all my strength. The cabinet splinters the glass, spiderwebs fissuring across the entire window. Growling, I kick out once more, and with a loud crack, the cabinet goes flying through it.

Tiny shards cut into my skin, but I hardly notice, just as the deafening crash from the cabinet barreling into the ground doesn't register, either.

I'm already making my way back down to the second floor, where the doctor lies dead, donning gloves and a mask from his supplies. The smell stabs at my nostrils and eyes; the N95 doing nothing to filter out the smell.

Snapping on two layers of gloves, I grab the corpse by the collar of his shirt and drag him back up to his studio, where the sick fuck used to take patients and rape them while unconscious.

Regardless of his extracurricular activities, the doctor was clearly involved in the skin trade, which means this won't only send a message to the Society, but it will also send a message to every trafficker who has had the misfortune of stepping foot inside this place.

They will know that Z knows.

Vomit swirls in my stomach from the pungent odor, threatening to rise up my throat as I drag the dead body to the window. I grab the last bottle of alcohol and dump the entire contents all over him.

Holding my breath, I grab the rope made out of bed sheets, tie one end around his torso beneath his arms, and the other end to his bed frame.

Then, I throw him out of the fucking window. The legs of the frame scream against the cement floor as it drags a few feet before holding tight.

Satisfied, I tear off the gloves and mask, pull out another cigarette and light it up, inhaling deeply as I sit on the edge of the bed. I hold the lighter to one of the drapes on the floor, the material bursting into flames and quickly spreading.

And then I enjoy my cigarette while my wrath comes to life before my eyes.

It's both loud and silent in my brain, filled with white noise that drowns out any coherent thoughts. I feel everything and nothing at all, and I've never been more dangerous.

Never been more lethal.

I laugh and enjoy watching this place fucking burn. So many awful things happened here. So many victims—so many women and children were brought through for a temporary fix just to be taken somewhere and broken all over again.

Slowly, I stand and make my way out of the room. My body physically registers the heat, sweat beading on my forehead and down the back of my neck. Smoke fills my lungs and the flames singe at my skin.

Yet, I can't feel a goddamn thing.

Right as I exit the building, I inhale fresh air and meet a frantic Jay. I cough a few times, clearing my lungs as best I can before I take another puff on my cigarette.

"*Seriously,* dude? You're smoking while burning down a building? You literally just inhaled a shit ton from the fire."

Ignoring him, I walk around to the back where the corpse hangs from the rope. Smoke licks at the edges of the window, and while the bedsheets are beginning to burn, I had purposely left them dry.

I bring the cigarette to my lips and inhale one last time before flicking it onto the doctor, his body instantly igniting.

I smile, smoke curling out from between my bared teeth.

That's better.

A beacon to let every motherfucker in my path know what is coming for them next—a beast that has made a home within the fire.

These flames will die, but the ones in Hell are eternal.

I'll see you there, fucker.

Satisfied, I turn my back to the inferno I've breathed to life and walk away.

I told my mouse I would stop littering, but something tells me she wouldn't mind just this once.

November 2021

   She fucking sabatoged me. Fuck, its hard to even write a letter right now because I'm shaking so hard.
   I was doing so good during practice. Francesca was my pursuer, and for a long while, she couldn't find me. And when she did, I discovered that it takes several seconds to reload an arrow.
   Seventeen to be exact.
   I was playing it smart. Timing how long I ran before hiding. Tricking her into firing the arrow so I could run again. She wasn't hitting me. I was doing SO.**FUCKING** GOOD.
   Then fucking Sydney pops out from behind a tree, as if the evil bitch was waiting for me.
   And then she fucking tripped me! <u>TRIPPED</u> ME! Like a child on a playground.
   Who fucking does that?
   I landed on my goddamn face and two seconds later, an arrow hits my leg. Luckily, they use plastic ones for practice, but that's far beside the point.
   Especially when my punishment will make an arrow in the back feel like child's play.

Chapter Twelve
The Diamond

"How's it feel to be a failure?" a voice whispers from behind me.

It instantly evokes chills down my spine. I whip around, her face inches from mine, causing me to jerk back. My fist curls, tempted to send it flying into her fucking nose.

I was standing in my room, just about to unbutton my jeans and look at the damage, when she snuck up behind me.

"What the hell is wrong with you?" I hiss. She just stares at me with wide dark eyes, a smile frozen on her creepy fucking face.

I swallow, unsettled, and thoroughly weirded the hell out.

"I think the better question is what *isn't* wrong with me," she retorts, giggling as she does. She rocks up on her toes, her eyes gliding up and down my ravaged body.

Francesca took us out into the back of the woods—a practice run for the Culling. She and her men used plastic arrows to track us down, shooting them at us like we're fawn running from a hunter's hungry stomach.

The objective is not to get hit, and the burning in the back of my thigh is a constant reminder of how epically I failed. I came so close to succeeding, but then Sydney happened.

She was waiting for me and stuck out her foot right as I passed by, Francesca's arrows nipping at my heels. I face-planted the cold earth, and by the time I got back up, an arrow was ripping through the air and piercing the back of my thigh.

It didn't break the skin, but I can tell I'm going to wake up with a nasty bruise tomorrow. Though, I'm sure it'll be swallowed up by the others when I receive my punishment.

"What the fuck did I ever do to you?" I snap, throwing my arms out to the sides. Her smile grows, the gleam in her eye a testament just how unhinged she is. "We are in the same exact situation. Why are you acting like this?"

"I heard Francesca talking about you soon after you got here. Said you were promising and might be her best girl yet if she can correct your attitude. Then yesterday, you went and got yourself raped, and I saw her face. I saw her almost step in. And she's never done that for me or any of the other girls. But then—" she holds a finger up in the air— "Then, you punch Rocco and break his nose. He wanted to punish you for it, and you know what she did? She took the punishment for you instead. That's definitely never been done for any of us."

My brows knit, confused as to why Francesca would do something like that.

"She's giving you privileges that we don't get because she thinks you're special. Well guess what, *diamond*, I don't think you're special at all."

Doesn't really matter what you think, does it, bitch?

I'm not exactly sure if Francesca will stand by her confidence in me now that I've failed the test today, but determination cements into my bones anyway.

If she sees potential in me—if she's going as far as to protect me—then there's a good chance I can get her to see me as a person.

We're seen as cattle. Product to mold to perfection and then ship off to the highest bidder. However, the more she sees me as something other than just a price tag, the more she'll soften toward me. That could mean letting her guard down. Letting information slip or getting privileges that could assist with my escape.

My thoughts race with the possibilities that could mean for me. I know that I won't be exempt from the horror that comes hand-in-hand with human trafficking, but I might be able to save myself from some of it.

Sydney understands this, and maybe rightfully so, she's not happy with it. There's a power imbalance, and the other girls might start to feel the same.

"We're all leaving this place," I remind her. "Soon, we'll be shipped off to whoever pays the most money, and how Francesca treats me won't matter anymore."

"It does matter," she snarls. "I want to stay here, and she won't let me now that you've shown up. You heard her."

I set my jaw. Sydney doesn't want to see the diamond shine because that means she'll be expected to as well. And when we shine, that means we are good enough to be sold. Francesca cares about one thing above all else—her reputation. And there's only one thing Sydney wants more than anything—not to be sold—which must be why she acts out so badly and causes trouble. Her punishments are worth it, as long as Francesca never sees her as fit to be auctioned.

"Why do you want to stay here so badly?"

"Because it's my *home*. I have nothing outside of this house, and I would rather be here than stuck with some fat, old man with a worm dick. And *you* are ruining that!"

I blink. Interesting depiction, but not entirely wrong either.

"You get raped here, too, Sydney," I point out.

She shrugs. "It's not so bad. It's what I'm used to and comfortable with."

Another blink. How one could settle into the life of being raped and beaten is beyond me, but she's hinted at having nowhere else to go. This tells me a life outside of this house for Sydney is bleak. Nonexistent. Most likely filled with nights on the streets and random men.

And I suppose being in a house with the monsters you know is safer than a man who paid money and believes they own her.

Men have this funny habit of thinking they're entitled to women, especially when they don't respect them. As if their respect is a determining factor on how women deserve to be treated.

At least the men in this house have rules and limitations on what they can do to us. Mainly mutilating or causing permanent damage. Men on the streets or the ones who buy us at an auction—they don't have rules.

"So that's it," I say. "You're going to continue to terrorize me because you want to cheat the system when none of us will get that option. Maybe it's *you* who thinks they're special when you're not."

She giggles a high-pitched sound that grinds my nerves to dust. And then she turns and walks away without a word, casting an indecipherable look over her shoulder.

Who we're fighting over would rather see us shipped off to the highest bidder, and she's not just causing me to fail a test, she's actively inflicting trauma on me.

Abuse. Rape. Things that no human being should ever have to suffer through—especially in the name of jealousy or pettiness.

"You sabotaged me, Sydney," I call out, causing her to stop in her tracks. "I won't forget that."

Keeping her back turned, she swivels her head to the side, and her hand drifts up and down the doorjamb airily, as if she's toying with the thought as her fingers are with the wood.

Finally, she glances over her shoulder at me, a grin on her thin lips.

"You're going to be a lot of fun, diamond." She winks at me and then leaves, sashaying down the hall before she disappears into a room at the end.

I glare at her the entire way, and I know damn well she can feel the heat of it burning into her back.

The cunt is probably getting off on it, and the vindictive side of me will be happy to fuck her in the worst of ways any chance I can get.

Raucous laughter booms from downstairs, nearly vibrating the floor beneath my knees. Francesca and Rocco are the only two who actually live here, but he likes to invite his rapist friends over every day to shoot copious amounts of drugs in their veins and have their way with the girls when permitted.

Though, I suppose Rio and Rick have been practically living here now that they can't be seen in public. I've been praying Rick makes it easy on me and leaves the house anyway, but the bozo is too fucking lazy and high off his rocker now that he has an endless stream of drugs coming in. He's got the money to get his junk hand-delivered.

Regardless, they're all fucking obnoxious, incapable of keeping their mouths shut and not making disgusting remarks anytime we're in their vicinity.

Damn, what I wouldn't give to fuck that tight ass.

Do you see the way it bounces? Imagine how it would look railing her from behind.

Jesus, her tits are to fucking die for. I can't wait to fuck them.

Each word twists my stomach further and further, wringing my insides like a wet rag until it's coiled into a knotted rope. Sydney's words are the only thing keeping my teeth glued together.

Francesca has high hopes for me, and I need to do everything in my power to stay in that light, even if it means cracking my molars from the force of keeping my mouth shut.

Sleep still clings to my eyes while Francesca paces before us. Yesterday was the Culling practice, and I spent the entire night waiting for our punishment, but it never came. So, when she barged in my room at the ass crack of dawn, I hadn't even closed my eyes yet.

"Etiquette is important," Francesca begins, walking back and forth down the line, her five-inch heels matching the pounding of my heart.

She's always ready to walk down a runway, and I wonder if she puts so much effort into making the outside look pretty because her insides are a cemetery of bones and decay. She should've looked into becoming a mortician with the way she's so good at dressing up a corpse.

She stops before me, and I keep my eyes casted down at her feet. The tip of her shoe is scuffed a little. Wonder how much that bothers her.

"Look at me."

My eyes instantly find hers, with no hesitation.

"Kiss my foot," she orders, tipping out her shoe with the mark. Part of me wonders if she could hear my thoughts and is punishing me for it. Nevertheless, I decide it's probably the She-Devil above. Now *She* just loves to punish me.

My immediate reaction is pure fire. My mouth works to gather saliva, ready to spit on her shoe instead, but I manage to refrain. Barely.

Hesitation races down my spine, and it takes physical force to bend my spine forward and do as she says, placing my lips gently on her dirty shoe.

"Now lick it."

My lips twitch, threatening to curl into a snarl, but I do as she says and quickly lick it, dirt and lord knows what else gathering on my tongue.

I imagine it tastes exactly how her soul looks.

I squeeze my eyes shut, working to regain control over the screaming in my head, before I rise up again, keeping my eyes downcast. If I look at her, she'll see death in my eyes.

As if sensing this, she bends at the waist and curls her finger beneath my chin, the cold metal of her ring seeping into my skin as she lifts my head.

"I know it hurts but hesitate again and your teeth will be kissing the floor instead."

Swallowing down vomit, I nod my head and whisper, "I'm sorry."

She smiles prettily and straightens, satisfied.

"Each second you hesitate is another reason to punish you. Your master will expect obedience. Mindless little zombies, you will be."

Sydney giggles, raises her arms, and moans like an actual zombie. My eyes widen, and none of us can contain the shock, staring at her like she's insane.

Well, no shit, I guess. The bitch *is* insane.

Francesca snarls, storms to her, and slaps her across the face, the sound of flesh hitting flesh echoing in the room. Her head snaps to the side, strands of hair flying across her face from the force. Disturbingly enough, Sydney peers up at Francesca through her hair, another laugh releasing from her tongue.

Francesca bends at the waist. "You keep laughing, Sydney, and I'll keep letting Rocco stretch your ass until my entire foot fits."

I swallow, looking back down to the floor. She's fucking certifiable, and I can't help but feel a stab of sympathy.

Was Sydney an average girl before she was stolen away? Did she live a normal life, have a job, friends, and go out on weekends to find a fling?

Who was she before she died inside?

After an entire day of grueling training on how to serve our future masters, dinner is served in our rooms. None of us are allowed to eat together and I imagine it's because they don't want any of us becoming friends—joining forces and planning to escape together or some shit. The more alone we feel, the more hopeless.

We're fed soup and crackers, a meager meal but something she claims won't fatten us up. Apparently even sex traffickers are fatphobic and body shame the women. Never mind that they can't get pussy unless they quite literally steal it.

I've just finished eating when it sounds like Francesca screeches from below, the enraged sound echoing throughout the house. I freeze, slowly setting my soup bowl on the nightstand when footsteps pound on the wood, though, it doesn't sound like she has her heels on. Her angry stride travels up the stairs and down the hall, my heart beating faster with each step toward me.

My door slams open, and she storms into my room, the doorknob deepening the crater in the wall from the force.

I flinch and jump up from my bed, heart racing as she stomps towards me and sticks her face in mine.

"You were doing so well," she spits.

My mouth parts and I shake my head, speechless as confusion and adrenaline war in my brain.

"Wha—"

"Don't play stupid," she hisses before backhanding me, fire lancing across my cheek and a gasp slipping free.

Instinctively, I grab my cheek, shock rendering me utterly paralyzed.

I look at her just as she shoves a shoe in my face. Or what used to be one. It's the same ones she was wearing earlier—the same ones she made me kiss and lick—black stilettos with gold heels. Except now, the gold spike is cracked off at the base, barely hanging on, and deep scratches mar every inch of it.

"You did this," she accuses. "You did this to all my fucking shoes!"

I shake my head again, eyes wide and protests falling from my lips. "I didn't, I *swear*, Francesca. I didn—"

Another sharp slap to the same cheek cuts off my truth. Her chest heaves with anger. Heat radiates from her in waves, solar flares of fury lashing at me as she seethes.

Tears rush to my eyes, and I shake from the effort to keep them from falling. I don't want to show an ounce of weakness. She'll take the tears for guilt. My vision blurs and colorful words gather on my tongue. It takes several swallows to force them back down my throat.

"I saw the look in your eyes earlier, *diamond*. Don't pretend like you weren't planning my death. You're a spoiled little brat and doing *this*—" she shoves the shoe in my face— "will do you no favors."

"Fran—"

"Shut up!" she screeches, completely losing her mind. She grabs my hair and yanks me down onto the ground, fire racing across my scalp. I cry out; the sound quickly muffled when she shoves my face into the wooden floor and starts yanking down my leggings.

My eyes blow wide, and panic begins to override my senses.

"Wait, wait, Francesca, I didn't do it!"

She's not listening, though.

"This will be the *last* time you disrespect me. Do you understand me?!" she shouts, finally getting the material down past my ass.

I twist, attempting to roll out of her hold, but her nails are clawing into my hip and forcing me back down. Still, I can't stop fighting, not when she's trying to spread my legs.

"Stop!" I yell, vision blackening with panic and a slew of tears.

"Get in here," she snaps to someone, but I don't see who. I only feel their weight pressing down on me, and my body truly begins to fight then.

"Wait, wait, *please, please,* I didn't do it! I didn't do it," I sob, desperate to get away but unable to. The weight is pressing down on my head, preventing me from seeing or moving, but I can feel everything.

Oh god, I can feel everything. The broken heel of her shoe is being shoved inside me, and I scream as it tears me apart.

"Please, please, please," I cry. I cry and cry and cry, but she's past listening.

Her hands disappear, along with the weight of the person on top of me being shoved off.

Francesca is yanking my head back, forcing me to stare at her contorted face, nearly spitting with ire. She's on her knees, eyes wild as she hisses, "Don't you *ever* destroy my things again, or you will suffer much worse than this. I swear to fucking God, I will make you wish you were dead. Am I understood?"

Sobs rack my throat, slobber nearly pouring from my mouth as I cry out, "I didn't do it."

Rearing back, she slaps me across the face again, my ears ringing as she continues to mindlessly hit me, over and over until I'm breathless from the onslaught of pain.

"You fucking useless bitch!" she screams. She lifts my head again, but I can no longer see her through the rivers pouring from my eyes. Indiscernible pleas fall past my lips, but even I don't know what I'm saying anymore.

"You know what happens when you become useless? You end up buried in an unmarked grave somewhere no one will ever find you."

Finally, she releases me, nearly smacking my head off the wood. Immediately, my body curls in on itself, the foreign object still lodged painfully inside me, but I don't have it in me to take it out.

Whimpers tear through my throat, so powerful that no noise is capable of slipping through, stealing my breath in the process. Francesca storms out of the room, leaving me violently shaking and bawling from the assault.

A mass comes back down on me, and my body uselessly flails, fists flying but making no contact.

"Shhh," the voice whispers. The moment it registers that it's Sydney's, I fight harder, screaming at her to get off, but she's too strong for me right now.

She's completely wrapped around my back, her legs circled tightly around my waist and locked on my stomach while her hand pets my hair.

"Shh, it's okay," she whispers. "We'll be together now."

The little energy I had left dissipates, and the only thing I am able to do is sob.

Grabbing my hot, reddened face, she tilts my chin up. Just barely, I make out her wide brown eyes and a gentle smile. Almost reverently, she pets my hair and down my cheeks, staring at me as if I'm a prized possession.

"Welcome home," she whispers.

November 2021

You know what's funny about pain? There's never really that moment where it just stops. Like an on or off switch. Pain fades. Slowly. Almost so gradually, that you don't even notice the moment where it fades completely. It's like one moment we feel it, then we learn how to live with it, and eventually, we realize that it's just... gone. Poof.

I wondered how long it would take for the pain to fade when Sydney was wrapped around me and wouldn't let go. Then when she did, it was because it was time for my punishment.

Another injustice because of the girl clinging to me. But of course, how the fuck are we supposed to ~~dis~~ discern injustice anyways when my being there at all is an injustice in itself. Whatever.

They pulled the bloody heel out of me, and replaced it with things far worse. Rocco's friends had a good night

They didn't feel pain. But I did.

I still do. istilldoistlldo.

You know? I think it's going to take a long time for it to fade. I just have this fucking feeling.

Chapter Thirteen
The Hunter

"They deal in the black market," Jay tells me. I'm staring at camera footage of the tattooed man from the video—the one that brought a little girl with a gunshot wound into Dr. Garrison's shoddy hospital. "Organ traffickers, to be specific."

"Who is 'they'?" I ask, carefully watching the man carry the injured child out of the hospital, gently set her in the backseat of a red Camaro, and then speed off. Whether he didn't care to avoid the one camera on the front of the building, or wasn't aware of it, doesn't actually matter. I got his license plate number.

Jay pulls up a photo. It's of the tattooed man with three other men. Based on their body language, they appear very comfortable with each other.

"Them. They call themselves the Basilisk Brotherhood. Widely known in the black market for trading in human organs. Ryker, Daire,

Kace, and Slade. No one knows their real last names."

I close my eyes, reining in my temper. I have little control over it these days.

"Before you get growly and go on a killing spree, Tony the Tiger, there's been some talk that they are not actually as bad as they're making themselves out to be."

I shoot Jay a look, but he ignores me. I'm scarier than Tony the Tiger, and he knows it.

"Why do you say that?"

"Just some comments on forums that I've come across on a few deep websites," he says, shrugging his shoulders. "I don't know what it is, but I have a feeling those rumors are true."

We'll see.

"Regardless, they would have knowledge on the comings and goings of the skin trade," I surmise.

Jay meets my heavy stare, a mutual agreement passing between us silently.

If Addie is traded or auctioned off, they might be able to track it, which means that I need to have a chat with the Basilisk Brotherhood.

"Give me a second, and I'll get in contact with them," I say, straightening and motioning for Jay to move aside. He grumbles something about this being *his* computer, but I don't pay him any mind.

Jay's great at what he does—amazing, even.

But I'm better.

I sit down and open up several programs. The first one is a software with facial recognition. It provides a hit on every single camera their face has appeared on. I'm almost impressed when very few pop up.

Ryker's face is the most popular—the same large, angry-looking man that brought in the little girl to the doctor. Unlike the grainy footage from the hospital, this camera catches a clear image of him.

He's interesting-looking, with sharp features, long hair that seems to always be tied up, pale gray-green eyes, light stubble, and a nose piercing. Type of face women would fall to their knees for.

The other three certainly aren't hurting for pussy either, though they're all incredibly different from each other. Definitely not real brothers, though I'm sure they act like it.

"You'll get along with them great," Jay says over my shoulder. "You all are in a business where being obscure is key, yet each one of you stands out like lollipops among moldy bread. Very lickable lollipops, too."

Yeah, whatever. I didn't ask to be beautiful.

I ignore him and narrow down my search to the most recent location they were spotted last. Portland, Oregon. Massive city and a great place to hide.

Also, a prime location for human trafficking. Prostitution runs rampant there—one of the most blatant and in-your-face forms of trafficking there is. The police spend more time arresting the girls for their crimes rather than trying to save them.

'Merica.

In the video, it appears as if they're doing some type of exchange. Could be drugs, but something like cocaine or heroin is child's play when you're dealing with human organs. Call it intuition, but none of them give off the vibe of a drug addict.

I sift through different programs until I finally get a hit on a residential house's Nest camera from two weeks ago. The red Camaro pulls into the driveway, and the four men pour out of the car.

An older woman steps out of the front door and waves her hand animatedly. The Nest picks up audio, so when her voice comes through, it's clear that whoever owns this house is either family or like family.

She's loud and boisterous as she greets them, and the men gravitate towards her like little boys would their grandma.

"I'll never get over how grown-up you boys are!" she exclaims, first hugging Ryker, and then the other three.

"'Sup, Mama T," Daire says, grinning at her. He slings an arm around the woman and ruffles her short silver hair with the other hand. Swatting at him, she berates him lovingly as they disappear into the house, their voices quickly fading.

Clicking off the program, I open up a browser and search the quickest route back to Portland. Seems I'm going to be spending a lot of time there.

"You're going to her house?"

I turn my head, spotting Jay from the corner of my eye, a disapproving look on his face.

"Where else would I go?"

"You're going to piss them off."

"I'm not going to *hurt* her," I scowl.

"Do you think that will matter to them? Your presence will be threatening enough."

I swivel my chair completely around, cocking my brow as I lean back and cross my arms.

"Do I look fucking scared?"

He tips his head back and sighs dramatically. "We know you're a bad bitch, Zade. That's not the point." I reach out and punch his thigh in response to being called a bad bitch, earning me a groaned *ow*.

"No, the point is that this is my quickest option. I will give them a very good reason to come to me, and I will ensure we come to a mutually beneficial agreement. I don't have time to learn the ins and outs of transporting humans. It's complicated as fuck, and my primary focus the past several years has been locating the rings once the girls have already been moved. Addie can be traded any day if she hasn't been already, so I need to cover my bases. While I try to find where she's being held, I need someone that understands the business to keep an eye out for if or when she's transported."

Jay sighs, sensing that I'm going to do what I want anyway. "Fine. Just don't be a dick to her."

I flash a grin. "Don't worry. The ladies love me."

"Get out of my house right now, you fucker!" Teresa, otherwise known as Mama T, yells, pointing a finger at me. "Do you think you can just waltz into my house? Who do you think you are?"

I lean back into the couch, wiggling my butt until I'm comfortable.

"A very desperate man, Teresa Baker," I say, looking over the house casually. She has a very cozy home, and everything has its place.

Cream walls with matching couches, maroon flower pictures spaced out perfectly, matching wooden furniture, the brown surfaces gleaming as if she dusted them not two seconds ago, and a white birdcage hanging in the corner, a little Tweety chirping away.

Does she have a Sylvester, too?

She scoffs, "What the hell does that have to do with me?"

"You know some men who I need to have a chat with. Does Ryker sound familiar? Slade, Daire or Kace, even?"

Her face visibly pales, and her thin red lips part as she scrambles for a response.

Too slow, Mama T.

"Call them. Bring them here. That's all I want."

She huffs out an amused laugh. "You know they're going to kill you, right?"

"Now why would they do that? We're having a lovely time."

She shoots me a look, sits down in her chair, and grabs the phone off the receiver. She's probably one out of fifteen people in the world who still have a landline.

Her green eyes spear me like sharpened knives as she slaps the phone to her ear. I smile wide at her in return, though I fear it came out a tad feral.

"Get over here, now. Bring your brothers," she says after someone picks up, glancing over at me with irritation.

"No, I'm not hurt," she assures quickly. "There's a man here to see you four."

He must agree because she hangs up the phone without another word. Still shooting me the evil eye, she sets the phone down a tad aggressively, and an uncomfortable silence descends.

Nothing about Mama T is typical, nor is she shy as she meets my stare head-on. Despite being in her fifties, she's got character—tattoos on her neck, a Monroe piercing, a nose ring, and dark red lipstick.

"My girl was kidnapped," I tell her, hoping to appease some of her anger.

Honestly, I have no interest in harming an old lady. I hate that I'm making her uncomfortable, but it's a necessary means to get what I need. I'd rather she feels relaxed in my presence—as much as she's capable of when a six-foot-six man with scars all over his body walks into your home.

She stares at me blankly, waiting for me to continue. "She was taken by some very bad and powerful people. Could be anywhere in the world at this point. Your boys happen to have a refined skill in what I need to possibly track her down."

She leans her elbows on her spread knees, and it feels like she's looking past my flesh and into my soul. I stay still. People seeing me for who I am has never bothered me.

"You're a powerful, bad man."

I shrug. "And also, someone with very little time to waste. I've got a firm hold on my manhood, and I can admit when I need help."

She raises her thin brows and gives me a look that suggests *at least you have that going for you.*

I'd like to think I'm pretty, too, but I'll let it slide.

"What makes you think my boys will help you? Is my life your bargaining chip?"

"Of course not," I chirp, much like the bird chattering in the cage. "Only a weaker man would hurt an innocent woman to get what they want."

She cocks a brow, unimpressed. I can't help but smile at that.

"Like you said, I'm a powerful, bad man. I have connections and capabilities of my own. Whatever they need, I can do, once my girl is safe and sound."

She nods her head, though she doesn't look convinced. I'm not worried about what they will ask of me. What I don't know, I can learn. When it comes time to collect, Addie will be by my side, and I'll have all the time in the world to get them whatever they need.

"Well, I don't approve of your methods, but I was married once and would've killed to have even a fraction of the love you have for your lady friend."

"Come on, there's time. You could still find your one and only."

She rolls her eyes. "I'm too old for that shit. I have my boys, and that's enough. Just next time, would ya knock? You almost gave me a goddamn heart attack."

"I'm sorry, Teresa," I say genuinely, my hand over my heart. It only earns me another eye roll.

"Call me Mama T."

I grin, pleased that I've been accepted. I told Jay—the ladies love me.

If the Basilisk Brotherhood didn't respect Teresa, they would've kicked the door down to get to me. Instead, they rush inside, the four of them nearly tripping on each other to get in.

Teresa is already waiting at the door, hands raised in a calming gesture.

"Now, calm down, boys. He's not here to hurt me."

Slade grips her by her arms and spins her around, assuming to check for injuries. She twists out of his grip and swats at him.

"Stop it, I'm fine. I can take care of my damn self."

Ryker's eyes immediately find mine, his pursuit never pausing for even a moment. He rushes toward me, but before he can make it another step, Teresa grabs him by the arm.

His head whips around to her in shock, and she glares at him.

"Are ya fucking deaf, or am I a mute now? What did I say? He ain't here to hurt me, so calm down."

Ryker faces me again, a mixture of anger and bewilderment on his face.

I take a bite of my chocolate chip cookie and give him a close-lipped smile while I chew.

These cookies are fucking delicious.

"Who the fuck are you?" Ryker barks while the other three flank him. Chests puffed, chins notched high, and hands ready to pull out their firearms.

Teresa rolls her eyes and mutters beneath her breath, storming out from behind them to sit in her chair with an irritated huff.

Boys will be boys.

Slowly, I stand, wiping the crumbs from my hands on my jeans.

"Z," is my only response and Ryker's brow quirks.

"Z," he echoes dryly as if he doesn't believe me.

"That's what I said."

"Like *the* Z?" Daire clarifies. Two tiny diamond dermals are pierced above a thick black brow, glinting as he arches it on his forehead.

"Yes," I say. Introductions are so tedious when very few have actually seen my face. Anyone could claim to be me, but all of them would fail when it came time to prove it.

Slade snorts, rolling his dark eyes, which make an interesting contrast to the waves of dirty blond hair falling into them.

The only one who doesn't have much to say is Kace, who stands back and observes me closely. If I were a lesser man, it'd make me uncomfortable.

"Let's say I give a shit that you're Z—why are you here and in Teresa's house?"

"Well, to get to you, of course. Excuse my impolite methods, however, time is of the essence," I answer, flashing a grin. Ryker snarls in response.

Touchy.

"Does Dr. Garrison ring any bells?"

A collective silence ensues for a few moments, and then Daire chuckles. "That was you, wasn't it? That set him and his place on fire?"

"Sure was. I happened across some intriguing footage with Ryker's face on it. Intriguing enough for me to investigate, and it's like Jesus himself handed me a gift. Word on the street is that you're all very particular... tradesmen. And I have a current need for that."

Ryker glances at Teresa, who's staring up at us with complete boredom on her face.

Sensing Ryker's need for secrecy, she waves her hand. "Leave. It's my nap time."

He glances at me before walking to an end table next to Teresa's chair and snatching a crumpled receipt and pen. She grumbles when he starts scribbling on it but doesn't stop him.

Straightening, he hands the slip of paper to me. "You caught us in the middle of something. Meet us at this address in four hours. Don't be late. Now get out."

I arch a brow when I spot hemorrhoid cream on the receipt but quickly decide it's not my business what's growing on Teresa's ass.

"I'll be early," I say. "Bye, Mama T."

"Good luck," she calls. I wave a hand in acknowledgment before opening and shutting the front door behind me.

I don't need luck, just the help of four men, who are probably going to be enough pains in my ass that *I'll* need the hemorrhoid cream next.

Chapter Fourteen
The Diamond

That's such a good girl, little mouse. Open that pretty mouth and taste me…

You've been naughty, mouse. You like it when I punish you, don't you?

I could eat you for days, and it would never be enough…

Fuck, baby, I'm so fucking addicted…

I jolt awake, and for one beautiful second, I thought I was back in Parsons Manor with Zade. Images of mismatched eyes and a wicked smirk clog my headspace, but the sudden movement lances sharp needles of pain throughout my skull. The memories dissipate, Zade's deep tenor fading as the dull throb that radiates from between my legs feels like a curse that was cast by an evil witch—a curse that won't let me forget.

Bright sunlight pierces through the dusty curtains, and it almost feels mocking. I squint my eyes, the migraine worsening as I train my tired eyes on the dirty window.

It's cold outside, but it doesn't look like we'll be plagued by the usual rainy forecast today.

The phantom in the sky really is a devil. Why else would She make such a gruesome day so bright and sunny?

Today is the Culling, and already the house seems to be filling up with chatter.

To make matters worse, my body doesn't feel nearly as broken as I thought it would. My soul? Completely shattered. But at least I can fart without feeling like I'm going to pass out, right?

Wrong. If I could hardly move, it might've provided me with an excuse to not participate in the Culling.

Despite the beating my body took three days ago from my punishment for failing the practice test, my wounds are healing, so lying to her about my physical well-being when the other girls will still have to take part… It makes me feel like a coward.

So, thank you, God, for the small blessings in life and for allowing me to see another day and pass gas properly. A-fucking-men, bitch.

Phoebe, Bethany, and Gloria were raped alongside me. Jillian kept her head down when she walked past us, but Sydney blatantly laughed in our faces, and all I wanted to do was grab her hair and drag her down on that dirty ground next to us. It was *her* fault I was on that floor to begin with, naked men crowding around me, and already injured from her stunt with Francesca.

All I could think about as we were passed around from man to man was how much I hated her. Hated her superiority and hated her for sabotaging me.

It was the only thing that got me through touches from dirty fingers and violent invasions from men that weren't my shadow.

Afterward, Rio carried me up to my bed, my legs physically unable to support me from the abuse my body endured. He couldn't look at me. Not when he did nothing while men stole from me, and then he picked up that broken girl and carried her to bed—only because Francesca demanded it of him.

But he did speak to me. He told me about a mythical being rumored to terrorize Puerto Rico. He told me when he was young, he was playing with his baby sister when he swears that he saw it. A creature that was there one moment and gone the next.

I don't know why he told me that story. Maybe to distract me, but I suppose it worked. He gave me a monster that didn't feel real instead of focusing on the monsters that are.

"Get up." The sharp slap that follows the harsh words startles me, and I yelp from both the surprise and pain. I hadn't even heard her come in, despite her loud-ass heels. She must've gotten new ones already.

I look up to find Francesca staring down at me, a frown marring her bright pink lips. She looks disappointed in me, and I hate how small that makes me feel.

I open my mouth, but no sound comes out. What am I supposed to do? Apologize?

After she assaulted me with her broken heel and I was gang-banged by Rocco's friends, she couldn't bear looking at me for a full day. Yesterday, I had finally broken through and managed to convince her that Sydney was the one to destroy her things.

She didn't apologize. Didn't even appear remorseful. But she did lock Sydney in an old cellar on the property for the entire day, and I'm almost ashamed to admit how much it soothed my soul to hear her screaming to be let out. Already, I'm changing, and the old Addie is unrecognizable.

I've never wanted to hurt someone until now. Never felt the urge to grab a knife and rip someone's throat open ear to ear.

I'm vibrating with it, but Sydney isn't the only one on the receiving end. I'm pissed at every single person in this house, save for the other innocent girls.

Especially with Francesca, and every man who stole a piece of my soul that night. A piece I don't even think Zade will ever be able to get back for me.

There will always be pockets missing where my innocence used to reside.

"Get ready in the beauty room. Our guests will be here soon." Her eyes flicker down my body snidely. "Look presentable," she tacks on, the words digging into my skin like a needle, before turning and walking out, her clicking heels echoing against the hardwood floor.

Grinding my teeth, it takes monumental effort not to fucking scream. From rage, pain, and just pure frustration.

Instead, I force my battered body into movement, slip out of the lumpy bed and pad my way towards the beauty room.

Men's voices drift from below, and the sound sends my heart flying to my throat. I work to swallow as I meet Phoebe at the threshold.

The second our eyes meet, both of us look away. Incapable of connecting over something that we both suffered through. Shame. Embarrassment. Sorrow. All are at the forefront as we walk into the room.

Bethany and Gloria are picking through the clothes on a rack Francesca must've set out for us. Instead of revealing outfits, warm clothing hangs from the metal rod. Guess it wouldn't be ideal for five girls to run for their life with a thong riding up their ass and tassels hanging from their nipples in freezing weather.

Jillian is sitting at a vanity and putting on concealer in hopes of covering up the dark circles rimming the underside of her eyes. Briefly, we make eye contact, but her gaze flickers away immediately. I haven't seen her since our punishment—apparently, she's been sick and has missed out on the last couple of lessons.

A swarm of angry bees rises up my throat, and I can't stop the uncontrollable bitterness from taking hold, seizing my heartstrings, and turning it into a puppet of mass destruction.

Did she sleep that night? Hearing three girls scream in pain and begging for them to stop? Begging and begging and begging.

Please.

Pleaaase, stop!

Please, I'm begging you!

Please… please… please…

Has she grown tired of the word? Does it sound funny to her now? When a word is said so many times, it doesn't even sound like a word anymore. It sounds like gibberish—a sound comprised of pitch and tones that hold no real meaning. A construct that humans have formed to communicate their wants and needs. But what do words fucking matter when no one listens?

Her eyes meet mine again, a glossy sheen over the surface of them. And there it is. Shame. Embarrassment. Sorrow.

She made it out unscathed, and it looks like survivor's guilt has been gnawing at her insides for the past few days.

I deflate, berating myself for taking my anger out on someone who doesn't deserve it. Jillian is just trying to survive like the rest of us. None of this is her fault.

Then, Sydney walks in, all high and mighty, and my unwarranted anger towards Jillian redirects itself towards the person who actually deserves it.

She acts as if she didn't spend an entire day screaming in a cellar.

Biting my tongue, I walk over to the vanity next to Jillian, my movements mechanical. My bones feel like rusty hinges as I reach for a bright pink sponge and concealer. It's going to take mounds of it to hide the distress, but I settle with a few dollops to start.

My hand trembles as I apply chemicals to my face that are meant to hide my pain. Bethany and Phoebe talk quietly in the background, whispers full of fear and comfort.

Bad, bad girls.

I consider listening in on their conversation, but I'm distracted when Sydney starts tearing off her clothes until she's naked. Jillian and I have a clear view of her through our vanity mirrors. We both pause, hands suspended in the air as we stare at the unhinged girl behind us, now picking through the clothes on the rack.

Bethany and Phoebe's whispers taper off, and soon the entire room is disturbingly enraptured by her.

I can't help but watch her as she hums, takes a shirt off the rack, and observes it as if she's a regular girl shopping in a fancy boutique. Entirely unbothered by the eyes burning into her exposed skin.

Forcing my attention away, I glance at Jillian. She's now staring hard at herself, most likely trying to avoid Sydney's naked form reflected in the mirror.

"You have any advice?" I ask, my voice weak and hoarse from all the screaming.

I watch her freeze from the corner of my eye. She collects herself and then resumes blending her concealer, clearing her throat.

"Cover your tracks," she says quietly, her Russian accent prominent. She has a beautiful voice, and Rocco's friends thinks so, too. "And run only when necessary. It isn't about how far you can get; it's about making sure they never find you. You can run for hours, and you'll always lead them right to you."

"They can't get you if they don't know where you are," I mutter aloud. The words come out raspy and broken, but I don't bother trying to repeat myself. "What about the traps?"

"I counted the distance between them the best I could. They're about thirty feet apart, roughly. They're uniform, so the hunters know how to avoid them."

I roll my lip between my teeth. "Thank you for helping me."

She glances at me. "Don't mention it."

Literally, or we'll both be in trouble.

We descend into silence after that. She doesn't offer any consolation, but it's not something I would ever want from her. From anyone.

Twenty-five minutes later, we're all dressed in jeans and long-sleeved shirts. They'll do virtually nothing to protect us from the elements, and certainly not any metal arrowheads plunging into our bodies at a breakneck speed. But considering we'll be running on adrenaline, it's enough to keep our bodies warm.

Francesca's heels resonate as she climbs the steps, and my system floods with panic, whatever control I was grasping onto slipping. So easily, like my fingers are covered in grease.

"You girls ready?" Her voice is like a punch to the kidneys. I glance at her through the mirror, her eyes perusing each of us, clicking her tongue when she must deem us presentable enough.

"Let's go. Time to eat, and then we will go over lessons on how to act properly tonight. When night falls, the Culling will begin, and if you pass, you will be required to mingle with our guests afterward."

Panicked glances are exchanged. Even surprise flashes across Sydney's gaze.

Bethany raises a trembling hand, requesting permission to speak.

"Are you saying that we have to do the Culling... in the dark?" she asks hesitantly.

Francesca raises an eyebrow. "That's what I said."

Then, she turns and walks out, the expectation to follow clear. Slowly, we trail after her, but not before we look at each other with the same panicked expression.

We're fucked. We're all fucked.

Single file, ladies. We must be in a uniform line to greet your potential rapists. Make a good impression, and they may be nice *when they rape you.*

Bursts of loud laughter and deep voices tighten my throat. It feels as if my heart is making an escape attempt, breaking through its gilded cage and clawing its way out of captivity.

Jesus, I think I'm going to pass out.

My legs wobble and my hand catches the railing, clutching it so tightly, my knuckles are bleached white. It's the only thing keeping me from pitching forward.

"Get it together," Jillian whispers harshly from behind me.

"Says the girl who wasn't punished for this three days ago," I snap back.

She quietens. That was rude of me. But fuck, there's not a manual on how to rewire my brain to be unafraid and calm. I'm nearly hyperventilating by the time we reach the landing and make our way into the living room where the hunters await.

These men don't belong here.

This house is run-down, and it doesn't matter how clean or tidy it is, it still looks like trash. And there are five men standing in the middle of it, wearing Armani suits, diamond-encrusted Rolex watches, and submerged in a shroud of expensive cologne that costs more than my car note.

Their conversation dies as they turn to us, and I realize the different colors in their eyes look the same when they're all lifeless.

"Francesca," one calls, drawing out her name with affection. "You've got yourself a beautiful lot here."

The man has short, dirty blond hair, blue eyes, and a deep tan to complement his toned body. He looks like he spends his days lounging on his yacht, most likely shacked up with a supermodel in a skimpy red bikini, who's blissfully unaware of her sugar daddy's taste for hunting innocent women for sport.

Lucky her.

His eyes slide to mine and lock, his grin growing as the other three men grunt their agreement. I'm supposed to appear meek and submissive, but it takes me too many seconds to drop my stare to the glossy wooden floor. Courtesy of yours truly. We had to make this place look presentable, and adding a coat of oil apparently accomplishes that feat.

Feeling the burn of his stare caressing my tender skin, I'm now confident that I was too slow. A spark of adrenaline ignites in my blood, worsening my nausea. Without a shadow of a doubt, I know he's going to be the one hunting me today.

"The one with the orange hair, does her pussy match, or did she ruin it by dyeing it that color?" another asks, and I have to clench my teeth and bite back a response. Phoebe trembles beside me as Francesca affirms something incredibly personal, her voice even and pleasant.

Nasty bitch.

"I like that one," he states. My gaze flickers to him, noting his bushy black brows, tiny eyes, and potbelly. "Her hair will look beautiful wrapped around my fist when she's sucking my cock."

A knot forms in my throat, and I take a risk by hooking my pinky around hers and squeezing briefly. We're crowded into each other tightly enough that the quick action goes unnoticed.

"Of course, Ben," Francesca responds pleasantly. The man, Ben, practically foams at the mouth while his cold eyes heat with wickedness. One thing we have in common at this moment—nefarious, evil things are running through both of our minds.

"And I think I want her," the blond man pipes in, nodding at me. His searing gaze hasn't lifted, causing sweat to pour down my spine and vomit to travel up to my throat.

"You're sure, Xavier?" Francesca questions. "She's not eligible, yet. Still has a lot of healing to do." My heart bottoms out when I realize he's the important man she told us about—Xavier Delano. And of fucking course, he's targeting me.

God? Why do I always attract the big, bad wolves?

He licks his lips, a crooked grin forming. "I've never been surer of anything in my life. I'm confident I'll get a taste of her soon. Whether it's tonight… or another time."

I feel my face bleach of color, and it's becoming increasingly harder to keep from blowing chunks all over his snakeskin Armani shoes. He would definitely blend in with the place then.

The remaining men choose their targets, and soon, Francesca is leading us out of the door and back toward the deep woods. Crickets chatter, and the biting wind ravages our brittle statures. If we weren't so tense, we'd bend like rubber beneath the strong gusts.

A massive bonfire rages directly behind the house, dozens of people crowded around it, bundled in warm clothing and drinks in hand. There are also several large TVs placed sporadically around. According to Francesca, the hunters will wear body cams, providing entertainment and viewing pleasure for the other guests.

My breathing escalates as I face the endless trees, shadows flickering from the fire behind us. The scent of fear emanates from the six of us as we line up, and I break out into a cold sweat. My boots sink into the mud, suctioning my feet deeply into the frigid earth. Part of me desperately wishes it was tar instead, granting me the fortune of getting stuck here.

Already, I'm plagued with memories of sprinting through these woods and coming so close to victory, only for Sydney to appear behind a tree, lips curled into an evil smile and reeking of malevolence.

What if she does it again? I think I'll kill her if she does. Rip the arrow out of my body myself and stab it into her instead.

Behind us, the men ready their crossbows, the clanging of metal as they load arrows into them grinding against my frayed nerves. Risking a glance behind me, my eyes round when I see headgear settled over their eyes.

Night vision goggles.

Fuckers. Everything about this stupid fucking game is rigged.

"All right, ladies," Francesca starts. "Let's go over the rules briefly. You will be given a ten-minute head start. You are required to stay within the maze walls. If caught going outside of them, it will result in immediate death. They will shoot to kill, not shoot to maim. At the end of the maze, there is an open area. If you reach this location, you are immediately deemed safe, and no harm will come to you. If you are still within the maze but have not been shot, and the allotted hour depletes, you are also deemed safe, and no harm will come to you. Is that understood?"

None of us speak, and our lack of protest is answer enough.

"How's it said from *The Hunger Games*, may the odds be ever in your favor?" a male cuts in, and it sounds like Xavier.

A round of laughter follows the bad joke, but before my lack of self-control can get me in trouble, he calls out, "Run!"

We take off, sprinting through the woods carefully, wary of traps. Strings will be tightened between two objects at foot level, and if tripped, we'll be strung up, easy for the picking. Walls of branches are piled high on either side of us, makeshift barriers to confine us in a maze. Not only is it redirecting our focus onto getting out rather than staying hidden, but it's also meant to disorient us and incite panic.

And fuck, does it work.

I bring myself to a halt and rush behind a trunk, my heart pounding rapidly. The walls of the maze are spread out, allowing plenty of trees in between.

There's no point in covering my tracks up until this point; it's from here on out that will matter. I tear through leaves and twigs, searching for a branch. My fingers are already red and stiff from the cold, but I hardly feel it with the adrenaline coursing through my system.

In the dead of night, it takes too long to find a suitable branch with leaves on it, brittle as they are, and even longer to accomplish what I'm doing.

After Jillian's advice, I racked my brain for all the ways to cover my tracks without having to consistently stop and sweep them away as I run. I settled on fashioning a sweeper to my back, using a belt I stole from the beauty room to keep it in place.

She said gaining distance isn't as important, but I want to accomplish both. Get as far away as I can and do so without a trace. I suppose one good thing is coming from this, and that's learning how exactly I'm going to escape when the time comes.

I grab onto the branch with leaves, poise it on my lower back, and use the satin belt to anchor it to me, tying the fabric in several tight knots. And then I start speed-walking, swiveling my head back and forth to both keep from kissing a tree, and ensuring the branch is doing its job.

It's too dark to tell for sure, but it appears as if it is, and that's good enough for me.

So I take off, counting my steps and lifting my branch carefully over the wire when I reach them. My pace is quick but steady, holding on to the belt tightly for extra security with one hand and keeping the other in front of me, preventing me from running into anything nature has to offer.

I dart from one tree to another, keeping myself concealed at all times. Several minutes later, I reach a dead end, and from the corner of my eye, I see a flash of dark orange to my left. Phoebe.

Of course, she doesn't know how to cover her tracks as she runs. And as dangerous as she is to be around right now, I refuse to keep my mouth shut and allow another woman to fail.

"Phoebe!" I call out, keeping my voice as quiet as possible.

She skids and turns to me, breathing heavily. I can't see much of her features, but I imagine her face matches mine. Panicked, and eyes dilated with fear.

"Cover your tracks. You're leading them right to you," I tell her in a whisper-shout, and then I take off in the opposite direction. I don't know if she'll listen, although I do know that it might be too late. She's led them this far, and to ensure my own survival, I need to get the hell away from her.

The branch dragging behind me is loud, so I force myself to slow, counting my thirty steps and keeping an eye out for any wires. I'm nearly gasping for breath, willing my heart rate to calm. I should've put enough distance between the two of us by now.

So, when I turn to see Phoebe running after me, I fucking spazz.

"What are you doing?!" I exclaim, attempting to keep my voice down, only causing it to break from the pitch.

"Please, let me stay with you," she pleads, no branch in her hands to cover her tracks. She didn't even bother to *try*.

"What the fuck is wrong with you, no! You're going to get me killed," I snap, chest pumping as my eyes pinball, searching for any movement in the darkness. I'm almost positive our ten-minute head start has passed. They have night vision goggles—we don't. Which means they could be anywhere.

Her pale hand clutches my arm and pulls me close, her nails digging in. Now that I can see her clearly, she looks crazed.

"Please, I can't let them do that to me again. Let me come with you, *please!*"

I try to wrangle my hand from her, but her grip tightens, and she refuses to let go.

"I'm not letting you go! I'm coming with you."

Shit. This is what I fucking get for not being like Sydney and gladly watching others fail.

"Okay, fuck. You can come, just let me go," I hiss, finally freeing my arm from her desperate clutches. Making a split-second decision, I run back the way we came about twenty feet, swivel my branch to my front and start brushing away her tracks, walking backwards until I reach her once more.

"Stay in front of me, and run as fast as you can," I demand. "And don't do anything to get us killed. Not more than you already have."

She winces from my harsh words, but I feel no remorse. I'm pissed off that my kindness has most likely just earned me an arrow in the back, and even more angry that I can't find it in me to knock her ass out and leave her behind.

It would benefit me, however, I wouldn't be able to live with myself. It's the whole reason I called out to her in the first place. She's young, desperate, and terrified and I'm putting on a good show of looking like I know what I'm doing. Of course, she's going to latch onto me.

Thankfully, Phoebe listens this time, keeping in front of me as we sprint. My branch is behind me again, clearing our tracks. Sweat coats nearly every inch of my skin, trickling down my forehead and spine, irritating the stitches in my skin. Clouds puff from my mouth, and I have an insane moment of panic when I wonder if my bad breath will leave a scent trail.

Several times we get turned around, and I swear we've passed the same fucking tree three times now. I'm growing frustrated and tired, so I skid to a stop and urge Phoebe to find a large tree to hide behind. I find one several feet southwest of her that provides a clear view of the space between both trees.

I'm heaving, desperate for oxygen, and on the verge of puking. I need to catch my breath, and I'm growing paranoid that even if they can't see our footprints, they'll be able to hear us.

"Stay quiet," I whisper, even though I'm struggling to accomplish that myself. My body doesn't care about keeping silent. All it's only focused on is greedily sucking in precious air, no matter the cost.

I split my focus on catching my breath and listening for any footsteps. An owl hoots and a cold yet soft breeze flows through the forest. Such a stark contrast to the dark and dangerous situation. It feels like there should be Michael Myers music playing in the background.

A rustle from a nearby brush nearly sends my heart flying out of my throat, but then a bunny emerges and sprints off. Just as I wrangle the muscle back down where it belongs, a voice calls out.

"Fiiirecraacker."

Fuck. I don't know if it was a good guess, or if my branch failed to conceal both sets of footprints, but Phoebe's pursuer caught up to us. Round eyes clash with mine, and I know that my irises are dilated with fear just as much as hers are.

"What do we do?" she mouths silently, and I shake my head, at a loss. I don't *know* what we fucking do. I've no idea where he is exactly, but if even an elbow pops out from behind a tree, he'll be able to spot it immediately.

Does it count if I'm hit with someone else's arrow? I'm sure I'll still be punished, even if I wasn't the intended target.

"Fiiiiirecrackeeer," Ben calls out again. I risk a glance around the tree trunk and see a shadow move about twenty feet behind us.

Fuck. Way too close.

If we stay silent, we might get lucky, and he'll wander off in another direction. He might think we've gone down a different trail and allow us to put distance between one another. But right now, the slightest sound, and he could hone in on us. It's not safe for either of us to even breathe.

Not that I can fucking breathe anyway.

Phoebe covers her nose and mouth with her hand, squeezing her eyes shut, tears crowding past her lashes and glinting in the moonlight. If she's not already, she's going to start having a panic attack. And in my experience, those are rarely silent.

I put my shaking finger to my lips, a tear of my own breaking free. My vision blurs as I face the very real possibility that I might get hit with an arrow, and then later be brutally raped for it. Again.

But she can't hold on, and a small whimper slips past her hand. My heart stalls, and almost in slow motion, I hear several footsteps taken in our direction.

"Was that you, firecracker?" he says in a hushed tone as if he's whispering right into our ears.

Shit, Addie, think. What would Zade do?

He'd be a fucking hero; that's what he'd do. Zade isn't interested in saving himself, only everyone else. So, what would he want *me* to do?

Save myself. He'd want me to save myself. But the Culling wasn't designed for the prey to safely get away.

Before I can decide, Phoebe's eyes widen into round discs, and she seems to shy away, her body beginning to emerge from the other side. Slowly, she raises a shaking hand and points behind me.

My heart drops, and for a moment, I'm paralyzed. My brain once again divides into two, one half panicking because she's no longer concealed, and the other half frozen in terror because there's somebody fucking behind me.

I know without a shadow of a doubt that it's Xavier. He's found me.

Leaves crunch and a twig snaps to my right. My head whips in that direction, and I scarcely see the shine of a crossbow glinting under the moonbeams.

And then time speeds up, slapping me in the face as two arrows barrel towards us at once. One from Ben, and the other from behind me.

The air whistles and my body moves purely on instinct, ducking low and veering off toward the tree to the left of me. The arrow flies between my tree and the one I'm aiming for, and a *thunk* stops me in my tracks. Mere inches separate the tip of the arrow now impaled in the bark, and my face.

My eyes blow wide, and I yelp. I look up and notice the first shot towards Phoebe also failed. We won't get that lucky again. And we only have about seventeen seconds to get away.

...*three, four, five...*

"Phoebe, run!"

Both of us scramble, dirt and leaves kicking up beneath our boots as we take off, our legs pumping and tearing through the foliage.

"Jump!" I screech, my mind scrambling to keep up with our steps. Scarcely, I lift the branch attached to me, and the both of us jump over the tripwire, coming incredibly close to snagging it.

Our pounding footsteps ruminate through the forest floor. There's no hiding now. There's only escaping a silver arrowhead. The paths we take are strategic only in the sense of losing them, rather than trying to find our way out.

We clear a few more traps, and after several minutes, I hear Phoebe's footfalls coming to a sudden stop. I skid, turning to see her bent at the waist, panting so hard, she's nearly choking. Her face is as bright as her hair, and her eyes seem to cross.

"I can't keep running," she chokes out, and then gags. "I can't."

"No, no, you can do it! Come on, Phoebe, you got this."

She shakes her head again, and I can't help but take a step back when I see a shadow dart to the side about ten yards away or so. A scream tears from my throat when the arrow goes flying, piercing Phoebe straight in the back of the shoulder.

She falls face first, an agonized wail following suit. Groaning, she manages to pick herself up and charge past me. Confused, I chase after her, then come skidding to a halt again when she steps over the tripwire, collapses to the ground, and grabs onto the string.

"Addie, fucking *go!*" she screams, her voice breaking from the force. My face contorts and tears spill over my eyelids, both from denial and guilt. But an arrow cutting through time and space has me diving ahead, another arrow coming within scant inches from my head.

My hands grapple at the cold ground to propel me forward, nearly face-planting again in my pursuit to get back on my feet.

Run, little mouse. They're coming for you.

I make it about fifteen feet before a loud cracking noise echoes in the brittle wind. Gasping, I turn my head in time to see a rope snap around Ben's ankle, sending him flying straight up into the air. His crossbow drops from his hands, thudding to the ground next to Phoebe.

My mouth drops, a shocked laugh tinkling out as Ben's shouts of fury fill the air, wiggling like a worm on a hook as he swings from above. Even from hundreds of feet away, you can hear the gasps of shock and outrage from the house.

Phoebe must've waited until Ben approached her and then released the wire right when he was in the crosshairs of it.

"Let me down right now!" Ben shouts, and though the shadows conceal his face, I know it's cherry red. "I will fucking *kill* you for this."

And he will. I know it.

Phoebe knows it, too.

Our eyes clash for a moment, and then her gaze slowly drops to the crossbow.

"Phoebe…" I warn.

"I'm dead, anyways," she rasps, grabbing the crossbow in her hands, and stumbling through reloading it. Glancing around nervously, I tuck myself behind a tree, wary of another arrow flying my way. I need to run—like ten seconds ago, but I can't pull myself away.

"Don't do it, little girl," Xavier calls out from the depths of the trees. I bristle, warring with the need to run and stay by Phoebe's side. Neither of us can see him, but his attention seems to be focused on the girl loading a dangerous weapon with the desire to kill on her fingertips.

"Help! Fucking help me!" Ben screams, wriggling fiercely but getting nowhere. He's suspended above a deadly angel, and her arrow will show no mercy to the wicked.

"God fucking dammit, Xavier, GET HER! GET HER—"

She ignores them both, takes aim, and right when she pulls the trigger, another arrow is zipping through the air and plunging into her other shoulder.

She cries out, the scream echoing, but her own arrow strikes true, embedding directly into the top of Ben's skull and killing him instantly, the rest of his sentence silenced by a metal arrowhead.

Covering my mouth, I watch as blood pours down like a waterfall directly on top of her, but she's too busy laughing maniacally to notice.

Once more, she meets my wide stare. So many words rise to the tip of my tongue, none of them sufficient. Goosebumps rise on my skin, and all I want to do is tell her how proud I am. How fucking admirable and brave she is. We both know she's not going to make it through the night, but this was *her* choice.

"Go," she mouths. With one last lingering look, I take off, hoping she can see everything I couldn't say in my eyes.

"You can run, little girl. But you can't escape me," Xavier shouts, his threat following me as I sprint through the maze. Phoebe's distraction provided me with the head start I needed to get away.

Determination takes hold, and I kick my legs as hard as I can. I continue to weave through the maze, holding my breath as another whistle pierces the air, and an arrow embeds in a trunk only a foot away.

These men may be skilled in hunting, but what they don't know is that I've been hunted by a far scarier man. I was a mouse caught in a trap before, scared, and helpless as I was taken between the teeth of an apex predator.

But I'm not their little mouse, and they are not Zade.

And I will never succumb to them.

Chapter Fifteen
The Diamond

I lost him.

Not only that, but I made it out of the maze, deeming me safe.

No harm will come to you.

Lies, but I'll take it for now.

I didn't stop there, though. I ran so deep into the woods that I'm thoroughly lost now, not even a whisper of human life. It reminds me so much of Parsons Manor, it makes my chest ache. Doesn't help that I'm breathing so heavily that I choke on the oxygen with every inhale. I'm on the verge of both vomiting and passing out, even though my body can't decide which to do first.

Feeling confident enough that they don't know where I am, I rip the branch off my waist, lean heavily against a tree and slide down, my legs incapable of holding me up any longer.

My eyes begin to roll, but I fight against the urge because despite being considered safe, that doesn't really exist in this world. Xavier could stumble upon me and take advantage of us being alone. My screams wouldn't be heard, and even if they were, no one would give a shit.

Wiping sweat from my eyes, I look over my surroundings. At first, I see nothing but trees. But then, off in the distance, I glimpse metal glinting in the moonlight.

A crease forms between my brows and my curiosity piques. I allow myself another minute to catch my breath before I force myself back to my feet and jog toward the foreign object while periodically checking over my shoulder to make sure that no one is behind me.

As I approach, the object becomes identifiable, and I lose my breath all over again when I realize what it is.

It's an abandoned train. A massive row of trailers stretches across the wooded area in either direction, the metal rusted and corroded from nature. My heart pounds and excitement blooms.

Escape.

That's the only word that comes to mind when I look at this abandoned train. I don't know how yet, but I do know that it could provide me shelter when I eventually leave this place.

Checking over my shoulder once more and seeing nobody there, I approach the train and run my hands over the cold metal. So badly, I want to seek asylum here instead of returning to that house. I've no idea whether they know of the train's location, but it won't be hard to find with the tracking device in the back of my neck.

If this train is going to offer me anything, then I need to utilize it when they aren't able to track me.

A loud horn breaks through the silence, causing critters to scatter and a yelp to escape, my heart jumping up my throat. Breathing heavily, I peer over my shoulder, hearing voices calling out, announcing the end of the Culling.

They'll be looking for me, and I'm tempted to dig out the tracking device with a sharp branch and make a run for it anyway, but fear has me in a chokehold. There are too many factors against me.

Be smart, little mouse.

I take off back in the direction I came from, now paranoid that they'll find me near the train and discover it if they weren't already aware of it. I don't want to chance it if they weren't.

After several minutes of jogging, I catch a glimpse of black hair and a feminine stature before it disappears behind a tree.

"Hey!" I call out, hoping whoever it is, they'll know the way back.

The person emerges from the other end of the tree, and I realize that it's Jillian.

She looks over to me, eyes wide and breathing heavily. She doesn't look much worse than I do, which is honestly relieving.

"You made it," she says softly. We meet each other in the middle and her eyes look me up and down, likely looking for injuries.

"I did," I respond, still breathless. Up until Zade's training, I've never exerted this much energy in my entire life.

"Do you know how to get back?" I ask.

She glances around. "I think so. If not, they'll come get us."

I nod, and we begin to walk.

"Have you been through the Culling before?" I ask.

She seems to have so much knowledge for it being her first time.

"No, you only go through it once," she answers.

"Except if you're Sydney," I mutter, though I'm relieved to hear that

I'll never have to do this again.

Jillian snorts. "That's true. She knows the maze like the back of her hand now."

"Is she the one who taught you how to get through it?"

She shakes her head. "When I first arrived, I was even more combative than you. Francesca considered me too much of a risk to put in the Culling until she could set me straight, so I had watched other girls go through it first. I learned a lot from them." She pauses. "And I also witnessed everything that happened after. Look, you need to prepare for—"

A deep booming laugh interrupts whatever she was going to say. Jillian and I both flinch and turn toward the sound. Xavier emerges from behind a tree, and my poor overused heart speeds up once more.

"Well, diamond, I guess you proved me wrong this time," he chuckles, his eyes sweeping my body up and down in a predatory way.

As much as it tickles their manhood to catch us during the Culling, it also means that we're deemed unworthy to be auctioned off. And that means they're allowed to dole out our punishment for tonight only. So, while escaping Xavier might've ruffled his feathers, it's still an accomplishment.

Because now he gets to keep me.

Swallowing nervously, I say, "I guess I did."

He purses his lips and nods, and then tips his chin in the direction that we need to go.

"I'd be happy to escort you fine ladies, if you don't mind," he offers, his voice deepening.

Jillian and I glance at each other, but ultimately, we nod our heads. Because what else are we supposed to fucking say?

No, go away, you have cooties.

If only it were that easy.

He directs us outside of the maze so we can avoid the tripwires. It takes thirty-five long grueling minutes to make it back to the house. Thirty-five minutes of bouts of uncomfortable silence, stilted conversation, and the anticipation of buying me.

Jillian and I are exhausted, both of us stumbling several times from our quaking knees and fried nerves.

When we arrive back at the house, Francesca is standing at the tree line, hands clasped as she watches the hunters and prey emerge. She looks a little unhinged, most likely because one of her girls killed someone, but when her eyes find mine, they quickly take me in, checking for injuries. A subtle smile tips the corners of her pink lips when she doesn't spot any, glee brightening her eyes. She may have a death on her hands, but the diamond still shines bright, I guess.

Glad to be of use, bitch.

Phoebe is already leaning against the back of the house, blood pouring from her wounds and staining her backside. They've already removed the arrows, and now they're working to staunch the bleeding. This surprises me as much as it scares me, considering she killed a man tonight. I would've thought she'd never make it out of those woods alive.

She's pale and looks delirious from the pain, but there's a sereneness to her face that I've never seen before. She forced me into saving her, then turned around and saved me instead.

All I want to do is hug her tight and tell her that everything is going to be okay. Not because either of us believes she's going to survive, but because once she's gone, she'll be in a better place than she is now.

Sydney comes running out, not a drop of blood in sight. I'm admittedly disappointed by that. Luckily, Gloria follows closely behind, pride shining in her eyes as she walks toward me, unscathed this time around. I begin to smile, but that small moment of elation quickly fizzles out when a large man emerges with Bethany slung over his shoulder, an arrow in her back. My eyes widen in horror, disgusted to see the arrow lodged deeply in her spine, blood soaking both her and the man who carries her.

It takes a monumental effort to keep the tears at bay, but I refuse to turn my head away from her. She doesn't deserve for any of us to ignore her pain. Another man gathers Phoebe, and together they carry her and Bethany off.

My lip trembles, and I quickly suck it between my teeth and bite down before Francesca can spot it. I don't know how Zade kept it together in situations like this. Maybe because he had the assurance he could kill them for it, and I... fuck, I'm so helpless.

I try to dissolve my face of any emotion, but I don't know how successful I am when I'm watching two girls be carried off to a fate worse than death.

Sydney comes to stand beside me, purposely bumping into my shoulder, and Jillian and Gloria flank the other side of me. Francesca turns to us, a mix of pride and exhaustion shining through her made-up face.

"Only two, that's wonderful news," she says, even going as far as to clap her hands like a little sea otter, though it's lackluster. I wonder if she's going to be punished for what Phoebe did, too.

I'd love to be the one to do it. I'd take one of those arrows and stab her in the eye with it. Then pluck that baby out of her skull and make her chew it.

"As a reward, you ladies will get to pick dinner tonight. Whatever you want! McDonald's even! Though, that stuff is *horrendous* for your bodies, but just this once should be okay."

My mouth opens, but fury chokes my words tighter than a Victorian corset. In the end, I'm glad for it because only poison would've spewed from my mouth.

We survived the Culling, and we get fucking *McDonald's* as a reward? It's too stupid to be real.

Sydney saves me and jumps up and down excitedly. "My favorite!" she exclaims, nearly bursting my eardrum. I flinch from the pitch, flattening my lips and working to swallow down the venomous words.

I'm *shaking.*

"Sounds good, Francesca. Their fries are always the best," Gloria says, her voice tight. One glance, and I can see she and Jillian are tense, struggling to keep their expressions pleasant.

"Wonderful, let's go in and get you girls cleaned up. There will be celebrations tonight, and you'll be expected to mingle with the guests. Make an impression and be respectful as they could be potential buyers."

She turns on one foot and walks off with the standard unspoken expectation for us to follow. Sydney skips after her, but not before throwing a demented look over her shoulder, turning my blood into ice.

Whatever the fuck that look meant—it's not good.

Nothing with Sydney is ever good.

"Suck it in tighter," Francesca snaps from behind me.

"I'm trying," I wheeze, right as she tugs on the strings for the thirtieth time. I ate the McDonald's. Of course, it didn't settle right because when has McDonald's *ever* made anyone feel better after eating it. And now, Francesca is intent on making it come right back up.

"I think it's tight enough," I groan.

Pretty sure I hear a rib crack in response. It feels cruel that I'm being forced to wear a corset with this dress, but men that operate within human trafficking rings are just as stereotypical as the men who blame sexual assault on the girls' clothing. Tiny waists are revered, but probably not as much as not having a gag reflex when a dick is shoved down your throat.

Francesca ties the knot and then helps me slip the dress over my head, the same dress all of us are required to wear. A black, silky number that accentuates my curves—my now greatly exaggerated curves. The material ends right below my ass cheeks. A butterfly could flutter by, and my dress would fly up like it's allergic to the winged creature.

If I pass gas, it's *over*.

Francesca runs her hands through my cinnamon tresses, observing me through the mirror. We're in the beauty room, the other girls putting on their makeup, already having gone through the same torture.

"You need to do something with this hair. It's beautiful but hides that elegant neck of yours. Don't cover up your freckles when you put makeup on either. They accentuate your unusual eyes."

I force a smile, scared that if I do anything more, my stomach will blow through the corset.

"I can figure something out with my hair, pin it up perhaps," I say agreeably.

"I can do it," Sydney chirps from behind me.

My smile drops, along with my heart. I don't want the bitch to come a mile within my vicinity because I know damn well she's going to pull something.

Just as I open my mouth to protest, Francesca turns to her and says dryly, "Fine, but if you do anything to her hair, I will personally see that you lose your hand."

Sydney's smile only grows, "Of course, I would never."

Francesca scoffs as if she doesn't believe her but walks away anyway.

If she doesn't believe her... then *why* is she walking away?

Setting my jaw, I narrow my eyes and carefully watch Sydney approach me from behind. She meets my gaze through the mirror, her cold eyes churning with an indecipherable emotion.

A secretive smile pulls her red lips up higher as she begins to sift through my hair. My shoulders are hiked up to my ears, and the tension between us thickens.

"How long have you been in this house?" I ask after a few moments of silence.

Her deft fingers start separating pieces on the side of my head and then begins French braiding a small section.

"Four years," she responds.

I raise an eyebrow. "You've avoided the auctions that long?"

She smirks. "I've worked hard to be too unstable to be sold but too valuable to be killed. I'm good at what I do," she finishes with a wink.

I swallow, not entirely sure how to respond to that.

She glances slyly at me, "Rio has been treating me so good lately, though. He comes to my room every night now. Says my pussy is the tightest he's ever had."

I arch a brow. Rio has refused to touch us during lessons, and I've never seen him show any interest otherwise. I'm not surprised that he's fucking one of the girls if it's consensual, but I am surprised that she thinks I'd give a shit.

"If that makes you happy, then good for you," I finally say in a monotone voice.

She pauses. "You don't care?"

"Why would I care?"

"He likes you."

I roll my eyes, annoyed by her school girl shit. She acts like we're two girls getting ready for prom, gossiping about boys. She plays the classic mean girl act well. Pretends to be nice but all her sugary sweet words are laced with salty insults. Too bad for her, I'm not interested in playing this game.

"You have a man at home, right? Z is his name?" she asks, noting my reaction. She pulls my hair particularly tight, and I hiss in response.

"Gentle," I snap. She only smiles, waiting for a response to her question.

"Why do you care?" I ask, my anger heightening when she runs her hands through the rest of my hair roughly, tearing through knots.

"A sexy Puerto Rican man has the hots for you, and you don't care." She shrugs. "And I guess I'm curious about the man that makes you so valuable. Is he looking for you?"

Rio does not have the hots for me, but I ignore that.

"Don't we all have someone looking for us?"

She shrugs. "No," she says simply, and I almost feel a pinch of sympathy. "Do you really believe he's going to be able to save you?"

I flatten my lips, debating on responding at all. If I say anything incriminating, she will immediately use it against me. Twist my words and tell Francesca that I'm trying to escape or something.

"I think all of our loved ones would at least try. That's what people do when they love you."

I hope that hurt.

She gathers my hair together, beginning to pull it into a ponytail in the middle of my head.

"Do you think he would save me, too?" she asks quietly.

She keeps her eyes downcast, leaving me bereft of her expression. Manipulative cunt.

"I think he would save everyone," I say. *And then kill her himself.*

Finally, she looks up at me, a twinkle in her eye that has my muscles tightening.

"If he does, I'd be happy to suck his cock for it. Let him fuck me in the ass, too, if he really wants."

I narrow my eyes, gritting my teeth so roughly, I'm close to cracking my molars.

"He would never touch you," I snap. "Nor would he let *you* touch *him.*"

A gleeful smile stretches across her face, and I internally slap myself for giving her the reaction she wanted.

"I think he would once he sees how much better I am than you. I've been here too long not to know how to make a man come in five seconds."

She fashions my hair into a messy coif that I'd probably consider beautiful if I knew that being anything but ugly is going to attract the wrong kinds of attention tonight.

The second her hands drop, I calmly stand and turn to face her. And then I take a page out of Zade's handbook of being a psychopath, grab her by the neck, whip her around and slam her against the vanity. Bottles of perfume and makeup brushes topple to the floor, and I hear a gasp from one of the girls behind me.

Surprise widens her dark eyes as I come nose-to-nose with her.

"Keep pushing my buttons, Sydney. If you perceived me as weak, then you're going to get quite the fucking reality check. I put up with your shit this long because I'm sympathetic that Mommy and Daddy don't love you, nor does Francesca. But I will *not* be bullied by you and continue to stay quiet."

She seethes at me, and her true face appears from behind that fragile, porcelain mask. The room is well lit, yet as her anger amplifies, it seems as if she pulls the shadows from the corners of the walls and shrouds them over her face. Her chin is dipped as she glares at me, but I'm not fucking scared of her.

I've faced far worse than her already. All it does is reignite that thrill that I've been missing for so long. My adrenaline is rushing, and this—this I could get off on.

"You're a *pest*, Sydney."

"And you're going to die," she murmurs. I laugh in her face.

"Then I'll take you down with me, bitch."

I shove her deeper into the vanity, pushing off her and causing a few more things to knock over.

When I turn my back to her, deliberately letting her know I'm not afraid, I find Gloria staring at me with wide eyes beneath her big glasses while Jillian gets dressed in the corner, minding her own business.

I make it two steps before Francesca's loud footsteps bound up the steps and into our room with a smile on her face. Sydney times it just right, creating a fake coughing fit the moment she heard Francesca coming.

And when she sees Sydney sprawled against the vanity, coughing as she clutches her neck dramatically, I already know what she's going to pull.

"What happened?" Francesca barks.

Sydney points at me. "She choked me! Pushed me against the vanity and choked me."

Francesca's eyes turn to me, and I meet her stare head-on, making sure to keep my face neutral.

I'm not going to get into a *she started it* fight and present myself as emotionally unstable as she is.

Her brown eyes assess me closely, but the adrenaline has taken hold in my bloodstream, and all I can feel is… elation. Heat has warmed every inch of my body, sinking low into my stomach.

If Zade were here…

I force those thoughts out of my head before they sweep me away. If I let that happen, I'd be humping the air, and not only would that be fucking embarrassing, but I'm also in the number one worst place in the world to get horny.

After a pregnant pause, Francesca meets Sydney's stare.

"You probably deserved it."

I smother the smile before it can emerge, but *fuck* is it hard when she gasps loudly in response.

"Go to your room until I call you down," she orders harshly.

Sydney rushes past me, but I feel her intention from a mile away. I step out of her path before she can knock into me, which only serves to make her angrier. Her head whips around, and the glare she shoots my way is pure hatred before she disappears.

Clearing my throat, I lower my head. Hopefully Francesca sees it as submission, and not a last-ditch effort to contain how pleased I am.

I feel her eyes boring into me, and a bead of sweat forms on my hairline. Knowing the drill, Gloria and Jillian line up beside me, effectively distracting her.

"Tonight, is about having fun, but make sure you present yourselves as ladies. Don't act like sluts but be docile and compliant. You all are allowed *one* drink tonight. I won't tolerate any of you making drunken fools out of yourselves." She pauses. "Make me proud tonight, girls."

Chapter Sixteen
The Hunter

The Basilisk Brotherhood lives in a bank in a suburb of Portland. Obviously, it was abandoned, though the sign outside the building still stands, the old name in bold blue letters. The entire front wall has been replaced with black slate, assumingly because it used to be glass when it was a business.

What's more interesting is that they turned it into a mini skyscraper. I know damn well this bank didn't look this good when it was active, and it sure as shit didn't have at least five floors on top of it.

I swing open my door and inhale my cigarette one last time before stubbing it on the ground with my boot.

Stop littering.

Yes, baby.

I grab the butt and throw it in a little trash bag hanging in my car, the recyclable sack full of orange filters already.

Exiting my Mustang, I slam the door shut and slowly approach the building. The parking lot is empty, so I'm assuming their cars are hidden in a garage somewhere.

Several cameras watch me as I approach the front door. Glancing up, I stare directly into the lens hanging above the entrance, and seconds later, the door clicks.

Two of the four brothers are waiting for me on the other side. Ryker and Kace, the former with his arms crossed and a frown tugging on his lips, and the latter with his hands tucked into his front pockets and a stoic expression.

They both eye me closely, so I put my hands up.

"I swear I'm not here to rob you. Scout's honor," I say with a grin.

"You'd be dead already if you were."

I drop my hands, the smile on my face growing. Deciding I'll push their buttons one at a time instead of all at once, I remain quiet.

We're standing in what used to be the main room; the teller station now closed off completely. Now, it's four walls, dimly lit with shiny gray wood flooring and deep navy blue walls. A single black leather couch is pushed up against the wall to my left, and I imagine this is where all unwelcome or untrusted guests are vetted before they're allowed into their home.

"You have two minutes to explain what the hell you want," Ryker says.

"Well, fuck, no pressure, right?" I widen my stance and cross my arms, appearing at ease. "Long story short, my girl was kidnapped by the Society. Sold off into the skin trade."

"You're Z, and can't find her?" Kace challenges.

I keep my face blank as I meet his stare. His blue eyes are ice cold and unflinching, unconcerned with questioning my skills.

"I'm capable of a lot of things, Kace," I say quietly, unleashing a little bit of the darkness that's been festering inside my body. "Including finding exactly where your twin sister stays. Claremont Drive, right? Her twin girls, Kacey and Karla, are getting so big already. Eleven years old, am I right?"

He snarls and takes a step towards me, the first sign of emotion sparking in his eyes. Ryker's hand snaps out and lands on his chest, stopping him from advancing.

I forge on before any threats can leave their mouths. I have no interest in Kace's family.

"Her name is Adeline Reilly. She was taken to Dr. Garrison's place to be treated for injuries from a car accident—one that they caused. The doctor had a penchant for taking his patients to his room and having his way with them, except with Addie, he tried to kidnap her. He was killed by one of her kidnappers, Rio Sanchez, and when they left, they shut down the entire grid. The last thing I am is incapable, but I am also aware that the more people I have searching for her, the faster I am to find her.

"I am a patient man, but not when it comes to getting my girl back."

They're quiet for a few beats, their brains churning.

"What do you need us for?" Ryker asks finally.

"You trade in human organs," I answer. "Do you not?"

Ryker tilts his head to the side, contemplating my question.

"If you know that, why would you want people who are in the market for people like your girlfriend to help you?"

I shrug casually. "You're not going to hurt her, and I'm willing to look the other way in the meantime."

If I find out they are getting people killed so they can profit off of their organs, then all bets are off. Though, I have a very strong feeling the rumors were true, and that's not the case.

Kace shakes his head as if he can't believe what he's hearing.

"You have extensive knowledge of the inner workings of the skin trade. I'm sure you know exactly how to track down product if it's being auctioned or traded," I continue.

"What's in it for us?"

I widen my arms, the shit-eating grin back on my face. I'm empty on the inside—nothing but white noise takes up residence, but I've grown accustomed to arranging my face into expressions just as easily as I can wipe my face clean of them.

"I'm a man of many talents. I'll write an IOU on a piece of paper, and you can tuck that in your pocket for when you need it. One-time admission. Can't be reused. Like a coupon."

Kace narrows his eyes, staring at me as if I'm a little sibling begging to play with him and his friends.

"What makes you think we'd have any use for you?" he questions dryly.

My ego—it hurts.

"Crazier shit has happened," I retort, dropping my arms.

Another pregnant pause, and I make sure to meet both of their gazes, not the least bit bothered by their intimidation tactics.

Ryker jerks his head towards the door, grumbling, "Follow me."

Kace stares at his brother, communicating something with his eyes that I don't care to interpret. Whatever silent conversation passes between them lasts all of three seconds before Kace gives in and follows after Ryker without argument.

But not before throwing a suspicious look over his shoulder.

Who hurt you, bro?

I don't care to find that out, either.

A fingerprint scanner is built into the door handle, the machine chirping when Ryker's print is recognized.

I follow them through the door, and my brows shoot up my forehead. I've walked into a bachelor's wet dream.

The room is gigantic and completely open, with the ceiling scaling up at least a hundred feet. The entire area is washed in browns and blacks and made up of only four walls. A staircase on the far right leads to a balcony that completely circles the building, housing dozens of doors and a black elevator on the back left side. The upper four floors have their own floating balconies, too, and I wonder what the fuck do they need all this space for.

Scratch that—I don't care.

Oh, but I might care about *that*. A massive vault is straight ahead, the door painted black. My curiosity piques, wondering what's beyond it.

I whistle, impressed and maybe even a tad jealous of their get-up.

"Human organs pay well, don't they?" I muse.

"Shut up," Kace bites out, heading for one of the black leather couches where a shirtless Daire lounges casually, knees spread wide.

I do a double take when I see a chain coiled around his hand, leading directly to a collar fastened around a girl's throat, who is currently kneeling at his feet. Only a black band covers her tits, the rest of her body is fully exposed. Her head is bowed, and her hands rest neatly on her pale thighs. A curtain of black hair obscures her face from view, and I can't tell if that's intentional or not.

I think Addie would sooner rip my balls off before she'd ever kneel at my feet. Lucky for her, I'd gladly kneel at hers. Kiss her little toes while I'm at it, too. Eventually, my mouth would lead up between her legs, but I don't think she'd mind that part.

Daire grins at me, the piercings above his brow glinting from the crackling flames in the fireplace next to him. He doesn't look the least bit bothered by my presence, though that doesn't erase the spark of challenge in his eyes.

Slade sits on the opposite side, his dark blond head turning to glare at me over the top of the couch.

Such hostility.

"I've agreed to help him," Ryker announces, taking a seat beside Daire. He doesn't even glance at the girl, and I assume he's used to Daire's sexual habits by now.

"Yeah? What's he doing for us?" Slade asks, his question directed at his brother, yet his dark eyes stay glued to me.

"Oh," I say, holding up a finger for them to hang on. I twist around until I find a piece of paper and pen on an end table, write the letters I, O, U on it, and hand it to him.

He looks at the paper with bewilderment, turning his glare back up to me.

"First off, don't write on people's shit. Secondly, you're fucking kidding me, right? We don't need you."

I grin. Is he nervous that I might find hemorrhoid cream on his receipts, too? He should know I don't need a piece of paper to tell me what Slade spends his money on.

"You can act like my skills wouldn't benefit the business you four are conducting, but that won't get you very far."

He crumples the paper and throws it in the fire, and I can't help but chuckle in response. Their attitudes don't bother me—it's expected when a stranger comes busting into their lives making demands.

But they *will* fucking help me, whether they want to or not.

"You'll have to let me know the source of these rumors," Ryker cuts in. "The last thing we want is word getting out."

"I'll point you to the forums they're posted on. You can handle it from there, yeah?"

Ryker nods. "They're dangerous."

"Because they're true," I finish, already understanding the ramifications that can have. They have a process, and it's built off their reputation.

"You trust him?" Slade asks, raising a brow.

Ryker shrugs, unconcerned. "There's one of him, and four of us."

My top lip pulls over my teeth, just as unconcerned. I settle into the couch next to Slade, earning a glare that I dutifully ignore. Not hard when it's like a chihuahua growling at you.

"So, if you're not bad guys, how the hell do you traffic in organs... politely?"

"We handle the extraction process of the organs before selling them. If they're already deceased, we purchase the body for an inflated price, remove the valuable organs and discard the rest. Then sell the organs in the market. If they're alive, we send them home."

He pauses, waiting for a reaction he's not going to receive. I keep quiet, and after another beat, he continues.

"Daire is the one who understands the trading system best. Locates the product and keeps track of what's going in and out of the market," Ryker informs me. Oddly, I'm surprised by that. Daire winks at me, the corner of his lips still curled up.

"Slade is our negotiator and accountant. Sets up the deals, negotiates prices, and handles the money. Kace removes and preserves the organs. And I conduct the deals once terms have been agreed to. Our priority is to intercept humans who are being sacrificed for their organs and get them back home."

"But you *do* sell people's organs?" I clarify.

"Absolutely, but who we sell to provides a service to families in desperate need. People who have been on waiting lists for transplants or those who can't properly afford it with our current healthcare system. Doesn't matter if it's underground, they still go to good people who deserve it. The black market is full of evil, but not all of us are. It's only necessary we appear that way."

"If you're only extracting organs from the dead, are you saying you only sell bone and skin? Doesn't seem like a profitable business."

Ryker and Slade glance at each other, a short conversation trading between them. I arch a brow, waiting for their decision.

Slade turns to me. "Kace used to be a mortician. He's not a doctor, which is why we went to Dr. Garrison for serious injuries, but outside of his mortuary knowledge, he's well-versed on how to painlessly put someone to sleep."

"For good," I say, filling in what he didn't say.

"Yes."

I glance between Ryker and Slade, narrowing my eyes as I figure out what exactly they're trying to say. Daire is now petting the girl's hair, zoned out of our conversation.

"You assist in suicides."

Slade's stare turns grave. "Consensually. These are people who have a low quality of life. Whether they're terminally ill, old and tired, or suffering from other mental illnesses. Whatever their reason, it's their choice, and they agree to donate their organs. Kace puts them in a deep sleep, extracts the organs, and then they pass. Completely painless."

I nod my head slowly, turning that information over in my head. People often only care about life when it's inside of a woman's stomach but stop caring once that life is born. Makes me wonder if people choose this route because they couldn't get the help they needed.

I purse my lips, then state, "Oregon is a state that passed the Death with Dignity Act."

"The people who come to us are not from the states who have passed that law. In order to qualify for a physician-assisted death, you have to prove your residency," Slade explains.

"And the money you get for their organs—where does it go?"

"Depends on their wishes. Sometimes they ask it to go to the family, and we honor that. But in most cases, whether it's because they are not on good terms with their family or they don't have any at all, they don't care what we do with it, as long as it's helping someone."

Ryker cuts in, "It's a stable income, and they pass with dignity when they otherwise would not be able to. It also allows us to maintain our secrecy. As much as we want to be like the big, bad Z and go around killing all the evil guys, they're the ones who deliver the victims directly into our hands so we can save them."

I cock my head. "The little girl that was shot. How did that happen?"

Shadows fall over Ryker's eyes, darkening them to a moss green. "That's how one of the traders brought her to us. He didn't say how it happened, just that she was now useless and that we could sell her organs since she was going to die, anyway."

In this corner of the world, even the dead are valuable.

"If you killed them, that's one less person capable of stealing innocent people from their lives. One less child getting shot and sold for their organs."

Ryker leans forward, resting his elbows on his spread knees.

"We do, when we're able to, which is why our reputation as ruthless, murderous assholes is important. But if every single tradesman in the black market were killed, it would raise suspicions. The second that happens, we're out. We don't have a worldwide organization like you, we're only four men. This means if people catch on to us, that's thousands of lives we *don't* save. You know as well as I do that they're parasites and breed like rabbits. Snuffing out a few doesn't even put a dent in the cesspool of sick fucks. We save more lives this way, but that doesn't mean we don't have our fair share of blood on our hands."

I nod, pursing my lips. "Fair enough," I concede. "Good thing you have a mass organization at your disposal now. Maybe hold on to the next IOU paper, yeah? You can even sell it on eBay after—those are valuable."

Slade tightens his lips and looks away.

"Fuck off, smartass."

Chapter Seventeen
The Diamond

If it weren't for the collar wrapped around my throat, I'd consider swiping one of the guest's pocketknives and slipping out the back door, disappearing into the night. I'd cut the tracking device out of my neck, and take off, uncaring if I'm wearing nothing to protect me from the elements. I'd rather die alone in the middle of the woods than at the hands of a sex trafficker.

And Francesca knows that. She knows all of us would risk that. That's why simple black metal collars with a ruby pendant in the middle are currently dressing our throats. Something she made very clear houses another tracking device—one that can't be removed without a key.

The house is engulfed in distraction and glamor. So many men, dressed to the nines with hundreds of thousands of dollars dripping from their icy wrists. So many opportunities to slip away unnoticed while eyes are turned.

I never understood why the sickest of humanity go out of their way to appear the prettiest. You can throw glitter on a snake, but the bitch still bites.

"You look beautiful," a deep voice whispers in my ear from behind me. I startle, turning to find Xavier, a salacious grin on his face.

Francesca ordered us to mingle with the men, so I've been camping out in the living room. Even with all the cleaning we did, the house still reeks of despair. Too much horror is caked into the crevices, and no amount of scrubbing will ever free this place of it.

I force a smile, stepping away from him an inch and dipping my chin. Heat washes throughout my body, but not the kind that feels good. It feels like when you've got a stomach bug and are stuck in a car—the cold sweat is sickening.

"Thank you," I say, loosening my voice. His stare is intense as he sweeps my curves slowly, taking his time. Naturally, I want to dropkick him in the balls and run. I can only stand there and take it, though. Straight and tall, refusing to curl in on myself like he wants. It's the only defiance I can muster other than grabbing the champagne flute in his hand and breaking it across his face.

Relax, little mouse.

He didn't catch me tonight, so he doesn't get to punish me. However, I have a dreadful feeling that Francesca will gladly allow this man to touch me, regardless.

Which means I need to play nice.

"You were incredible today, despite the little distraction that vile girl caused," he says pleasantly. I can tell that he's trying to insert warmth into his presence, but it feels like sticking my hand into a fireplace that hasn't been used in centuries.

"Though I must admit, the Culling always seemed counterproductive to me," he continues. "Even if it is fun."

Clearing my throat softly, I ask, "May I ask why?"

He grins as if he sees straight through the thin façade. "It teaches you how to run away from us. It's been a tradition for centuries, but if you ask me, I'd prefer my women to be incapable of getting away."

I nod my head slowly. "That makes sense," I admit.

And really, it does.

The Culling is designed to test our endurance. I get that. If we're too weak and broken, we'll be lifeless little things, resulting in them constantly having to replace us. It's designed to break us mentally—spiritually. Induce terror and hope of escape, just to be dragged back again.

Nonetheless, Xavier is right, too. It does teach us how to run.

He takes a step closer to me, his woodsy cologne burning my sinuses as he invades my space. I want to tell him to get the fuck out of my no-no square, but I can't imagine that going over well.

Try as I might, I can't stop my limbs from stiffening, and my shoulders from hiking up an inch. My fingers twitch with the need to curl into fists, but I refrain.

"Tell me, Adeline, would you run from me if I made you mine?"

God, yes. I'd run until my feet were worn down to the bone. Even then, I'd still run.

"Of course not," I answer, keeping my voice quiet.

He chuckles, a mixture of amusement and condescension. Hot breath fans across the side of my face as he leans in close, his coarse beard scraping against the shell of my ear.

"You wouldn't be able to, even if you wanted to," he whispers. "You wouldn't be able to stand. Your legs would be shaking too badly from how hard I fuck you."

A hand drifting across my backside accompanies his words. I close my eyes, searching for the strength to not tremble beneath his touch. To not run the hell away from him and pray to the She-Devil above that he never finds me.

"Does that sound good, diamond? Do you think you'd even remember Z after I'm done with you?"

My eyes snap open, and red clouds my vision. This time, I do tremble, but only from rage.

God? I need you right now. I need you to bestow whatever voodoo shit you got up your sleeve, so I don't fucking murder this man.

He leans back, his cold gaze searching my face for a reaction. I look away, incapable of keeping the fire from my eyes, and firmly keep my mouth shut.

What the fuck does he expect me to say to that? *Yes, pedo master, I would forget all about Zade and only think of you and your small, puny cock.*

Fuck out of here, dickhead.

He grunts out another sound of amusement, and I bite the inside of my cheek until the taste of copper fills my mouth. And then I bite harder.

"Answer me," he clips.

"No," I whisper, casting my gaze down to conceal the lie. "I think it would be very difficult to think of anything else but you."

And how much I want to kill you.

"Yeah?" he asks, his voice hitching with excitement.

"Yeah," I squeak, right as his hand roughly grips my ass, jerking me deeper into his broad chest. My muscles tighten impossibly further, feeling his length digging into my stomach. Revulsion twists my insides, and I swear it'll be some form of justice if I just allow the vomit to spew right in his face.

He rolls his hips into me, and just as I'm reaching my snapping point, someone clears their throat loudly from behind me.

Xavier releases me, and I take a few steps away, immediately correcting my disheveled dress from his groping. When I risk a glance up, I find Rio standing beside me, hands linked behind his back and a neutral expression on his face.

"Excuse my intrusion," he says, bowing his head for a moment. "I'm required to change the dressings on her back before the event. It's also time for you to head into the red room," he informs, his tone clinical but pleasant.

Xavier straightens his jacket, casting me a look I refuse to meet. It burns the side of my face as he dips his chin in acknowledgment, before taking off. Flicking my eyes to Rio again, he nods his head towards the kitchen entryway, which leads back toward a bathroom.

Still shaking, I follow in step, hoping I'm not too unsteady and roll my ankles in these heels. Francesca would probably reopen my stitches herself from a stupid mistake like that.

Even after we enter the bathroom, we keep quiet, and he shuts the door behind us. My shoulders relax a smidge now that we're alone.

I wonder when Rio started feeling *safe*.

But I'll admit, I'm grateful. He's not an ally by any means, but he's the least of my enemies in this fucking house.

"What the hell is the red room?" I question.

Rio glances at me. "A room in the back of the house full of tarp and torture devices. I'm sure you can conclude why they've dubbed it the red room," he answers dryly.

I swallow. "Are they... taking Phoebe and Bethany back there?" I ask.

"Yes. It's only used for those who fail the Culling."

My chest clenches and my stomach twists. They're doing unspeakable things to them right now, and that makes me fucking sick.

"Turn around," he demands.

I narrow my eyes, not appreciating the way he's ordering me around. Noting the look on my face, he sighs, and says, "*Por favor.*"

Flattening my lips, I turn.

"Why did you save me anyway?" I ask quietly, peeking over my shoulder to watch him dig out the first aid kit from beneath the sink and set it on the yellowed countertop. I'm sure they were white back in their heyday.

"What makes you think I saved you?" he counters, glancing at me as he digs out bandages and Neosporin. "You're going to have to lift up your dress."

I sigh, doing as he asks. I know the drill with him, and this isn't the first time I've had to expose my body so he can change the bandages. I hike the dress up underneath my armpits, and it makes me sad how desensitized I've become to baring myself to men.

I'm wearing a thong, but that might as well be nothing with how scrappy it is. Slowly, he unlaces the corset, and with each loop undone, I can breathe a little easier. When it falls from my torso, I suck in a deep breath, the bliss almost painful. My stomach is red and indented from how tightly Francesca laced it.

"You have to re-lace that, you know," I tell him.

He grunts. "Then you better be nice. I can make that tighter than she did."

A shiver rolls down my spine when his fingers brush against me, picking at the tape until he catches the edge and peels the old bandages from my skin.

"So, you're going to act like needing to change these wasn't intentional?" I prod. "You just changed them before the party." Which was only two hours ago.

"Would you like me to leave you next time?" he volleys back, his tone tight and a tad impatient.

"No," I whisper.

"Then accept it for what it is and shut the fuck up about it."

I snap my mouth closed. This time, I have no problem listening to his demands. Regardless of him wanting to admit it, he saw Xavier getting handsy, and stepped in. Something that is very unlike a human trafficker to do. I'd rather just be grateful for the intrusion than question him, and then he never does it again.

Lord fucking knows this won't be the last time a man will get too handsy. And that knowledge makes my skin crawl.

Rio is the reason I'm in this situation to begin with. Or at least one of the reasons. He played a massive role in it, and that's something I'll never forget. But I also won't forget the little bits of kindness he showed me when he'll soon be facing the barrel of Zade's gun.

I don't know if I can spare his life, but I'll try to make sure his death is quick.

Clearing my throat, I wet my dry lips. "Are you going to help Phoebe and Bethany, too?"

He sighs. "I *can't* help them."

I snarl. "So, that's it? You're going to stand by and do nothing while two innocent girls are being raped and tortured?"

He doesn't answer immediately, and it seems I've managed to strike a nerve.

"That's who I am, baby. A bad, bad man with no remorse."

Liar. If he felt no remorse, we wouldn't be in this bathroom right now, cleaning a wound that didn't need it.

"Why do you do it?" I ask in a whisper, hissing when the alcohol hits a sore spot. "Is it for the money?"

He scoffs. "I don't give a shit about money. Can't take it with me when I'm dead, so what good is it to me?"

"Then, why?" I push. He sighs, ripping open a fresh package of gauze.

"You're not the only one who's enslaved to powerful people," he clips shortly, his tone signaling the end of this conversation. But I don't listen.

"Zade is going to kill you, and you know this. So, if you know you're going to die anyway, then why continue?"

He slaps a strip of tape on me a bit harshly, growing frustrated with my needling.

"*Puñeta*. How about you use that pretty little head of yours, and figure it out," he snaps, his accent deepening with anger. "If someone doesn't stay for their own life, what else could make them stay?"

My face drops as realization dawns. "They're using someone against you," I breathe. "Family?"

"My little sister," he grumbles. "As long as I'm a good boy, she won't be sold."

A knot forms between my brows. "Why not just take off with her and run?"

"Because I *can't* take her. They have her and I can't get to her, *entiendes?* You done playing twenty questions, or should I tell you about how I lost my virginity, too?"

I clamp my mouth shut. He's given me more than enough. It's not fair of me to keep pushing.

Rio finishes up, placing fresh gauze over my stitches.

"These are about ready to come out," he says, stepping back to discard the trash and put away the kit. Then, he bends and grabs the corset, fashioning it back around my waist and quickly tying it up, leaving it considerably looser than Francesca did.

Once he's finished, I release my dress, fixing it as an awkward silence compresses the air around us.

"Thank you," I say quickly, the words burning my tongue on the way out.

He glances at me. "Don't thank me yet, *princesa*."

He opens the door and exits the bathroom without another word, leaving me to my own devices. My heart pounds, not liking how fucking ominous that sounded. Then, his excuse to Xavier smacks me over the side of the head.

I need to change her dressings before the event.

What fucking event? Didn't we already have one? Isn't this the afterparty *to* the event?

Dread replaces the marrow in my bones, and as I walk out of the bathroom and back toward the living room, I realize the Culling was only a preliminary event. A few men linger in the corners of the living room, drinking and laughing, looking every bit unconcerned with life. And the girls are gathered in the center, shoulders high and eyes cast down.

With the exception of Sydney, of course. She wears her defiance on her sleeves. Directly meeting the gazes of all the onlookers and even going as far as to smile at them.

I stand beside Jillian and keep my voice as low as possible as I ask, "What's happening?"

Her eyes flicker to me, and I note how ashen her skin is.

"The worst part of the entire night," she whispers back. Anxiety mingles with the dread, merging in my system until I'm nothing but a ball of frayed nerves. Is this what she was trying to tell me to prepare for in the woods?

Just as I open my mouth to ask more questions, loud screaming reaches my ears. My teeth click and then grind when the sound gradually increases. My heart pounds and my palms slicken. That's Phoebe and Bethany, and whatever is about to happen, it's bad.

Really fucking bad.

I grow nervous and fidgety, confused about what's happening, but still desperate to never find out.

Yet their screeching heads straight for us, almost painful to the ears. Two men are dragging them in by their hair, completely naked and bloodied beyond recognition. Since Ben is dead, the one handling Phoebe has thick black hair and a beard, appearing just as ruthless as his partners. And the one handling Bethany is a skinny, older man with thin lips and glasses.

I barely manage to stifle a gasp, incapable of feeling anything outside of horror and panic. Jillian and Gloria shift uncomfortably, both on the verge of tears. Sydney watches them with cool detachment, even as they're tossed at our feet.

Phoebe and Bethany lay there, nearly lifeless. Vomit climbs further up my throat, glimpsing the mutilation they've suffered. I have to look away, physically unable to stomach it. Limbs and skin are missing. Pieces of their body have been cut and completely removed. Blood steadily pools beneath them, the puddle growing larger until it begins to seep beneath our feet.

"They're all yours, girls!" the black-haired man announces proudly, heaving from the exertion and excitement. Blood paints their clothing, and while everyone's eyes are alit with excitement, these two, in particular, look like they're riding a high. Most likely from torturing two young girls.

Their slacks are still undone, shirts unbuttoned, and hair ruffled. Sweat drips from the tip of the black-haired man's nose, while the other has pit stains marring his white shirt.

I take in all these details with wide eyes, my brain slow to process what's going on.

Francesca walks in a moment later, staring down at the girls with her lip curled. Then she trains her gaze on us, appearing calm and collected. She's seen so much—done so much. Does nothing faze her anymore?

"Thank you, gentlemen, for bringing them in here," Francesca says kindly.

Gloria breaks first, turning and slapping a hand over her mouth. Tears stream from her eyes as she gags beneath her palm. A fire lights in Francesca's eyes, her head whipping towards the mousy girl.

"Don't you dare vomit on my floor, little girl. I will cut your tongue from your mouth," she hisses, her makeup cracking from the tension in her face.

Gloria nods her head, though her face is green and she's still on the precipice of losing it altogether. All I can do is chant to myself over and over not to puke and completely lose my shit.

Francesca approaches, making sure to keep her precious heels out of the blood. She stares at us with an unreadable expression.

"You will take them outside, and you will put them out of their misery."

My eyes widen, and Sydney giggles from beside me. It takes effort not to whip my hand out and slap her in the mouth.

"What do you mean?" The question slips out before I can stop it, and I feel instant regret when all eyes turn to me.

"It means," Francesca snarls through gritted teeth, "that you will end their miserable existence. And then you will dig their graves and hope to God that you aren't next."

Chapter Eighteen
The Diamond

My thoughts are running through mud. I'm slow to process her words, even as Rocco and one of his friends break through the crowd of guests and scoop up the girls in their arms, before heading for the door.

My mouth is hanging open, speechless and horrified as I watch the other girls slowly begin to follow after them.

This isn't real.

This can't be real.

But when I meet Francesca's golden-brown eyes, blank and dull, I realize that there's no escaping this nightmare.

"Go," she mouths. Blinking, my body follows her command and heads toward the door. But I can't feel it. It's an out-of-body experience—I'm only capable of watching myself go through the motions. My feet carry me down the porch steps and to the back of the house where the bonfire still rages, the flames licking the frigid air. Flickers of orange light lash across the night sky, clouds of smoke curling up from the orange glow.

Guests pour out of the house behind me, their excitable chattering rising above the crickets. The air has a pulse to it, thrumming with anticipation and glee, but that's all wrong.

Two girls are dying tonight, yet all that coats my tongue is the rapture of their glorious deaths.

Phoebe and Bethany are thrown to the ground, their wails heightening from the impact. Tension lines the muscles in my legs, weighing me down and making it nearly impossible to line up with the other three girls in formation.

We stand before them, various emotions clogging the space between us. Resignation and enthusiasm from Jillian and Sydney respectively, but Gloria and I look at each other, absolutely petrified for what's to come.

Francesca stands on the other side of the bonfire, deep shadows, and bright red accentuating her features. A demon risen from Hell.

"These girls were deemed unworthy in the Culling," Francesca announces loudly. The men quieten, and I imagine it's the only time they've been inclined to shut up and listen to a woman speak.

"For centuries, we've carried on this tradition. In our world, only the strongest can survive. Only those who can endure and persevere no matter what we throw their way. These girls standing before you—*they* are worthy of you. And they will prove their worth to you by snuffing out those that were not good enough."

Francesca's dark eyes turn to us expectantly, but all I can do is stare.

I see Rocco advance towards us, large stones in his hands. Sydney grabs for hers quickly, nearly vibrating with delight.

He stares down at me with expectation, a delighted look on his face.

Reluctantly, I grab a rock, surprised by how heavy it is.

Jillian and Gloria grab for theirs, quivering hands curling over hard stone. A tear drips down Gloria's cherub cheeks.

Noticing it, Rocco leans down, grabs her by the cheeks, and licks her tears; his disgusting tongue sliding up the entirety of her face. She squeals in response, and Rocco snickers darkly.

"Show me one more tear, little girl. I'll be happy to throw you down next to them."

"Don't make me do this," she pleads quietly, barely above a whisper. Her entire body is quaking in his palms.

"Do you prefer to be the one throwing the stone or to be the one beneath it? Choose now."

She squeezes her eyes shut and nods her head, accepting her fate silently.

Pleased, Rocco forcefully pushes her away and stands beside Francesca, chest puffed, and hands clasped behind his back. As if he's a soldier honoring the death of his comrade.

A black hole swirls in my chest, eating up anything good left inside of me. I glare at the duo, the fire in my eyes fiercer and brighter than the one before me.

I can't decide which I'm more eager to kill. Him, or his sister.

A collective silence ensues, the energy thick and heavy. Not even a cricket chirps, as if the wildlife can feel the tension, too.

Sydney breaks first, cocking her arm and hitting Phoebe with the rock on her shoulder, directly over one of her wounds, a savage cackle echoing in the air.

I wince, my horror growing as she swings mindlessly. Phoebe's cries reach my ears mere seconds later, and finally, I react on instinct. I push Sydney to the side, ignoring her outraged wail when she lands awkwardly on her hand holding the rock.

Out of the corner of my eye, I see Jillian and Gloria kneel, raising their hands and bringing the rock down on Bethany's head—attempting to give her a quick death.

Adrenaline pumps through my veins, and my heart races. I quickly roll Phoebe to her side, blurring out her extensive injuries.

Sydney clambers to her knees, rushing toward the both of us with murder in her eyes. Growling, I whip my rock directly at her head, ignoring Francesca's sharp gasp as the rock strikes true, knocking the crazy bitch out cold.

Turning my attention back to Phoebe, I carefully gather her in my arms, cradling her head in the juncture of my shoulder and curling myself over her.

"I will not let you suffer," I whisper in her ear, desperately and rushed. A hot tear breaks free, burning a path down my cheek. "You saved me, Phoebe. You were so fucking strong and brave, and you will always be my hero. Do you hear me?"

"I… I h-hear you," she chokes, sobs racking her chest. Inhaling deeply, I lunge for a branch in the pit, barely feeling the flames licking at my flesh.

Rocco rushes towards me, but it's too late. I'm jabbing the sharp tip of the branch deep into her jugular. Phoebe convulses beneath me, blood pouring from her neck in rivulets. I hold on to her tightly, but I cannot say the same for my shattering soul.

A sob bursts from my throat, and I press my forehead against hers, hardly feeling the blood soaking my skin.

Tears of sorrow and rage track down my cheeks, and all I can do is just squeeze her harder, rocking us back and forth as she dies in my arms.

"Sleep, Phoebe," I whisper against her, my voice cracking. "Go to sleep now."

Nearly as quickly as it began, she stills. But I can't let her go. I weep into her lifeless body, battling with relief that she's no longer suffering, and despair that she had to die at all.

Someone's daughter died today.

And all I can hope is that whoever loved her, will forgive me for being the one to take her from them.

Two Months Later

I twirl the tube of red lipstick until it's completely exposed. Carefully, I apply it to the bow of my top lip, taking great care to stay within the lines.

Then, I move to my bottom lip before rubbing them together and popping them.

I stare at my reflection, hardly recognizing the person staring back at me. Black circles rim the underside of my eyes, and I remind myself to put extra concealer there before I meet with Xavier tonight. He only likes to see how exhausted I am *after* he fucks me.

I haven't been placed up for auction yet. Francesca says I'm almost ready and that when the time comes, Xavier will ensure he is the highest bidder.

It's unofficially official that he will be my master. Because of this, Francesca has allowed him to visit me once a week for the past month.

Tonight will be the fourth night that we spend together. Afterwards, I'll curl up into a ball while Rio cleans me up. Xavier gets off on drawing blood, and now that I'm essentially spoken for, he's allowed to mark me. Within reason, Francesca says, but honestly—what's reasonable about any of this?

I hold the lipstick up and wonder if it's the color of my blood that excites Xavier or the feel of his knife breaking past that weak barrier of skin.

I drop my hand and meet my caramel eyes in the mirror.

When's the last time I genuinely smiled? The last night I was with Zade, I think. How long ago was that? I believe it's January now, and the last time I saw him was not too long after Satan's Affair. I've missed my first holidays with him. Thanksgiving and Christmas, and maybe his birthday, although I don't even know when that is. My New Year's kiss was Xavier's dick down my throat, and if I didn't have a desire to kill myself before, I did then.

What had Zade said to make me grin? He had said something ridiculous, but I can't recall what it was anymore. I do remember him laughing when I struggled for a response. And I remember my traitorous lips tipping up, as much as I tried not to.

I wish I never suppressed my smiles with him. Because now I don't know if I'm capable of one anymore.

The muscles in my face twitch as I force the corners of my mouth up, stretching it wide and baring all of my teeth. Despite how hard I try, it doesn't reach my dead eyes. It's unnatural. Awkward.

Terrifying.

I smooth out my face, contemplating how I can smile again.

"Duh, Addie," I whisper. "You know how to do it."

I lift the lipstick and place it on the corner of my lip and draw it out across my cheek, curving it up towards my eyes. Then the other side, until a big red smile is painted across my face.

The Joker had the right idea, I decide.

Feeling slightly better, I cap the tube and let it roll across the floor.

Heavy footsteps travel down the hallway and toward my room.

My heart speeds up, and I wonder if Francesca will let me keep my smile. Just for a night.

But the second she walks up behind me and spots what I did, her eyes widen. Her hand flies out and smacks into the side of my head, sending me toppling over.

"What is wrong with you?" she hisses.

I brush the strands of my hair out of my face, looking up at her outraged expression.

"I'm sorry, Francesca," I say quietly. "I just wanted to smile."

She huffs. "You need to keep it together. I don't need another fucking Sydney on my hands. You are mere *weeks* away from being sold off, diamond. Don't you dare ruin this for me."

I frown and nod my head, apologizing again. It looks funny with my face painted the opposite.

"Wipe that shit off and get ready. Xavier will be here in ten minutes."

Sad. No smiles for me tonight.

A deep shuddering breath fans across my face, his excitement growing as the sharp bite of metal digs into my stomach. He hasn't broken skin yet, though my pain receptors are screaming at me like he has.

"I want to see you covered in red, diamond," Xavier whispers from above me, his hard length poised at my entrance.

I *am* covered in red. He's made so many cuts around my body that I've turned the white bedsheets scarlet.

It's never enough for him.

A whimper falls past my lips when I feel him push inside of me, and my gag reflex threatens to spew bile all over him. There's nothing in my stomach. Francesca doesn't allow me to eat much on the days he visits— she says that she doesn't want me to get bloated.

"You like feeling me don't you, baby?"

I screw my eyes shut and nod, though it's the furthest from the truth.

He invades my body like a parasite would, an unwelcome tenant that leeches from my life force to feed his own.

The sharp point of his knife finally breaks skin, and his blade glides across my stomach, drawing out a sharp yelp. Blood bubbles from the wound, and he moves his hips faster in response.

"Fuck, that's so pretty," he groans breathlessly.

A tear slips past my eye, and I pray he's too distracted to notice. He only cuts me deeper when I cry.

He wants me to writhe beneath the piercing metal and get off on the pain as he does. He wants me to enjoy this, and when he sees that I'm not, it makes him angry. He says I just need to get used to it—I just need to *adjust.* But I don't know how anyone could get used to being sliced open like a fucking pig.

Another cry leaves my lips when he finds a new spot and starts applying pressure—slowly—as if he's giving me time to get accustomed.

I'd rather he just get it the fuck over with but I think he knows that.

He thrusts harder, causing his knife to slip and cut me deep. Pinching my eyes shut, I inhale sharply. Xavier shudders while my soul cracks.

I don't think Xavier plans to keep me for long. How could he when I will eventually bleed out?

"Once I take you home with me," he pants, "I'm going to drink that fucking blood. Dine on it at all hours of the day."

My stomach revolts and I nearly gag again. The picture he's painting in my head is vile and disturbing. He might as well declare himself as a cannibal or an aspiring-vampire.

Noting the abhorrence twisted into my features, he snarls and moves his blade to my throat.

"This vein right here? One little slice, and I could drink from you until you're nothing more than a wilted corpse. Do you want that?"

Yes. God, please, let me die. Here and now, and I'll be fucking happy.

"No," I choke out, my voice tight with pain. I wouldn't dare tell him to do it because then he won't. Xavier would never go as far as to give me what I actually fucking want. Especially because he knows it isn't *him.*

"Then tell me you want me," he demands, as if hearing my thoughts.

"I want you," I immediately echo, though it rings hollow. He wants to claim a place in my heart, but that place is a vacuum of emptiness that he will never be capable of filling.

He snarls, hearing the vacancy in my voice, and buries himself inside me. Though if he thinks he's deep, I'd hate for him to see the size of Zade.

The only reason his cock will ever cause me pain is purely because it's attached to him.

Working to swallow, I suck my trembling lip between my teeth. Maliciousness sprouts in his blue eyes, and it's like watching him pull a black coat over them, the bright color shrouded beneath the darkness.

His hand travels down the planes of my stomach, pausing to dig his thumb into a wound and wring a cry from my throat, before continuing down. He swirls his fingers over my flesh in a taunting manner, an evil smirk curling his lips.

There's a little sponge in my windpipe, collecting hatred like water and swelling until my throat is hermetically sealed.

Lightly, he brushes across my center, his eyes sparkling as his fingers find that spot that has my muscles tensing.

"Oh, God," I breathe, more tears burning the backs of my eyes. I hate that spot—yet another thing he's aware of.

His eyes blaze, excitement radiating from him.

"Tell me again," he orders, his voice dipped in sin. I close my eyes, imagining a scarred face with devilish yin-yang eyes, grinning at me from beneath his hood.

Working to swallow, I rasp out, "I want you."

It takes effort not to crack when I hear him groan. It's all wrong. He sounds wrong, he feels wrong, he's just… fucking *wrong*. He smiles when he hears it and rubs harder.

"Say my name, diamond," he demands.

I set my jaw in response.

I'll never say it. Never.

He's been trying since he started visiting, and every effort has been wasted.

When I keep my mouth firmly glued shut, he starts thrusting again while continuing to stimulate me. My body tenses, a traitorous feeling congregating in the pit of my stomach. Still, I keep silent, refusing to relinquish more than I already have.

Xavier thinks I've given him nothing, but that's not true. I've given him everything—he just finds no value in what he's taken from me.

The smooth, unmarked skin he mutilates.

The fragments of my sanity that chip away with every brush of his skin, and every whispered omen of the day I will be his.

My ability to touch and be touched without wanting to slit my throat open.

My dignity, self-esteem, and the comfort within my body.

My fucking worth.

All meaningless.

Because what he really wants is every broken piece of my soul, and for me to cherish every broken piece of his.

But my soul is already spoken for—already claimed by a wicked man with every intention to keep it to himself. And I suppose he's given me his in return.

I'm just not sure what the fuck to do with it now.

"You'll say it one day, diamond. You have the rest of your life with me," he promises.

My legs clench around his hips as he fucks me harder, bending down to drag his tongue across my nipple. I grit my teeth, the bile rising in my throat.

"This is mine," he groans. "All of this is mine."

His teeth close over the abused peak, biting until my vision blackens with agony, and a scream is tearing from my throat. Even then, he doesn't relent. Not until blood leaks through the cracks of his teeth, and I'm begging for the knife instead.

What a tragedy.

Finally, he releases me, a smear of crimson staining his bottom lip. His eyes are dilated as he pumps his hips faster, his ministrations on my clit quickening.

Gradually, it pulls me away from the fire lancing through the peak of my breast. I inhale sharply—a staccato breath full of sorrow.

The orgasm ravages my body, and oh look—*there it goes*. Another piece of my sanity.

"I'm getting really tired of looking at fucking Neosporin," Rio says from behind me.

Xavier just left for the night. He was particularly brutal, slicing over the healed scars on my back and all across my breasts and stomach. He pushes it a little farther every time.

They said the Culling is designed to weed out those who have endurance—who can survive anything. But I'm not sure I'll survive another night with him.

"Sorry," I mumble, too exhausted to snap at him. My eyes are pinned on the dozens of tally marks carved into the nightstand, and it's only depressing me more.

"You're giving up, *princesa*," he sighs, dropping the first aid kit on the bed. He started calling me that after the Culling, now sounding more like an endearment than an insult.

Francesca never did relieve him of taking care of me, and neither of us have bothered to stop it. It will never be said aloud, but I think we both find solace in one another.

"What do you care?" I grouse, training my eyes on the wall. He grabs a few paper towels and lightly pads the wounds on my back, soaking up the blood. They just started to scab over from the last time.

Turns out, Francesca didn't need to be worried about my scars from the car accident. I got lucky enough to find someone who happens to enjoy the sight of them, and then some.

I'm still completely nude, but I've grown accustomed to being naked in front of men considering it happens all the fucking time now. All because I live with a psycho bitch.

Sydney was particularly pissed about me knocking her out the night of the Culling, so she attempted to cut off my hair with scissors in retaliation. Luckily, Jillian stepped in, and she only earned herself a punishment.

Since then, she has made it her personal mission to frame me for the stupidest shit any chance she gets—drawing on the walls like a toddler, breaking dishes, dropping food, and ruining clothing in the beauty room.

Most of the time, I think Francesca knows it wasn't me, but she's grown tired of the incessant squabbling and takes it out on both of us now. Sydney is happy to accept her fate as long as I'm suffering, too.

I've accepted the punishments, though—which always result in a night with Rocco and his friends. I tried to defend myself at first, but it never made a difference.

"Lucky for you, these have to heal, so no more nights with him until he's officially paid for you."

I glance at him, surprised by that. Francesca hadn't told me, but I'm relieved anyway. Sometimes he gives me information he's not supposed to. I've never questioned why, too scared he'll stop if I do. After he told me about his sister, we've fallen into an easy camaraderie. Both of us chained to our woes and accepting that neither of us can help one another get out of the metal confines wrapped around our wrists.

I shrug. "Doesn't make a difference. The others will still have their fun. Want to take a crack at me next?" I ask dryly.

Normally, I'd be horrified by saying that to someone, but I feel nothing.

Rio chortles. "I have no interest in you."

"No? Not any of the others, either?"

I remember Sydney attempting to get a rise out of me, claiming Rio was sneaking into her bedroom at night. I hadn't cared then, and I wouldn't care now. Regardless, I'm almost positive she was lying.

Rio has had every opportunity to fuck me or one of the other girls. Yet, I've never seen him lay a finger on anyone outside of what was necessary. In the beginning, he deliberately made me uncomfortable, but he hasn't even done that since he first kidnapped me. Now, he acts as if I don't exist when in the company of others.

One day, I had asked him why—why the initial cruelty and the silence around people, and then be so different when we're alone? He stared dead into my eyes and said, *"The men in this house search for weaknesses. I never want to be yours."*

He presses particularly hard on a cut, drawing a hiss from between my teeth.

"No. Now, shut up, or I'll leave your wounds to fester."

I snort but leave him alone. His threats run hollow now, and we both know I'm not scared of him anymore. And I think we both know he doesn't want me to be, either.

"Francesca said weeks until I'm his. How many?" I ask, my voice still hoarse from my time with the man in question.

"Three."

I close my eyes and nod my head, gritting my teeth when he cleans another sore spot.

"New girls are coming in next week," Rio continues.

"How many?" I whisper.

"Three. Plenty of room now that it's just you and the *loco* one."

My heart pangs from the reminder. Gloria and Jillian were sent off to auction a week ago, leaving Sydney and me alone with each other. After the night we were forced to end Phoebe and Bethany's lives, our training became more intense.

Just because we were considered worthy, doesn't mean there still wasn't an opportunity for us to fail. Francesca put us through grueling etiquette classes. How to address our masters, how to speak, eat, and sexually service them.

They're specifically designed to break us mentally. We were whipped, raped, and starved if we made mistakes. And just like the night of the Culling, we were forced to punish each other. By the time those two girls were auctioned, we could barely stand one another.

Even after Jillian and Gloria were successfully sold, the grueling lessons haven't let up. The bruises have faded, and the stitches have been removed, leaving two large white lines marring my back, yet Francesca wouldn't allow for me and Sydney to be auctioned. And still, I have no idea why.

Although I'm spoken for, Francesca is still required to follow protocol. I have to stand on a stage, and others will be given a chance to bid on me. It's just guaranteed that Xavier will win.

He's one of the richest men in the world, he claims. Not even sure what he does for a living, or if he's even a citizen of the country, but I suppose it doesn't matter.

Despite what Rio thinks, I am never going to give up. I have no plans of skipping off into the sunset with Xavier, but I do plan on letting him take me out of here.

They've made it their mission to keep me exhausted, compliant, and ignorant. I haven't been outside these walls since the Culling. Haven't felt the sun warming my cheeks or the snow on my tongue. They're scared of Zade and what he can do, so the safest bet is to keep me holed up, never to see the light of day.

Three weeks. That's when Xavier will have no choice but to take me out of this house and risk Zade finding me. And that's when I will do everything in my power to make sure he does.

Rio finishes bandaging my back before rolling me over and moving on to the wound on my stomach next, keeping his eyes fixed on his task.

Not even a peek at a nipple.

"Try not to miss me when I'm gone," I murmur, staring up sightlessly at the ceiling.

I feel him glance up at me before focusing back on a particularly deep wound. He'll need a butterfly bandage for that one.

"I'll pray your life is short," he responds finally. I smile, the first real one in months. Turns out I didn't need that red lipstick after all.

That was sweet of him to say.

Francesca's footsteps pound down the hallway, but Rio and I don't bother moving considering he still has a few wounds to clean.

I meet her stare when she breaches the doorway. For a brief moment, she glances down at my body, an unreadable emotion in her eyes.

Do I look pretty, Francesca?

"Finish cleaning her up quickly, Rio." He stops and tips his chin over his shoulder to look at her, her face cast in a severe expression. "Claire's here, and she wants to speak with her."

January 2022

When people think of New Year's Eve, they imagine who they're going to kiss when the ball drops. Mine was spent with a stranger's lips all over my body, and his dick in places they have no right to be.

There was a moment that I felt relief when Francesca first told me Xavier would be visiting me once a week. Now, after the second time he's come to see me, I can't imagine why. He's crueler than Rocco and his friends.

They just aim to get their rocks off, but Xavier draws out my pain until I'm a sobbing mess. I hate that he makes me cry. It makes me feel weak and powerless.

Even worse, it makes him angry. He wants me to enjoy it and the last thing I will ever do is fucking enjoy what he does to me.

And while he digs his knife into my skin, staring at me closely, ~~until~~ anticipating the moment I break, I picture all the ways I could make him bleed.

That isn't the worst thing he's done to me. No.

He can't be a normal rapist and worry about his own pleasure. Shit, that's most of the male population as is. Instead, he made it his goal to make me orgasm too.

He succeeded. And it made me want to die.

Chapter Nineteen
The Hunter

Rubies and emeralds drip from the woman's body, clasped around her curves with thin metal chains. Aside from the jewels, she's bared completely, open to the males' demeaning gaze.

"Going bid, two hundred thousand dollars," the woman's voice announces through the speaker built into my leather chair. Her voice sounds just as hollow as the woman spinning around on the stage looks.

These auctions are luxurious. The bidding area is one massive pinwheel made up of fifteen glass cubicles surrounding a small stage in the center, providing each bidder with privacy while they fight over stolen women. The glass is heavily tinted, allowing bidders to see the stage clearly, while still keeping us hidden from those looking in. Jay and I have found that the tint on them is adjustable and can allow each bidder a clear view of one another.

I plan to utilize that feature later.

Inhaling my cigarette, smoke unfurls in the confined space as I press the button, placing my bid.

"Going bid, two hundred and fifty thousand dollars," the woman drones directly after I hit the button.

Someone else bids, and before the speaker can finish, I click the button again, prompting her to announce the bid as three hundred thousand dollars.

She will be the fifth girl I bought tonight. She's also the fifth girl that has been auctioned. Every single girl—they will be leaving with me.

The payment is wired out of my account with each confirmed sale, but everyone will be dead by the end of the night, and Jay will have transferred it right back to me. Not that I'm hard up for it, but my money will never line the pockets of the Society.

My finger presses that button three more times before getting the confirmed sale. I inhale again, a low buzz vibrating beneath my skin as another girl is pushed onto the stage. She stumbles but manages to catch herself in the five-inch heels before she face-plants.

She's a mousy girl with big doe eyes and glasses that cover half her face. The others will fight over her purely because she appears young and childish. Just like the last five, she's draped in fine jewels that cost more than what these men are willing to pay for the body beneath them.

Click.

"Going bid, fifty thousand dollars."

"Three more girls after this one," Jay tells me, his voice soft in my ear.

I don't speak. These rooms are bugged, and I want their deaths to be a surprise.

Click.

"I don't think Addie is here, man."

I knew that already, but Jay—sweet Jay—was hoping for the best. I'm not here because I thought Addie was going to scamper on this stage where I can buy her and whisk her away from all this evil.

She's never going to be auctioned. Claire would never risk it—not with me watching. She's very aware I have the means to track down victims within human trafficking, so it defeats the purpose to sell Addie into a trade that I'm very well acquainted with, just for me to rescue her anyway.

She's going to be handled differently—that I'm sure of.

It's been over two months since Addie's been gone. Each day that passes, the black circles under my eyes deepen and the angrier I grow.

I've lost my mind. My patience. My strength. Everything. The only thing puppeteering my body is sheer will and desperation.

Wherever she's being held, it's off-grid, and she hasn't been moved, most likely because they know I'd find her if she were. When girls are stationary in an undisclosed location, it's almost impossible to find them in the skin trade. If they're not being handled through proper channels where they're being transported or sold, then there's nothing to fucking track. She hasn't even been taken into town. No cameras on this entire fucking planet have seen Addie's face since she left that hospital.

Nor have they seen Rio or Rick—two of the three people that could lead me to her. I assume her kidnappers are wherever Addie is, but Claire... she knows how to move under the radar. The few times I've been able to locate her, an army surrounds her, and infiltrating takes planning, which is impossible to do when she disappears again. She's a red herring, moving in a way that's designed to distract me. I have every intention of taking out Claire but using her to get to Addie has only proven to waste my time and resources.

And that… that just isn't going to work.

Which is why I'm here tonight, intent on destroying yet another facet of the shadow government. More importantly, I'm hoping one of these girls has seen Addie. Jay has identified each of the girls being auctioned tonight, and several of them are native to Oregon. Which means if Addie is still in this state—one of them could've come from the same household as her.

Click.

"Going bid, four hundred and fifty thousand dollars."

Sold.

I buy the next three girls, too, and though I can't hear or see the outrage from other bidders, I can tell from the increasingly competitive bidding wars as each girl is sold. They all fold eventually, most likely with the intent to buy a girl from a different auction.

Moments after the last girl steps down from the stage, there's a soft knock at the door.

"Jay, lock all the doors in the building and barricade the exits. No one gets out except me," I tell him quickly before calling out louder, "Enter."

"Got it," Jay responds, just as Lee Morrison enters the room. While he's not the owner of this auction house, he keeps this well-oiled machine running. His job is to escort the bidders to their rooms, make sure their accommodations are satisfactory, and oversee the women coming in and out, ensuring the auction runs smoothly and without a hitch.

"Shut the door, please," I instruct, keeping my back turned to him. Seconds later, I hear it click shut.

"Sir, where would you like us to transport your winnings?" Lee asks, his voice respectful, yet timid. He's uncomfortable.

Good.

"My winnings," I repeat. "You do know they are human beings, correct? Just as you are?"

Lee clears his throat. "I apologize, sir. Where would you like us to transport your girls?"

"There's a limousine pulled up to the back entrance. Make sure none of them are hurt from here on out."

"Yes, sir," he says.

"Tell them now," I demand softly. "On your radio. Tell them that now."

He stammers, caught off guard from my odd request, but ultimately, does as I say. He radios for my *winnings* to be transported into the limo unharmed, and once he receives the confirmation, he clears his throat again.

"Will that be all, sir?"

"In that regard, yes."

Assuming I'm done with him entirely, I hear his feet pivot on the thin black carpet and his hand jiggles the doorknob when he grips it.

"Before you go," I assert, stopping him in his tracks. "Have you ever bought any girls for yourself?"

Lee stutters. "Well, not here, no."

"But elsewhere?"

After a beat, he says, "Yes, of course."

I hum noncommittally, though his answer has my body tightening with rage.

"Sir, may I ask why—" His question comes to a crashing halt when I stand and turn to face him. I'm not sure if it's my scars, or the look of cold murderous rage in my eyes, but something about my face has his words fading and his eyes widening.

Blindly, his hand reaches behind him, searching desperately for the door handle as I approach him.

As quick as a whip, my hands grip him by his throat, cutting off his shout. I lift him to my height level while he kicks and claws for me to release him, and I stare into his dilated eyes.

All I see is my own monstrous reflection.

I had told him those girls were human beings, but I never said that I was.

Pulling my top lip over my teeth, I snarl at him. "How many women have you thrown onto that stage, just to be carted off to a life of misery and suffering? How many have you taken for yourself and did unspeakable things to them?"

His face turns purple and his mouth flops like a fish, but no sound escapes from his constricted throat. I only squeeze tighter, relishing in the way his veins pop from his forehead. I wonder if I can make them burst open.

"Come on, Lee, I know you have a wife and children. How do you face them every night, knowing that you've condemned people just like them to a sickening fate?"

Just before he goes unconscious, I release him. He sucks in a huge breath while I force him into the chair that I've been occupying for the last two hours. Purchasing women that he proudly presented to me and fourteen other men.

I deliver one punch to his face, nearly knocking him out cold. It provides me enough time to grab the black bag I had brought in with me, full of rope and tape. Of course, the two bouncers, Beavis and Butt-Head, checked my bag before allowing me to enter the building, but they had only smiled—assuming the items were for the girls I planned to buy.

I had smiled back because they're idiots, and because they were going to die.

Quickly, I dig out the roll of duct tape and bind his hands and feet. He pleads with me relentlessly, and when that fails, he flops around like a worm on a hook, but I can't imagine what he thinks that'll accomplish.

Next, I fish out my can of lighter fluid and squirt some all over his body. His eyes widen, and he struggles harder, attempting to break through the tape like he's the Incredible Hulk.

"Jay? Send them in," I order.

"On it."

Leaving Lee to struggle for a bit, I step out to find several of my men pouring into the building, engaging in a shoot-out, and taking down security in a matter of minutes. No one is making it out of this auction alive.

While they take care of the employees and guards, I meticulously make my way into each cubicle. Jay unlocks each door for me one at a time, and I walk in, incapacitate the grimy rapist inside, then tie them up just like Lee.

By the time I make my way through all fifteen cubicles, a sheen of sweat is coating my skin. Most of them were old, but there were a few younger ones who put up a fight. A very pathetic fight—but one all the same.

Rolling my neck, I release some of the tension in my shoulders.

"All the girls safely in the limo?"

"Yep, and everyone else is dead," Jay reports.

"Have Michael set up the camera on the stage," I command, while sliding out a cigarette and lighting it.

I'm still in the fifteenth cubicle, which is, of course, on the other side of Lee. The man bound in the leather chair is squirming, begging for me to release him. Makes me wonder how many children or women have asked the same of him.

Michael saunters on the stage with a tripod and camera in his hand. While he sets it up, I ask Jay, "Did you figure out how to turn the glass transparent?"

"Obviously," he sasses.

"Let's see it then, genius."

Seconds later, the glass walls gradually lighten until all fifteen cubicles are transparent, and I'm surrounded by men strapped in leather chairs, fighting like hell to get free and failing.

Jay whistles. "Damn, dude."

It seems all at once, the fifteen men freeze, confused, and petrified as they take in the sight of fourteen others in the same situation as them. Even Michael pauses on the stage, taking in the scene around him with a grin on his face. Eventually, I watch all their heads turn toward me.

"You see this?" I ask the man next to me. "How exciting. You get to show them their fate."

"Hail Mary, full of grace. The Lord is with thee."

I cock a brow and patiently wait as he prays for a salvation he'll never receive.

"Blessed art thou amongst women, and blessed is the fruit of thy womb, Jesus. Holy Mary, Mother of God, pray for us sinners, now and at the hour of our death. Amen."

"Do you think you've been saved?" I ask.

"Yes," he says with conviction.

I smile. "Nine more Hail Marys to go. I want to hear you say them even as you burn."

He starts shaking his head vigorously, restarting his prayers as tears fall down his cheeks.

"Hail Mary, full of grace. The Lord is with thee…"

I inhale one last time, then flick my lit cigarette onto the chanting man. Just like the others, he's covered in lighter fluid, and instantly bursts into flames.

His prayer bleeds into screams, and I'm disappointed that he couldn't even make it through his second Hail Mary before he succumbed to the agony.

He's a god-fearing man, but I'm confident the devil will take good care of him.

Leaving the sick fuck to burn, I make my way next door to Lee.

"Miss me?" I ask, pulling out my matchbook and lighting one up.

"Pleasepleaseplease, I'll do anything! *Please* don't do this!"

"Anything?"

"Yes! Whatever you want!"

I bend at the waist, and pin him with a devilish look. "You know what I want, Lee? I want you to feel the same pain I feel every day. I want you to fucking suffer. Can you do that for me?"

He loudly protests but it's no match for the wails of agony that tear from his throat when I throw the match onto him, his body engulfed in flames within seconds.

Once more, I make my way into each of the rooms and set every single one of them aflame. Just as the last body catches fire, I signal Michael to start recording through the glass.

He presses play, and the camera slowly begins to rotate on the tripod, while Michael and I make our way out of the building.

The camera will spin in circles, broadcasting fifteen men burning alive on the dark web. There for all the traffickers' and pedophilic assholes' viewing pleasure. And there for Claire's viewing pleasure as well.

The bitch is going to burn, too. Mark my fucking words.

"I have to admit, ladies, I've been in a limousine full of women before, and this… is not how it went down," Michael announces loudly.

Ruby berates him while I smack him upside the head, which wrings out a snort from the girl sitting next to me.

Michael and I hitched a ride with the eight girls who were auctioned off tonight. Luckily, I had the foresight to bring a shit ton of extra clothing.

While I was busy catching a bunch of pedos on fire, Ruby was in the limo with the girls, reassuring them that they were safe and going home. Still, as men, mine and Michael's presence cause them a bit of discomfort; the poor girls wary of our intentions.

Certainly doesn't help with Michael acting like an ass.

"I actually appreciate the humor," the girl next to me says in a heavy Russian accent. "Makes me feel less broken when people don't treat me like glass."

"See?" Michael mutters indignantly, still rubbing the back of his head.

"Fair enough," I concede. "He still deserved it."

"Did you kill them?" she asks, peering up at me. She's a pretty girl, with long brown hair and hazel eyes that remind me of Jay's. I remember her standing on the stage while I bid, her chin tipped high and posture ramrod straight.

She's not one to cower, that much is clear.

I arch a brow. "You mean the people bidding on you?"

"Aside from you? Yes."

"I did," I confirm.

She pauses for a beat, then looks away. "Good."

I turn my gaze away, too, relieving her of my probing stare. "Anyone else you want me to kill?"

She sniffs. "I can think of a few."

"How about we trade, then. I'll kill whoever you want me to if you can tell me if you've seen someone for me."

I feel her stare once more, so I meet it.

"Show me her," she whispers. Pulling out my phone, I bring up Addie's author photo. My chest clenches painfully, and I turn the screen towards the Russian girl.

"Her name is—"

"Addie," she murmurs, and my heart stops.

"You know her?"

"She was in the house with me. Still there, last time I checked."

"Where?" I snap, incapable of minding my tone.

"I don't know," she answers, her voice hardening. "Are we in Oregon?"

"Yes. We're in Jacksonville."

"Then she is close. I was blindfolded on the way to and from the house, so I've no idea where it is, but I counted the minutes, and we were in the car no more than an hour. All I can tell you is that the owner's name is Francesca, she runs the place with her brother, and it's somewhere in the middle of the woods."

I take a deep breath, briefly meeting Michael's wide stare. Hearing that Addie could only be an hour away has my heart racing. Out the window goes my patience and discipline. My fingers are itching to search nearby towns and go house-to-house, kicking in their doors until I fucking find her.

Part of the reason I came here tonight was in the hope that someone would have seen her. But truth be told, I didn't think I'd get this lucky.

"What's your name?" I ask, voice strained.

"Jillian."

"Can you tell me… fuck, is she—"

"She's alive," Jillian cuts in, understanding my need to ask how she is but knowing the answer is obviously *not good*. "She's had a hard time with one of the girls in the house—Sydney. They're at each other's throats, and it gets them punished a lot."

Low tremors radiate through my limbs, gradually increasing as Jillian goes on.

"And she has a buyer already, last I heard. He's been visiting her."

I clench my jaw so hard, the muscle nearly bursts from the pressure.

"His name?" I ask through gritted teeth.

She's quiet, seemingly struggling to remember. Then a mousy voice pipes up, answering the question for her.

"Xavier Delano," she says. Jillian and I turn to the girl with short brown hair and round glasses.

"That's his name," she reaffirms. "I-I was in the house with Addie, too."

"Thank you…"

"Gloria," she supplies when I trail off.

"Thank you, Gloria. You need me to kill any assholes, too?"

She smiles and shakes her head no. "I have enough blood on my hands."

Funny, I feel the opposite. I'll *never* have enough on mine.

Chapter Twenty
The Diamond

Present

"S hit," Rio mutters after Francesca leaves, his movements quickening.

My brows plunge, and my heart picks up speed from his obvious concern. "Claire?" Who's Claire?"

He glances at me, and I watch him visibly shut down, like pulling a string and the blinds slamming over his eyes. Whoever Claire is, she's to be feared.

Ignoring me, Rio finishes bandaging me up, and then grabs my arm and forces me into an upright position. He walks to my dresser and opens the drawers, throwing random articles of clothes at me.

"What—Rio, what the fuck is wrong with you?" I snap, a shirt smacking me directly in the face.

"Claire is the one who put the target on your head," he says, keeping his voice an octave above a whisper. Then, he walks to me and helps me slip into my clothing like I'm a toddler, but I'm too scatter-brained to stop him. My heart thuds heavily, panic circulating throughout my system.

I've no idea who the fuck this woman is, but it's clear she has some type of connection with Zade. That's the only reason a random woman would put a target on my head, right?

However, I swear I've met a Claire before... but my brain is too muddled to recall where and what she looked like. Or her significance to me or Zade.

He grabs me by the shoulders, his face severe. "Be very careful with that mouth of yours, *princesa*. Matter of fact, keep it shut."

I tighten my lips and nod my head. Lately, I've been too tired—too *weak*—to fight back. I walked into this house with my fire lit, and within two months, the proverbial fingers have pinched the flame, leaving only a trail of smoke behind.

All I need is a spark, and maybe... maybe it can be reignited.

My stomach twists with anxiety as I follow Rio down the hallway. A dull ache throbs between my thighs, reminding me with every step of what I'm desperately trying to forget. Something Xavier aims explicitly for. It's also a reminder that Zade may not want me anymore—something I've come to terms with already. I never thought I'd want to lose his obsession... but how could I not? I'm filthy now.

Rio walks ahead of me without a glance, tightening the knot forming in my stomach. There's an ice-cold fortress shrouded around him, as solid as the tension in his shoulders. It feels as if he's distancing himself from me because I'm about to be sent off to war, and he's never going to see me again.

Some days, I still hate him for what he's done to me, but I won't lie to myself and say that we haven't built a bond, either. He's been an emotional crutch for me these last two months, and I've begun to figure him out by now. If he's acting this way, it's for a reason.

And that makes me really fucking nervous.

I pad down the stairs, quiet voices rising from the living room. Rocco stands in the kitchen, drinking a glass of water and staring at me with his beady little eyes.

I keep my head down, watching my bare feet travel across the dirty floor. I just cleaned it two days ago, but Rocco and his friends act like there's glass on the floor and insist on wearing their muddy boots around the house.

My eyes focus on a perfect set of footprints that trail into the living room, leading right to two sets of heels. The new incomer has mud caked on her shoes, too. How fucking rude.

A throat softly clears, and I finally lift my stare. Immediately, I regret it. The shock of who I'm looking at nearly knocks me right onto the dirty footprints.

Claire... I've definitely met her before. She's Mark's wife. The senator who had tried to abduct me before, and the one Zade viciously murdered the night of Satan's Affair.

I remember meeting her the night Mark invited us to a charity event at his house. She was frail, subdued, and seemed so nice.

Why did *she* put a target on my head? Out of revenge for her husband? That has to be it. Zade murdered Mark, so now she's taking her anger out on him by getting me kidnapped and sold.

But Jesus, what's there to be mad about? The man obviously abused her.

"Hello, Adeline," Claire greets, smiling at me behind her red lipstick. She looks significantly different than the first time I met her. Not because of her appearance—she still has bright red hair curled perfectly around her face and a beautiful, albeit aging, appearance.

It's because she looks... happy. Like she's thriving. She doesn't look upset or distraught over the death of her husband.

I'm muddled with surprise and confusion, so it takes me a moment to say, "Hi, Claire."

She clasps her black-gloved hands together and takes a step towards me.

"I know you're probably very confused, my dear," she starts. "And I'm terribly sorry you were brought into the middle of all this." She waves a hand, indicating 'all this' as the house I'm currently being held captive in.

Let's not pretend that I wouldn't have been taken anyway.

But I keep quiet, not sure how exactly I'm supposed to respond to that. Wave a hand and say *aw, shucks, it's all right. I'm having the time of my life.*

"It's very unfortunate you got involved with someone such as Z. He came in and wrecked your life like a bull in a china shop, didn't he?"

Yes. Yes, he did.

"I suppose so," I admit.

"He's caused a lot of trouble for me as of late. Most recently, gratuitously murdering several important buyers at an auction house, then stealing the girls."

My heart drops into my stomach, sending the butterflies inside scattering. Tears burn behind my eyes, but I force them down. Hearing about Zade, and the havoc he's wreaking is... God, it's almost comforting. In a way, the people in my life before I was taken have begun to feel like ghosts rather than real, living people. Zade, Daya, my mom... none of them feel absolute anymore.

But Claire telling me about the trouble Zade is causing makes him feel real again. And I didn't realize how much I needed that.

"He took Jillian and Gloria?" I ask, my voice raspy with unshed tears. My chest is cracking wide open with countless emotions, and at the forefront of it all is relief.

"That he did. And I'm not going to allow that to happen with you. There's been a change in plans, so I figured I'd take this opportunity to see the precious diamond in the flesh once more before you're shipped off. Whatever luck Jillian and Gloria have on their side—is not on yours."

My throat dries. "I'm not being auctioned off?"

"Of course not, dear. You were never going to be."

Did Francesca know this? Since I arrived, she's been telling me that I'd be auctioned, yet she doesn't appear surprised by the news.

When I just stare at Claire blankly, she continues, "A very intelligent and resourceful man has attached himself to you. Which means that he will have the capabilities to find you once you step foot outside of this property."

That knowledge kicks my heart up a notch, swirling with a burst of excitement. Obviously, Zade knows how to find people. I assume it's only taken him this long because I've been locked inside a house in the middle of nowhere for over two months. Finding a lead on me is probably next to impossible, but the second they take me out of here, they'll no longer have that advantage.

"Francesca has informed me that a very high-profile buyer has set his eyes on you. So, in order to keep you hidden, we will be conducting a direct sale."

My mouth parts, and I'm honestly unsure of how to feel. A direct sale will give them plenty of opportunity to conceal me, but I've never had any intention of hiding.

Heart thudding, I nod my head. "Okay," I say.

She smiles condescendingly, as if I'm a child agreeing to go to bed when I never really had a choice anyway. I suppose that wouldn't be wrong.

"Xavier has already paid for you and will collect you in three days. Francesca will continue to prepare you for your new life, providing you with all the knowledge you need to ensure you and Xavier live happy lives together."

Ah. Claire is just as psychotic as Mark.

Maybe she's a byproduct of Mark's abuse, maybe not. Regardless, she's no better than her husband. Her pain does not justify inflicting pain on others. Not like this.

"Francesca and I will go over the details. Nothing for you to concern yourself with. I just wanted to deliver the good news to you myself," she goes on, her eyes glittering with delight. They are what stars look like when they die. No life left in them yet blazing with a light that ensures everything in its path will die, too.

I had hoped with being auctioned that I'd be able to make a run for it, or ensure my face was seen on a camera, at the very least. Maybe steal a phone and send a text—anything to give Zade a location. Those options won't be as easy now, but still not impossible.

I lick my dry, cracked lips and meet the twin dead stars in her skull. "Can I ask one thing?" I ask softly.

Her red lips flatten, but she nods her head.

"Can I ask why?"

Francesca hisses, but Claire holds up a hand, silencing her. That alone is satisfying to watch. She takes a few steps toward me.

"When someone as beautiful as you catches our attention, it's hard to look away. Normally, I prefer to plant someone in your life. A boyfriend, if you will. Someone you would fall in love with and trust. They would've handled you, and you would've been able to have some sort of freedom, while also bringing in money. However, you got someone else's attention first, and suddenly, you became so much more valuable."

My brows knit, and it's hard to swallow. It's not hard to conclude that Claire is just like Mark. Someone who finds women and children and brings them to the Society. But the way she speaks...

"This trade, this *world*—I own it. I own it all," Claire supplies. "I am the Society, dear. Me and my two associates. Mark thought he was the man in our marriage, but he never knew that I was the one pulling the strings all along. Zade did me a favor by getting rid of that scumbag, despite how fun it was to hang my husband by the balls. I'm not angry because your boyfriend killed my husband. I'm angry because he's attempting to ruin what I've worked hard to build. The sad, little lives you all live are my empire. I'll be damned if *Z* tries to take that from me." She spits out his name like it's a bug that flew into her mouth, ire and disgust twisting her features.

All I can do is stare at her in utter disbelief. Confounded that Claire is the ultimate puppeteer. The president—shit, *all* of the world leaders— they're guppies compared to her.

Taking advantage of my speechlessness, she turns to Francesca. "Let's have a chat, Franny. We have some things to discuss."

Francesca smiles graciously at Claire. "Of course!" She turns to me, her smile dropping long enough to say, "Go back to your room and don't come out until dinner." And then she's back to smiling at Claire again.

Her face must hurt from all that exercise it's getting.

Nodding, I pivot on my heels and hurry towards the stairs. Rio stands at the doorway to the kitchen, hands threaded behind his back. Briefly, we make eye contact, but for the life of me, I can't decipher the emotion swirling in his dark irises. He stays behind, but I'm glad for it. Being confined to my room is exactly what I need right now so I can adequately plan my escape.

Xavier was right about one thing—the Culling is a double-edged sword. It taught me how to run, and that's precisely what I plan on doing.

Hot breath fans across my face, disturbing the deep sleep I've fallen into. I twitch, feeling strands of hair tickle my nose.

It takes me several seconds to pull myself out of the weird dream I was having. With reality setting in, so does a sense of animosity and danger, and it takes another few seconds to realize someone is breathing in my face.

Immediately, my instincts blare on red alert, adrenaline and fear flooding my system.

Slowly, I crack open my eyes, then choke on a startled scream, my eyes rounding into discs when I see Sydney standing above me, her face mere inches away from mine.

Her eyes are wide, a psychotic glimmer in them as she stares down at me with a crazed smile. She's breathing heavily, little sounds of excitement bubbling out of her throat with each exhale.

I press myself deeper into the bed, my heart tearing through my chest as I struggle to find my breath.

"What the fuck, Sydney?" I gasp, attempting to keep my voice down but failing.

I'm seconds away from releasing my bladder all over the bed, my horror growing as she climbs on top of me, her blonde strands brushing across my face and blocking my vision.

My body moves on instinct, I kick my feet on the bed, attempting to gain traction and slide myself upright, but her hands wrap around my throat, holding me in place. She's not cutting off my air supply yet, but I panic anyway, all of those moves I learned from Zade evading me.

"I know what you're going to do," she whispers. I almost miss what she says, with my heart thudding loudly in my ears.

"You're going to try to escape, and I'm going to tell them," she breathes, giggling maniacally when I flail against her. "And hopefully they fucking kill you for it."

Her hands begin to tighten further, and finally—*fucking finally*—my training kicks in. I shoot my arm up between hers and twist my body with all my strength, sending her flying off the side of the bed.

The impact is loud, and we both freeze, waiting to hear if anyone woke. Francesca stays on the bottom floor on the opposite side of the house, but that doesn't mean we can't be heard.

There are also always two or three men standing guard outside of the house, ensuring none of us try to run.

Sydney's eyes narrow, and I know she's about to attack again. My legs are tangled in the blankets, so I react first, freeing my legs and then diving towards the end of the bed.

She charges at me, wrapping a hand around my ankle and attempting to drag me back. I kick out hard, and her grip loosens enough for me to break free and scramble off the other side of the bed.

Slowly, she stands, her chin dipped low as she stares up at me with pure evil as we face off on either side of the bed.

"What the fuck is your problem?" I whisper-shout.

"I know what you have planned, and I'm not going to let it happen."

It takes effort to keep my eyes from widening, and the stricken look off my face.

"I don't have anything planned," I vehemently deny.

She ignores me. "You don't get to be treated better than the rest of us, then escape your fate," she growls.

"Treated better?" I echo on a bewildered laugh. "You've been getting me in trouble since I got here!"

"And yet she still loves you more," she hisses back. I shake my head, absolutely astonished that she believes that. Francesca sees me as a dollar sign—a substantial one. She doesn't love anyone more than herself.

"Maybe she *would* love you if you didn't act like a fucking psycho bitch," I clip, growing angry. She begins to circle the bed toward me, and I realize belatedly that I'm cornered.

"I'm telling Francesca about your plans," she says, ignoring my jab.

"What plans?" I ask, playing stupid and hoping she doesn't actually know a damn thing. For the past two months, I've been working out different ways to escape once I'm taken out of here, and after Claire blindsided me last night, I came up with a few ideas that could work now that I'm no longer being auctioned. But Sydney is about to fucking ruin them.

She points to my floor, and my face drops in horror. My head snaps back to her in shock.

"How did you know about that?"

She shrugs, a joyous grin curling her lips. Gradually, a sick realization sets in.

She was the person standing inside the wall, watching me sleep that night. She must've hid when I spotted her, then resumed watching me when I found the journal.

Jesus, how long has she been reading it? And how often has she watched me fucking sleep?

"How did you get behind the wall?"

She shrugs, grinning wildly. "There's a lot of things you don't know about this house, *diamond*. I know everyone's secrets, including Francesca's. Why do you think she's allowed me to stay for so long?"

"What secrets?"

"Like I'd ever tell you," she scoffs.

I've no idea what she could possibly have on Francesca, but I don't care. What I *do* know is that one of us is not walking out of this room alive tonight.

If Francesca finds out I'm planning to escape and how, they'll do everything in their power to make sure I never get away.

Not going to fucking happen.

They'll have to lock me in a submarine in the middle of the goddamn ocean to keep me away from Zade.

I stand in the corner of the room, while she lingers at the edge of my bed, possibly sensing the conclusion I've come to. Whether it's because she notes the determination that must be etched into my expression, or the fact that I'm not leaping over the bed to escape.

Time slows for a few seconds, both of us still. And then we're springing into action simultaneously. She charges for me while I dart toward my nightstand. I hoarded a couple of pens in the drawer in the case I ran out of ink, and now, they're the only things that may save my life. Not from Sydney—but from Xavier.

She grabs ahold of my hair just as I rip open the drawer and locate one of them, my fingers curling around it while she swings me towards the wall. I crash into it painfully, the back of my fist swinging out sightlessly to dislodge her from my hair.

Teeth sink into my shoulder, clamping down with all her strength. A high-pitched yelp escapes past my lips. I bite back the scream threatening to rip from my throat, feeling blood spurting from around her teeth.

Blinded with pain, I raise my hand and stab the pen anywhere I can reach, feeling the pen sink past flesh and sinew. She releases me with a strangled yelp, but before she can move away, I grab ahold of her and send us both careening to the ground, no longer caring if we're caught.

Fuck this bitch.

We roll for a few seconds, fighting for control. I manage to gain purchase and twist on top of her, using one hand to slap away her claws, and the other to plunge the pen into her neck. My hand slips, the pen slick from her blood as I impale it into flesh.

Her nails rake across my face, leaving stinging trails, but they fade into the background as I keep stabbing her blindly, managing to hold on to the slippery pen only by sheer determination. Over and over, I stab her, exhaustion sinking into my bones quickly, but pure adrenaline and panic keep me going. Finally, she goes limp, blood pooling around us.

I'm panting heavily, soaked in blood, and delirious from the adrenaline. My body is going into shock, and all five of my senses are on lockdown, nothing penetrating past the shroud of numbness.

I just gaze down at her body, now riddled with holes. She stares sightlessly up at the ceiling, and I find that her eyes don't look any different than when she was alive.

My door creaks open, and Rio rushes in. He stops in his tracks when he sees Sydney on the ground and me straddling her, painted in crimson. It's… warm. I think I feel warm.

"Fuck, *princesa*. What did you do?"

I barely hear him, only interpreting his words from the way his lips move. I point at her, and croak, "I killed her."

He quietly steps in and shuts the door, but not before peeking out to see if anyone else is coming.

The soft click is inaudible to the typhoon raging in my ears. He keeps his steps light as he comes around the other side of the bed to get a better look. His lips form a circle, and he must whistle, but I don't hear that either.

All I can do is stare.

"Come here," he mouths, waving me towards him. Blinking, I stand on quaking knees and manage a single step before slipping on the blood, barely catching myself on the bed. Rio's hand grips my arm and pulls me up and away from the growing pool.

He grips my face in his palms, his dark eyes searching mine. And then he slaps me hard enough to knock my head to the side. The white noise bleeds into a sharp ring, and then all my senses come rushing back in. I hear, see, feel, taste, and smell everything.

Copper. That's the first thing my senses notice. And then Rio is gripping my face again, forcing my concentration back to him.

"Look at me, *mama*. What the fuck are you going to do now, huh?"

I open my mouth, at a loss for words. Finally, I just say, "Escape."

He shakes his head, drops his hands, and steps away. He stares at me, but as usual, I can't decipher the emotion churning in his irises.

"I shouldn't have said that," I whisper, realization dawning that he's not going to let me. Fuck. The situation catches up to me all at once, and I enter into panic mode.

I killed Sydney because she was going to out my escape plan, and now I'm going to be locked in a submarine somewhere, forced to live out my life alongside the fish.

With Rio catching me in the act—any chance of escape just went to complete shit and now I'm never going to get the fuck out of here. Rio isn't going to let me go. There's no fucking way. His *sister* is on the line.

"Shit," I mutter, uncaring of my bloody hands and sliding them through my hair, pulling tight as I try to come to terms with being caught before I've even stepped foot out of the fucking house. "I can't live with the fish, Rio. I don't like sharks."

Rio's brows plunge. "The fuck are you talking about?"

"Shit, shit, shit. Fuck—"

Muttering something Spanish beneath his breath, he grabs my arms and brings me in close.

"As much as I appreciate the vocabulary lesson, I'm going to need you to shut the hell up," he cuts in. "Look at me."

I do, but my thoughts are elsewhere.

"You need to tell me how the hell you would even escape. Your two options are acres of forest that you will get lost and probably die in or walk a road that you can be easily found on."

I drop my hands and clench them into fists in an attempt to abate the shaking. The volcano has fucking erupted, and I'm still vibrating from the aftershocks.

"There's an abandoned train somewhere out there. I found it the night of the Culling. I was going to follow that out," I say. In the back of my brain, my logical side is screaming at me to stop telling him my plans in case he betrays me. But the larger side of me wants to trust Rio. So fucking badly, just this once.

"And the guards outside?" he questions, voice low.

I shake my head, a tear wiggling free. "I don't know," I cry. "I don't—there's no way—"

"Shut up, *estúpida*," he barks again, keeping his voice quiet. "I'm going to go downstairs, and I'll take care of the guards. I'll leave the front door unlocked. Whatever you decide to do, and wherever you go, that's your decision."

A knot forms between my brow, and it takes several seconds to wrangle my scattered thoughts back into one direction.

"Rio, you can't," I protest. "You can't risk your sister's life for me."

The muscle in his jaw pulsates, and his dark eyes bore into mine. I've no idea what the hell he's thinking.

He swallows. "I'll figure something out with her. I think I know where she is."

Then, it clicks.

"Let's make a deal," I rush out. "You help me get out of here, Z will save your sister. Tell me her name and where she is, and he will get her out."

His mouth opens and closes, and for the first time, I've made Rio speechless.

"You have yourself a deal."

"Wait, my tracking device. I-I can't leave with it in me."

"Turn around," he demands, swirling his finger. Biting my lip, I do as he says, shivering when he roughly sweeps my hair to the side.

"How are—" A sharp gasp cuts off my question when I feel something sharp slice and dig into the back of my neck.

"*Jesus,* a fucking warning next time," I spit, cringing as the tip of the blade digs into my skin.

"He's not here, *mama,* but I am. And I need you to stop wiggling."

I huff, feeling warm liquid trailing down my back from the wound, and after several painful seconds, the metal pops out. He flicks the device onto my bed and then leans in, his breath brushing across the shell of my ear.

"Katerina Sanchez, she's fifteen years old. I believe she's with a groomer by the name of Lillian Berez. Last time I saw a picture of her was three months ago, and she was standing in front of a sunflower field."

He releases me, and steps away while I turn to face him. "Thank you," I say quietly. "I'll make sure she's safe."

He gives me a look that tells me he'll figure out a way to haunt me if I don't. Maybe he'll come to Parsons and join the rest of the ghosts in my house.

"One of Rocco's friends is sleeping on the couch. Be quiet, and it should be fine. He's out cold from the drugs."

"Okay," I nod, feeling a burst of gratitude that I've no idea how the fuck to express. He'll probably smack me if I try. Rio hates any type of appreciation as much as he does attention. And maybe that's more because he hates himself.

"Tell your man to give me a head start, yeah?" he says, backing away.

I frown. "Run fast."

Slowly, his tongue swipes along his bottom lip, and his gaze drifts over me one last time as if committing me to memory.

"Bye, *princesa*."

"Bye, Rio," I whisper.

And then he leaves, his footsteps silent.

I don't waste another second. I rush over to my dresser—which happens to be right by Sydney's body—slipping and sliding in the blood coating my feet. I tear through the drawers and hastily pull on a long-sleeved shirt and then a sweatshirt. I grab a pair of socks next, round the bed, and start wiping the bottoms of my feet as best as I can on the thin blanket.

I pull my socks and shoes on next, grab my journal from the floorboard, and quietly make my way down the steps.

Fear has kept me in my bedroom at night. It prevented me from going down the steps and out the front door, knowing that there was going to be someone outside waiting for me.

It's controlled me for over two months, kept me compliant, and now I no longer have that option. I've killed someone, and if I don't leave, I'll be next. No, I'll be praying for it, but I know they wouldn't let death embrace me so easily.

I snag a grocery bag under the sink, cringing every time it crinkles. Then, I find a few bottles of water in the cabinet and a box of granola bars. It'll have to be enough. I can't afford any more weight than that. Next, I slide open the drawer and grab two large knives for protection.

My plan is to make it to the tracks and then follow them out of here. Hopefully, I'll find shelter in one of the trailers when I need to take a break. I'm anticipating that they'll assume I took the road and focus their search party in that direction when they find me missing.

They see me as a diamond because I have Zade's love, but they fail to remember that's what forged me into a stone so unbreakable. He's taught me a lot about myself and who I really am. But most importantly, he's taught me how to persevere.

Just as I'm leaving the kitchen, I hear a loud snore, and I pause, my heart picking up speed. Rocco's friends tend to stay the night when they get too fucked up, and I imagine it'd take a stampede of elephants to wake them. But I can't be too sure—it just depends on the amount of drugs that are running through their systems.

Peeking around past the entryway, I see a grungy man laid out on the couch, mouth half-open. It's Jerry. He's one of the regulars here and also one of the more vindictive ones when Sydney and I receive punishments.

There's a small part of me tempted to walk over and stab one of my knives into his throat, yet I can't bring myself to do it. Despite how badly

I want to murder every single person in this house, I'm not a ruthless killer like Zade.

At least, I didn't use to be. I guess I'm not so sure anymore.

Heart in my throat, I slowly and silently make my way towards the door, jumping when one of his snores is particularly loud and obnoxious.

I'm halfway through the room when I hear my plastic bag give out, and one of the water bottles breaks right through, loudly smacking off the floor and rolling several feet.

Just barely, I bite back a gasp, trapping it on the tip of my tongue right alongside my erratic heartbeat. My wide eyes snap to Jerry. His snores have cut off, but he appears to be sleeping still.

A dangerous amount of adrenaline is coursing through my bloodstream, and my vision goes spotty from how hard my heart is pounding.

I cup the bottom of the bag and tiptoe to the water bottle, cringing when the sack crinkles in my hand. Then I crouch down and grab the water bottle, keeping my movements slow.

Screwing my eyes shut, it takes several seconds to try and calm my heartbeat. My hands are clammy, and sweat is breaking out alongside my hairline and lower back. I don't think I've ever been this fucking terrified, and I'm too consumed in it to feel any type of thrill. It's just that… pure terror.

Breathing out softly, I stand again and try to recover the bottom of the bag, but before I can, another water bottle slips through, once more crashing to the floor.

I choke, and as if moving through molasses, I lift my head to look at Jerry.

His eyes are wide open and pinned directly on me.

For several beats, we just stare at one another, suspended in time.

"What do you think you're doing?" he asks, sitting up and swinging his legs over the edge of the couch.

I can barely hear past the thrum of my pulse, and my vision tunnels, on the verge of blacking out from the fear. If he calls out for Rocco or Francesca, I'm done for. *Rio's* done for if they find out he was involved. Then, his sister will be sold, and I'll never get out of here—

Focus, little mouse.

Swallowing, I straighten, deciding that keeping my mouth shut for now is the best option. I have no explanation.

"You trying to escape, diamond?"

I shake my head, eyes widening further as he stands, and starts walking toward me. Instinctively, I take a step back, kicking the fallen water bottle.

"Then you want to explain what the fuck you're doing?"

Once more, I shake my head. The only excuse that comes to mind is that I was bringing snacks to the guards. Which is honestly laughable, and the last thing I want this man to do is fucking laugh. He certainly wouldn't be quiet about it considering he's always been the loudest one in the group.

He pauses, scanning over my form, and the moment I see the spark in his dark eyes, I know precisely what the fucker has planned. A slow, insidious smile grows on his face.

"Come here," he directs.

All I can do is shake my head again, like a broken toy that can only perform one trick.

He snarls, snapping his hand out and seizing me by the arm. I wince as he tugs me into him, my senses overwhelmed by body odor, stale cigarettes, and rank breath.

"You fucking listen to what I tell you to do, diamond, or I'll have

Rocco come out and join in on the fun. Which do you prefer, huh? Me, or both of us?" he spits harshly, though keeping his tone hushed. It would seem he wants me to himself, so he'll stay quiet for now.

Tears burn the backs of my eyes, and I nod my head quickly, hoping to assuage him. The drugs tend to get them riled up, and their tempers are unpredictable.

"Good girl," he croons, loosening his grip. "I want you to turn around, push down those pants, and touch your toes. I want to fuck you from behind."

My mind races as I pivot, keeping my movements slow as I try to figure out what the hell I'm going to do. There's no way I'm just going to let this asshole rape me again.

He nudges me firmly, "Hurry up."

"Let me set my bag down first," I whisper, voice shaky. He harrumphs but doesn't protest, so I bend down, deftly grab the knife and slide it out, hoping my body is concealing what I'm doing.

"Fucking slow-ass bitch," he curses, growing impatient and tugging at my waistband, attempting to slide them down for me.

I straighten, which allows him to get them halfway down my ass before I'm twisting at the waist and slashing out my knife. The blade cuts through his throat, and his eyes widen, nearly silent from the shock.

And I spring into action, pulling up my pants, quickly grabbing the sack, the stupid fucking water bottles, and booking it out of the door, leaving Jerry to choke on his blood.

The muscle in my chest pounds so hard that it hurts as I skitter across the porch and down the rickety steps, barely pausing when I spot the two dead bodies piled next to the stairs. The guards—their throats are slit open.

Panting, I round the house towards the back. Rio is nowhere to be found, and I pray to god he got the hell away already.

Because he may be the only one to get out of here alive.

Chapter Twenty One
The Hunter

"Motherfucker, I will fuck you up," Daire snaps from his computer chair, his chin tipped over his shoulder as he glares at me.

I roll my eyes. "You say that every time and never do."

I wouldn't mind if he tried. These men are trained killers just as I am, and a good old-fashioned fistfight might serve to release some of the tension crammed in my muscles. The weight of carrying frustration, anger, and anxiety in my bones is taking a toll. I've gone out on a few missions to take down rings in Oregon to relieve some stress, but it's never enough.

I push away and pace the floor behind him. His office is inside the vault, but you wouldn't be able to tell if it wasn't for the door. They hollowed out the room and transformed it into a basement. Right at the round entrance is a staircase that leads you down to the bottom, which has been expanded to run beneath the ground floor, where Kace's work area is. Just like the rest of the bank, it's washed in browns, creams, and blacks; all of it screams money.

So of course, his get-up is a computer nerd's wet dream. His desk takes up an entire wall, filled with monitors and TV screens hanging above. LED lights flash colorfully around the room, highlighting the sharp edges of Daire's face as he searches through his channels again, checking to see if Addie was tagged in any locations.

"You're looming over me. I can feel your breath on the back of my fucking neck."

I exhale extra heavily, prompting him to whip around and send a fist flying towards my dick. I easily avoid it, but he manages to surprise me and stomp on my foot with his, forcing me to step back.

Touché.

"You hover worse than a wife checking over her cheating husband's shoulder," he snips.

"I would say the scorned wife and I both have valid reasons."

He grumbles something under his breath, leaning his face farther into the computer as he checks over the grid. His pet kneels beside us, head cast down, but I catch the hint of a smile on her face.

"Did you find out where Jillian and Gloria came from?" I ask.

Daire shakes his head. "Not yet. I can easily trace the ones kept in a holding facility—like the ones you take down—because those are checkpoints for girls to be transported to and from. But many of the victims are taken to groomers before they're auctioned, and those are usually residential houses and oftentimes off-grid to protect the homeowners. Whoever Francesca is, she's obviously a groomer and a well-hidden one."

He has an entire map of transportation routes and checkpoints and insists that he would know if Addie were put up for sale or transported. There are minimal places to list girls for sale on the dark web, even for those who are selling their own children for profit, and Daire has access to every one of those channels. There is also an entire network for the auctions, moving girls to and from holding facilities, and other events where high-profile people can buy women and children, which Daire also has access to.

But Addie is too high-risk to be put through those standard processes. Claire is smarter than that. So, we've shifted our focus to tracking down this Francesca woman, but there are no homes in the state of Oregon owned by her.

"What was their last known location before they disappeared?" I ask. We've been narrowing our search down to surrounding towns within an hour's drive from Jacksonville—where the auction was held—but unless they have cameras within or outside of the house, we have no way to confirm if Addie is inside any of them.

"Prior to being auctioned, Gloria was last seen getting into a vehicle in Grants Pass, and Jillian was picked up in Portland. She has records for prostitution, so she most likely was being trafficked beforehand that way."

"Those cars are dead ends?"

"Yep," he confirms. "Drove somewhere with no cameras and never seen again from there."

"Fuck," I curse, beginning to pace again. It's the same ordeal with Xavier Delano. We were able to track his flight to Portland, Oregon, and a town car that drove him to the outskirts, but he fucking disappears again after that. They've taken every fucking precaution to make sure there is no trail leading to this house.

Daire clicks through a map as he says, "There are hundreds of thousands of homes in our targeted areas. Addie has to be in one of them, but narrowing down *where* is—" He cuts himself off, his eyes narrowing in concentration as he murmurs, "Interesting."

"What?"

"There's an old train system that used to operate in transporting girls near Grants Pass. It says it's still active, even though this railroad line has been closed for decades."

He goes onto Google Maps and tags the coordinates of the railroad, and then zooms in until it shows us a 3D view of it. The train is left abandoned on the railroad, the trailers corroded with nature and rust.

It's in the middle of woods, with nothing but trees surrounding it. Another decade and most of the wildlife will have taken over completely.

"It's just odd that it's still considered an active channel," Daire says, his brows pinching and a frown tugging down his lips.

"Are there any residential homes nearby?"

"Doesn't hurt to look," he replies. He looks up at me. "Keep in mind, there's no way to legitimately confirm that they're holding girls in them unless you storm the place. My advice? Don't do that."

I arch a brow in response. He rolls his eyes and turns back to his computer, realizing he's talking to a person that just barged into Mama T's house unannounced to get to them. What's stopping me from doing it to anyone else?

The answer is *nothing*.

"I'm going to need a long session with my pet after dealing with you," he mumbles.

"You're welcome."

He smirks but focuses on the screen as he navigates through the forest. For a long while, he doesn't find anything. Long enough that I start pacing a hole in the floor behind him.

"Found something," Daire announces about twenty minutes later, drawing my attention back to him. I come up behind him and lean down to get a better view.

If the fucker says I'm hovering again, I'll steal his pet and drop her off somewhere random just to inconvenience him. Asshole is fucking blessed to have me so close.

A massive run-down house emerges from the trees. It looks like its prime was in the early 1900s. Still, it's livable, big, and definitely well-hidden.

My heart picks up speed, and for the first time, I feel an inkling of excitement.

"Where is it located?"

"Merlin, Oregon. Only about fifteen minutes from Grants Pass, give or take." He pauses. "And about an hour from Jacksonville."

By the time he finishes his sentence, I'm nearly vibrating.

When the satellite picture was taken, only a rusted red pickup truck was parked outside of the house. I snatch my laptop, quickly searching the license plate to find the owner.

"Rocco Bellucci," I mumble, immediately digging into his background. "Got a few charges for public intoxication, domestic violence, and battery."

Daire shrugs. "Pretty standard charges for ninety percent of the male population."

Next, I check to see who owns the house, Rocco's name appearing once more. I rap my fingers on the laptop, anxiousness buzzing through my nerve endings. This house is suspicious, but nothing about it indicates this is a grooming house.

It's not registered under a name I recognize, and there isn't any physical evidence that girls are being held here.

Digging my phone out of my pocket, I pull up Jillian's number. After promising she'd help any way she could if I had more questions about Addie, I had Ruby get her a burner phone.

It rings for several long seconds before her bored, accented voice comes through, "Yeah?"

What a fluffy, warm person she is.

"You mentioned before that Francesca had a brother," I state.

"Yeah, he's one of the people I'd love for you to murder," she answers.

"Well, what's his fucking name?"

"Rocco. Don't know his last name."

My world tilts on its axis. The possibility that we just found Addie is almost too much.

"Helloooo?" her voice rings out.

"Were you kept in a three-story colonial home?" I name off a few more attributes of the property that might be recognizable, and when she doesn't answer right away, I almost crack the phone in half.

"That's it," she says finally.

Fuck.

"Jillian?"

"Yeah?"

"I'm going to murder so many fucking people for you."

The last thing I hear is her snorting before I hang up the phone, and I look up to meet Daire's rounded eyes.

"We found her?"

"We fucking found her," I confirm, immediately pulling up directions to the house.

It'll take about four hours to get to Merlin from Portland, but I'll need to prepare first. I won't know how many people will be occupying the house beforehand, so it'll be necessary to have Jay in my ear and Michael and Ruby with me in case there are more girls being held there. I'll have several more mercenaries following close behind if I need backup.

"Z?" I look up. "What if she isn't there anymore?"

My eye twitches from the mere thought. The possibility is high, but at least I'll have the people in my hands that can lead me straight to her.

I meet his stare, and for just a moment, I unleash the darkness.

"Then a lot of people are going to die."

"I have news," Jay says through the car speaker. It's six o'clock in the morning and still pitch-black, the sun not even broaching the horizon yet. Dense fog is shrouding the roads, making it hard to see.

I'm five minutes away from Francesca and Rocco Belluccis' house, Daya in the passenger seat next to me, while Michael and Ruby are driving behind me. It's only about ten minutes from the Rogue River, so acres and acres of National Forest surround the property.

Last night, I managed to hack into a few of the satellites. The government likes to tell people that satellites aren't interested in your house, but that doesn't mean they don't intermittently take images.

Jay's flipping through them now, but he hasn't seen any sightings of Addie.

"What?"

"I sent a drone over the house," he starts. "And the entire property is in an absolute upheaval. There are about thirty men currently searching around the property. Half are in the woods behind the house, and the other half are walking the road."

Right when he finishes, two black SUVs fly past me, and I spot several men on foot up ahead.

"Shit," I mutter, slowing down until I come to a stop right beside a man. "Jay, let Michael know what's going on and keep a drone on us."

I roll down my passenger window, and the guy bends at the waist, eyeing Daya and me with impatience.

"Everything okay, sir?" I ask.

"Everything's fine, nothing you need to worry about."

"Looks like you're having a search party. Do you need help?" I push.

"Nah, just looking for my dog."

I arch a brow, and Daya gives him a look. "You must really care about this dog," she remarks.

"Yeah, the bitch is priceless," he retorts. "Now keep it movin', you got cars behind you, dickhead."

But I'm already rolling my window up and pressing hard on the gas.

"Hear that, Jay?" I ask, my chest tightening.

"Yep. Do you think it's Addie?"

I shake my head, my thoughts racing faster than my car.

"Jillian mentioned other girls in the house, so it could be any one of them, but there's a really good fucking chance. I don't think they'd have a massive search party like this for a regular girl."

"It sounds like Addie. She's brave."

I bite my lip, a plethora of emotions rising in my chest—excitement, fear, and pride.

I make a quick decision to head towards the train. I have no idea what direction she's gone in, but I know she's too smart to take the road. Too many possibilities to get caught and brought right back to the house. But there's a chance she found that train, and is using it as a guide out of the woods. Or seeking refuge in it.

Daya's phone buzzes for the millionth time, and she sighs as she taps on it.

"Her mother again?"

"Yeah," she says softly. "She's been a wreck since Addie went missing, and I think she's told every police officer in the state about themselves and their momma because they haven't found her yet."

"She knows we might get her today?"

She nods, "Yeah, I probably should've waited, but I've just never seen Serena like this before, and I guess I just wanted to give her a little bit of hope, ya know? It's been over two months, and I think she was all but convinced Addie's dead."

I flick my gaze to Daya. "She's going to get her daughter back today. Call me psycho, but my girl is close. I can feel it."

Before Daya can respond, Jay's voice cuts in. "Oh, shit."

"What?" I snap.

"About two months ago, there are a couple satellite images of a massive gathering at the house. I looked to see if there was an influx of flights and hotel bookings, and sure as shit, there was. I mean, dozens and dozens of high-profile men from all around the world flew in and stayed in surrounding hotels. One of them was Xavier Delano; he has booked into a hotel forty-five minutes away every week for the past month."

Just like Jillian had said—he's been visiting her often.

"Fucker," Daya mutters.

White-hot fury builds in my chest, an ever-present volcano ready to erupt at any second. And it has, many times. Resulting in a lot of traffickers dying and a couple of buildings burnt down. I try to concentrate, otherwise I'll go blind with rage again, and my car will go careening off the side of the road.

I come up to a dead end, my only option being to turn left or right.

"Jay, is the railroad line up ahead?"

"Yep, a few hundred feet," he confirms a moment later.

"We're going to search on foot, but I have a few men on standby, and I want you to send them to the house just in case. I don't want anyone to leave."

"Got it."

I turn left and drive for a few seconds before coming across a hiking trail. There's a small lot, so I quickly whip into a parking space.

"Put your Bluetooth in," I tell Daya, sticking my own in my ear. Michael has pulled in the spot beside me, and the four of us exit the cars.

"Is it Addie?" Michael asks immediately.

"We don't know for sure, but I think it is, and she can't be far."

Ruby gasps and puts a hand over her heart, always one to be theatrical. "Oh! We best hurry then. She's probably so scared, poor girl."

Michael nods, a small hopeful smile tipping up his lips.

"Help direct us to the railroad line," I tell Jay after calling him on the Bluetooth while pulling out a cigarette from the pack.

"Those will kill you," Jay complains. I look up, noting the drone stationed fifty feet above my head. I raise my hand and give it the finger. Jay chuckles through my Bluetooth and tells us where to head.

It takes us about five minutes of speed-walking to find the train.

"How long is the train?"

"This one is larger than most. Stretches about two miles. You've got about a half-mile to your right, and the rest to your left."

I turn to Michael, "You and Ruby go right, and Daya and I will go left."

He nods, already taking off in the direction. "See you soon," he says, waving a hand, Ruby quickly following after him.

"Ruby!" I call. "You got a gun, right?"

"You're damn right I do," she shouts back, not even glancing behind her. Smiling in approval, I head in the other direction, my bones rattling with anticipation.

I'm coming home with my little mouse tonight. And then?

We're going to burn down the world together.

Chapter Twenty Two
The Diamond

The tip of my toe catches on a rock, and I stumble forward, managing to right myself before I eat dirt. The cold has settled deep in my bones, and all feeling in my hands and feet have depleted.

I don't know how long I've been running now, but I've counted the trailers I've passed.

Twelve. Only twelve.

It's pitch-black outside still, and an owl is hooting somewhere in the distance, easily drowned out by my namesake.

"Diiiamond!"

I heard Rocco's friends calling for me right as I reached the train, and I'm seconds away from bending over and puking, which would lead them straight to me. If not by the sound of my retching, then by the puddle of vomit I would be leaving behind.

It took me a while to find the train again, being so unfamiliar with these woods. I've only run through them twice, and both times was through a large maze filled with traps. Considering I'm not thinking clearly at the moment, I didn't want to risk tripping over a wire, so I went around it.

"Diiiiiiamoonddd!" a man calls again, and I gag, the adrenaline too powerful.

Their voices are still relatively far off, but I haven't covered any of my tracks. Haven't had the time to. I've no idea if they know how to follow them—probably not—but it doesn't matter. Francesca will, since she hunted me when we practiced for the Culling.

I'm on the twentieth trailer when I stumble again, and this time, I'm unable to catch myself. I topple forward, landing awkwardly on my hands and knees, agony flaring from the impact. My bag goes flying, and another fucking water bottle tumbles out. Dropping my head low between my shoulders, I work on breathing.

In, and out. In—fuck, I *can't* breathe.

My numb face contorts, and a sob crawls up my throat like the itsy-bitsy spider.

Keep fighting, baby. Keep fighting.

I don't know how to anymore, Zade. I don't fucking know how.

I shake my head, sucking in sharply, working on getting it fucking together. Another inhale, and I force myself up, bits of rock, leaves, and sticks embedded into my palms.

Brushing them off, I scan my eyes over the trailer next to me. It doesn't look much different than the others—white, rusted, and corroded—but there is a ladder anchored to the side of it.

If I stay out much longer, they'll find me, so I need to find a place to hide and regain my strength. I'm still deep in shock, and my body is beginning to shut down from it and the adrenaline.

Wiping the snot from my nose, I gather my meager belongings again, cradle them in one arm and grab onto the cold metal with the other, and start climbing.

"The itsy-bitsy spider climbs up the waterspout," I croak, missing a rung and slipping again. My knee hits the metal, sending waves of pain up my leg. Hissing, I finish my climb and clamber toward the middle of the trailer. Once I reach the hatch door, I turn the lever and yank it open, the last threads of my energy expended.

"Down came the rain and washed the spider out." I peek into the trailer, seeing nothing but plant life snaking through the crevices. I may very well be climbing into my grave, but I'd much rather die here.

Yeah, I think this is a good place to die.

I awake to the feeling of something skittering across my leg. I'm instantly gripped in panic and shoot forward, a sharp yelp on the tip of my tongue.

For a moment, I'm convinced I'm back in that house, straddling Sydney with that pen in my hand.

It takes several moments of taking deep breaths for the panic to subside, and my surroundings to bleed back into my vision.

Panting, I look down, noting that my hands are still covered in blood. It's soaked through my clothing on my arms and legs, too. My skin is itchy and irritated, and I can feel it flaking off me.

Groggy, freezing, and uncomfortable, I look around the inside of the trailer I'm in. Vines grow up through the cracks, and it's dirty and stifling in here but otherwise empty. I left the top hatch cracked, and a strand of morning light filters in, providing enough illumination to see clearly.

A groan rumbles from my throat, my back aching from my stiff position. Just as I readjust, I pause, noticing a brown squirrel sitting several feet away, sniffing the ground and keeping a close eye on me.

"Hey, cutie," I whisper, my voice hoarse with sleep. I titter, and with absolute fascination, watch it slowly come closer until it's within inches from me. It darts out of the way when I try to pet it, so I back off.

"What's your name?" I whisper, smiling when it hops on my leg, its tiny claws digging past the fabric of my joggers.

For several minutes, the curious squirrel and I observe each other, and for the first time in months, I feel a little lighter. This little creature is so small and insignificant to most, yet watching it clean its little face has my eyes filling with tears. I've been surrounded by hollow corpses for so long that it's shocking to see something so alive.

I sniffle, wiping away the wet trails from my cheeks, only for them to be replaced with more.

"My Nana loved watching the squirrels from the bay window, ya know?" I say aloud. "So, I'm going to call you May. Her birthday was in May, and I think she'd love you."

The squirrel titters, crawling down my leg towards my foot. I laugh when it nibbles at the tip of my shoe, tugging on the material slightly.

I gasp when I see another squirrel come rushing toward us out of the corner of my eye.

"Oh my God, there's two of you!" I squeak, keeping my voice quiet. May hops off my leg and meets up with her companion. The couple chases after each other, pulling another laugh from my chest. Several vines cling up the side of the trailer, directly up towards the hatch.

With both fondness and sadness, I watch the couple climb up the vines and squeeze their fluffy little bodies out of the crack.

"Bye, May," I whisper, loneliness settling in.

Instead of letting it sink its claws into me too deep, I force myself to stand, my back and legs aching painfully.

I don't remember much after dropping down in the trailer except that I nearly twisted my ankle, but I must've fallen asleep soon after. Considering there's a blue tint to the light peeking through, it's still early morning, and no more than a few hours could've passed.

There's no doubt that they're still looking for me, and I battle with the decision of whether I should keep moving or wait it out and hope they give up on searching the forest. I'm terrified to reach the point where I no longer have the protection of the abandoned train.

After that, I'll be out in the open, with only two kitchen knives to keep me safe.

Deciding to forge ahead, I take a moment to gobble down a granola bar and chug half a bottle of water, determined to eat and drink sparingly. I want to throw these stupid water bottles for nearly getting me caught, but I have no idea how long I'm going to be stranded for, so I need them.

When I dropped in here, I hadn't really given much consideration on how I was going to get out. And now, I really regret that decision.

I look around, hoping to find something that will give me a boost, but there's nothing in here.

Shit.

God? Can we barter or something? If you help me get out of here, you have my permission to knock off ten years of my life. That'll leave me with like five years left with all this stress, and I'm content with that.

Now that my head is clearer, I can say with absolute certainty that I don't, in fact, want to die here.

But it looks like I'm going to.

Another bout of tears floods my eyes, and my throat tightens.

Just as I'm about to start hyperventilating, I hear voices outside of the trailer. Inhaling sharply, I'm paralyzed with terror as I listen to two people speaking.

I can't hear what they're saying, but I do hear the distinct noise of a radio.

Oh, my fuck, that's them.

Hyperventilating commence.

I slap a hand over my mouth, suddenly paranoid that they can hear me breathe through thick steel. Glancing up at the hatch door, my heart drops when I hear a muffled voice say, "The hatch looks open."

Absolute terror consumes me, and the only thing I can think to do is quietly grab both of my knives, fisting one in each hand, and head towards the far corner of the trailer where most of the shadows are converged.

Obviously, that's going to accomplish absolutely nothing when they open the door and look inside, but there's literally nothing else I can do. Not until they come down here.

The sound of someone jumping on the side of the trailer reverberates throughout the metal and along my body, sending my heart flying into my throat.

I grip the knives tightly, shaking violently as I hear the man crawl up the trailer.

"Hey!" a voice calls loudly. The man pauses, and with him much closer to the door, I can hear him better.

"Who the fuck are you?"

I can't hear what the person's response is, but whatever it is, the guy doesn't like it.

"The fuck did you just say, asshole? You have no business being here."

The other person is closer now, though I still can't make out what they're saying.

"I don't give a fuck if it's not private property. Who the fuck are you to question me?"

Confused and relieved, I hear the man climb back down the trailer, assumingly standing off with the intruder.

I try to listen past the loud heartbeat in my ears, but I can't make out a damn word.

Their shouting increases, though most of it seems to derive from the man who came very close to finding me.

Just when it seems it's about to get physical, it goes deadly silent for a beat, followed by a sharp sound of metal pinging off of metal. A bullet? I didn't hear a gunshot, but it's so hard to hear past my roaring heartbeat.

It sounds like a man says, "Fucker," though I can't be sure.

Eyes wide, I stare up at the hatch, my nerves in tatters as I hear someone jump back up on the ladder of the trailer.

Oh, no.

No, no, no, no.

He's back.

A sob rackets up my throat, muffled by my hand as I hear the man loudly approach the hatch.

If he wants me to come out, he's going to have to come get me, and there's no way I'm going without a fight.

I would sooner slit my throat than go back to that house. Go back to Xavier.

The hatch creaks open, and vomit rises up my throat. I'm on the verge of fainting, until I see his face.

My eyes widen further, the fear quickly replaced with disbelief.

One blue eye so light, it's nearly white, with a wicked scar slashing straight down through it. And one brown eye so dark, it appears obsidian. I can still see his features clearly, even with the black hood drawn over his head. And right now, utter relief is staring right back at me.

"Zade?"

"*Fuck,* baby, stay right there. Don't you fucking move."

"She's in there?" a female calls out urgently, her footsteps climbing the trailer now as well. But I'm too blinded by shock to pay attention. Zade drops down into the trailer a second later, his weight reverberating throughout the heavy metal.

A whimper bursts from my throat, nearly choking on relief as I stumble towards him, colliding in a tangle of limbs.

He immediately lifts me into his arms, my legs circling his waist before he collapses to his knees, holding me so tightly that I can hardly draw in a breath.

Total disbelief has me in a chokehold and I'm heaving around the sobs pouring from my throat. They rack my body so profoundly that my bones rattle from the force.

"I'm here, little mouse, I'm here," he chants. "Fuck, you're so cold." His voice breaks, and he rocks us both, vibrations rolling through him as he fights to keep it together.

Piece by piece, we both crumble, the chips falling around us in a waterfall of anguish. And I just know that when Zade picks up our scattered pieces and stitches us back together, we'll be forever entwined.

He places soft but urgent kisses on any surface of my body within range. My head, cheeks, neck, and across my shoulders, while his hands roam mindlessly, heating my chilled skin, though it feels more like he's worshiping.

I don't know how long we stay there, but eventually, my weeping dies down, yet Zade never stops holding me.

"Addie?" a voice calls softly. My eyes widen, and my head snaps up, seeing Daya's face peering down in the hatch. Her smooth dark brown skin is wet with tears, and her sage green eyes are flooded.

"Oh my God, Daya," I croak, once more overcome with disbelief.

"Let's get you up, baby," Zade urges. "It's cold, and the place is still swarming with people looking for you."

I sniff, wipe my nose, and nod. He boosts me up, and Daya grabs onto my hands, helping me out of the trailer. When I climb out, she immediately embraces me in a hug; her hold is nearly as tight as Zade's.

"Don't you ever leave me again," she cries, voice shaky and tight. I nod, on the verge of breaking down all over again.

But then a woman screeches from behind us, erupting in jumbled words that sound a lot like *oh my God, you found her, she must be freezing*. Or something like that.

Daya and I pull apart to watch a red-headed woman and another man I don't recognize rush toward us. A moment later, Zade jumps up, dangling onto the hatch and lifting himself up with ease.

"You found her!" the woman shouts again.

"Jesus, Ruby, don't announce it to the world. There are still people around searching for her," Zade snaps.

She waves a hand, unconcerned. "You'll get 'em."

And he will. On the ground are two dead bodies, bleeding from what looks like their chests.

"How did you…?"

"Literally took two steps to the side and shot them both through the chest with one damn bullet," Daya answers for him, glancing at me with a look that says, *he's fucking crazy but also kind of cool.*

Approaching the trailer, Ruby pinches her hands, indicating for me to climb down to her. "Come on, honey. I'll get you warmed up."

I just stare at her, my brain submerged in a pool of gelatin, slow to process what's happening. After Daya softly nudges me, I shakily descend the ladder, my feet nearly slipping on the rungs. The woman, who must be Ruby, wraps an arm around me the moment my feet hit the dirt.

"You're safe now, honey," she croons, rubbing my bicep to warm me up as she walks me along the abandoned train.

I glance over my shoulder and spot Zade a few feet behind; his eyes laser-focused on me as if he's convinced I'll disappear if he looks away for even a second.

I'm safe now. Yet it still feels like I'm in Hell.

PART II

January 21st, 2022

I don't think my body is ready to accept freedom yet. It doesn't feel real. I'm just waiting for someone to draw back the curtain and **TA-DA**, I'm still trapped in that house, with a random man's nasty dick in my face.
Fuck.
I'm free.
Yet, I still want to fucking die.

My lipstick isn't the same color and I cried about that

Chapter Twenty Three
The Hunter

"No good news?" I ask, crossing my arms across my chest.

Jay's lips tighten, and he shakes his head. Francesca and Rocco Bellucci were nowhere to be found when my men arrived at their house. In fact, the entire house was vacant, except for a dead man in the living room with his throat slit open, and a couple men piled outside of the porch steps. Which means Rio and Rick fled, too. I suspect they all left the moment they found Addie missing, hightailing it out of there before I could get to them.

The worms are slippery, but they won't be able to hide from me for long.

"How is Addie doing?" Jay asks, concern etched into the lines of his face. He glances over my shoulder as if he can see her from the front door.

It's the first time he's been in Parsons Manor, and his body language suggests he's ready to get the fuck out. He took one step in, and the front door shut on its own behind him. Since Addie's been home, the activity has increased. Her energy has been dark, and the manor never had any warmth to begin with.

I wanted to take her back to my place, but Addie refused—stating she's been holed up in one prison for long enough and doesn't want to find herself in another. So I stationed heavy security around the property, using advanced—and illegal—technology to ensure nothing gets by without my knowledge. Whatever Claire has up her sleeve next, she knows there's no chance of touching Parsons.

After I found her, I took her straight to trusted old friends of mine, Teddy Angler, and his son, Tanner. Teddy is a retired surgeon but has been working for Z since I built the organization, taking in any survivors that need care. His son is a nurse, and often assists Teddy now that he's getting older.

We stayed with him for a week so he could treat the lacerations all over her body, the open wound on the back of her neck, and pump her with fluids. She was dehydrated, malnourished, and ravaged by the abuse.

I refused to turn away from what was done to her, though all I wanted to do was walk right back out of his door and shred anyone who inhabited that house with my bare fucking teeth.

I'm not sure if she even recalls much of her time with Teddy. She was catatonic the entire stay.

It's been a month since she's been home, and in the beginning, we were swarmed with police officers and media outlets. Law enforcement were requesting her statement, and wanted information on her kidnapping. And of course, because Addie's a popular author, it got media attention. I'm not ashamed that I've lost count on how many paparazzi I've threatened bodily harm to due to them trying to sneak onto the property.

I would've loved to make a fucking example of one of them. String them up at the end of the driveway as a friendly reminder of what will happen if even their toe touches the goddamn property line.

The chaos has died down, but it sent Addie further into herself, and she's been confined to her bedroom and cocooned under her black silk sheets as if she's allergic to the outside air. For the first couple weeks after her rescue, she would hardly speak at all.

Addie often flipped between complete desolation, where she stared blankly and gave no reaction, to crying and inconsolable. I've had a therapist, Dr. Maybell, come in to talk to her a few times to help draw her out, and it has helped.

Seeing her like this breaks my fucking heart, and all I want is to hand her the pieces and give her something to hold on to.

But she won't hold on to anything. Won't even let me come near. If I get within a foot of her, she flips out. She absolutely refuses to let me touch her, and it's fucking killing me because that's all I want to do.

Daya and Serena have both visited frequently, as Addie is far more comfortable with their embrace than she is with mine.

"Alive," I answer, though I'm not entirely sure that's the truth. She's breathing, but she's not living. "And slowly getting better. She's talking now and will smile and laugh sometimes. She'll be up, down, and sideways for a long time."

I glance down at the deep gouges in my hands, still bright red from last night.

Every night, she thrashes in the bed, screams tearing from her throat and body flailing. I've learned to be careful when I wake her. Some nights she goes into full attack mode. Sightless as she scratches at me, convinced I'm one of the demons haunting her nightmares.

During the day, she's back to being a ghost. Though that doesn't seem right, either—the ghosts in Parsons Manor are more active than she is.

And to be frank, I'm growing frustrated. Not because she's lost in her trauma, but because I have no fucking idea how to bring her out of it.

Helplessness is a feeling I've become intimate with. I can't save every girl, but I'll be damned if I can't save Addie, even if it's from herself.

"She's going to get through it, Z," Jay assures, seeming to note the distress darkening the underside of my eyes.

"I know she will. She's the strongest woman I know," I agree.

Jay nods, and hands over a bouquet of red roses. "I don't want to bother her right now, so give these to her for me, yeah?"

"Of course, thanks, man," I say, grabbing the bundle from his hand. His nails are painted neon pink today, and they're chipping already.

"Have you checked in on Katerina?"

Jay nods. "Yeah, she's kind of like Addie right now. Doesn't speak much and her emotions are unstable. She's so young and has been through a lot."

Once Addie had gotten in my car, she had given me two names, along with a plea to save one of them from a sunflower field. Rio's sister, Katerina Sanchez, and her groomer, Lillian Berez.

I don't know why Addie had asked me to rescue Rio's sister, only that it was important to her that I do. Katerina is a fifteen-year-old girl who was enslaved to a wicked woman. Regardless of who her brother is—and how badly I want to kill him—she's not responsible for her brother's sins and needed saving.

Caught up with Addie and getting her settled, I sent Michael and another one of my mercenaries to take care of it. If it wasn't for Addie insisting Katerina was by a sunflower field, it might've taken a lot longer to find her, but they were able to track her down within a couple of days and get her out of there. Unlike Addie, they didn't go through great lengths to keep her hidden.

Now, she's in one of my safe houses, getting treatment for her extensive trauma.

"Her brother still attempting to hide?"

Jay gives me a look. "You know he is. He's still in Arizona." When I nod, he hikes a thumb over his shoulder and says, "I'm going to head out. Let her know I'm thinking about her."

He casts another glance at the living room, sweeping his eyes over every nook and cranny as if a spirit is going to be standing there staring at him.

I can feel the eyes on my back, but whoever they are, they aren't making themselves known. Jay turns and softly shuts the door behind him, while a cold draft brushes across the back of my neck.

Ignoring the phantom, I head upstairs to check on my girl. Her mother left only an hour ago, and she tends to take naps after those visits.

The first time meeting Serena Reilly was... interesting. Addie never told her about me—which I had expected, considering their relationship was in shambles long before I came along. And regardless of the fact that I found her daughter, her spidey senses are tingling, and she is sensing just how dangerous I am.

She's not wrong.

Cracking open the door, I peer inside, finding Addie sitting up, balancing her journal on her knee as she scribbles in it like she can't get the words out fast enough. A shot of relief floods my system. Today seems to be a good day for her—as good as it's capable of being.

She doesn't acknowledge me, so I lean against the doorframe, content with watching her write. The balcony doors are cracked open, letting in the cool, fresh air. It's freezing in here, but it doesn't seem like she notices.

Over the last few days, she's been writing in that journal more often. I'm not sure where it came from, but it's her lifeline, and it seems to be helping her. Dr. Maybell recommends journaling and shit all the time with the girls I rescue. Better than bottling up all those emotions and letting them fester and eat away at them slowly.

After a few more minutes, she grabs a tube of lipstick, blindly applies it to her plump lips, then smacks a kiss on the journal. Glancing at me, she snaps the journal shut, sets it on the nightstand, and grabs a tissue to wipe off the crimson stain on her mouth, finally meeting my eyes.

"I see you're still creepy," she comments dryly, crumbling the tissue up and tossing it on the table beside her.

I grin and slowly approach her. She visibly tenses, so I sit at the end of the bed and give her space.

I'm all for pushing Addie's boundaries, but this isn't one I'm willing to. Despite my less than honorable methods with her in the past, the last thing I want to do is worsen her trauma. She's been through enough; she doesn't need another self-serving man taking something from her that she's not willing to give.

When she's ready to accept me again, I can't promise I won't push her past her comfort zone and work to reawaken a part of her I'm sure she feels is lost.

But that takes time and trust.

And I'm a very patient man.

"Forever and always, baby," I murmur, shooting her a roguish grin. It feels like my heart explodes when she offers a small smile in return.

That small gesture feels like she just handed me the entire fucking world in her tiny palms.

"Jay got you roses," I tell her, handing her the bouquet. Her hand curls around the stems, and she sniffs the petals.

"That was sweet of him. I probably should've met him… He's your friend, and he helped save both of our lives. I need to thank him personally," she says, her brows knitted with guilt.

I had given her a brief rundown of what happened the night of the ritual—how Jay realized the Society set me up and came to warn me. He was stationed in a van a block away in case shit went awry and we needed a quick escape, but by the time he got to me, the bomb had already gone off. But I haven't told her who the Society is yet, and she hasn't seemed inclined to get into it.

I shrug. "Jay isn't going anywhere, and he understands that you're not ready for people yet."

She snorts dryly. "People-ing sounds exhausting. And speaking of exhausting tasks… I need to shower," she admits, wrinkling her nose.

"You do stink," I say, my grin widening when she shoots me a glare.

More often, I've been seeing her old self poke through. Sometimes it's a jab at something I said, other times it's a little smile, and then there are moments like now—where she looks like she wants to give me the one-two to my eyeballs.

I eat it all up.

"You're supposed to say I smell like flowers."

"Baby, there are flowers out there that smell like straight ass. So sure, you smell like *those* flowers."

She stares at me for a beat, and then her face cracks, and a full-blown grin stretches her lips.

Fuck.

I'm so in love with her.

"Fine, I guess I can't really argue with that anyway." She glances at the door leading to her personal bathroom. "There are no cameras in there, right?"

I arch a brow, enjoying the way her lips part. "I haven't taken them out."

She glowers. "Why not?"

I hold her gaze, ensuring she can see how serious I am. "I'm not going to watch you, Addie. But the second you give me a reason to, I will."

Her brow lowers, picking up on my meaning. "I'm not going to hurt myself."

"Okay," I say, taking her word for it. "I'll change out the sheets, and they'll be fresh by the time you're done."

Slowly, she drags herself out of bed, and the burst of pride is uncontainable. I'm pulling up the corner of the silk sheet when she pauses at the door leading to her bathroom, peeking over her shoulder at me.

"Hey, Zade?"

"Yeah, baby?"

"Thank you."

"Your mom is coming here tomorrow, just to remind you."

It's only been a few days since Serena visited last, but she's been trying hard to reconnect with her daughter. Something I'm actually glad for, despite how exhausting she can be.

Addie rolls over to face me, once more a little burrito in her bed. She's intent on wasting away for now, but I plan on channeling her trauma into better, more healthy avenues when she's ready.

Her sweet caramel pools peer up at me, a slight frown on her face. Shadows stain the underside of her eyes, so dark that some of her freckles are lost.

"Does she have to?"

I shrug a shoulder. "No. Say the word, and I'll lock the doors."

She drops her gaze, but not quick enough to hide the guilt. "That was rude of me to say," she admits. "She's still my mom."

I settle in deeper next to her, slumping against the stone wall, careful not to touch her, though my body is vibrating with the need to.

We haven't touched since I found her in the train, and each second feels like a stab in the chest. Fiending for Adeline Reilly is a feeling I'm old friends with, but this is the first time I refuse to act on it.

"Tell me about her," I say. "Tell me everything about *you*."

She raises an eyebrow, and I smile because it's cute. "You mean you don't know everything about me already?"

"Of course, I don't, baby. Not the things that matter. I may know what high school you graduated from or where you went to college before you dropped out, but that doesn't mean I know how happy you were. If you were lonely or sad. Or if a boy cornered you in a library and made you scared." I pause, that particular scenario angering me. "If that happened, I just need a name, that's all."

She snorts, rolling her eyes.

Addie resisted pillow talk before she was abducted, intent on hating me. And when she stopped hating me, we only had a couple of nights together before she was taken.

She wiggles deeper into the sheets, glancing at me through thick lashes. My heart clenches painfully, and I have an uncontrollable urge to kiss every single freckle dotting her cheeks and nose.

"My mom hates me," she starts. "Or maybe she doesn't hate me, but she's never *liked* me. I think it's because she never understood me. My mom is all about being prim, proper, and classy. Enter beauty pageants, marry a rich man, and live lavishly. I think she just wanted me to have the life she couldn't have, and when I did the opposite, she resented me for it."

"At least you'll end up marrying a rich man," I comment. She pins me with a dry look.

"Now I can never marry you. It's my life's purpose to disappoint her in every decision I make."

I arch a brow. "Don't underestimate me, Addie. I'll become a poor man for you."

She shakes her head. "I don't even know your last name. Or your birthday."

I grin. "I'm sorry, I didn't realize those things were so important."

She glares at me, conjuring all the sass from the fellow women around the world and inserting it into that single look. It only makes me smile wider.

"Aren't we having a heart-to-heart? Plus, you keep threatening me with marriage. Shouldn't I know your last name?"

"Does this mean you're actually going to take my threats seriously and marry me?"

She sighs, waltzing right into that one. She knows it, too.

"It's a simple question. The kind of question anyone would ask on the first date. Or even before the first date just in case the man ends up being an obsessive stalker who murders people."

I tip my head back, a deep laugh pouring from my throat.

"My birthday is September 7th," I tell her.

"Doesn't surprise me that you're a Virgo. Next," she prompts sassily, waiting for my next answer. I bite my lip, tempted to spank her ass and give her a reason to be sassy.

"Meadows, baby. Our last name is Meadows."

"*Yours.* Don't get ahead of yourself. You'll be expected to beg."

There's no stopping the savage grin from gracing my lips. "I *love* to beg."

"Whatever, creep. We were talking about my mom, not marriage."

I get comfortable, fully facing her and propping my head on my hand. Her eyes flutter when I notch my finger under her chin, demanding her full attention. Gently, she pulls away, but I don't let it bother me. It's a start.

"Your mom doesn't hate you, Addie. She hates herself. And she doesn't resent you because you're not living the life she wanted for herself, she resents you because you were living the life you wanted, and she wasn't."

She stares at me, seeming to contemplate that.

"The best thing you can do is keep living that life, little mouse. Continue being a successful author who loves horror movies and haunted fairs. Who loves her Nana and the gothic mansion she inherited and finds a thrill out of the ghosts that walk the halls. You've always been unapologetically you."

She wrinkles her nose as if she's disgusted. "So, you're wise and shit, too?" She scoffs, a sound of abhorrence, though there's a faint glimmer in her eye. "Despicable. What are you bad at?"

My smile turns salacious, enjoying the way red tints her cheeks. "I'm very bad at lots of things. And I hear that practice makes perfect."

She groans and shoves me, and I laugh when she flips over, turning her back to me. We both know she's laughing, too, but she just isn't ready to admit it yet.

That's okay. I've got nothing but time.

February 18th, 2022

One time, Sydney told Francesca that I drew on the walls with a sharpie. The picture was of a stick figure with their head severed off. There was red smeared all over it, and later I found out Sydney was on her period.

Of course, I was blamed for it. Francesca made me clean off the blood with my toothbrush.

Don't worry, I didn't use it again after that. Rio snuck me a new one, and they were none the wiser, thinking I was brushing my teeth with the same brush that I scrubbed period blood with.

I ~~was~~ considered sharpening the end of that toothbrush like I was in an actual prison, and stabbing Sydney in the eye with it. Then, I really would draw on the walls, except it'd be a figure with a missing eyeball, her blood smeared over it.

Now that would be funny.

Chapter Twenty Four
The Diamond

"I have an awkward question," I start, and I almost immediately regret saying anything at all when Zade grins slyly at me. He probably thinks I'm going to ask him to do something weird.

This will be the first time I'm planning on leaving the property since I've been home, and my anxiety is high. It's been a little over a week since I had talked about my mom with Zade, and it made me feel… better. Enough to get up every day, shower, take walks to the cliff, get some fresh air, and just… live.

I think I've reached the point where I need to feel human again, but there's been one nagging concern in my head that's keeping me from feeling that.

"Can… Would you mind driving me to the clinic?"

Usually, I'd drive myself, but the thought of getting behind the wheel again makes me break out in hives. My car was totaled in the accident, and even though Zade bought me a new one, I can hardly get in it without having an anxiety attack. Plus, it's missing the ketchup stain on the roof, and I miss that stain. I still don't remember where it came from, but I'm pretty sure it was from a fly-away French fry after I hit a speed bump too hard.

So anyway, I decided Zade taking me would cause more annoyance, but less panic.

His face relaxes, and I think he knows what I'm asking.

"Sure, baby," he agrees, nodding toward the door. "I'll be in the car."

He stands, then pauses and looks at me. "And by the way, nothing is awkward between us. If you need me to pluck a butthole hair, I'll do it." He shrugs, "Or you know, pop an ingrown hair on your vagina."

My mouth drops open, but then my eyes narrow, and I cross my arms.

"How much shit did you watch me do when you were being a little creep?"

His grin only widens in response before he walks out of the door.

I swear I hate him.

But I'm thankful that he's not asking questions. How does one say, *hey, I want to get tested for STDs because I had a bunch of dicks in me* without at least one person feeling uncomfortable? Doesn't really come out right, no matter how you word it.

I will forever be thankful for Francesca forcing Rocco and his friends to use condoms, aside from the first time Rocco assaulted me. She said we would be worthless if they gave us diseases. But it was useless anyway—they certainly didn't use condoms when they forced us to perform oral. I think it just made Francesca feel like she was being responsible.

According to Rio, there was an incident long before I arrived, where one of the guys gave all the girls syphilis. Since then, Francesca has been diligent about them getting tested if they wanted to partake in our 'lessons,' but I wouldn't trust any of them to actually keep their dicks clean.

Xavier used condoms, too, but there was one occurrence when the condom broke. I bite my lip, anxiety flaring just thinking about that minuscule chance that I got knocked up anyway, despite that I have the IUD. It's improbable, but not impossible.

My heart drops, picturing the disgusted look on Zade's face when finding out that I'm pregnant with another man's baby.

I know him well enough by now that I'm confident he wouldn't actually give me that look, but that image plagues me anyway.

I wouldn't blame him if he did. That disgust is what I feel every time I stare in the mirror. Which is why I tend to avoid it at all costs.

I'm getting a pregnancy test, and if I did get that unlucky, I'm throwing myself off the building next.

I've been out of the house for a total of two hours and forty-seven minutes, and I'm fucking exhausted. I'm still riddled with anxiety, nauseated by the possibility that I'm as filthy as I feel.

"You look like you need ice cream," Zade announces, his palm flat on the steering wheel as he makes a left turn. It's… hot. Watching Zade drive is foreplay.

Even worse, he's wearing a leather jacket over his hoodie today, and I still haven't been able to unstick my tongue from the roof of my mouth.

I blink, the loss of blood making me a little woozy. I told the doctor to test me for every STD known to man—especially herpes since that's one of the scarier and mostly silent ones—and I lost count of how many tubes of blood she drew. She stared at the barcode on my wrist almost the entire time, and after the gauze stemmed the bleeding, she slapped a Band-Aid with smiley faces on my arm. I laughed, then cried when the pregnancy test came back negative.

"Ice cream?" I echo dumbly.

"Do you like ice cream?"

"I—well, yes," I stutter, my brain slow to catch up with the randomness.

"What's your favorite flavor?"

"Mint chocolate," I answer, watching him make another turn. He's heading in the opposite direction of Parsons now, and I think he's aiming for *Lick n' Crunch* a few blocks away—a mom-and-pop shop that sells the best soft-serve ice cream in Seattle.

The thought of getting ice cream with Zade is so normal and mundane that it feels like the most exciting thing to happen since sliced bread. And watching Zade lick an ice cream cone will probably be just as weird as it will be hot.

"So toothpaste?"

I sigh. "Et tu, Brute? It's not *toothpaste*. They taste nothing alike."

A grin tips up one side of Zade's mouth, and his eyes glitter as he pulls into the parking lot. The bastard of a man is just trying to get a rise out of me.

"It's toothpaste," he reaffirms, though I'm not sure if he actually believes that. He looks too damn mischievous, but I can't help arguing anyway.

I unbuckle and swivel toward him, my eyes thinning.

"Mint is a delicacy, and you're just a simpleton incapable of appreciating it."

He laughs outright, putting the car in park. Mint is definitely not a delicacy—quite the opposite, actually—but I'm sticking with it.

"Are you saying I need to refine my food palette?"

"Obviously," I answer dryly.

He leans in close, the leather groaning beneath his weight, and my breath hitches, all my senses invaded by the pure intensity that shrouds this man. His scent envelopes me, causing me to stiffen as his lips scarcely brush the side of my jaw.

"Your pussy is a delicacy, baby, and I could eat it forever and never grow tired of the taste of you. Is that refined enough?"

A flush crawls up my neck, burning a path to my cheeks, while my mouth opens in shock. I'm entirely embarrassed by the traitorous squeak that breaks free from my throat, only causing my cheeks to grow hotter. He chuckles, then he's out of the car in the next blink. I glance around, trying to locate where my heart fell out of my ass.

Surely that's the only explanation of why I feel so empty now that he's gone. Or the asshole took it with him.

I sigh.

That's definitely what happened.

Daylight savings is approaching, relieving the world of its depressive claws. Something about the sun setting before five in the afternoon really puts a damper on your day.

It's still cold outside, yet we're sitting on a bench outside of *Lick n' Crunch*, people-watching and shivering my ass off while I slowly eat my dessert.

Zade got a mint chocolate chip cone for himself, and he smiled wider than the damn Cheshire Cat when I just stared at him.

"My entire world revolves around you. If you want mint chocolate chip, then that's what I want, too," he had said.

"Do you even *like* it?"

"I like you, does that count?"

"*No.*"

He just went and sat down, a satisfied look on his face as he lapped up the sweet cream. He doesn't appear disgusted, and I admit that I've spent half of my time trying to figure out if he's fucking with me or if he truly does like the flavor.

I still haven't figured that out.

Shooting him a narrow-eyed look when he catches me staring and winks, I turn away before he can see the smile threatening to curl my lips.

People are bundled up in their coats, bustling down the street and in and out of shops.

My attention snags on a person walking down the road. They have masculine features and are dressed in a big poofy purple dress. Then I do smile. My mother would turn her nose up at the eccentrics in Seattle, but I've always admired their confidence and ability to be comfortable with who they are.

"I hope they're happy," I murmur. When Zade looks at me curiously, I nod towards the individual in the purple dress. "This world can be so cruel. So, I hope they're happy."

Zade is quiet for a beat. "Happiness is fleeting. All that matters is that they're living their life the way they want to."

"You believe that?" I ask, facing him. "That happiness is fleeting?"

He shrugs, tossing the last bite of his cone into his mouth, and chews as he contemplates something.

"Absolutely," he says finally. "It's not something solid you can hold on to. It's vapor in the wind, and all you can do is inhale it when it's near and hope it comes around again when it blows away."

I nod, having to agree with that.

Shivering, I eat the last of my cone, the icy breeze stirring up my hair, sending the tendrils dancing. Zade catches them and gathers my hair until it's lying straight down my back. I can't help but tense, though I don't stop him from whatever he's doing. He removes his leather jacket and wraps it around me, trapping my flyaway hair beneath the heavy warmth.

"Thank you," I whisper, bundling further into the jacket, overcome with emotion for a reason I can't explain. His jacket smells of leather, spice, and a hint of smoke, and as I inhale his comforting scent, tears burn the backs of my eyes.

Maybe because this is the best I've felt in so long, and that kind of makes me want to cry.

He gives me a soft smile, his mismatched orbs bright. Even the scar slashing down his white eye can't take away from how at peace he looks right now.

"You're welcome, baby."

My heart thuds, and I finally recognize why I feel so emotional.

Turning back to watch the city, I lean my head on his shoulder and inhale deeply.

This happiness may be fleeting, but I've never been surer that it'll be back.

March 2nd, 2022

When I was first kidnapped, I expected them to take a lot from me. Mainly my sanity. And they definitely succeeded there.

But what I didn't expect them to take was my ability to be touched by Zade. I mean, don't get me wrong, it makes sense. But the one thing I've never been able to resist was Zade's touch.

And now I want to light myself on fire every time he does.

That's not fair of me. I just don't want to be touched. It makes my fucking skin crawl. Even the thought of it reminds me of all the dirty hands that have touched me all over.

One of Rocco's friends used to rub lotion over my skin because he was **obsessed** with how soft it is. He would come from doing that alone, I didn't even have to touch him back. All I could think about was that one movie with Hannibal Lector. "It puts the lotion on its skin or it getsthe hose again."

Fuck, I think Rocco's friend was worse. It was like receiving a bad massage from a forty year old drug addict who could only locate a clit if it was covered in coke. Even then, he'd lose it again.

Chapter Twenty Five
The Diamond

"Can I take you somewhere?" Zade asks. I've just stepped out of the bathroom from my shower, yanking a brush through my wet, tangled hair. I tear the bristles through a particularly brutal knot, uncaring of the way the strands tear.

"Baby, you're hurting your hair. Let me brush it."

Feeling defeated, I slump my shoulders, trudge over to him, and sit on the floor between his spread knees.

He takes the brush from me and gently starts running it through the sopping tresses, slowly detangling the mop on my head.

It feels nice, but I'm too tired to appreciate it.

Another two weeks have passed, and it's a constant up and down battle. Turns out, one of the men did give me chlamydia, and it only cemented that feeling of filth ingrained deep in my bones.

I cried, confessed my diagnosis to Zade, and then cried even harder when he was nothing but supportive. It's been treated, but that lingering repulsion lingers, sinking its claws deep into my membrane.

He's probably used every word in the English language to assure me that I'm not disgusting or that he doesn't see me differently, but it didn't change how I viewed myself.

Zade was right. Happiness is fleeting, however, over the past weeks, he's done everything in his power to help me hold on to any semblance of peace.

Finishing with the brush, he sets it down on the bed and gathers my hair together. I nearly choke when he begins braiding it.

"Where the hell did you learn to do that?" I ask. I'm tempted to twist around like a dog chasing its tail, just so I can witness this.

"Ruby taught me," he answers quietly. "There was a young girl that I rescued a few years ago, and she wouldn't let anyone else touch her but me at first. She loved braids in her hair, so I learned how to do them for her. Got pretty fucking good at it, too."

My lip trembles, and I'm forced to suck it between my teeth to keep the sob in.

Bastard of a man.

Just when I think I can't fall in love with him any more than I already have, he goes and does this shit.

There's no denying that he's going to be a great father one day, and though the thought scares me, I don't want anyone else but me to have the privilege of seeing it happen.

"Oh," I whisper.

"Let me see your wrist band," he says. I raise my arm, and he drags it off my hand and ties off the braid.

"Thank you," I murmur, standing and turning to face him. I'm in a weird internal war where I want to crawl onto his lap, but the thought of actually doing it makes me break out into hives. "Where did you want to take me?"

"I want to show you something—someone, too. But I thought maybe seeing this would... help you."

My brows pinch, but I nod, curious about what he thinks could possibly help me. As far as I'm concerned, I'm a lost cause. Hopeless. Helpless. And all the synonyms for those words, too.

During the forty-five-minute drive, Zade tells me all about how he got suspended in high school and almost didn't graduate. It was a senior prank—he glitter-bombed the entire school, and they had to spend the rest of the year surrounded by pink sparkles.

One of these days, I'm going to have to make him show me pictures of his younger self. He says he's always had heterochromia, and I can only imagine how much the ladies loved that.

Eventually, we pull up to a massive gate with several armed guards standing outside. As soon as they spot Zade's car, they let him through without hesitation.

We drive down a long dirt driveway that leads to what appears to be a mini village. There's a massive, long building in the center with several smaller one's surrounding it.

There's also an enormous greenhouse, which is where most of the activity is. People are milling about, carrying baskets of fruits and vegetables. A group of girls walk together, giggling and whispering to one another as they make their way towards one of the smaller buildings. All of them are kids or women that I can see.

"Where are we?"

"This is where the survivors go if they don't have a safe home to return to."

My gaze snaps to him, then quickly turns back to my surroundings, taking everything in with a whole new perspective.

"Really? How many are here?"

"One hundred and thirty-two survivors," he answers, and the fact that he knows the exact number does weird shit to my heart. Shit I didn't consent to.

"How many people do you have room for?"

He shrugs casually, parking outside the largest of the buildings. "However many I need it to. I own hundreds of acres, so if I need to build another dorm, I do."

I blink. "You really are stupid rich, aren't you?"

"Sure, but it goes back into my organization."

Mouth open in awe, I scan the area, overcome with how… peaceful it appears.

"Are these the only safe houses you have?"

"No, they're all around the country. Eventually, Z is going to expand to other countries, and I'll start building there, too, and offer a safe place for survivors."

"How do you keep it hidden from Claire?"

"I've gone through great lengths to make it impossible to trace any of my assets. Everything is under an alias and doesn't tie back to me in any way. There's also an incredible amount of security, and it's a no-fly zone for aircraft. This is the safest place anyone could be, I've made sure of that."

I shake my head, at a loss for words. I remember him saying before that he offers a home to those who didn't have one, but seeing it just cements how incredible Zade truly is. Aside from his psychotic tendencies, he's doing something that no one has done before.

"Come on, baby. There are a couple of people I want you to meet."

I frown, unsure of who that could be, but follow him out of the car anyway. As we're walking down a path, we see Ruby heading toward us, a group of children running behind her, giggling as they try to keep up. When she spots us, she screams in excitement, quickening her footsteps.

"Oh my goodness, Addie baby, you look so beautiful!" she coos loudly. She immediately embraces me in a warm hug when she's close enough, and for a moment, I'm too stunned to react. Eventually, I wrap my arms around her, and embarrassingly enough, I feel a little like crying.

She pulls away, crooning over me some more.

"Are you coming here to stay, sweetie?"

"Oh no, he was just showing me the place," I answer.

"Well, you'll have to come visit more often. These little kiddos are good for the soul."

I smile, peering down at the three little girls and one boy standing in a circle and babbling to each other. I think I believe her. They're adorable, and I can see how a place like this would be comforting.

"I think I will," I say softly.

Ruby lets us pass after that, and Zade directs me inside the greenhouse.

I pause, losing my breath as I take it all in.

Mist clings to the air, coating the plant life with dew, while bright pops of color break up the never ending green.

It can only be described as a contained jungle, sans the wild animals. Though I almost retract that statement when two little boys go zipping past me, laughing wildly with huge turnips in their little fists. A woman chases after them, pleading with them to stop running.

Zade grabs my hand and leads me to where two young women dig at the soil, planting seeds.

"Katerina Sanchez," Zade calls out quietly, and my heart stops when one girl's head turns to the side, a familiar face staring back at me, though feminine and younger, and one eye is permanently closed.

"Oh my God," I whisper, paralyzed as the girl's brows knit, confused on who we are.

"Yeah?" she says cautiously.

Zade grins. "My name is Zade. I haven't gotten the chance to introduce myself yet, but I—" He abruptly cuts off when the girl rips off her gloves and then proceeds to nearly tackle him into a hug. While surprised, he recovers quickly and wraps his long arms around her, gently patting her back.

"You're the one responsible for getting me out," she says into his chest, her words muffled. "Thank you. So much."

He chuckles. "I think you should be thanking the woman standing behind you. She's the one who told me to help you."

Without hesitation, the girl turns to me and embraces me in a hug next, squeezing tighter than I expected. Try as I might to hold in the tears, I can't. They break loose, and a whimper escapes as I hold her tightly.

"Was it Rio?" she asks softly, her voice watery from her own tears.

"Yes," I rasp. She pulls back enough to get a good look at my face, her dark brown eye tracing over my features.

"How did you know him?"

I glance at Zade, but he doesn't seem bothered by the conversation, even though he wants to murder her brother.

"He—he was in the house I was in when I was kidnapped." I clear my throat. "He took care of me and helped me get out."

Her lip trembles. "He's not a very good person," she says, and I'm so surprised, I laugh. "But he's not a good person because he's such a great brother. He's sacrificed a lot for me."

I nod, wiping my cheeks, although it's useless when a few more tears slip free.

"I don't think people are black and white, Katerina, but I do know that his love for you is."

She smiles and nods, accepting that easily.

"They took my eye because he tried to escape from Francesca. I was ten years old, our parents had just died the year before, and he was trapped with that evil woman. He never forgave himself, and even though I haven't seen him since, I know he's done everything that's been asked of him so I wouldn't get hurt."

"And did you?" I ask. "Did you get hurt again?"

She shakes her head, but there's a darkness swirling in her eyes. "Lillian wasn't very nice, but she didn't hurt me anymore." Something tells me that even though *she* wasn't hurt anymore, other girls were.

She was trapped in that house for at least five years—I can only imagine the horrors she's witnessed.

"Katerina, can I ask why they, uh, needed Rio so badly? Enough to use you as collateral?"

It's something I've been wondering since Rio told me about her. Why would they go as far as holding his sister over his head just so that he would work for them? They could find plenty of men willing to do their bidding, if offered the right amount of money.

She swallows. "I think… I think he was Francesca's… favorite."

I frown, not really sure what she's getting at. "Like favorite guard or—"

She shakes her head, her lips tightening. "I've heard Lillian say nasty things about them. About how much Francesca likes the way Rio… tends to her."

My mouth pops open, realization dawning.

"Oh."

Then, my eyes widen, another realization hitting.

"*Oh.*"

Francesca was fucking Rio. But I have a feeling it wasn't mutual. She was raping him, regardless of his compliance, and it sounds like she was quite attached to him.

My eyes drift to Zade, his expression tight. An overwhelming sadness washes through me, muddling my feelings toward Rio further. In a way, he became my friend while I was trapped in that house. And for over two months, I was being forced to do things against my will, never realizing Francesca was ordering him to do the same.

There's a part of me that still clings to that hate, but it's weakening.

He kidnapped me. Ruthlessly fed me to the wolves and stood by while faceless men repeatedly broke me. Yet, he picked up the pieces afterward. Gathered them in his hands and carried them to my room, where he meticulously placed them back together—as janky as it was.

I want to hate him. But I don't know that I do.

"Thank you for telling me that," I say softly.

Her bottom lip trembles. "I know I lost an eye, but I think Rio has lost so much more than I have. I hope he's okay, and safe, wherever he is."

I blink back fresh tears and nod my head. "Me too."

We let Katerina get back to her gardening after promising I'd visit again. Sensing my inner turmoil, Zade keeps quiet as he leads me to another part of the sanctuary. There are two girls tending to chicken pens, plucking the eggs from underneath them.

I gasp, coming to a halt when one of them turns, and I get a good look at her features.

"Jillian," I breathe. She turns at her name, and her eyes bug from her head.

"Oh my God," she says, her accent deepening from shock. Then, she's hurriedly setting down the basket of eggs and rushing toward me.

We meet in the middle, our arms instantly wrapping around each other in a fierce hug.

Due to Francesca's mind games, we could hardly stand to look at each other when she and Gloria were sold. But all of that immediately bleeds away now that we're free.

My vision blurs, and when we pull away, I can see tears swimming in her eyes, too.

"How are you?" I choke out, chuckling when her nose wrinkles.

"As good as I can be, which isn't saying much," she answers.

I nod, "Same. Kind of feels like a slow death."

Her lips twist, and she shrugs, attempting nonchalance. "I feel that, too. I've been seeing Dr. Maybell, though. And all this—" she twirls her finger, gesturing to this farm— "has helped a lot, as well. Being surrounded by others with similar experiences and having something to keep me busy prevents me from spiraling. I was on the streets before, and part of me didn't want to be rescued because I'd have to go back to that. So, this… this has really saved me."

She glances at Zade, clearly uncomfortable with her admission, but she only straightens her spine instead of hiding. Sharing feelings is… hard.

"Happy to help," Zade says simply, his face smooth but his orbs glitter with warmth.

He's a cold-blooded killer yet easily melts beneath a survivor's hopeful gaze. It impacts him as much as it does me because when you're trapped and terrified, hope is the first thing you lose, and the most devastating. So, getting it back... that's one of the best gifts we could ask for.

My lip trembles, and I can't decide if I want to hug her again or turn and smack a large one right on Zade's lips. I'm incredibly happy for Jillian, and it feels like some of the cracks in my soul mend just a little more.

We find a spot by one of the pens and talk for a good hour while Zade helps the other girl with the chickens, leaving us alone. She tells me a little about her life before she was taken, and I tell her about mine. She made me promise to bring her a signed copy of one of my books, and it honestly tore my heart out as much as it mended it. I miss writing, but I know I'm not ready for that yet.

Eventually, we leave Jillian to her work while Zade shows me around the rest of the small village. There are classrooms for the children, workshops for the elder kids, and plenty of activities to give them all something to work toward. The adults are also taught skills and trades that will allow them to get jobs, along with teaching life skills and giving them the necessary tools to support themselves.

Of course, no one is required to leave, but the last thing Zade wants to do is strip people of their independence, so those who want to go out and experience the world and lead normal lives are able to do so.

There's even a stable with horses, offering equine therapy for the survivors. And of course, there's several on-site therapists, Dr. Maybell being one of them.

My memory is a little spotty from when I first came home, but I never forgot her warmth. The few times she visited, she helped more than I realized. And sometime soon, I plan on seeing her again and more regularly.

We spend hours playing with the children and speaking with other survivors. I even met Sarah, the little girl who is still very insistent on

Zade becoming her daddy. His eyes were a warm gooey mess when they looked over to me while Sarah jumped all over him, and for one insane second, I almost said yes right then and there.

He's going to make a great father one day, but that day isn't today. Not when I'm still learning how to pick up the pieces without cutting myself.

By the time I get back in the car, I'm overwhelmed with emotion. From getting to see what Zade built and how fucking beautiful it is, to seeing Jillian and hearing about Rio—I'm a damn mess.

"Do you still want to kill him?" I ask, not bothering to clarify. He knows who I'm talking about.

"Yes," he admits.

"Even after meeting his sister and hearing that he's suffered, too?"

He's silent for a beat. "One person's suffering does not justify the pain they inflict on others."

"You're right, but he also didn't have a choice," I argue.

Zade sets his jaw, pulling out of the parking space and heading down the dirt road.

"Baby, there's no good answer for this. If you want me to forgive him, that will never fucking happen. He's directly responsible for nearly killing you in a car accident, kidnapping you, and bringing you into a place where you were repeatedly raped and abused. What do you want me to fucking say? He's a victim, too, and all's forgiven?"

I snap my mouth shut. Just like people aren't black and white, neither are our emotions toward them. Rio caused me a lot of pain, and regardless of the person I came to know in that house, Zade didn't experience that. He didn't get to know Rio like I did, and the only thing he'll ever see is the man who helped ruin my life. I can't fault him for that. Especially when I don't think I'd be so forgiving either if the roles were reversed.

"I'm sorry," I say.

He sighs. "You have nothing to be sorry for, little mouse."

The gates open for us again, and he pulls out onto the road.

"Can you take me to one more place?" I ask.

"Anywhere," he answers.

I hold up my arm, showing him the barcode Rio tattooed on my wrist.

"I want to get a tattoo."

He smiles. "Of my name?"

I snort. "Keep dreaming, buddy."

March 14th, 2022

Zade tried his best to convince me to get his name tattooed over my wrist, but I told him that's a curse to all relationships. He even offered to get my name tattooed on his asscheek, and as tempting as that was, I declined.

Instead, I got an elaborate rose that completely covers the barcode, the stem wrapping around my arm. I told Zade that I have my own rose that will never die, and I'm pretty sure his eyes got a little glassy.

It's beautiful, and it feels like taking another step in the right direction.

Almost all of the women and children at the safe house had barcodes too. Some of them covered, most of them not. Some choose to keep them as a reminder, much like Zade does with his scars. Others, like myself, want to move on from that part of our lives.

And for the first time since I've been home, I feel a little lighter than I did before. It feels a little like healing.

Chapter Twenty Six
The Diamond

You bleed so pretty, diamond. Like your body was meant to be cut up by my knife.

I set my trembling hand down, still clutching the knife until my knuckles turn white. Maybe I don't need to make this salad.

Fuck, I know it hurts so good, doesn't it, diamond? Look at all that blood.

My favorite color has always been red, and my God, do you look beautiful covered in it.

A hand brushes across my shoulder, and all of those memories come to life. Xavier is standing behind me, ready to take from me again. And I can't let it happen. I won't survive it.

"No!" I scream, whipping around and sending the knife flying straight toward his face. Does he like the sight of his *own* blood? I'll show him how glorious it looks on him, too.

A hand closes around my wrist, halting my progress, but fuck him. He's not going to stop me—not this time.

"Little mouse," he whispers, and that confuses my brain. Enough for Xavier's face to fade, only for Zade's to appear.

Heart racing and vision blurred with tears, my hand flies open, the knife clattering loudly against the tile.

Fuck me, I almost just stabbed Zade in the face. Eyes widened with shock; the only thing I'm capable of is to stare, unsure if Zade is an apparition, too. He studies me closely, face carefully blank as he lowers my hand.

"Careful, little mouse, that's my strongest asset."

Blinking, I finally choke out, "Don't ever tell my mother about this."

Zade's brows pinch, and his mouth opens, then closes, before finally settling on, "What?"

I extract my wrist from his grip, my blood spiking hot from the lingering adrenaline, and now embarrassment.

"What just happened was entirely dramatic, and if she ever finds out I'm just like her, I'll die."

He blinks, amusement filtering in his yin-yang irises. "You'll die, huh?"

I nod once, sharply. "In absolute misery."

His mouth quirks up. "I wouldn't dream of it then."

Sniffing, I nod once more, straighten out my shirt purely just to give my hands something to do other than stabbing people, and then turn, open a drawer, and pull out another knife.

"Good."

He's silent for a beat. "Do you want to talk about the attempted murder that just occurred?"

"Not really," I answer, chopping off another piece of carrot.

"But I do."

I sigh, setting the knife down and pivoting to face him again.

"Zade, I think I'd rather talk about my mother trying to convince me that chastity belts were the latest fashion when I was fourteen than talk about trying to stab you."

Another pause. "Okay, so there's a lot to unpack here, and I'm not sure where to start."

"Exactly, can you believe her? I told her she might as well make the chastity belt into an electric fence, too, so I don't have to suffer through that."

He arches a brow, fighting a smile. "Yeah, baby, not dramatic at all."

I shoot him a droll look. "You're here. Why are you here? Did you need something?"

"Just you, little mouse."

Dammit. Why does he have to say all the right things? He knows exactly what he's doing, too, and how much I secretly enjoy it.

I narrow my eyes, and he forges on, a slight curl to his lip as he speaks.

"While I'm not scared of the Society, we are currently sitting ducks, and I need to handle a few things with Jay. And there are a few things I need to discuss with you, starting with who put a target on your head."

"Claire, right?" I ask. Surprise flashes across his face.

"How did you know?"

"She came to visit me."

His face smooths into a blank slate, but it's a mirage. Anger swirls beneath the surface, bubbling out through his hardened tone. "What did she say?"

"Pretty much just bitch-slapped me with the knowledge that she's been the big man behind the screen the entire time. She was there because she knew you were looking for me, and I was going to be handled differently to ensure that you wouldn't find me."

He nods slowly. "I'm not going to rush you, but eventually, I'll need to know if you saw anyth—"

"I want to help," I cut in. It doesn't give me anxiety like I thought it would. Instead, it gives me a sense of relief.

When he took me to the sanctuary a few days ago, it changed something in me. Seeing all those survivors getting better, working on healing, and seeing them shrouded in all kinds of happy vapors, it shifted something in my chest.

It made me realize that's what I really need. A goal—something to work toward that would genuinely make me happy. And now, I know what that is.

"Add—"

"Don't tell me I'm not capable, or not ready. I've had a lot of fucking time to think. And I don't want to be this insufferable victim, okay? I don't want to let them win, and more importantly, I want—no, I *need* to help."

He crosses his arms. "Okay. How would you like to help?"

I shrug. "I'll tell you everything I know. And if you go out on missions, I want to come."

His brow cocks, and his gaze flickers over me before returning to my eyes.

"Okay," he acquiesces again. I'm almost suspicious of how agreeable he is. I was expecting him to lock me in my proverbial tower like Rapunzel.

Noting the look on my face, he says, "I'll never treat you like you're helpless or incapable. I've always known how strong you are. So, if you want to help, fine. I'm more than happy to bring you along for the ride, baby, but that comes with stipulations."

"What stipulations?" I ask, growing wary.

"We start training again. We'll pick up where we left off, and I'll teach you not only how to defend yourself but how to fight, too. You need to learn how to use a weapon properly, and so help me God, Adeline, you will not do stupid shit when we're working in the field."

My mouth opens, offended by his accusation. "What makes you think I'd do anything stupid?"

His brow jumps up to his forehead again. "You're going to tell me that confronting your stalker in the middle of the night wasn't stupid?"

My teeth click shut. So, maybe he has a point there.

"You're brave. *Incredibly* brave, and a goddamn survivor, and it's admirable as fuck. You have no idea how proud of you I am. But you're also impulsive, and reactive, and I refuse to lose you again, do you hear me? I won't. Which means that you have to listen to me, and you cannot go off and do your own thing because you think you're helping. We're a team, baby. Got it?"

I chew my lip, mulling that over. If I've learned anything, it's that I am underwhelmingly out of my league when it comes to this corner of the world.

"I understand," I agree. "I'm not going to pretend like I'm the big bad wolf... yet."

His answering smirk suggests that he *is* the big bad wolf, and honestly, I'd have to agree.

But I won't admit it. His head will blow up, and then I will need to jab that knife in his face just to pop his oversized ego.

"Aim for the jugular, not the ear, baby," Zade instructs patiently. It grinds on my nerves anyway, and I'm a hairsbreadth away from turning the knife on him instead. "Adjust your feet—" He gently kicks one of them back. "You're unbalanced and not holding the knife correctly."

Since I started training with Zade three weeks ago, I've improved, but it doesn't feel like enough. It never does.

Before me is a gelatin mannequin with countless stab marks in it, most of them far off from where I'm supposed to be hitting.

A reel of people clicks through my head, picturing each one in place of the mannequin. It helps for the most part, but then I freeze up, remembering Sydney's lifeless body beneath me, or the feel of my knife cutting through Jerry's throat.

Claws dipped in guilt have me in a chokehold, and I'm growing frustrated with myself. With *him*. I'm not like him. I can't just kill someone and… get over it.

I whip around, shooting daggers at him with my eyes instead of my hands.

"You're so unapologetic for what you've done. For how many people you've killed. How are you okay with that?"

"Why wouldn't I be?" he challenges, tilting his head with an amused grin. I'd say he looks like a cute puppy, but that would be a lie. He looks like a vicious beast that's been locked up too long and is ravenous. For me, in particular.

"I don't know—morals?" I say, like the answer is obvious. Because it is. "Guilt? Remorse?"

"The very people you want to kill are the founding fathers of society's morals. I killed their expectations of me, and then I sliced open their throats to show them that they would never control me. They will only ever answer for their crimes, and I have no problem being the executioner. If you don't want to do this, y—"

I slash my hand in the air, cutting him off. "Don't do that. Don't give me an out."

"It's not an out, it's an option. I want you to do whatever you can handle, Addie. If that means staying home, I support you. If that means going on a massive murder spree, I'll be right by your side, baby. You're still having nightmares about Sydney and Jerry, and carrying around that guilt for protecting yourself. If you can't learn to accept that, how will you accept taking anyone else's life? Because believe me when I say, this won't be self-defense from here on out."

"I don't know *how* to accept it, Zade. I feel like I'm justifying murder."

"Just like I 'justified' stalking you?" He puts air quotes around the word because we both know Zade was well aware of what he was doing and how wrong it was.

"Forcing a gun into that pussy and making you come all over it? Or all the other times you told me no, and I did it anyway?" he volleys back. The flush in my cheeks deepens, and my face burns from the reminder of that stupid gun. "Did I know it was wrong? Of course, I did. But it clearly didn't stop me from doing it. You need to figure out *your* morals, and what you're okay living with. Not what you've been taught, but what you feel in your gut."

"So, stalking and assaulting me is written in your book of morals?"

"No," he says, his smile widening. "I was obsessed with you from the moment I saw you. All those dark, twisted emotions I felt were the rawest form of who I am. I made the decision to show you that instead of concealing it. I never claimed to be a good person, little mouse, and that was something I decided I could live with. Just like murdering a bunch of pedophiles and human traffickers."

"I'm pretty sure the people you kill tell themselves the same thing you do to help them sleep at night," I comment dryly.

"I'm sure they do," he agrees easily, taking a step toward me. My breath hitches, but I stand my ground, even as his voice deepens sinfully, "And I'm sure there are many who claim to be good and honest, and that they would be willing to kill me for my crimes against you. But that's the difference. I've never made those claims."

A flush crawls up my face, warming my cheeks beneath his intense stare.

"You make it sound so easy to just be… bad."

"I've had a lot of practice."

He has, which raises more questions. I roll my lips, my pulse beating erratically, working up the nerve to ask the question on the tip of my tongue. I'm afraid of what might happen once I do.

I've explained to Zade before that it was going to take me time to get used to some things about him. And now that I've been through what I've been through… all those old feelings are resurfacing. Not the hate or the desire to get away but accepting and understanding his contradictions and skewed morals.

"So, what's been stopping you then?" I rush out.

Cocking his head, he waits. "From fucking me," I say bluntly. "You didn't stop before. What's stopping you now?"

He's silent for a few beats. "Because I wouldn't be able to live with myself," he murmurs, staring at me thoughtfully. "There would be a very different reaction this time around—you already know that."

I cross my arms, popping out a hip. "Would there?"

"Yes," he says firmly. "Do you think if I pinned you to the ground, you'd fight me at first only to end up grinding your pussy into my face because I've awakened something in you? Or do you think you'd fight like your life depended on it, only to end up mentally checking out from the trauma?"

I swallow, the truth tasting like dirt on my tongue.

"You will never hear me call myself a good man. Or kind. Or even honorable. There is very little left of that in me, and the truth is that it was never really there to begin with. I was born with a blackened soul and good intentions. And there is a difference between those who are needlessly evil and those who do bad things hoping that something good will come out of it. I'll let you decide for yourself which one I am."

He doesn't wait for me to answer—I get the distinct feeling that he wants me to think about it first.

He steps towards me, and my muscles instantly stiffen. That's when I realize I don't need to think about it at all. Trauma has a tight hold on me, but all I want him to do is hold me tighter.

"You want the simple answer, too?" he asks, his voice deepening, causing my pulse to skyrocket. "It's because I love you, Adeline Reilly. And I know you love me back. When I'm inside you, you won't be thinking of anything else but how to get me deeper. The only fear you'll taste is from a God sending you to heaven too soon."

My heart skids and comes to a crashing halt against my rib cage, giving out on me completely. My knees will be next, and that would be fucking embarrassing.

He grins, his gaze turning predatory. "That won't be the only fear I'll instill in you."

Slowly, he begins to circle me while I stand frozen. His heat presses into my back, and his breath warms the side of my neck. My fight or flight instincts are kicking in, and my control over it is slipping.

"You will always be the little mouse, and I will always hunt you. I'll patiently wait until you're ready for me to touch you, but make no mistake,

Adeline, it'll still hurt when I do."

An icy chill washes through me at his ominous words, colder than the ghosts who haunt this manor. Before, that might have scared me. Even more, after being hunted by the cruelest of humankind, I should be tired of it.

Yet I feel nothing but a small thrill and… comfort. Somehow, Zade has managed to warp our cat and mouse game. Now, I find solace in the knowledge that he will always find me. And knowing this… despite me not being quite ready for him yet—it makes me want to run.

Just so he can catch me.

With tension polluting the air, he grabs my hand, spins us around, and points the knife at the mannequin.

"Stop picturing all the people you want to kill and picture the people you have killed. Recreate that night in your head. Replay it over and over until stabbing that knife in their necks feels liberating."

It takes too long to pull my headspace away from the predator standing behind me, but eventually, I manage it.

The moment that night replays in my head, I want to curl in on myself. Remembering how I plunged that pen into Sydney's body until the life was snuffed from her eyes. Or slashing my knife across Jerry's neck and watching his eyes bug from his head.

I was protecting myself. Yet, I still carry their deaths on my shoulders as if they were innocent.

For the next hour, I continue to struggle. I'm growing frustrated with myself and picking myself apart to figure out *why* I feel guilty, particularly over Sydney. Is it because she was a victim too? She was forced into the same things I was, enduring the brutality of sex trafficking that ultimately sent her into a psychotic break.

Over and over, I turn it in my head until it clicks.

Sydney may have been deranged, but she was broken too. She deserved my sympathy, but that doesn't excuse her from her actions. It doesn't give her the right to hurt other people. And it doesn't mean I was wrong for ending her life.

Though, with Jerry, Claire, Xavier, and all the others who decided I was nothing more than an object—they don't deserve anything more from me than what they've already stolen. Not my sympathy, remorse, or guilt. It wasn't my decision to be raped and brutalized, but it *is* my decision to slit their throats for it.

As I come up to the second hour, going through the movements with Zade becomes natural. Sliding the knife into the dummy's neck feels just as he said it would. Liberating.

Others may believe it is never okay to take a life under any circumstances. We are not the judge. At one point, I might have even believed that, too. But then I came face-to-face with true evil. People who are not human at all, but vile *things* that will continue to destroy this world and anything good that inhabits it.

Now, I realize that choosing to look the other way and let *God handle it* is a fucking cop-out. It's allowing evil to continue to live because they believe the afterlife is scarier.

If it's so scary, then why wait to send them there?

Now, I realize it's selfish. They're too fucking scared about making it into heaven to condone murder, even if it saves innocent women and children's lives.

Doesn't that make them just as evil?

Condemning those who are capable of being the executioner doesn't make them better people. It makes them compliant.

By the time the third hour passes, I'm panting heavily, sweat pours down my face and back, and I feel invigorated.

When I face Zade again, it feels as if I'm viewing him from a different set of lenses. I wonder if he sees me differently, too, and if he'll be able to let go of who I used to be and love the person I've become.

"Adeline, I feel as if this house is taxing your mental health," Mom announces with finality, brushing off imaginary lint on her Calvin Klein jeans. It's not very often I even see her in anything other than a dress, skirt, or pantsuit.

I feel so special.

"Why do you say that?" I ask, voice monotone and un-fucking-interested. I'm rocking in Gigi's chair, staring out at the gloomy landscape. It's storming today, and the windows are foggy from the rain. I tilt my head, fairly certain I'm seeing a handprint forming on the window.

Aside from the creepy hand, sitting here brings back a sense of comfort and nostalgia. Where a different version of myself would stare out the window, my shadow lurking in the darkness and watching me. Where I loathed every second of it, yet I would war with the fact of not knowing if I hated it because I was scared or if I hated it because I enjoyed it.

"Honey, have you seen the circles under your eyes? You can hardly miss them. They're very dark. And on your birthday, no less."

This is my mother being sweet. Caring. Concerned. And frankly, it's fucking exhausting. She's been trying harder to… I don't know—fix things with me or something—since I've come home. Of course, my father has no interest in joining her efforts, but I can't find it in me to care.

Her daughter getting kidnapped must've made her realize a thing or two about the state of our relationship and how utterly in shambles it was—*is*. Whose fault it is, I'm sure she'd have a different response depending on her mood.

But she's trying. Therefore, it's only fair that I try not to kick her out of the house. On my birthday. I'm already exhausted, and it would seem my dark circles are showing now.

Zade woke me up to my bedroom covered in roses and a gorgeous black knife with purple weaved throughout the handle. I'm getting better at handling them, but it's a work in progress and his present was a testament to his faith in me.

Then, Daya wanted to do brunch, and now Mom is here and I'm ready for a nap. People-ing is still tiring.

"Concealer will fix it."

"Maybe you should come stay with me again. Get away from that... *heathen*—" I snort, which then turns into a full-out laugh. Something about my mother calling Zade a heathen is just... well, funny. True, but funny.

My mother is gaping at me as if I've told her I'm shaving my head bald and going to live the rest of my life in a van and smoking hookah.

Doesn't sound so bad, actually. Except maybe the going bald part.

I bite my lip to hold in the laughter, grinning while she only grows more ruffled.

"I don't see how shacking up with a criminal is funny," she mutters, turning away with an affronted look on her face.

"What if *I'm* the criminal?" I question.

She sighs. "Adeline, if he has coerced you to do something..."

I roll my eyes. "He hasn't made me do anything, Mother, chill. And I'm fine. Really. I went through something traumatic—obviously—and sleeping doesn't always come easy to me."

She shifts on the leather couch, gearing up to say something else, but I cut her off. "And I'm good here. In Parsons Manor."

Her mouth shuts, a frown tugging down her pink-painted lips. I sigh, a stab of guilt hitting me in the chest.

"Mom, I appreciate your concern, I do. But it's going to take me a while to get readjusted and back to normal." *Normal.* Saying the word feels like swallowing a handful of rusty nails. I'll never be normal. I don't think I ever was.

And if anyone could attest to that, it would be my mother—the woman who's called me a freak most of my life.

She's quiet for a moment, staring down at the checkered tile and lost in whatever hurricane is sifting through her skull and ready to come out of her mouth. I've always felt like storms rage through her head since her words were always so fucking destructive.

"Why didn't you tell me about him?" she asks quietly. She lifts her head to look up at me, her crystal blue eyes swirling with hurt. I can't decide if the sight of it twists the guilt deeper or if it makes me angry.

"Because you've never made me feel safe enough to tell you anything," I answer bluntly.

Her throat works, swallowing that bitter pill.

"Why... why did you need to feel safe to tell me about him, Addie?" she asks, her sculpted brows pinching. "I mean, if he were... normal, it shouldn't have been a big deal. If he were someone you met in a bookstore, or at one of your events, or even in a grocery store." She pauses. "Why did you need to feel safe?"

I roll my lips and turn back towards the window.

"Addie, does he hurt you?"

My neck nearly snaps from how quickly I turn back to her. "No," I say sternly, though that's not entirely true.

Did he hurt me? Yes, but not how she's thinking. He would never lay a finger on me out of anger. The type of pain Zade delivers is unorthodox, and while there's always been a part of me that enjoys it—it still hurts.

Yet, I crave it anyway.

"Then why?"

I sigh, debating on how much I should say. He kills people for a living? Too much. He stalked me? Would never live that one down, no matter how guilty she feels.

So, I just settle with the truth. The part that doesn't announce him as a psychopath with a bit of an attachment issue.

"He saves women and children from human trafficking, Mom. He's very deeply involved in that dark corner of the world."

She sucks in a sharp breath, her spine snapping straight and her eyes widening with outrage. "Is he the reason you were kidnapped?"

"No," I snap. "He is not why, and you need to remember that he *saved* me. I would not be here—be alive—if it wasn't for him."

She shakes her head in confusion, and asks, "Then why were you? If he's involved with the same people?"

I shrug, feigning a nonchalance I don't feel. "There were many factors, but none of them were his doing. That's all that's important."

She sighs, a sound of both frustration and acceptance. "Is he dangerous?"

"Yes," I admit. "But not to me. He loves me, and not only that, he loves me for who I am. *He's* never wanted to change me."

She flinches at the dig but refrains from defending herself this time.

"Just because he loves you, that doesn't mean he's good for you," she says with finality.

I purse my lips, considering that for a moment. "What is good for me then, Mom? You know best, right? A real stand-up guy that's a lawyer or doctor?"

"Don't be obtuse," she snips. "How about someone like a police officer, who only carries a gun because they're—"

"Protecting people," I cut in. "Because you think they're protecting people. You really want to get in that debate right now? And wouldn't you say Zade is doing the same? By rescuing innocent people from being kidnapped and enslaved?"

She tightens her lips, clearly still in disagreement but not willing to keep arguing. That's a first, but I don't expect it to last.

This time, I'm the one sighing. I throw myself back in the chair.

"I don't want to fight about him with you because it's not going to change anything. I know him better than you ever will, and if you want to hate him, fine. But do it where I don't have to hear about it," I say tiredly and resolutely.

I'm too exhausted to keep fighting with her. That's all we ever do, and it got old over a decade ago.

"Fine," she huffs, irritated and contrite. "Let me take you to a nice dinner for your birthday, at least. Can we do that? No talk about your boyfriend."

I stare at her, and the tightness in my chest eases a little. Smiling, I nod my head.

"That sounds good. Let me get ready."

I stand and head towards the stairs when she calls out, "Don't forget the concealer, honey. You need it."

April 7th, 2022

I think Mom could tell I was anxious to be out of the house again. Half way through the dinner, she finally broke down and made some comment about getting medication, and I told her that I'd rather smoke weed.

Of course, she broke her promise and asked if Zade is the one supplying me "the marijuana." I told her I'm the drug dealer, loud enough for the waiter to hear, so she chewed her food extra hard the entire dinner, irritated and ~~\[redacted\]~~ embarrassed by my jokes.

I got a kick out of it though. Eventually, she realized that and relented, laughing with me when the waiter wrote his phone number on the reciept.

She thinks he wants sex. I think he just wants free weed.

Well, maybe sex too. But definitely free weed.

Regardless, it felt good to laugh, and I have a feeling my mom will let me get away with a lot of shit now just to see me smile again.

And the fact that she's even putting in that effort, well... it makes me smile.

Chapter Twenty Seven
The Diamond

The sound of Francesca's heels rebound against the ceiling, sending my heart flying into my throat. Daya glances upward, unsettled by the sound but used to Parsons Manor's shenanigans.

I, on the other hand, am having a silent heart attack. I've been hearing those sharp footsteps since I've been home, and though they're not actually Francesca's, I think the wicked ghosts in this house know they haunt my nightmares and enjoy bringing them to life.

I curl my hands into tight fists to abate the shaking, racking my brain for something to distract me.

"Maybe I should just become a nun," I announce, causing Daya to pause mid-pour. She's filling up a glass of red wine, and it feels... weird. Like I shouldn't be standing here enjoying wine when I've murdered people and escaped sex trafficking.

We're sitting at my kitchen island, and I can't help but bask in the nostalgia. I was gone for two and a half months, but it feels like years. It's weird, but it feels good, too. To be here with her again, drinking like no time has passed at all.

Daya blinks at me, thrown off from my declaration, and slides the glass over to me. "I love you, but you wouldn't even last a day."

"Rude," I mutter, taking a sip of the wine. I cringe, the bitter taste invading my taste buds. I like my wine sweet, but it's what Daya had in her fridge.

"You want to become a nun because you can't tolerate touch in general, or touch from a man?"

I pick at a hangnail. "Men, which is proving very difficult with training. He has to touch me, and every time he does, I fucking panic, then waffle between freezing up and going ballistic."

After Zade and I agreed to take down the Society together a month ago, I felt something shift inside my chest. A purpose was born, and it serves to get me out of bed every morning and train.

But it's not a magical fix-all. I look at Zade, and I feel everything I felt after giving in to him. The magnetism, the connection, and the love. He's given me the space I so desperately need, even though I can see that it's killing him inside. While I feel guilty every time I pull away, I also feel relief.

But now I feel other things—things that I know have nothing to do with him, but with sex. The thought of it makes me want to vomit, and there's this fear ingrained in me that every time Zade shows me any affection, that's what it's going to lead to.

It played such a huge part in our relationship before I was kidnapped; it's difficult to train my brain to think it's going to be anything else. Zade is a flirt, and while he's made plenty of sexual remarks, he hasn't made a single attempt to seduce me.

"And then I get angry," I continue, frowning into my Merlot. "I lash out at him and say horrible things, and he just fucking takes it."

"Baby girl, it's going to take a while for you to work through your trauma. You have PTSD, as anyone would. Don't rush yourself."

"I think it'd be easier if I wasn't in love with him," I admit, circling my finger around the glass. It creates a soft sound that is soothing to the turmoil in my head.

"I still feel attraction, ya know? Like every time he touches me, I *want* to enjoy it. I just can't. He hasn't even made any advances. Nothing sexual, but that's where my head immediately goes, and then I'm right back in that house with Xavier."

"Did you talk to Zade about him?"

I take another gulp of Merlot before responding, "Yes. After we agreed to work together, we sat down, and I told him everything. Well… not *everything*. Not the gruesome details. But he knows the CliffsNotes of what I went through, and he explained how he found me. Talked about some brotherhood and told me all about Max."

A sadness cloaks her sage eyes, and I can tell she's anxious because she starts fiddling with her nose ring.

"Yeah, he… saved me, too. From Luke."

I reach over and grab her hand, squeezing tightly. Zade told me what happened with Daya, but I was waiting for her to bring it up to me first. If there's anything I understand, it's not wanting to relive certain things.

We've all been suffering in very different ways, yet the source of our pain is the same.

The Society. Claire.

Daya was the decoy to draw me out of Parsons Manor so Rio and Rick could kidnap me. Of course, Luke was the one to put her through hell, but none of that would've happened if it wasn't for Claire leading Max to believe that Zade killed his father, and then putting a target on my head. One that Max immediately jumped on, angry and intent on getting revenge.

"I'm so sorry, Daya. I'm so sorry he did that to you." My voice cracks by the last word, an unexpected rush of tears blurring my vision.

Daya covers her face, trying to hold in her own tears. "Goddammit, Addie," she snips without heat. "Don't you dare make me cry."

But it's too late, a sob hiccups from her throat by the last word. I scoot my chair closer to her and pull her into a hug; my own demons be damned. Her arms circle around my waist, and we both let go.

Grief pours out through the cracks while we hold each other, like two pillars falling together, both incapable of standing without the other's support.

By the time we pull apart, snot is running down my splotchy, red face, and I just know mascara is running down my cheeks. She's got drool on her cheek and makeup circles around her eyes. With how bloodshot they are, coupled with her dark brown skin, her light green eyes are almost startling.

Regardless, we both look ridiculous, and immediately we burst into laughter, which fades into another round of tears. In the end, neither one of us can tell if we're laughing or crying, but it feels good either way.

"My head hurts now," I croak, wiping my blackened tears away, and then I grab a tissue and loudly blow my nose.

"Drink more wine, it'll make it worse, but at least you'll be buzzed."

I laugh, taking a sip as she also blows her nose.

"Where is Zade, by the way?" she asks.

"I don't know, actually. After our training session, he dipped out pretty quickly, saying he had to take care of something. He didn't say what it was about, and I was too sweaty and mentally exhausted to care at that moment."

We both shrug it off. He could've realized we ran out of toilet paper and needed to replenish for all I know. I think if it were anything important, he would've said.

For the next hour, Daya and I finish off the bottle of Merlot and I'm pleasantly buzzed. I also decide that I'm going to have to be very careful with drinking from now on. It feels a little *too* nice, and I refuse to use it as a crutch.

I'd rather work through my trauma the healthy way. You know—by murdering Claire with my bare hands.

We're in the middle of laughing over a stupid video someone posted on social media when the front door bangs open, and two voices are snapping at each other.

One is Zade's. The other is a girl's.

Sage and caramel eyes meet in a collision of confusion, and *what the fuck*.

With a slight wobble, I stand up and make my way toward the front door. And then turn right back around, rushing for my friend when I see who Zade brought home.

"Daya, there's a crazy chick in the house. Run."

"What?" she asks, alarm in her tone.

"Don't call me crazy!" the girl screeches from the front, and I grimace. I've never had the pleasure of meeting her, and I was okay with living life without that pleasure.

Shoulders hiked up to my ears, I slowly pivot and watch Zade stalk toward me, appearing exhausted and annoyed. Behind him is the murderous girl who lurked behind the walls in Satan's Affair.

Sibel.

"Baby, we have a guest."

Glancing at the girl, I shift uncomfortably, unsure of how the fuck to respond.

Clearing my throat, I settle with, "I can see that."

Sibel is staring at Daya and me with a broad smile on her face. The last time I saw her, she was dressed as a doll with makeup that made it appear like her porcelain face was fissured.

While her chocolate brown hair is still piled high in pigtails, her face is bare of doll makeup. She would be beautiful if the unhinged look in her eyes wasn't so distracting. She looks exactly how she did on the TV after she was apprehended for murdering four politicians.

With Zade.

Except he was never caught for those murders.

"Ladies, this is Sibby," Zade introduces tiredly, waving a hand at her before coming over to my side. I tense as he nears, splitting my attention between watching the space between Zade and me close while keeping an eye on the crazy girl.

The four men she murdered doesn't even begin to scratch the surface of the number of people she's killed. For five years, she stayed in that haunted fair and went on a spree. Whoever she deemed as evil was killed in very gruesome ways.

I've had enough experience with murderous girls, and I really, really don't want any more.

She waves her hand animatedly at us, excitement twinkling in her brown eyes. Then she turns them to my house, slowly taking in Parsons Manor.

"Wow," she breathes. "It's creepy in here. This is so perfect." Her head whips back to me, and I'm not proud of the not-so-subtle flinch. "I hope you don't mind my henchmen and me staying for a bit," she says.

"There's more?" I ask Zade, turning to him with pinched brows.

He sighs.

"Some people say they're not real, but they are," Sibel explains, not looking the least bit ashamed of admitting she sees people that others can't see.

Zade meets my stare, a grin on his face.

"Sibby is crazy," he says.

She stomps her foot, shooting a glare at him. "I'm not crazy, Zade. Just because *you* can't see what I see, doesn't mean *I'm* the weird one."

I cock my head, completely baffled at how she's even here. Last I heard, she was locked up in a psych ward awaiting trial.

"She escaped," Zade supplies, noting the confusion on my face.

"Oh," I say, because I have no idea what the hell else to say.

"That's… good?" Daya chips in, sounding wholly unsure if that is actually good.

Zade sighs for the millionth time. "Sibby is on the Most Wanted list. She took matters into her own hands—" Zade pauses to send a scathing look her way— "and broke out of the psych ward. Considering she took the fall for something we both did, I felt that it was only fair I gave her a place to stay. *Temporarily.*"

She nods once, as if Zade summed up her entire life story perfectly.

"I'm going to take her back to my place. I'm not expecting you to let her stay here—"

"But it's so creepy here!" she exclaims, as if that's a good reason to stay. And well… it kind of is.

"—so, I'll be dropping her off soon. I just wanted you to properly meet her since I'm…" he trails off, glancing at her. "Stuck with her," he decides, turning to look back at me. "I'm most definitely stuck with her."

Sibel frowns, opening her mouth to say something, but Daya cuts in.

"Uh, wait a second, took matters into her own hands *how?*" she questions, sending Sibel a suspicious look.

"I killed my therapist," she answers, her smile dropping. "I didn't want to kill her. She smelled like pine trees, so she wasn't a demon. The first and last person I've ever hurt who wasn't deserving, I promise."

My mouth drops. "Zade," I whisper, my discomfort growing. Sibel looks to me, noting my deepening fear.

"Please don't be scared of me. You smell like the most wonderful flowers. I would *never* hurt you."

"She's not going to hurt you, baby," Zade reassures quietly. I look up to meet his gaze, mismatched eyes full of sincerity.

"I would've discussed this with you first, if I had any idea this was going to happen," he swears. "I was meeting up with Jay when the news broke that Sibby escaped. She happened to be hiding out in the area. Helicopters and shit everywhere. I went looking for her and found her trying to get into a sewer drain. It was a split-second decision."

"Okay," I say, offering a tight smile to let him know I'm not angry. Despite Sibel's presence being a little disconcerting, I understand why Zade made that decision.

She took all the blame for what they both did, and she never ratted him out. That's something very few people would do, especially when they owe you nothing. And that, I can respect the hell out of.

Sibel holds up a wicked, pink knife. "And he got my knife back! The police had it as a murder weapon, and Zade got it out for me."

"She was literally losing her mind over it, and didn't give me much choice," he clarifies dryly.

She shrugs, content with having her knife back regardless of how it happened.

I stare at her and toss around an idea in my head, a little hesitant but deciding it'd be easier for Zade to only be in one place. He's pretty much moved in with me, and it's been oddly comforting. The selfish part of me doesn't want to give that up.

"There's plenty of room here. Sibel can stay."

She yips loudly, bouncing on her toes and clapping her hands like a little girl. Her reaction makes me feel slightly better, only because it's a little cute.

"My friends call me Sibby," she says, and based on the eager look on her face, it seems like she's hoping I'll consider her as one.

"Or demon slayer," Zade cuts in. She pins him with a sassy look in response.

"Okay, Sibby. Welcome… home."

Her dark eyes snap back to me, pure delight radiating from them. A wide smile takes over her face, resuming her bouncing once again, and it eases my concern a little more.

"Addie, you don't have to do that."

I wave a hand. "It's fine. She said she's not going to hurt us, and if you trust her, that's enough for me."

He looks like he wants to kiss me, which makes me a little nervous, but he quickly smooths out his expression and offers me a simple, appreciative smile.

"The second you want her gone, she's out. No questions asked." While Sibby doesn't look too thrilled to hear that based on how she stops bouncing and glares at him, Zade clearly gives no shits.

I nod, the last of my tension bleeding out.

"Sibby is already really good at fighting. Partly because she's—"

"—*Not* crazy," she cuts in, narrowing her eyes.

Zade shoots her a look, one that says, *yeah, okay, and I'm Jackie Chan.* "Regardless, she can fight. She could help you with training."

My heart softens, hearing what he's not saying.

You can't stand my touch, so here's someone who can give you what I can't.

"Thank you," I whisper. Now more than ever, I'm frustrated with myself. I will take him up on that offer because I recognize it won't change overnight. But I vow to try harder, so I can give Zade what he deserves, too.

All of me.

Zade plops an ice pack on my shoulders, and I groan both from the freezing temperature and how good it feels. Training has been taking a toll on my body, but also in the best of ways. I'm stronger than I've ever been, and that feeling is addictive.

Since Sibby arrived a couple of weeks ago, I've only gotten better. She's smaller and moves with a quickness even Zade doesn't quite possess, and she's far more unpredictable.

We've been sitting around my kitchen island for the past several hours, working out the kinks of drawing Claire out of hiding. Not only did everyone in Francesca's house disappear, but she did, too. And now that Zade has me, there's not a damn thing in this world that's stopping him from finding her.

Zade believes the best way to locate her is through her lawyer, Jimmy Lynch. He's been working for Claire and her late husband for twenty-seven years, making him a trusted friend.

He also has a taste for children.

Last week, Zade was able to hack into his phone, noting the copious amounts of child pornography he has downloaded. So, he started pushing ads on the child porn sites Jimmy uses, waiting for him to take the bait. Unsurprisingly, he did, both on his phone and laptop over a period of three days.

Of course, Zade designed the virus, so unbeknownst to Jimmy, it was released on his devices as soon as he clicked on the ad. Within seconds, Zade was able to infiltrate his system and implement spyware on them.

From there, he watched the email interactions between him and Claire. While he could try to implement a virus onto Claire's computer through a phishing email, she's too intelligent for that, so Zade's only other option is to manipulate her into putting a drive into her computer, which will contain the virus. And our best way to do that is to create a massive lawsuit against her. It's common practice for lawyers to transmit information through drives, especially if there's a mass amount of evidence stacked against them.

Unfortunately for Claire, since she's gone into hiding, she's fired a lot of staff who've worked at her estate. Cleaning crew, a couple of chefs, and a groundskeeper. Evidently, she has no plans to return to her mansion—or to keep it.

Zade has spent the last week contacting these staff workers, asking them about their experiences, and ultimately encouraging them to sue Claire for workplace harassment as well as assault.

In return, Zade will offer his protection and money. Thankfully, they all agreed. Because honestly, their lack of safety and resources was the only thing keeping any of them silent. Mark sexually assaulted many of his employees and threatened to harm them and their families if they spoke out. And Claire was physically abusive and prone to getting violent when something didn't meet her standards.

They've already filed their lawsuits, so tomorrow, we'll be putting the second step of the plan into action by replacing Jimmy's drives with Zade's.

Once Zade has access to Claire's laptop, he's going to take his time watching her. In the meantime, we'll be focusing on our other goal.

"Francesca and Rocco are slimy little snakes," Daya informs us, ire in her glare as her fingers fly over the keyboard. "And Xavier is a pussy."

Daya is assisting us with tracking down my former captors—and rapists—while Jay continues to focus on Claire.

"Satellite image showed a red pickup truck parked in their driveway under Rocco's name. That hasn't been seen anywhere?" Zade asks, adding extra shredded cheddar on the mac 'n' cheese before sticking the casserole dish back in the oven to crisp. Seeing him doing something so domestic is… odd.

I never thought I'd see oven mitts on a stalker and professional killer, but here we are… All he needs is an apron, and I'd be convinced I've fallen down the rabbit hole and hit my head on a tree root.

Shit, I think I already have because now all I can imagine is Zade in nothing *but* an apron. That… shouldn't be enticing, yet it is.

"We found the truck abandoned in Northern California. From there, we lost track," Daya answers, unknowingly saving me from traveling down that dangerous road. I have a feeling that fantasy would've only gotten weirder.

"No street cams nearby?" I ask.

"Nope," she replies, popping the P. "They haven't made it this long by dumb luck. They know how to avoid cameras. I imagine the car they switched to has also been abandoned by now."

Zade nods, keeping silent as he processes the information. From here, I can see his inner gears turning.

"Since we can assume they're driving, look at cameras in gas stations in the surrounding area to start with. It'll take time but check in on anyone you deem suspicious. It's possible that they will stay hidden in the car and use a decoy to pump and pay. I'll get a few more of my men on it to help you. And while they're probably paying in cash only, it doesn't hurt to check if they used credit cards as well."

"Francesca is eventually going to have to use the bathroom," I chip in. "I mean, I honestly can't see her squatting on the side of the road or using a porta-potty. So facial recognition would be valuable."

"It would," Zade agrees, shooting me a small smile. I wrestle down the pride that wants to bloom throughout my body. My inner feminist doesn't need no man's approval.

"You can set up a facial recognition bot that'll alert you if any cameras spot her. Whether it's from restaurants, stores, or gas stations. We can't rely on it, though, because while Francesca is the one most likely to appear in public, she also has the advantage of disguising herself better than men. Facial recognition is advanced, but it's not foolproof."

I tip my head side to side in a *you have a point* gesture. "If anyone knows how to use makeup, it's her," I concede. She's had a lot of practice bringing the dead to life—with her own face and with the girls she held captive.

Daya's hands continue to fly, following Zade's directions without hesitation.

Sibby has her chin in one hand and drums her fingers on the table with the other—clearly bored. Her interests lie more in taking action than the planning aspect.

"I'll track down Xavier Delano," Zade says, shooting a loaded glance my way. "We should be able to find him easily. I have a good feeling he's not as smart about covering his tracks as the others."

"That'd be awfully egotistical of him. It's not like he didn't know that I was… uh, *with* Z… or whatever." Zade smirks over my stumble. I roll my eyes, intent on ignoring him, but then Daya betrays me and snorts, flicking her gaze at me with amusement.

Assholes.

The lot of them.

"Shut up," I snap. "I don't know what to label it."

"Fuck buddy?" Daya provides, but that doesn't sound quite right. The brow cocked on Zade's forehead tells me he feels the same.

"Lover!" Sibby chips in cheerfully.

My lip curls in disgust. Hate that label.

"Oh, admirer," Daya says, snapping her fingers as if she hit the nail on the head.

"One true love," Sibby sighs wistfully. She glances off to the side, seeming to listen to something before she rolls her eyes. "Okay, *five* true loves."

My eyes pinball between the two idiots as they continue to toss out words that could define mine and Zade's relationship.

"How about just stalker," I cut in dryly.

"Come on, baby, that's not what you were calling me when you were screa—"

"Shut *up*, or I'll start screaming other men's names and I promise I don't need your dick anywhere near me to do it."

Challenge sparks in his eyes, signaling that this conversation is quickly taking a nosedive.

"You really want to cause mass extinction for those names? Moan them, little mouse, I dare you. Whichever ones you choose, not a single man by that name will fucking exist anymore. How about we start with Chad? We can definitely live without the Chads in the world."

My mouth pops open. "That is so… excessive."

He shrugs, turning to take the mac 'n' cheese out of the oven, "Doesn't change a damn thing."

My wide eyes drift back down to Daya's, hers equally as rounded as mine. I give her a look that says, *you see what I have to deal with?* in which she returns, *good luck, Sister Susie.*

I look at Sibby and find her staring off into space, whispering to one of her henchmen about unsanitary ways to use the popsicles in the freezer.

Oh my God. I'm living with nothing but psychopaths.

I knew this but fuck me.

Hey, God? Do ya mind sending down some medication to correct your gross mishandling of these two demented souls?

Shaking my head, I turn to Zade, who is now serving the mac 'n' cheese on plates for us, alongside the steaks he cooked on the grill. Something I was surprised to learn—Zade can fucking cook.

"How long do you think it'll take to locate Xavier?"

"It depends on how accessible he is. I may find him within an hour, but if he's stationed on a remote island with an army surrounding him, it'll take time to get to him. Keep in mind that this man is stupid rich and has nothing better to spend his money on, so this is entirely possible."

I tilt my head in curiosity. "Richer than you?"

"Absolutely. I have no interest in collecting more than what's necessary. Money is an illusion, and a powerful one. It turns men into spineless assholes with no real regard for human life except their own. Xavier will use his money to protect himself. Especially because he's a little bitch and, well…" he peers up at me with a savage smile. "I'm pretty fucking scary."

He serves dinner, saving me for last. The hairs on the back of my neck rise as he approaches me; my body warming as he draws near. He crowds over me when he sets my plate down, the heat radiating from him sinking beneath my skin. Then, he leans down, and my brain short-circuits. I can't decide if I want to embrace the darkness or run from it.

Hot breath fans across my ear as he whispers, "Not only am I scary, baby, but I'm really, really angry. And when I'm angry, I'll make them pray for Hell."

A shiver rolls down my spine, and goosebumps spread across my body like the Black Plague. I tip my head towards him, meeting his stare. My pounding heart climbs into my throat, creating an erratic pulse in my neck, and a palpable tension circulates the space between us.

Against my better judgment, my eyes slide down to his mouth, thickening the tension. Deliberately, he skates his tongue across his lip, and like a magnet, my gaze latches on to the slow and sinful act.

By the time I force my eyes back up to his, my mouth is parted, and my lungs are deprived of oxygen.

"I hate to cut into this beautiful moment, but Sibby is taking her clothes off."

Daya's voice snaps me out of whatever trance Zade has pulled me into, and almost violently, my head whips towards Sibby.

Sure as shit, she's in the process of slipping off her neon green tights.

"Sibby!" I shout exasperatedly. "Stop taking your clothes off, we are not having a fucking orgy!"

April 28th, 2022

Not to be dramatic, but I'd rather watch Rocco kill a prositute again than listen to Sibby have sex with her henchmen. I think it bothers me because she's so free with sex, and I'm... not. Not anymore at least.

I think it reminds me how fucking broken I am.

Maybe because I was in a house where people killed prostitutes.

The woman accidentally grazed her teeth on his dick. That's why she died. We were doing another lesson, and this time, we had to learn how to pleasure our masters with other women. We needed to learn *teamwork*. They brought in prostitutes all the time for lessons, but this one was scared. She saw what was happening, and couldn't keep her teeth from chattering.

The woman was giving Rocco a blowjob one second, the next, her teeth were quite literally on the fucking floor. He punched her so hard, it knocked her two front teeth out. Of course, OBVIOUSLY, blood was spilling from her mouth, and it got on him, and that pissed him off more.

So he whipped out a gun and shot her in the head.

He was going to make us bury her body, but Francesca stepped in and said we couldn't get blisters on our hands.

How nice of her.

Chapter Twenty Eight
The Hunter

I pinch the bridge of my nose and wonder how much Tylenol it's going to take to kill a Sibby-induced headache.

She's currently in a fucking argument.

With her goddamn self.

"Mortis, I *told you*, the police are looking for me everywhere. We can't go outside for a walk, or to get some alone time—we're trapped!"

She quietens, listening to whatever her imaginary boyfriend is telling her.

A disgruntled sound leaves her throat. "I miss those things, too, but this is the way things have to be. Timmy—stop trying to take my clothes off in front of Zade!"

"If you do that, I will literally lose my shit," I snap, shooting her a murderous look. I'm already two seconds away from losing it anyway. Her eyes snap to mine, wide with innocence.

"It's not *my* fault!" she screeches. She points her finger to a random spot, assumingly where she thinks the culprit is. "It's his."

Groaning, I rub my hands over my face roughly. The whole argument started because Sibby wanted to be the one to plant the USB drives in Jimmy Lynch's office. I simply reminded her she couldn't be seen, and the conversation took off in a different direction.

Apparently, her henchmen wanted to go to some fucking sex shop a few blocks from Jimmy's office. I said no, and here we are.

Seeing her in her element, fully believing that her henchmen are real despite people telling her they're not, it's as fascinating as it is sad.

I know her childhood was horrific—so much so that she created people to keep her company and get her through something incredibly difficult. A young girl that's known nothing outside of a diabolical cult, wandering a strange city aimlessly, all alone.

Her brain was protecting itself, and the henchmen were born.

"It's cold outside today. We can bundle you up in winter clothing, and no one should notice you," I reason with her. "But you *cannot* go anywhere else. No detours. No pit stops. Nothing. Not unless you want to end up in the psych ward again."

She looks off in the distance. "You hear that, Mortis? So, don't try to convince me to be bad. I'll get locked up again, and you'll never see me for the rest of your life."

He must agree with her because she turns to me, a satisfied smile on her face. "We're all in agreement. Don't worry about me, Zade. You can trust me."

"You know what? I believe you, demon slayer."

Her answering grin lights up her entire face. And I realize that Sibby is a beautiful girl.

I hope to God she finds something real one day.

"You look fucking ridiculous," I state dryly, looking her over with a critical eye.

She stares at me like I've personally wounded her.

"Why?" she asks, dropping her gaze to her outfit.

She looks like a fucking Cheetos puff, but in bright neon pink. She's wrapped in several layers of clothing, with a massive puffer jacket three sizes too big, ending at her ankles and barely concealing the yellow polka-dot rain boots. To top it off, she's been doing her makeup again, however, she has shied away from the broken doll look. I suppose it was too raw of a wound. Thankfully, Addie has been teaching her how to properly apply it, and it wouldn't be half bad if it weren't for the monstrosity of a fucking outfit.

I allowed Sibby to do some online shopping soon after she arrived, and it turns out, she has no idea what size she is nor how to dress herself.

She's only ever worn the clothes provided to her by her father and the costumes Satan's Affair had in their houses. So, she just ordered a bunch of random shit in whatever size, most of it ill-fitting.

Sibby is tiny. Her stature only comes to about five-two, and she has very little meat on her bones. Addie glances at me, regret on both of our faces for not monitoring her while she shopped.

"Literally, everyone is going to notice you. You're supposed to blend in, not stand out like a sore thumb."

Her brows pinch. "You're saying I look like someone's thumb?"

Addie bites her lip. "Let's trade jackets. You can wear mine, Sibby."

Sibby grumbles but ultimately switches with her. Addie slides on the hot pink puffer and zips it up, the coat not fitting her any better. The grin that slides on my face is nearly slapped off the second Addie spots it.

She points a finger at me, the material swishing from the movement. "I will fuck you up."

"It's cute, baby," I say, grinning wider when she narrows her eyes, giving me a look that promises death and destruction.

I'd love to see her try.

I grab a black beanie and slide it over Sibby's head and then wrap a thick, black scarf around her neck to help conceal the bottom half of her face, feeling every bit like a father dressing their child.

Despite her wanted status, she's the least recognizable, aside from Daya. And as much as I would prefer Addie's best friend instead, Sibby was very excited about being helpful. She's been cooped up in the manor for the past month, going even more insane than she already is.

It was vital we get her out of the house before she says fuck it and openly fucks her imaginary henchmen on the dining room table. She's already come close to it, and Addie and I were both deeply traumatized by that event.

I hand her a Bluetooth and instruct her on how to use it, sighing when she asks if her henchmen can have one, too. She claims they'll get worried if they can't hear what's happening.

"You know they can't all come, right?" I remind her. She twists her lips and nods.

"Mortis and Jackal are gonna come this time. So only they need one."

I indulge her and hand over two more, which she promptly passes to empty air, the devices dropping to the ground. I'll have to pick those up when she's not looking.

When she smiles, satisfied, I move on to the body cam, hooking it to her coat and adjusting it to make sure it's at a good angle.

"Don't touch this. I need to see everything you're doing. I'll be in your ear guiding you, so listen to everything I say," I tell her sternly.

She waves a hand, and giggles. "I know. You don't have to worry, Zade. I promise I'm not going to run off."

"Or murder someone," Addie grumbles from beside me.

Sibby looks to Addie. "If a demon is around, I'll let that one go. I can sacrifice one or two if it means taking out the biggest one of them all."

Good enough for me. As long as she listens.

After she's set to go, Addie stuffs herself into the passenger seat next to me, and we drive to Jimmy's office, forced to park a couple of blocks away. Sibby will have to walk the rest of the way, and this is the part I'm the most worried about. She's bundled up and hardly recognizable beneath all the material, but Sibby has a definite… uniqueness to her.

Which she instantly proves when she hops out of the backseat, slams the door, and starts skipping down the sidewalk like a goddamn buffoon.

I groan, swiveling my laptop towards me and pulling up the live feed from her body cam. Addie leans into me to get a better view of the screen, enveloping me in her sweet jasmine scent. I inhale deeply, tempted to take a bite out of her just because she smells divine.

Soon. I'll do that soon.

Her face is twisted into a mixture of amusement and concern.

Concern for the mission or concern for Sibby's mental state, it's hard to tell.

Addie has softened to Sibby, though. While still wary of her—which is the smartest thing to be—I think she sees Sibby for who she is. A lost girl looking for love and friendship. Even when she's talking to her henchmen or irrationally angry because I ate the last Pop Tart—Pop Tarts

I bought, by the way—she's sweet, incredibly loyal, and pretty funny.

I still don't know what the hell we're going to do with her yet, but I'll figure it out after Claire is taken care of.

Sibby is still skipping down 5th Avenue, earning looks ranging from *I see this shit every day* to *I'm so tired of seeing this shit every day*. She's not the slightest bit perturbed by the negative attention.

I suppose she's used to it.

Finally, she makes it to the block Jimmy's office is on. Instead of continuing straight, she turns right and heads down a side street so she can get to his office from the rear entrance.

There's not a lot of foot traffic on that side, making it a little less likely for her to be caught.

When she makes it to the door, she pauses, waiting for my signal. Jimmy has great alarm systems for an unruly teenager, but for me, it's like breaking past a saltine cracker. His defense system crumbles beneath my fingers and within ten seconds, I'm giving Sibby the go-ahead.

She bends and starts picking the lock, making quick work of it, and opening the door moments later.

The office building isn't very big, and I have the blueprints already pulled up on my computer.

"Turn left," I direct when she comes up to a dead end. She does as I ask, making her way down a short hallway before it opens up to the receptionist area.

The obnoxiously large wooden desk smack-dab in the middle of the room is empty, Jimmy's name displayed across the front. In case anyone was lost and wasn't sure where they were, I guess.

The area is extravagant. Shiny white tile floors, gray walls, and plants placed around the room to bring life to it.

"Go past the desk. You see that door with Jimmy's name on the plaque? That's his office."

"Isn't his name all over the entire building?" she gripes. Addie snorts from beside me, listening in on the call with her own Bluetooth earpiece.

Sibby jiggles the door but finds that it's locked, and no keyhole in the handle.

"Give me a second," I say, opening my program to check the security system within the building. He has an automated lock on his door that can only be opened through the app on his phone.

I roll my eyes. Shit like this is so tacky and such a waste of money. Fancy security systems like these appear advanced, but really, it's incredibly easy to hack into the app and unlock the door.

Pathetic, but it benefits me nicely.

"It's open," I confirm.

Quickly, she creeps into the room and shuts the door behind her.

"Is it safe to turn on a light?" she asks, her voice slightly muffled from the scarf.

"Yes, but use the flashlight I gave you," I tell her. His office faces the backside of the building, but you can never be too sure.

He's currently at a dinner with some colleagues and on his way to getting toasted on overpriced whiskey. I have Daya keeping an eye on him while I ensure that Sibby has no unexpected surprises. All it takes is an employee showing up because they forgot something.

She flips on her flashlight, displaying Jimmy's ostentatious office.

"Does he seriously have his name engraved into his own desk?" Addie asks beside me, her tone dry.

"Maybe he's a proactive boss and has reminders everywhere in case anyone gets early-onset Alzheimer's and forgets his name."

"I think that would be a blessing if I had to work for him."

Sibby travels farther into the office, looking around at the several filing cabinets.

"Where does he keep the jumpers?" she asks. Another snort from Addie.

"Jump drive," I correct, though I'm not even sure why I bother. I've told her what they're called a million times, and she still calls them that.

"They could be in his desk. It has his name on it in case you're confused about where it is."

"I'm not confused, silly," Sibby giggles.

Addie and I look at each other, grins on our faces. Sarcasm gets lost on her sometimes.

We watch Sibby approach his desk, the cherry wood gleaming, not a speck of dust in sight.

Everything has its own place atop it, arranged neatly and positioned in straight lines. Either Jimmy or his cleaning service has OCD.

She tugs on the top drawer, groaning dramatically when it sticks.

"He locks his own drawers?" she whines.

"Just pick the lock," I tell her calmly, praying she doesn't throw a tantrum and start stabbing the leather computer chair with the letter opener.

Sighing, she rifles through her jacket pocket before pulling out her kit and getting to work, grumbling to herself the entire time.

It takes her all of fifteen seconds to get it unlocked, and I'm tempted to ask her if it was as big of a deal as she made it out to be. But I'd rather not risk her getting angry. There have been quite a few dishes broken over the last month—unnecessarily. She has no idea how to regulate her emotions, but it's something I've been working on with her.

She slides open the door, finds a basket of drives and gets to work by replacing them with mine while stuffing his in her coat pocket. Later, I'll pick through them on a spare laptop to see if there's anything of value.

Next to me, Addie unzips the puffer jacket and nearly rips it off, a sheen of sweat on her forehead. She glances at me, and then crosses her arms.

"Don't stop on my account, little mouse."

"I feel like you're making it super-hot in here on purpose," she grumbles, reaching forward to turn down the heat.

"If I wanted your clothes off, I would just remove them myself."

She arches a brow. "You're saying you currently don't want them off?" she challenges.

The tips of my mouth curl, and I make sure to keep my gaze slow and blazing as I sweep it down her body. If she thinks the car is overheating her, I'll show her how hot I can make her with one look.

She flushes brightly, red staining her cheeks as she shifts, those thick thighs clenching. My cock hardens painfully in my jeans, picturing them wrapped around my head instead. She likes to try and suffocate me between them, but I would gladly die between her thighs.

"Quit being inappropriate," she snaps, her caramel eyes wide.

She's so goddamn beautiful, it hurts. Especially when she's angry.

"Impossible," I murmur, but I leave her be for now, turning my attention back to the screen.

Sibby places the basket of drives back in the drawer, softly shuts it, then relocks it with her picks. Afterward, she heads for the door.

"Did you need me to get anything else?" she asks. Before I can say anything, she barks, "Jackal, quit touching things. You're going to get us in trouble."

"Sibby, focus," I snap.

"Sorry," she mutters, but not before hissing out another demand to Jackal. Nothing is actually being touched, but if Sibby believes it is, she might try to fix it and then actually mess something up.

It's vital that Jimmy doesn't notice anyone's been in his office, even more so with it being so tidy. He might get paranoid and forgo using any of the USB drives.

I'll completely wipe the cameras, but you can't wipe physical evidence so easily.

"You did great, Sibby. Leave the room. Don't touch anything else."

"It wasn't me touching things—*yes*, I'm telling on you, Jackal. You're the one acting like an idiot."

Addie stifles a smile, and I decide that while Sibby is a complete pain in my ass, she's good for Addie. She makes us all feel a little more… normal.

Sibby makes her way out of the building without a hitch, up until she rounds the corner and smacks right into someone's chest.

The bodycam is knocked off, the camera rolling so only the sidewalk can be seen.

"Sibby?" I ask, my heart rate kicking up a notch. Her face is plastered all over the country. News outlets, social media, and so forth. If this person recognizes her, we're fucked.

"Oh, shit," the guy says, his voice muted. "Are you okay, miss?"

"That really hurt," Sibby groans. "You smell like a berry tree, though, so I'll let it slide."

"Oh, no," Addie whispers. "Sibby, you can't say stuff like that. It's known that you associate your victims with smell."

Sibby quietens, which allows us to hear the man's response clearly.

"What an odd thing to say."

"I am an oddball," Sibby says in a strained laugh. He must help her up based on the grunt and ruffling sound.

"Thank you for helping me," she says, a hint of nervousness in her tone.

"Yeah, of course. Guess I should look where I'm going next time," he responds easily. Some of the anxiety seizing my chest lessens until I hear him speak again.

"Hey, do I know you from somewhere?"

"No, I'm new to town," Sibby says. Her voice hardening.

"Stay calm," Addie says softly.

"Man, you look so familiar. You don't have any family around here?"

"I'm from the East Coast, silly. But I have to go, see ya!"

"Don't rush," I tell her.

"He's still staring at me," she informs, her breathing escalated. "Mortis was probably freaking him out. People don't take kindly to them outside of the haunted houses. Not used to their makeup and all that."

"I'm sure Mortis was fine," Addie assures, staring intently at the computer, even though the camera was left behind.

Luckily, it only takes her a few more moments to get to the car. She swings open the door and nearly dives into the backseat with a relieved sigh.

I waste no time backing out of the parking space. For several tense minutes, everything is quiet. But in typical Seattle fashion, we're balls deep in traffic and getting even a few blocks away takes more time than I'd like. Just as Addie releases a relieved sigh, convinced we're in the clear, a cop car rings their sirens from a couple blocks down, followed by flashing lights.

"Shit," I mutter, confident that we're the target. We're both trapped between cars, but already the other vehicles are starting to veer to the side to let the cop through.

That man did fucking recognize her. He must've called the police as soon as she left. And as luck would have it, an officer happens to be too fucking close.

"They might not know what car she got into," Addie assures, yet her voice betrays her nerves.

Just as the words leave her mouth, the cop's voice blares from their loudspeaker, naming my make and model and demanding I pull over.

"Okay, scratch that," she says, her tone pitching with fear. I glance at her, noticing how she clenches her thighs again, her nipples hardening beneath her long-sleeved shirt. Fright is palpable on her face, sweat beading alongside her hairline.

Her body responds to fear like metal does to electricity. When she's at the mercy of the currents, she comes alive.

I smirk but keep my mouth shut considering Sibby is in the backseat, and I have a cop about to ride up and raw dog my asshole. I need to focus, and I have a feeling Addie is going to test my discipline.

It's not the first time I've been in a car chase, but it's the first time I've had to worry about someone else's life other than my own during one.

"Hold on, ladies," I say. The cop car rushes right up on me, continuing to shout demands over the loudspeaker.

I take one second to look both ways before whipping my car into a U-turn and speeding off.

The police car quickly follows suit, almost bashing into oncoming traffic and narrowly missing an SUV.

"He sucks already," Sibby comments, completely turned around as she watches our pursuer from the back window.

"I got in a car chase, too, you know that?"

"I do," I say, gritting my teeth when I take a turn a tad too fast. My Mustang tilts on one side before dropping back down on all fours, causing Addie to gasp and dig her nails into my leather seat, followed by a little whimper in her throat.

This... this is actually Hell. If we were alone, I'd drive with one hand and reach over and take care of her with the other. I'm tempted to do it anyway, but I know Addie wouldn't appreciate the little demon slayer in the back witnessing it.

I straighten the car and then take another turn down a side street. Soon, the entire city will be flooding with police cars, with my make, model, and license plate broadcasted across their radios.

I have an extremely small window not only to lose them but get back to Addie's before I'm spotted again.

"It didn't go very well," Sibby shares, unbothered by our current situation.

"Mine didn't either," Addie grits out.

"You're safe with me, little mouse," I say, my attention snagged on a cop car barreling down a side street toward us.

My bloodstream is drowning in adrenaline, yet my muscles are languid and loose as I weave through traffic and take odd turns. Within minutes, several officers are coming at me from all directions.

I call out to Jay several times, but he doesn't answer.

Just as I'm getting ready to lead the cops straight to his house, he comes onto the speaker. "I go take a shit for five minutes, and you're in a high-speed car chase when I come back," he says with exasperation.

"A man knocked into Sibby on her way out and recognized her. Called the cops, and here we are."

I hear a flood of sirens in all directions, and my leather groans beneath Addie's nails, her chest heaving. Her eyes are dilated with fear and pinging in every direction.

"I got a drone tracking you down now," he says. "I'll tell you where to turn."

She shifts again, rubbing her thighs together and making throaty little noises.

Goddamn it.

"Addie, baby," I say, glancing her way.

"Yeah?" she croaks, her wide eyes locked onto the road.

"I'm going to need you to stop distracting me."

Her mouth parts, and she meets my flickering gaze, half of my attention on the road, the other half on my girl.

"I'm not doing anything," she insists, yet her flushed cheeks and hard nipples say otherwise.

Sibby pops her head through the seats, swiveling her head back and forth between us.

"My henchmen are already uncomfortable back here as it is," she says, giving us an evil eye. "If you're going to be doing dirty things, make sure all of us can join in."

Addie covers her red face. "Oh, my God, Sibby. First off, we're not doing anything. Secondly, even if we were, you would *not* be joining us."

Sibby appears affronted by that news as I take another sharp turn. Jay tells me to turn left a second later, sending the car careening to the side again.

"Well, that's not very nice," Sibby remarks.

"Sibby, not everyone likes to have group sex like you," I bite out, in disbelief that we're even having this conversation right now.

Her head whips to me, her brown eyes wide. "Really? Why? It's so much fun!"

Addie shakes her head. "Maybe for *you*. Zade already has a long list of heads to rip off for seeing me naked as it is."

"Damn right," I agree distractedly, listening to another direction from Jay. The sirens are beginning to fade as I gain more and more distance between us.

Until one comes racing out from a side street, nearly hitting the back end of my Mustang.

I growl out, "Jay. Warning next time?"

"Shit, sorry, my brother came in asking if I could order pizza."

Jesus fucking Christ.

"Zade, you really should consider letting Addie explore."

"Hey, demon slayer?" I prompt. "I'm going to need you to be quiet now."

She huffs, but ultimately sits back down in her seat. I still hear her whisper, "He's such a possessive dickhead. I'm glad you guys like to share me."

Addie muffles a smile by biting her lip, almost distracting me enough to go flying into a ditch. That's it. I'm doing this shit by myself from now on.

I have my writhing girlfriend next to me, and a horndog in the backseat who's testing my patience. I swear to God, if she makes a move on Addie, I'll kick her little ass.

Another cop car comes sweeping out fifty feet in front of me, nearly colliding into oncoming traffic. They right themselves before heading straight towards me. They're trying to fake me out by making me think they're not going to move. They like to do that to force people's hands. But the dumbass doesn't realize there's a side street coming up, and I have really good fucking control over this car.

"You see the street?"

"Yep."

"Once you go down that road, take a right and two lefts directly after. You should lose them all after that."

Addie's hand reaches out, clutching my arm as her back presses deeper into the seat as if that's going to save her.

"Zade," she groans, her eyes wide.

"I got it, baby girl," I reassure gently. I stomp on the brakes and whip the wheel to the side, perfectly fitting my Mustang in the small alleyway. The car fishtails a little, but I easily regain control. Seconds later, the cop car goes careening into the side of a building, failing to accomplish what I just did.

I follow Jay's directions afterwards and take the turns he directed me to. Just as he said, I lose them all. I expect helicopters are going to be here any second, so I stomp on the gas. Parsons Manor is ten minutes away, but I make it there in three. They're going to be searching for my car, but luckily, I can fit my Mustang in the trees until it's safe to get rid of it.

I come to a hard stop right past the tree line, forcing Addie and Sibby to catch themselves from pitching forward.

Silence descends, broken periodically by Addie's heavy breathing. The sun is dipping low below the Bay, the light slowly drowning beneath the surface.

"Did we die?" she squeaks.

Sibby leans forward again. "You're silly. If you're still breathing, that means you're alive." She sniffs loudly. "And you still smell as pretty as ever."

Addie's wide eyes drift to her, shock bleaching the color from her face. If heat wasn't rolling off her in waves and turning my dick into granite, I'd laugh.

"Sibby, exit the vehicle please," I tell her sternly. She rolls her eyes but listens, herding her imaginary men out of the car before slamming the door shut.

"You're safe?" Jay asks through the phone.

"We're good," I say. "Thanks, man. I'll call you soon."

Disconnecting the call before he can get another word out, I train my gaze on Addie. She seems to stiffen further under my stare, and I'd be lying if I said that didn't excite me.

Without looking away, I find the lever on the side of my seat and crank it, allowing me to slide it all the way back. She jumps, the soft leather groaning beneath her fingers again, while her gaze bounces around. Likely determining how quickly she can get out of the car before I pounce.

The tension is incredibly thick, and my dick is pressing firmly against the zipper of my jeans. It fucking hurts, but I welcome the pain.

"Come here," I order roughly.

"Zade…" Her husky voice trails off, uncertainty polluting her decision. She teeters between listening to my command and making a run for it.

Fuck, I hope she does run. God knows how much I love to chase her.

She must remember this because she swallows, and with unsteady movements, she crawls onto my lap. Tendrils of her cinnamon hair fall over my shoulders and chest as she adjusts herself, settling lightly on my thighs. I know she can feel me between her legs, proven by the sharp inhale.

For now, I keep my hands to myself. She's choosing to touch me—to get close to me—and I know it's only because she's still in the throes of fear and adrenaline from the car chase. It's the same combination that drove her to fight me at every turn while burning and writhing beneath my touch. The second she comes down, reality will smack her upside the head, and she will go back to cowering from me.

I want to remind her how good it feels. Give her something to latch on to when she's too lost in her head and can't find her way past the demons screaming at her.

My fingers drift through the curtain of hair hiding us from the outside world, strands lacing around my fingers. It's dark in here now, and the cool April air is seeping through the cracks. The water ate the sun, and I wonder if she'll let me devour her, too.

She grips either side of my seat, once more digging her nails in deep, and I feel an irrational surge of jealousy that they're not clawing into me instead.

"Closer, little mouse," I whisper. "I need to feel if you're real, and not just another ghost haunting Parsons Manor."

A shaky exhale skitters across my cheek as she relaxes her body into mine until every inch of her is molded into me. I can feel every beat of her heart drumming against my chest, syncing to mine in a ballad of longing and sorrow.

One of her hands releases the seat, moving to the center console, in search of something. My brows jump in surprise when she produces a cigarette and my black lighter.

Then, she grabs my hands and places them on her backside. "You have until this cigarette burns out to touch me."

I grin, delighting in her ultimatum. She'll expect me to squeeze her tits and run my hand across her cunt, but she's wrong. I'm not a pussy-deprived teenager that doesn't know restraint any better than he knows how to last more than thirty seconds.

I'll touch her in all the places that won't feel good enough. Her inner thighs and up to where they meet her ass, and her tiny waist up to her ribs and the side of her tits. When she's left with nothing but the taste of ash on her tongue, I'll show her that regret tastes worse.

She turns her chin towards the window, but keeps her stare pinned to me as she sticks the cigarette between her lips and lights it, the flame dangerously close to my face. The flare brightens her unusual light brown eyes, creating a startling effect beneath the flickering orange light. Shadows dance across the lines of her face, darkening the freckles on her cheeks.

At that moment, I decide she can't be real, and that I've gone mad just like the little doll who used to haunt the inside of the walls.

I'm ready to set this entire car on fire, content with watching it burn around us if it means I can stare at her beneath the blazing glow. The flame goes out, casting us back in darkness, only the glimmer of moonlight allowing me to see her shadowed curves.

The cherry flares as she sucks in and then softly exhales, smoke whirling between us. My eyes are riveted on her mouth, desperate to see those lips wrapped around me instead.

"Am I tangible, or will you let me slip through your fingers like the smoke from this cigarette?" she asks, her voice raspy. Every single nerve ending lights up from how sensual she sounds.

Instead of allowing me to answer, she twists her hand and sticks the cigarette between my lips. The burn from the nicotine and menthol spreads down my throat and into my chest. She pulls it away and leans forward, brushing her parted lips against mine.

My hands begin to move, whispering across her ribs, causing her to shiver as I flutter them down to her hips, squeezing firmly before sliding to her inner thighs.

I exhale, the smoke trading from my mouth to hers before swirling out between the crevices. She doesn't kiss me, but remains suspended above me and allows the smallest of brushes.

Then, she's retreating again, inhaling the cigarette once more. Back and forth, she twists it between us, periodically ashing through the cracked window. My hands never pause, though it only took moments before she began to tremble.

The air crackles around us, and it's clear that I don't need to set this car on fire when our chemistry is like dynamite and burns everything around us.

"Our mouths are touching the same spot," she says shakily. "Does that count as kissing?"

"You tell me, little mouse. When I make you cry out for God, does that count as praying?"

Her bottom lip curls beneath her straight teeth, and a growl forms deep in my chest.

"If you're showing me where to bite, I can assure you those sweet lips will only be the beginning."

She doesn't deign me a response right away and puffs on the cigarette again, then ashes it.

"Would you make me bleed?" she asks, her voice hoarse as the smoke swirls around us.

"If you ask me to," I murmur. "I'd prefer to see you covered in my own blood, though."

My answer seems to surprise her, so I take advantage and lean forward, brushing my lips across her jawline. She said I could touch her, but she never limited me to my hands.

"Whatever those men made you feel is not what I'm going to make you feel, little mouse. Whether your skin is between my teeth, beneath my blade, or under my tongue."

She shivers, and I nip at her jaw to prove my point.

"It's gone," she rasps, pulling away, throwing the cigarette out the window, and rolling it up. "Don't forget to pick that up."

The tension deepens as I wait for her to open the door and slide from my lap. Sensing her turmoil, I slide my lips along her jaw and toward her mouth until they're centimeters apart.

"You have until the smoke dissipates to kiss me," I murmur.

Only a hairsbreadth of a pause passes before she's crashing her lips onto mine. My hands dive into her hair, curling tightly as I devour her lips. She tastes sublime, and the feel of her tongue sliding against mine is intoxicating.

The world could fall to pieces around us, crumble to ashes as the cigarette did between our lips, and I wouldn't notice.

Staccato pants and desperate moans blend between my teeth, and all I can think of is all the ways I could make this last forever.

As if hearing my thoughts, she rips herself away, nearly crashing into the steering wheel in her pursuit to get away. Her hair is scattered across her face, and she stares at me with wide, panicked eyes.

She's strung tight, and those strings are on the verge of snapping.

"Smoke is gone," she whispers before opening the door and scrambling out, disappearing in a flash.

I grit my teeth and curl my hand into a tight fist, seconds away from sending it into the steering wheel.

Growling, I nearly kick open the door, grab the cigarette butt and throw it in the trash bag in my car, then slam the door shut behind me. Tension and anger build in my muscles, and rolling my neck does little to ease it.

Only my runaway mouse will, and deep down in that dark part of me, I hope she's suffering from the loss of me as much as I am her.

Chapter Twenty Nine
The Hunter

I cock my head to the side, staring at the running man with bewilderment.

"Why does he run like that?" I ask, genuinely concerned if Rick likes to peg himself with foreign objects. Maybe one got stuck because Jesus fucking Christ, *who runs like that?*

"That… that's a good question," Jay answers through my earpiece, sounding just as bemused as I am. He's watching through the drone hovering over the awkwardly running dude.

We've been tracking Rick Boreman since he fled from Francesca's house. He wasn't hard to find despite his best efforts to stay hidden. I'm sure it hurt his shriveled little soul to have millions of dollars and not be able to fuck off to a tropical island with strippers and blow. Guess the dude hasn't fried his brain with drugs so badly that he's not aware of the massive target on his back.

One of two people responsible for abducting my girl, and that's just not something I will take lightly.

I sigh, point my gun and shoot, the bullet hitting him in the back of the knee and sending him to the concrete with a sharp yelp.

"Fucking cocksucker!" he shouts, his voice breaking like a twelve-year-old boy. He even sounded like a kid who just learned to curse and does it every other word because he's trying to be cool.

"You really want to call me a cocksucker when that's what you've been doing the past four years just to get by?" I retort, arching a brow as I approach him.

We're in a dank alleyway, with trash littered on either side, spilling over from the dumpsters. Or maybe there's a family of raccoons in there tossing out the undesirable rot. Makes me wonder if they'd keep Rick's body after he's dead.

The pavement is wet and cold, and a whirring, orange bulb hangs at the mouth of the alleyway, offering enough light to bless me with a pock-marked face and greasy hair tucked under a beanie.

"Fuck you," he spits, his trembling hands holding his bloody knee. Or what's left of it. He's rocking back and forth, moaning through the agony as he glowers up at me with hatred.

Even Addie has more oomph in her glares than that, and she's never truly hated me. Not like Rickety Dick here is about to.

I crouch down and sweep my gaze across his form, dissecting him like bones out of fossilized shit. The summer camp counselors made us do that one year, and all I could feel was utter disgust. Feels about the same as I stare down at the sad excuse of a man.

At the time, I couldn't fathom what the fuck the point of that exercise was. Now, I suppose it was useful because Rick here is no different. A pile of shit with bones lodged somewhere inside, and unlike the first time, I'll enjoy pulling each one out of him.

One by one.

"That's not the part you should be ashamed of. It's *whose* cocks you're sucking. Xavier Delano ring a bell?"

He snarls, looking away and refusing to answer.

Max gave him three million dollars for kidnapping Addie. More than half of it is already gone.

Aside from his drug addiction, Rick also has a gambling problem. Horses, specifically. And he's really fucking bad at it, too. Any money he makes, he sinks into the wrong horse's ass and comes out with shit in the end. To make up for his habit, he's tended to some wealthy men over the years. Xavier being one of them.

"Do you know who I am?"

He sputters out what's supposed to be a laugh but sounds like a wet cough.

"Am I supposed to?" he snips.

"Aimin' for the heart today, my guy," I respond, grinning.

He snarls. "Let me guess—Z. No wonder you hide your face; you're fucking ugly."

"Don't make me cry, Rick. I'm having too much fun," I deadpan.

"This is about that stupid fucking diamond, isn't it? Did ya kill Max already, because I hope to see him in Hell so I can kick his ass for getting me involved in that shit." He laughs again, similar to a hyena. "That fucking bi—"

A rush of fury hits me in the chest, and I snap out my hand and grab him by the jowls, squeezing until he squeals like the fucking pig he is.

"Finish that sentence, and I'll rip out your tongue with my bare hands and make you choke on it. And I wouldn't call my girl stupid when you're the one lying on trash with a bullet in your knee," I bite out.

He seethes but locks away all the insults he had ready to spew. I'd say he was getting smarter if he wasn't trying to slyly sneak his hand toward the knife in his back pocket. The handle is sticking completely out. Some think that my left eye is blind because of the discoloration and the scar slashing through it, but even if I was, a grandma with bifocals could see what he's up to.

Patiently, I wait for him to think he has a chance. He wraps his fingers around the handle and then rips it out of his pocket and slashes it towards my face. I catch his wrist and snap it before he can blink, the knife dropping from his grip.

He screams, eyes widening with shock as he stares at his limp, useless hand. I squeeze his face tighter, his fighting renewed.

"Really, dude? A fucking *kitchen* knife?" I ask, picking up the pathetic weapon. It's what Addie used to carry around when she was attempting to hate me, and I laughed every time I saw it clutched in her tiny fist.

Addie has the power to cut me. This bozo doesn't stand a fucking chance.

He groans and thrashes in my grip, shaking his head roughly in an effort to dislodge my hand from his face.

"Let me fucking go!"

"Well, shit, since you asked so nicely, I guess I will," I say, releasing him. His eyes widen once more in surprise, and then he's scrambling up. Or at least trying to. He instantly drops back down, but he's not deterred. Desperation is more potent than a bullet wound to the knee.

If the government could bottle that particular emotion, they could create an army of superhumans. It's the driving force that creates extraordinary abilities.

Lifting a car off your dying child trapped beneath the tire. Running with a broken leg. Or rather, running with a kneecap shot out.

I lift my gun and fire off another bullet to his other knee, sending him crashing back down to the ground. Let's see if he can run with both blown out. He might even make it on Guinness World Records. Person to run the longest with no knees.

He cries out again, repeatedly tries to get up, and fails every time. I tip my head back and laugh my ass off. Shame, I would've liked to see Rick's picture in one of their books.

"Sorry, dude, I couldn't help myself. I really wanted to shoot you again."

Expletives burst past his yellow, chipped teeth while he rolls across the ground, shouting at the top of his lungs.

"Would you shut the fuck up? Someone could hear you, and then I'll get in trouble," I reprimand, smiling wider when another string of colorful words spills from his mouth.

Truthfully, we're in a shitty part of town. He can't legally leave the country, considering the government suspended his passport due to unpaid child support, and he doesn't have enough money anymore to buy a fake one. So, he was trying to hide in the boonies a few hours out from Seattle, but that is currently backfiring. There are probably several people who heard him scream, but no one is going to help him.

Not when they've got their own criminal activities taking place and their noses or veins clogged with whatever drug they could find. Pretty sure a dead guy is lying on the side of the street up the road, and several people stepped over him and kept it moving.

It's a very *mind your own fucking business* type of neighborhood. Perfect place to commit homicide. Weather's nice, too.

"Z, are you playing with your food again?" Jay pitches in with exasperation.

"What gave it away?" I ask, standing up and walking over to where Rick lies on the ground.

He's attempting to crawl away, dragging himself little by little with his arms. Desperation is running out, and resignation is setting in.

"You're going to burn in fucking Hell with me," the sad little man spits, saliva shooting from his mouth. "Just you fucking wait."

I sigh wistfully, rolling up each of my sleeves. "I sure hope so, Rick. That way I can torture you there, too."

I kick the side of his stomach until he rolls onto his back, what's left of his kneecaps bleeding profusely.

He's limp, now praying for death instead of trying to escape it. Even if he did survive, what kind of life would he have with no fucking knees? The dude is short as it is, he can't afford to lose any more inches.

Crouching again, I tip up his chin and press the sharp edge of the knife to his throat. He doesn't fight, only seethes at the Grim Reaper from beneath his blade.

"Any last words?"

"I—" I slice his neck, cutting off more than just his response.

"I don't actually care," I say, his eyes widening in surprise and mouth parting as he begins to choke on his blood.

"Ugh, can you mute your earpiece? I can hear him gurgling from here," Jay groans in my ear. I roll my eyes and ignore him, continuing to saw at his throat.

The knife is duller than a grandma's sex life, and getting through muscle and bone takes much longer than I'd like.

Eventually, I remove his head from his body, my arm aching from the effort. His blood covers me like oil, and I feel like I just walked off the *Carrie* movie set.

After tossing his head on top of his chest, I wipe my hands on my jeans then fish into my hoodie pocket and pull out a cigarette. Rolling the tension out of my neck, I light the stick and inhale deeply. Tobacco fills my lungs, instantly calming me.

I inhale death in order to erase the urge to create it.

"Rio booked a flight to Greece," Jay informs me. He's been jumping all over the country since Addie escaped, and just like Rick, what's in his bank account isn't enough to manufacture a new alias which means he's easily traceable. And if I can find him, so can Claire.

He's on borrowed time regardless of who gets to him first. Personally, I'd like to be the one to stick my knife through his throat, but a particular little mouse is keeping me from doing so.

She hasn't said it aloud, but she doesn't want Rio dead. What pisses me off more is that I can't *entirely* blame her. She formed a trauma bond with him, and as much as that irritates the hell out of me, I'm also glad she had someone kinda-sorta looking out for her in that house.

Doesn't negate the fact that she was there because of him. He may have helped her escape and cleaned up her wounds, but he still helped destroy her first. Just because you take the time to pick up the pieces after shattering a dish doesn't mean that it's not your fucking fault that it broke.

So, therefore, he should die.

Exhaling a thick plume of smoke, I take out a small container of lighter fluid from my pocket next.

"Continue to keep an eye out for other intelligence tracking him, especially from Claire. Send out one of my mercenaries to trail him, too. I'm sure he has a massive hit out on him, and they will need to be taken care of," I order Jay. "Only I will be the one to put a bullet in his brain."

"Roger," he murmurs, and the sound of keys clicking arises, causing my eye to twitch in irritation. So. Fucking. Obnoxious.

"Have fun on your... adventure."

I grunt, the earpiece clicking to indicate the call ended. Then, I uncap the lighter fluid and drench Rick's body and severed head in it.

Taking one more deep pull first, I flick the cigarette onto his corpse, stepping back as it bursts into flames.

"The ride to Hell is going to be a tough one, Rickety Dick. Have fun on *your* adventure."

Chapter Thirty

The Diamond

"Does Francesca happen to have short blonde hair?" Daya asks, storming into the living room with her laptop in hand.

"No," I answer, sweat dripping into my eyes. Sibby drops her hand, which was curled into a fist and ready to drive right into my face.

I rub my eyes, feeling the heat pressing in now that I'm no longer distracted with the screaming banshee that likes to use me for a punching bag.

"Well, she does now."

My eyes light up, forgetting all about how hot and exhausted I am.

"You found her?"

"You're goddamn right, I did. Fucking freak accident too. Cam from an old diner tagged her in a small town in South Carolina about eight hours ago. She was walking to the restroom and a waitress collided with her. Her sunglasses went flying, and bam—"

The second the words come out of Daya's mouth. Sibby's fist is flying into my stomach.

I tip over, the oxygen ripped from my lungs as pain explodes throughout my abdomen.

My eyes bug from my head, and only a wheeze escapes.

"What the hell, Sibby?" Daya barks.

"We weren't done sparring," Sibby shrugs. "Never fool yourself into thinking you're safe, even if you do smell like pretty flowers. Did you forget I murder people?"

I cough, hunched over as I turn my head and glower at the evil witch.

She giggles and skips away, satisfied that she taught me a valuable lesson for the day.

"I'm gonna kill her," I wheeze, straightening and shooting another round of daggers into the corridor she disappeared through. Another cough bursts from my throat. "After I catch my breath, though," I rasp, dropping to the checkered tile with exhaustion.

I've been sparring with her and Zade every day, all day. Between the two of them, I'd be happy to take the coward's way out and poison them in their sleep just so a girl can get some peace and quiet.

However, I can't lie and say that I'm not slowly becoming a badass.

The past month has been full of ups and downs. Zade was forced to buy a new car since his was not only identified at Satan's Affair when Sibby was caught but now as a getaway car for her this time.

Thankfully, Zade never puts anything under his name, so they still weren't able to identify him. Regardless, driving it is no longer safe, and for a second there, I thought he was going to have a memorial for the damn thing.

The USBs that Sibby stole from Jimmy were useless, and due to her being caught outside of his office, his paranoia got the best of him, and he trashed everything.

Normally, it could be chalked up to happenstance that she was outside of his building, but Claire is well aware of the connection between Sibby and Zade, considering her husband was one of their victims, which means Jimmy is aware, too.

Hence, why all of his devices were wiped and discarded, including the jump drives. Zade saw it coming, though, and sent one of his mercenaries into Jimmy's house to plant extra USBs in his home office.

It paid off.

Two weeks ago, Zade got an alert that Claire had connected one of his drives to her laptop. All of her previous employees are in the thick of their lawsuits against her, and it's safe to say Jimmy's hair has turned two shades whiter. There's no expectation for them to win, but Zade has made sure to compensate them already for their time and effort. They all have stable jobs and protection from Claire now.

Since then, our time has been spent decoding her messages and pulling as much information as possible from her business dealings. We were able to pin her location on a remote island on the other side of the world. We're going over the best way to draw her out from it, but Zade wants to get as much intel on the Society before we kill her.

It was daunting to learn that Claire's influence runs much deeper than we'd ever imagined. She has her hands in *everything*. Charities, hundreds of thousands of organizations and businesses, banks, big pharmas and the medical industry, the judicial system, and of course, the entire fucking government. It will take *years* to undo all the damage she's done and erase her influence.

"I'll help you kill her," Daya says, sitting next to me and crossing her legs. "But first, Francesca. So after she and the waitress collided, Francesca threw a huge fit and slapped the woman. Authorities were called, but Rocco strong-armed their way out of the diner and into their rusty brown Chevy Impala. They took off, and I was able to track them all the way back to the motel they're staying in."

"Holy shit," I breathe, eyes wide. "You fucking found them."

She grins. "Showtime, baby."

I'm jittery as fuck.

I wipe my clammy hands on my jeans, taking deep breaths to calm my nerves.

You can do this, I tell myself, then immediately turn my attention to the She-Devil above.

Right, God? Tell me I'm right.

Zade and I hopped on his private jet within twenty-four hours of finding out where Francesca and Rocco had been hiding. Since he has mercenaries in every state, he had one of them get a car ready for us at the airport, and an hour later, I'm standing outside their door.

And slightly panicking.

The motel I'm standing in front of looks like it comes straight out of *Bates Motel*. Run-down and owned by a serial killer.

The siblings have been staying here for the past three nights, and the vindictive part of me is overjoyed by it. My former groomer has always lived in filth but would walk around like she was dripping in money and class. She wanted nothing more than to live lavishly but was forced to stay in a shitty house with her brother by Claire's demand.

The house's location was perfect for hiding girls and hosting the Culling, so Claire wouldn't allow her to relocate somewhere nicer— something Francesca would complain about often. So instead, she sank all her money into her wardrobe to give off the illusion that she was thriving.

And this… this is the bottom of the barrel when it comes to filth.

Just as the bitch deserves.

"Room service!" I call out, rapping my knuckles on the red door.

Shouting can be heard from inside, but they're not any louder than the domestic violence case two doors down.

Nor is it any louder than the other strung-out couple three doors ahead, loud moaning and grunting coming from their room.

"Go away!" Francesca calls from the other side, followed by a fleshy slap.

"You stupid bitch, that right there is why we're in this situation! You can't keep your fucking hands to yourself!"

"Oh, that's rich coming from you," she hisses back. "What about all my girls, huh? You think they'd tell you that you kept your hands to yourself?"

"You shut the fuck up right now, or I'll kill you."

"Do it!" she screams. "We lost everything anyway, Rocco. We haven't heard from Claire for damn near a month now, except to be told we can't leave the goddamn country. We're running out of money because we can't fucking access our cards, I'm tired of this stupid-ass wig, and this motel has cockroaches!"

My hand is suspended in the air, ready to knock again, but I must admit, that little pity party entertained me.

"Room service!" I call again, smiling when Francesca screeches loudly in response.

Sibby would be proud.

That telltale sign of her heels stomping towards the door wipes the smile off my face. For a moment, I forget to breathe as I'm transported back into that house, dreading every step that pounded through the wooden floors.

The door is swinging open, snapping me out of my nightmares, only for them to materialize before me.

She's seething, breathing heavily like a bull with her wide eyes locked on me.

"Hey, Francesca. Miss me?" I ask, forcing a broad smile on my face. Seeing her is affecting me far more than I anticipated, but it doesn't minimize the murderous rage I feel toward her.

If anything, it heightens it more.

Rocco comes up behind her, his jowls wiggling as he walks. Francesca is frozen in the doorway, a stricken look on her face, while I stand equally paralyzed.

Breathe, Addie. They can't hurt you anymore.

"You've got to be shitting me," Rocco says, snapping Francesca and I both out of the stare down we found ourselves in.

She goes to slam the door shut, but I'm throwing my shoulder back into it, the wood reverberating off the door stopper.

Zade took EpiPen dispensers and filled them with small doses of anesthesia for me. Quickly, I grab one of them out of my front pocket and stab it into the side of her neck before her nails have the chance to claw at my face.

Francesca drops right as Rocco barrels into me like a linebacker, his body smashing me into the wall and knocking the breath from my lungs. My head knocks against it, learning the hard way that the walls are concrete. Stars explode in my eyes, and all I can do is blindly knock away Rocco's hands until I shake them from my vision. I manage to land one hit to Rocco's throat—weak as it is—and swerve under his arm. He chokes and hacks, providing me enough time to regain my bearings.

The last time he raped me was also the last time he would ever see me helpless.

Growling, he whips around, swinging out his arm as he does, aiming towards my face. I duck, and land a kick to his stomach, taking him by surprise. Before he can recover, I kick out once more. This time between his legs.

He shouts, eyes bulging and tipping over from the pain. I grab the other dispenser and jam it into his neck, his groans soon fading into silence.

Rock 'n' roll plays loudly from one neighbor, and the other has the news channel blasting from the TV. Thankfully, neither of them seems inclined to check on us.

Panting, I turn to find Zade leaning in the doorframe, arms crossed and a smirk on his face. A mixture of heat and pride swirl in his yin-yang eyes, and I can't help but feel on top of the fucking world.

"Good job, little mouse," he praises, his voice deep and smooth as butter. "Didn't want to join in?"

He smirks. "My girl had it handled."

My chest swells. Having Zade's love feels like a dream, but having his trust and confidence feels like a dream come true.

"Thanks," I breathe, a bead of sweat dripping down my back. I plant my hands on my hips, peering down at the duo passed out on the floor.

They look heavy.

Dusting my hands off, I head towards him and pat his chest, saying, "I'll let you carry them out," before slipping past him.

Zade's answering growl quickens my steps, a genuine smile blooming on my face. When I glance behind me, his head is turned over his shoulder, and he's staring at me like he has plans for me later.

He won't act on them, but I won't lie and say the idea doesn't sound a little intriguing.

After checking for passersby, Zade quickly drags Rocco into the back seat, and Francesca in the trunk.

They'll be out for a while still, but he speeds us back to the airport anyway.

Thankfully, they don't wake up until halfway through the flight home, and we knock them right back out again before they can give either of us a headache.

It's after midnight by the time we pull up to the looming gothic mansion, the gargoyles stationed on either side of the roof staring down at us.

I imagine they'd approve of what we're doing if they were alive.

This time, I help Zade. He takes Rocco and I wrangle Francesca out of the trunk. I accidentally drop her, which earns a chuckle from Zade as he heaves Rocco up the porch steps and through the front door.

Luckily, Francesca is rail thin. She was obsessed with her image and ate like a rabbit. Bending down, I lift her up by the arms and throw her over my shoulder, and then quickly make my way into the manor.

The weight I lost during my captivity has been packed back on with muscle. Not only am I back to a healthy weight, but I'm in better shape than ever. Toned in all the right places, muscle lining my arms and legs, and even my ass has rounded.

Most days, I still struggle with looking in the mirror and seeing something beautiful like I used to. Not because of how I look, but how I feel. In my eyes, my body is stained with dirty handprints, and no amount of scrubbing will set me free of them.

I let Francesca drop to the floor, her head cracking into the checkered tile. Sweat lines my hairline, and I take a moment to catch my breath.

Francesca and Rocco will assume that Zade will quickly torture and kill them. But that's where they're wrong. I have far grander plans in mind. Not just for them, but for Xavier Delano, too.

He's been hiding away on his private island with a mini army surrounding him, but Zade has gotten word that he has an L.A. trip planned at the end of the month. The island isn't far off the West Coast, and it'll only be a two-hour flight, but it's still impossible to hide a big black jet from air traffic control. Not unless he wants to risk flying nose-first into another plane and come crashing right back down in several pieces.

That would be fucking embarrassing.

So, until we get our hands on Xavier, Francesca and Rocco will be hanging out with the ghosts in the basement. It was finished when I renovated Parsons Manor, but it's still creepy as fuck down there.

When Sibby spots our new arrivals, she jumps up and down excitedly.

"They smell positively rotten," she shouts, curling her lip in disgust. Pointing to Rocco, she says, "That one smells like rotten eggs. And the other smells like a rotten pumpkin."

Mine and Zade's eyes clash, a *what the fuck* look on both of our faces.

"Pumpkin?" he mouths silently with confusion. I shrug, too exhausted to give a shit. Most of this day has been spent traveling, and I'm ready for bed.

"Sibby, get her legs. We'll carry her down together," I direct.

She turns around and speaks to one of her henchmen. "You guys are bathing their stench off me later."

"Oh my God," I say, turning my gaze back to Zade's. "I'm going to have to give the tub a bath tomorrow."

He shakes his head, appearing disturbed. "Use holy water. Lots of holy water."

May 29th, 2022

I'm in love with Zade.

It feels good to write it down considering I'm too chicken shit to say it to his face. Not because I'm worried about what he'll say back. I'm quite confident of that part actually.

But because I want to be able to say it when I'm not still thinking of someone else. Okay, gross. I **don't** think of my rapists in that way. That made me sound like I'm longing for them or something.

Really, I hate them. I hate them all. And they won't leave me alone. Every time I close my eyes, there they are.

And how the fuck am I supposed to say I love you when seconds later, I'll remember the feel of another man inside me?

It's fucked. **I'm** fucked.

Chapter
Thirty One
The Diamond

I fucking hate turbulence.

Just as I begin to swipe my red lipstick on my lips, the plane rumbles, and crimson is now on my goddamn cheek.

Huffing, I grab a baby wipe from my carry-on bag and swipe it off.

Xavier flew into L.A. last night, so we're on Zade's private jet and about halfway there. We have intel that he'll be attending an exclusive underground club tonight, so looking expensive is required. I'm anxious about seeing Xavier again, so I decided to occupy my time by getting ready during the flight rather than drowning in the anxiety and sweating off my makeup.

Makes me wonder if Xavier has ever felt that way. His arrogance is a testament to how stupid he is. He's gone several months without hearing from Z, and he thinks he's safe enough to come out of hiding for a weekend.

Honestly, I find it fitting. If he thought he could buy me and keep me as his personal sex slave without Zade finding him, surely he'd be confident enough to walk into a club and think he'll come back out on his own free will.

The club he'll be frequenting is geared towards those with dark desires. According to Zade's research, all the women are there of their own free will, which will allow us to focus solely on Xavier.

That is nothing short of a blessing. It would be that much harder for the both of us to walk into a place where women are being trafficked or abused, and not take the entire building down.

And honestly, I would be worried for Zade if that were the case.

He has positively burnt down the world to find me, and he hasn't stopped since. He tracked down Rocco's friends, and several of the guests who attended the Culling and sent them all six feet under. Well, technically, they're dust in the wind now.

Between training and keeping watch over me, to hunting down Claire, Xavier, my captors, and anyone that stepped foot in that house—I don't know how he has any headspace left to think.

He tried to take down a few more auctions too, but I drew the line there and demanded he brings in his other mercenaries to take his place in the meantime. It didn't take much to convince him, which only proved how exhausted he was.

He's a machine, and lately, I've been having to coerce him with make-out sessions to get him to relax. The asshole succeeded in getting me addicted to his lips since the car chase, and I can't even be mad when it's the only thing that seems to keep either of us sane.

"You look beautiful," a deep, baritone voice says from behind me. I turn to find Zade leaning against the doorframe to the mini suite, staring at me like I'm a glass of the finest whiskey, and he would kill for just a sip.

"Thank you," I murmur, swiping my hands nervously over my dress. It's a blood red strapless number, cut below the curve of my ass on one side and then dramatically tapers down, the silk flowing to my ankle on the other.

It reminds me of the dress I wore when he took me to Mark's estate last year. Pretty sure I'll never look at a red dress and not think of what he did to me in that movie theater.

Especially now, when he's prowling towards me with my black and purple blade and a strap in his hand, accompanied by a devilish glint in his eyes.

I'm wearing five-inch black heels, yet still, I feel like a little girl standing next to Zade. He has to be pushing six-foot-six.

"Don't forget these," he says, holding up the knife and lacy strap. "You're not going unprotected."

"Wouldn't dream of it," I murmur, enraptured by him. My heart clogs in my throat when he lowers himself before me.

"What are you doing?" I breathe, watching his long fingers reach out and grab my ankle. His touch feels electric, my leg twitching from the feel of his skin slowly grazing my skin. I hold my breath, my heart speeding as his hand disappears beneath the silk and travels farther up.

"Placing the crown on my queen," he croons.

"What do you mean?" I mumble distractedly, shivering from the electric currents traveling up my leg.

"A crown symbolizes power. That's what this knife is for you."

I'm trembling, and liquid heat is pooling low in my stomach. Something I'm still getting used to feeling again whenever Zade is brave enough to touch me.

He's grown more daring the past month, brushing up against me any chance he gets, and taking advantage of any excuse to touch me, his fingers always lingering longer than necessary. At night, when I'm lost in a nightmare, I let him hold me for a little while, feeling safer with him than I do in my own skin.

Sometimes in those moments, he'll place soft kisses along my jaw, never pushing it too far, but familiarizing me with the feel of his affection. More and more, I crave it and seek it out. And lately, I've begun to feel like it's not enough. Like I need more.

Sensing my growing arousal, he turns his head and places a soft kiss on my knee, peeking up at me through thick, black lashes. My teeth trap my bottom lip between them, and his eyes blaze in return.

Dropping his burning stare, he brushes the material of my dress to the side, both legs now bared. I decided to forgo panties with this dress, the silk too thin to conceal panty lines. If he lifted the material another inch, he'd be able to see between my thighs.

His nostrils flare, and I feel my face grow hot, flushing hotter when he leans in closer.

I can smell you.

Something he said to me so long ago, when he told me to run and hide in Parsons Manor, promising a punishment if he found me.

I have a feeling he can smell me now, and just how much my body weeps for him.

"Lift your leg, baby," he orders roughly, voice hoarse with desire. I listen, watching him loop the lacy strap around my foot and raise it to my upper thigh, his knuckles coming dangerously close to my center.

"Do you remember how to use this?" he asks, flipping the blade in his deft fingers. For the life of me, I can't fathom why that was one of the hottest things I've ever seen him do.

"Uh-huh," I squeak. It takes effort to drag my eyes away from the twirling blade to meet his gaze. There's a hint of challenge swirling in his mismatched pools, and I feel myself rising to meet it. "Do *you* know how to use it?"

I'll never know why I instigate him, even when wariness lingers behind the cloud of lust.

The smirk that curls his lips is wicked, causing my body to flush. I'm overheating, and he's hardly touched me.

I'm not sure what he intends to do, but that look on his face tells me it's going to be something nefarious.

"You can't cut me with it," I say seriously. For a moment, I see a flash of rage in his eyes, gone before the fire can spread. And I know he knows the reasoning behind my request. There have been several nights where I confessed the things that had been done to me in that house, including Xavier's kink with slicing me open while he raped me.

For a moment, I panic, fearing he'll stop at the reminder that other men have used my body. Tensing, I wait for the disgust. I wouldn't blame him if he was repulsed by me, but it'd tear my heart out anyway.

Instead, he flips the blade until he's gripping the sharp edge in his hand. Then he slides the handle against my thigh, gentle and teasing. The fear begins to dissipate, relief soaking my bones. But even that quickly fades when the handle caresses my pussy, just a whisper of a touch.

Now, I feel nothing but anticipation and that lingering wariness.

Turbulence rocks the plane again, a physical representation of how my heart feels.

"Did you know that reclaiming something that was stolen from you can help with trauma?" he asks.

"Yes," I murmur.

"And if something hurt you before, giving it a new meaning can help."

His eyes lift, focusing on me intently.

"Do you want me to show you a new meaning to this knife?"

I hesitate but then nod my head. A different kind of fear is seizing my body—the kind that I've always been attracted to. And I've missed it so much.

"Pull up your dress," he demands roughly, his voice deep and raspy. Quickly, I do as he says, bunching the material up just high enough to bare the apex of my thighs.

His nostrils flare, and he clenches his jaw briefly before ordering, "Now wrap your hand around mine."

Furrowing my brows, I do as he says, grabbing ahold of his hand that's curled tightly around the blade. "Wouldn't want to cut up those pretty hands of yours. So, you're going to guide me."

I shake my head, feeling myself start to retreat.

"I won't touch you," he promises. "You're in control, little mouse. I'm only here to protect your hand. Instead of allowing this knife to cause you pain, use it to give yourself pleasure instead."

My throat constricts, and I have the strongest urge to run away. But that feeling is what keeps me still. I don't want Xavier to win. To haunt my life so terribly that an inanimate object has the power to control me.

Nodding my head, I guide his hand up, my breath hitching when the handle slides along my slit.

Zade watches my movements closely, his teeth clenched and the muscle in his jaw pulsating. Blood begins to trickle down his wrist, and for reasons I can't explain, I squeeze his hand tighter, eliciting more trails of blood. He growls deep in his chest but doesn't stop me.

I bite my lip, a whimper breaking free when I slowly insert it inside of me, my legs trembling.

Normally, I don't think I could ever get enjoyment out of fucking myself with a knife handle. But using Zade's hand to do it adds a layer of pleasure I wouldn't be able to find on my own. Seeing his blood drip from our hands instead of my own—it does something to me that I can't explain.

My breath escalates when I slide the handle inside me to the hilt, Zade's fingers pressed up against my flesh. A groan rumbles deep in his chest, but he keeps his promise, his hand not even twitching against me.

"Tell me how it feels," he rasps, enthralled by the sight of me tugging our hands down just to drive it back up, eliciting a sharp jolt of bliss.

"S-so good," I breathe around a moan, my eyes fluttering as I continue, finding a pace that threatens to make me forget my own name.

"Go slower," he urges, his hand flexing beneath mine. I force myself to listen, keeping the pace gradual and drawing out the pleasure.

"Now watch yourself. Look how pretty you are when you fuck yourself."

Mouth parted and chest heaving, I look down between my slick thighs, the euphoria heightening from the sight.

"See how you're dripping all over our hands, baby?"

Both of our hands are covered in his blood, my arousal mixing in and carving paths through the crimson staining our skin.

My stomach tightens, an orgasm building low in my stomach.

"Yes," I moan.

"You know what I see? I can see how tightly your pussy is clenching the knife," he growls, face strained with need. "Like it's just begging to be filled."

"Do you wish it was your cock instead?" I pant, enjoying the way his eyes flare. Absolutely loving that he can only dream of fucking me, forced to watch a knife handle do it instead. A rush of power flows through me, and I can't contain the smile.

His eyes lift to mine, something dangerous whirling in his irises. My stomach clenches, the orgasm cresting higher. But I don't fear him. I pity him.

"Does it hurt knowing that you can't touch me?" I ask, another moan slipping free when I hit that spot inside me. "Does it cut deeper than this knife?"

"Yes," he confesses, his tone low and dark.

"You can't have it," I taunt. He eyes me closely, understanding what I'm doing and not liking it. Yet, he'll never disobey me, knowing that the trust I've placed on him will be shattered.

Giving respect hurts like a bitch when your hands are tied.

I drive the knife deeper and faster, reaching that peak, and I decide that giving him a small taste will deepen the agony.

All I need is a little nudge, but this time, I'm not the one that will be begging him to let me come.

He will be begging *me*.

"Do you want to lick me, Zade?" I ask, eyes threatening to cross. "I'm so ready to come."

He drops his gaze to our hands, baring his teeth from the restraint.

"Yes," he chokes out.

"Say please."

A flick of his dangerous gaze and savage curl to his lips that promise retribution, but he doesn't hesitate. "Please, little mouse."

"One lick," I allow. "Make it count."

Giving me one last weighted look, he leans forward, and I shiver when I feel his hot breath fan over my core.

And then his tongue is sliding against my clit, slow and firm. He groans around me, and I can no longer hold on. I shatter around him, crying out as my world breaks apart. My free hand flies into his hair, grasping for something to hold on to as my knees buckle.

He quickly stands, catching me and holding me up against him, our hands pressed tightly against my pussy as I ride out the waves.

I press my forehead into his chest, squeezing my eyes shut as the remnants of the orgasm slowly fade.

Both hands cup my face before sliding into my locks, pulling my head back and nudging his mouth against my cheek.

"Give me them," he demands sharply.

With aftershocks still attacking my nerves, I let him in, turning my mouth towards his. His lips capture mine immediately, and it rivals the pleasure radiating between my thighs.

He kisses me deeply, drawing out a small, husky moan before pulling away, only to brush his lips across my ear. Surprise renders me still when he reaches into his pocket, pulls out a rose, and slips it behind my ear.

"One day, you're going to feel safe with me again," he whispers, his voice dangerously soft. "And when that day comes, you better pray I'm feeling generous."

The second I walk into the club, *Supple*, it feels like a sinister entity reaches out and wraps itself around me.

A black studded half-mask rests over my eyes, concealing the upper half of my face. While they're not required in this club, more attendees wear them than not, preferring to keep their identities anonymous. Which translates to keeping their reputations intact.

A heavy bass vibrates the black and gold marble that stretches across the main floor with two bars on either side and a stage straight ahead with seating surrounding it.

Instead of the typical club bangers, slow and heavy music plays, the woman on stage performing a sensual dance to the heavy beat. She's wearing a black bra and panty set with a diamond-encrusted mesh dress over top of it. A red mask covers her face, dark hair spilling out from around it in waves.

For several moments, I'm entranced. Her lithe curves roll and move to the music with perfect precision, drawing onlookers in like moths to a roaring flame.

She keeps her clothes on, but she doesn't even need to undress in order to perform the sexiest dance I have ever witnessed.

"Focus, baby," Zade whispers from the Bluetooth in my ear. His voice is deep and lined with gravel, sending a shiver down my spine. Most likely from watching me watch her. He's hacked into the cameras in every corner of the room, and even through grainy footage, he must've seen how enraptured I was.

I feel my cheeks flush, spreading down to the pit of my belly. This place is already sinking its claws into me, and I've barely made it past the front door.

"She's a good dancer," I defend, refusing to be embarrassed over appreciating another woman's beauty.

"Didn't notice," he replies.

Oddly, I believe him, and something about that deepens the heat swirling in my stomach.

Several people line the barstools, though the room is far from crowded.

I spot an empty seat in the middle of the left bar, so I beeline for it.

I need a drink before I make my way downstairs—where all the real debauchery takes place according to Zade.

The bartender is a young man wearing a suit and bowtie with a sleek black vest. His glossy black hair is slicked back, and only a thin mustache covers his upper lip. He reminds me of what Edgar Allan Poe would've looked like in his younger years.

"What can I get for you, miss?" he asks politely, his dark eyes pinned to mine.

"A martini, please," I answer.

He's sliding over my drink a couple of minutes later, accepting my cash with a pleasant smile. Thankfully, he doesn't try to engage in small talk and focuses on his bar and the other patrons.

I subtly glance around while I sip my martini, the burn of the alcohol sliding down my throat soothing to my nerves. I can't help but feel like I'm being watched, though I suppose that's the purpose of this place. Apparently, voyeurism and exhibitionism are a given here. There's only so many places to go for privacy, and most patrons don't bother with it.

It's not exactly uncomfortable as it is unnerving. It makes me wonder what the woman on stage must feel, with so many sets of eyes tracing her every curve. Does it make her feel good? Or does she tune out the weight of people's stares and lose herself in the music?

Finishing off my drink, I slide the glass away and slip off the stool before I'm tempted to order another. As much as I'd like to succumb to the pleasant buzz a few drinks bring, I want to have all my wits when dealing with Xavier.

I prepared myself to see him again as much as I'm capable of in such a short amount of time, but I'm not delusional enough to believe that he's not going to rip open old wounds in a matter of seconds. But I'm stronger than I was, and I will never bleed for him again.

Once I make my way downstairs, Zade will follow soon after. While he trusts me to handle myself, he still refuses to leave me on my own.

I can't deny that his presence brings me strength, and when facing one of my abusers, I'll take as much as I can get.

Releasing a slow exhale, I find the curtain that leads downstairs, where men and women come and go. Ducking my head, I follow behind a couple, their hands roaming all over each other with every step.

The smell of sex permeates the air when I emerge from another curtained entryway.

Down here, a significant number of bodies occupy the space—at least half of them is in a state of undress. Several women bare their breasts for others to touch and kiss. A few men have their hands up dresses or deep inside another man's trousers.

Nothing is off-limits down here, and I have to remind myself that this is consensual. This isn't like when me and the other girls were punished together, a room full of naked bodies but several of us unwilling.

For a moment, I stop to take it all in. Familiarize myself with sex that creeps along the edge of innately wicked yet brings nothing short of pleasure and desire. For *everyone* involved.

Truthfully, I'm envious. I miss the freedom of sex, and my comfort with it. Even when a dangerous, imposing man forced it on me, my body still crowed for it, even if my head screamed otherwise. Now, the thought of it feels like taking a strong drug and getting too high. It's a nerve-racking feeling because control is unattainable, and it becomes a constant battle of talking yourself down from panicking.

Forcing my shoulders to ease, I glance around the room, looking for anyone who resembles Xavier. Most are wearing half-masks, leaving their mouths uncovered for… purposes.

Heart pounding, I weave through the bodies, searching for him and coming up empty.

It isn't until fifteen minutes later that Zade directs, "Found him. He's down the hallway in the viewing rooms."

I spot the hallway to my left, swallowing when I find how dark and uninviting it looks. Holding my breath, I sidle past writhing bodies, ducking away from a few wandering hands.

My heart hammers in my chest when I enter the hallway. Neon red lights line the ceiling on either side, illuminating the space in the color that represents debauchery. It reminds me of a haunted house in a way, but instead of screams of terror, it's screams of pleasure.

"You can do this, Addie," Zade encourages, voice soft. He must be able to hear my heavy breathing. Perspiration coats my forehead and the back of my neck as I walk into a room I would've thought I'd only see in movies.

There are three massive glass windows in each wall surrounding me. Behind each window is a room, a couple in various stages of sex. Straight ahead, a woman is on all fours while a man stands behind her and whips her ass with a cane.

The couple to my left is trading oral sex. The man stands with the woman in his arms, flipped upside down. I cock my head, a little curious how hard that would be to do.

To my right, the woman is chained to the bed, writhing as a man in a leather suit whips her.

There must be speakers in the rooms because their moans are just as loud as they would be if I were standing next to them.

Several voyeurs stand both in and outside the rooms, watching the couples while subtly touching themselves or the person next to them.

I shift apprehensively, beginning to feel way out of my element.

"Incoming, baby," Zade warns, but I hardly hear him. I'm so hypnotized by what's happening in front of me that I don't notice the person approaching, not until their voice is in my ear.

"Which one intrigues you the most?"

I startle, unable to contain the gasp. My heart pounds in my chest, and my stomach flutters from the fright.

I'd recognize his voice anywhere. I hear it so often in my nightmares; I fear I'll never forget it.

Xavier stands next to me, hands casually in his pockets as he watches on. Half of his face is covered by a black mask with a silver diamond painted over one eye.

"Terribly sorry to scare you," he murmurs, the smirk on his face indicating he's not sorry at all.

He doesn't recognize me yet. I'm wearing a dark brown wig to help conceal my identity, but I imagine he'll figure out who I am the moment he hears me speak. My huskier voice has always been easily identifiable.

Xavier's presence is suffocating, and it takes several more seconds to drag my gaze away, fighting to wrestle my heart back down.

Swallowing nervously, I face the couple straight ahead where the man is now fucking the woman from behind, bright red welts across her ass and thighs. Her hands are cuffed behind her back while the man uses her locked hands as an anchor. Her screams are high-pitched and sharp with pleasure, and once more, I feel a stab of envy.

"Too shy?" he prompts. Rolling my red-stained lips, I nod, hoping that'll satisfy him.

Don't be shy, diamond, let me see how good you suck cock.

I squeeze my eyes shut, tilting my face away, so he doesn't see how hard I have to fight to pull myself together.

"I'm right behind you, baby," Zade whispers. I don't turn to look, but I feel him anyway. He's a force far stronger than the man standing next to me.

Instantly, I relax. Zade may be Hades, but the dark God has never been known to bow for anyone but his woman. It gives me a small dose of power, enough to reignite my confidence.

Xavier can't hurt me anymore. He can't touch me, cut me, or use me. He's a pitiful soul posing as a powerful being. Soon, I will remind him that he is only a man, and I am the reaper forged beneath his own hands.

"I can help relax you if you'd like," Xavier suggests from beside me, his voice deepening. "There are private rooms to your left."

"Okay," I agree quietly.

He grabs my hand, the touch of his skin sending a cold chill throughout my body. I'd forgotten how dead he feels. He pulls me toward a double set of doors in the corner of the room. Subtly, I glance back to Zade, finding him in a full-face mask. All black with geometric points, a dramatic frown, and a slash through the eye. His yin-yang eyes are hidden, only bottomless pits where they should be.

Admittedly, he looks terrifying. And I'd be lying if I said that didn't spark something low in my stomach, sinking between my thighs.

Turning away, I focus as Xavier leads us into a hallway full of black doors. It's deathly silent in here.

"Soundproof rooms," Xavier supplies, glancing back at me with a wicked smirk on his face.

I bite my lip, my nerves running wild as he walks us into a private room. The white walls are tinted blue from the LED lights surrounding the ceiling. A single black bed sits in the middle with handcuffs on the headboard and footboard. And a dresser is next to it, likely filled with different kinds of toys.

"Should I be worried that these rooms are soundproof, Xavier?" I ask, no longer concerned with him recognizing my voice.

He slowly turns his head to me, his blue eyes widened with surprise. Even beneath the mask, he can't hide his reaction.

"I see my diamond has come back to me," he drawls, his lips curling into a smile. His eyes drop to my body, taking his time as he slowly takes me in, pausing on the rose tattoo on my forearm.

"My god, you look fantastic. Must be why I didn't immediately recognize you." His eyes kick up to my hair. "And your hair is darker. Can't say I'm a fan of that."

"Truly, I'm hurt," I respond dryly.

Anger flashes across his irises. That reaction makes the smile impossible to contain.

He nods his head, seemingly to himself.

"I suspect you've come back to kill me."

I cock my head. "You think I could?" I query, though I'm not the least bit interested in his approval.

He laughs, tipping his head back and exposing his throat. One slash to the jugular. That's all I'd need. But I don't want to kill Xavier.

Not tonight, I don't.

His laugh tapers, and if I were breathing any louder, I wouldn't have heard the subtle click from behind me.

I turn, my heart dropping when I tug on the handle, finding that he locked the door. Which means it's automated.

"I'm good friends with the owner here," Xavier explains darkly. "If we want a little extra time with the girls than they're willing to give, we have… means to get them to stay a little longer."

I face Xavier again, noting his hand in his pocket. He must have some type of button in there to engage the locks.

My pulse is hammering, but I force my chin high, exuding a confidence I'm having trouble feeling.

This… was not something Zade, or I, was aware of. One of the biggest rules in this club is no locks to offer security and comfort to the women. Seems the owner is a slimy bastard and knows how to hide it. Makes me wonder how many women have gotten trapped in these rooms, and how they were kept silent. The reputation of *Supple* is impeccable, which means their scare tactics are effective.

"You locked the doors," I say aloud so Zade can hear me.

"The fuck did you just say, baby?" His voice comes in a second later, and I just know he's rushing toward my door.

In order to protect the privacy of those who use private rooms, they don't allow cameras in here. And surprisingly, there's not even a shady camera hidden in the room like Zade would have thought. Which means now that I'm locked in here, he won't be able to see a damn thing that happens.

Adrenaline pumps into my system, and dread pools in my gut.

I may be stronger than I was, but that doesn't mean that PTSD doesn't have me by the throat still. Trauma isn't something that just *poofs* away. I've been improving, but it's a work in progress, and I have a sick feeling Xavier will roundhouse kick me back into that dark place it took me weeks to crawl out of.

He's the boogeyman in my nightmares. The face I can't get out of my head. The things he put me through were far worse than any of the things

Rocco and his friends did to me. What he did to me was fucking personal.

I wasn't just another body being passed around from man to man. I was a possession that he took his sweet time with. He drew out my suffering for as long as he could, and those are the moments that haunt me most.

I pleaded for a death he'd never grant me, giving him power over a life that was never his to take.

But I refuse to cower now. I refuse to give him any control over me ever again. Tonight, I'm going to take back that power and make him wish he'd just stuck the knife in my fucking throat.

The doorknob wiggles behind me, attracting Xavier's attention. I seize the opportunity and drive my fist directly into his nose in a snap movement.

His head knocks back, eyes bulging with surprise. Before he can recover, I'm lunging at him, landing another punch to his stomach and then to his temple.

He roars, his arm whipping out and catching me on the side of my head, the gold ring on his finger slicing across my cheek. Blood pours from his nose as he tackles me, a snarl on his face.

We land against the door harshly, knocking the breath from my lungs. He then grips me by the biceps and throws me with all his strength, pure rage on his face.

I fly to the ground, crying out as I land awkwardly on my shoulder, my temple knocking on the tile floor. Stars explode in my vision, drowning out Zade's now panicked voice in my ear.

He'll have Jay working to unlock the doors, and it won't take him long to figure out how, but all Xavier needs is a second to kill me.

Through blurred vision, I see Xavier's fist fly towards my face. Instinctively, I roll out of the way, causing his hand to bound off the hard floor. He shouts, shaking out his hand to rid himself of the pain.

Gritting my teeth, I kick out my leg, but he manages to catch me by the ankle and drags me towards him.

His face is contorted with animalistic fury. Blood pours from his broken nose, leaking into the cracks of his bared teeth.

I struggle against him, kicking my leg with all my might, managing to dislodge his hand long enough to drive my foot into his face.

He turns just in time, my heel only clipping his temple.

"Fucking bitch," he snarls, grabbing at my legs again and climbing on top of me. I thrash violently, only assisting him in rolling me to my stomach and pinning my hands to my sides with his knees. He tears at my dress, and for a moment, I lose control and descend into panic. A scream rips from my throat as he lifts my dress up past my ass.

No matter how hard I fight, he only squeezes me tighter between his thighs, and my efforts are useless.

The clang of his buckle is what snaps me out of it.

I'll be damned if this fucker ever puts his dick anywhere near me again.

Panting heavily, I stop moving and lie my face onto the cool tile.

He chuckles, believing I've given up just like every other time. I used to lie there and just take it, knowing that fighting would only make it worse.

"There ya go, diamond. That's a good—"

Growling, I buck against him, catching him off guard and causing him to pitch forward. And then I rear my head back, bashing it directly into his nose.

He lets out an agonized wail, his grip on me loosening. Twisting, I drive my fist directly into his trachea.

His eyes nearly pop out of their sockets, his cries depleting as he struggles for oxygen. Right at that moment, the door bashes open, the sound thunderous.

Zade strides in, the fury on his face so potent that all his distinguishable features get lost in it.

"Zade, don't kill him," I shout, a different kind of panic sprouting when he grabs Xavier by the back of his blazer and lifts him like he's holding up a goddamn cat by the scruff of its neck. He grips him tight enough that it reopens the cut on his hand, his blood beginning to trail down his wrist.

"Zade!" I shout, scrambling towards them when I see him slide his gun from the back of his pants, a silencer already screwed on. He doesn't hear me, so I do the only thing I can think of and grab the barrel of his gun, twisting it towards me.

His head snaps to me, his eyes wide with a mixture of rage and disbelief. "Don't. Kill. Him."

Breathing heavily, he growls and yanks the gun from my grip, shoving it back into his pants. He punches the side of Xavier's head, knocking him out cold. Despite that he is now dead weight in Zade's hand, he still holds him up like he's as light as a feather.

He's too busy getting in my face, baring his teeth. "You ever do that again, little mouse, I will bend you over my knee and use that barrel in your tight little ass. You understand me?"

I grimace and nod my head, realizing now how close he came to shooting me. Even if it were my fault, he would've never forgiven himself.

"Slap me, punch me, kick me in the goddamn balls. But do *not* point my gun at yourself."

I nod my head again, reality starting to catch up to me now that I'm no longer under attack. Zade's voice becomes a distant whisper, and I grapple with the tunnel vision, slowly narrowing my sight.

My system is crashing, and I struggle to hold on to my sanity.

Xavier tried to rape me. He came close to succeeding.

Spread those legs, diamond.

You're so pink. I can't wait to turn it red with blood.

Jay must say something to Zade because he quickly drops Xavier, his head hitting the tile with a fleshy smack, and slides his mask back over his face.

Security comes barreling into the room a moment later, distracting him before he can see just how panicked I am. Two men wearing three-piece suits are pointing their guns right at us.

"Drop your weapons!" one of them shouts. Zade raises his hands, and mine go up on instinct as well.

"No need to shout, gentlemen. I was simply saving my girl from getting assaulted by this man right here."

The two guards glance down at an unconscious Xavier, but they don't seem inclined to drop their weapons.

"Is that Xavier Delano?" one of them asks, trying to get a good look at him.

"No," Zade lies. Xavier's face is still covered, but if he's been coming here often enough, he might be recognizable by his hair or stature. Sometimes something as simple as their hands can be easily identified if you know them well enough.

I know I could recognize those hands from a mile away…

The guards shuffle deeper into the room, attempting to get a better view of Xavier. My heart pounds so heavily that my chest aches, and my vision is blackening.

I'm spiraling, and the knowledge that it could get me shot isn't enough to set me straight.

"P-please," I whisper. "He was trying to hurt me."

The guards look at each other and slowly lower their guns, appearing slightly concerned by my garbled words. It won't matter in the end. Xavier is too important, and they're not going to just let us go.

"Addie," Zade whispers, and at first, I'm not sure what he's trying to convey, but then he tips his chin up, as if telling me to *keep it up.*

Distract them. That's what he wants.

Though by the tension lining his muscles and how he's stepping in my direction, he's ready to say fuck them and rush to me. He can see that I'm breaking, and he's caught between comforting me and getting us out alive.

I dip my chin in acknowledgement. It's not hard when I'm on the verge of losing it anyway. The tears in my eyes spill over, and my lip trembles. I let out a cry, grip my hair in my hands, and pull.

"H-he was tr-trying to r-rape me," I sob.

"Whoa, whoa, hey, it's okay. We'll get this sorted out."

I let out a shout and thrash my head, and the guards are so taken aback by my outburst that they drop their weapons altogether. Their wide eyes turn to each other and have a silent conversation, one asking, *what the fuck do we do, bro?* and the other responding, *I don't fucking know, she's cracked.*

"Hey, uh, just relax, all right?" the first guard says, his words the least calming thing I've ever fucking heard. Then he turns to his partner. "Call for back-up."

But there's a bullet flying through the second guard's skull before the first can fully finish his demand.

In mere seconds, Zade has whipped out his gun and shot him; the silencer screwed on the end keeping his crime quiet.

The first guard's eyes widen, scrambling to take aim, but a bullet is tearing through his forehead next. His head snaps back, and he tumbles to the ground alongside his partner.

Zade wastes no time. He picks Xavier up and slings him over his shoulder, grabs my hand, and pulls me out behind him.

"Let's go, baby girl. And when we get on our plane, I'm fucking holding you."

I don't recall if I answer as Zade tugs me toward the end of the hallway. He mutters under his breath, most likely ordering Jay to do something, but the screaming in my head drowns out his words.

My body is moving on pure autopilot. I don't remember how he got us out of there. I don't remember the three-hour flight home. I don't remember anything at all but the weight of Xavier on top of me, the clang of his buckle ringing in my head.

May 31st, 2022

When Xavier would finish with me, he would pet me. Yeah. Fucking weird.

While he did though, he would tell me that Zade was going to fall out of love with me eventually. He said men like Zade can't stand the thought of another man touching what's theirs. For awhile there, I believed him.

He wasn't wrong though. But he also was.

He underestimated Zade's obsession, and I've never been more thankful for that.

Jesus, there's something wrong with me.

I guess it would be weirder if I was normal at this point, right?

Chapter Thirty Two
The Diamond

I'm fucking rattled, like an old A/C unit on its last leg.

We just arrived home. Zade is in the basement taking care of Xavier, and I'm desperately grasping onto my last shred of sanity. Restlessness gathers in my bones, and I feel like an animal confined within my own cage.

Heart pounding, I close my bedroom door behind me and then pace the floor, running my hands through my hair and pulling tight—a pathetic attempt to calm the anxiety.

Don't worry, diamond, I'll make this nice and slow for you. I want you to feel every inch of me.

No, I don't want to.

Tears build in my eyes, and I shake my head, attempting to rid myself of that demonic fucking voice.

I must've forgotten to lock the damn door because minutes later, Zade bursts in and slams it shut, a wildfire raging in his eyes.

"We need to have a talk, Adeline. I've let you process for over four hours now. I need you to talk to me."

Hysteria is consuming me, and what doesn't he get? I don't want to hear his fucking *words*, nor do I want to give him mine. There's too many of those in my head, and I'm drowning in them.

Whirling away, I bolt for my balcony doors. I've no idea what I'm going to do once I get there—maybe just pitch myself over the rail and end it all—but his arm is curling around my waist and turning me right back around.

The second my feet touch the ground, I wiggle out of his hold and turn to face him.

"Stop it," I snap. "Just leave me be, Zade."

"How many times will you run away before you learn that you can't escape me?" he growls, getting in my personal space before I can even take a breath.

I take a step back, retreating from his intensity. He doesn't let me go, though, stepping back into me until I'm pressed against the wall.

"However many times it takes before you realize I don't *want* to be caught," I snarl, my own anger rising. I'm not even sure what I'm angry at, just mad that he's mad.

Let me feel every inch of this sweet body, diamond. Fuck, you feel so good. Don't I feel good too, baby?

"You're drowning, Addie. Just let me help you."

I narrow my eyes, my mouth thinning into a straight line. "I've been doing fine!" I argue heatedly, growing defensive purely because he's right.

I am drowning. And the scariest part—I don't feel the need to come up for air.

"You're not fine. And you know what? Neither am I. I'm not fucking fine at all."

His hand trembles as he brushes a strand of hair behind my ear.

The man who's borne so much strength, a pillar of stone despite the ruthless attempts made to knock him down. But the thing is, stone still crumbles. It still breaks and chips and cracks. Even when it's left standing, there will always be missing pieces.

Here he stands before me, crumbling as we speak.

"I dream of all the ways I will make them suffer," he whispers. "I dream of their blood on my hands—between my teeth. I will kill every last one of them for you, little mouse, and I will fucking rejoice in it."

I stare up at him, my lip trembling as I force myself to keep the emotions down. At first, I felt everything while trapped in that house. And then, I felt nothing.

And now, I'm left with a pile of broken pieces in my hands where my heart is supposed to be, and I don't know how to mend it without cutting myself deeper.

"I don't need you, Zade. I don't need you to do anything for me."

He clutches the back of my neck and pulls me in. "See, that's what we're not going to do, Adeline," he barks, baring his teeth. "We're not going to act like you're so tough that you don't need me anymore. Because you want to know something, baby? There are very few men in this world capable of killing me. And I fucking need *you*. Do you understand me?"

I grit my teeth, refusing to answer.

"Do you think needing me somehow makes you weak?"

"Doesn't it?" I snap.

"No, baby, it makes you strong." He bends down, putting his face directly into mine. "I may own every breath in your body, but make no mistake, Adeline, you own mine, too. I am yours to command. To bend and break. To mold and manipulate. Do you think that makes me weak? Or do you think I'm strong enough to admit that even though my body can physically live on without you, I would never get my fucking soul back?"

His hand slides into my hair and fists the strands tightly.

"Without you, I will shatter. But with you, I am indestructible."

I suck in a sharp breath and clench my jaw against the different reactions circulating inside me.

But the most prominent—the worst one—is to do everything in my power to get this man away from me.

My skin bristles beneath his electric touch. Those sparks that used to feel so divine now feel like spikes cutting through my flesh.

"Every single man that laid eyes on you while in that house will die slow fucking deaths. I've killed so many already... and it's still not enough."

He pulls me into him, and I tense as he wraps himself around me.

So many men have done the same. Sweat soaking my skin as they take my body, their skin sliding against my own. Sliding inside of me. Over me. Around me.

How can he feel like home, feel so safe, yet make me feel like I'm being buried alive?

His lips whisper across my cheekbone, and panic sparks. My breath falls shorter, and my lungs constrict as his other hand reaches up to touch me. I tremble as memories flash through my eyes. Faces, *so many* faces. Smiling at me as they take from me.

Whispering filthy words from their fucking rotten mouths.

Such a pretty girl.

You're going to look so good with those lips wrapped around my cock.

Fuck, I could come from just touching you.

These tits are perfect, how much did you pay for these?

I can't control myself. I need you now.

I can't control myself.

I can't control my...

"Let me go," I whisper.

He stills, his mouth poised over my cheek.

"Stop... stop fucking *touching me*."

I hear him swallow. "That's like asking me to cut out my own fucking heart."

"If I can live without one, so can you," I snap.

He's solid stone as he processes my words. And all I want to do is fucking break it. Make him crumble beneath my fists.

Slowly, he pulls away, his mismatched eyes catching hold of mine.

What does he see when he looks at me?

Does he see the anger churning beneath the surface? Like looking down into the mouth of a volcano to see what the insides look like. Red. So much fucking red.

That's what the inside of every human looks like—but I'm no longer full of blood. Only fire.

"Do you think of them when I touch you?" he asks, his voice turning hard.

That fire rises, building in the pit of my stomach and ascending up my chest like lava.

Who gave him the *right* to touch me? Who gives anybody the fucking right to?

The trembling increases until my bones are rattling and my teeth chatter.

Fire.

I move without thinking, my hand wrapping around the gun tucked in the waistband of his jeans and yanking it out. The second he realizes what I've done, he backs away, raising his hands in surrender.

I point the gun right at his fucking head, and all I want to do is blow it off. All I want to see is his brain explode beneath the bullet.

Because I'm not looking into the face of the man I love.

I don't see him at all.

All I see is a faceless man trying to take what he wants from me without my permission.

And I want him to fucking *burn* for it.

Tears build in my eyes, my vision blurring. The gun is vibrating from how hard my hand trembles, but he's close enough that I'd strike true. Whether the bullet hits his head, his throat, or his chest, I don't care.

"Little mouse," he whispers. I squeeze my eyes shut, forcing the sweet whisper out of my head. I don't want to hear it. I don't want it to mix with the other voices.

So many of them.

Fuck, you're so tight. You sure you've been fucked before?

Shh, don't cry diamond, it'll only hurt for a second.

I can't wait to hear you scream.

Let me see that blood, baby. Show me how hard I tear you apart with my cock.

"You're no different, right?" I bite out, my voice cracking. "You've forced yourself on me before, remember? Taken from me—*stolen* from me. What makes you so different, huh?"

My eyes burn from the tears welling up. And within seconds, they spill, running down my cheeks.

"Do those memories keep you up at night?" he asks, his voice soft. "Do they torment you?"

He bares his teeth, his own ire flashing in his eyes. "Do you think about my touch as anything other than a fucking godsend?"

"I do now!" I shout, thrusting the gun at him. I suck in a sharp breath as a sob crawls up my throat.

He nods slowly, the anger dimming in his eyes. Deep down, I know better. I know he's not angry with me.

He's angry because he's helpless.

Hopeless.

A goddamn lost cause.

Because I will never be the same. And he knows that.

But what he doesn't know is what that means for him. *For us.*

The sob escapes, but the rage persists.

Slowly, he steps towards me like approaching a scared animal with vicious teeth. His eyes don't stray from mine as he advances, and I'm so close to slipping back into that paralyzing hold he has on me. And then he's right before me again, pressing his forehead into the barrel of the gun.

"Does this make you feel powerful?" he murmurs.

Another sob breaks free, but I don't lower the weapon.

"Does this make you feel alive again?"

I scowl but can't muster the courage to respond. I can't articulate what it makes me feel—I just know that it makes me feel *something.*

"What you've forgotten is that the heart beating inside your chest isn't fucking yours," he snarls. "It's *mine.* And if my heart has stopped working, then pull that trigger, little mouse. Kill the rest of me. I'm nothing if I'm not the reason you breathe."

I break, and screw my eyes shut against the flood of tears, but it's like putting a piece of paper over a bursting pipe.

My face contorts as pure agony consumes me.

"I don't want to feel anymore," I choke out, barely getting the words out before a gut-wrenching sob bursts past my lips.

"Let me—*fuck* Addie, just let me fucking hold you," he bites, his voice breaking.

He tears the gun from my grip and tosses it on the bed, and then I'm being swooped up into his arms, weightless as he lifts me up against his solid chest.

I open my mouth, and I scream. I scream and scream until my voice cracks beneath the pressure. Until I fear my throat will shred from the force.

I want to crawl outside of my body so desperately. Just so I can escape this feeling.

No. What I want is that gun back in my hand so I can turn it on myself.

One last shout rips out of my throat, this one so full of pain that it brings Zade to his knees.

And finally, the pillar crumbles.

The raw sound tapers off, fading into a hoarse, staccato cry.

I suck in a deep breath, filling my lungs with oxygen that I don't want, but I'm too lost in my grief to scream like I want to.

Zade's hold tightens painfully, trembles racking his body as he clings to me. He stuffs his face in my neck and he just... listens.

Listens to his heart breaking inside my chest.

The voices in my head amplify, and I'm clawing at my skull, desperate to get them out. But his hands stop me, grabbing onto them and trapping them between our chests.

"They are not here anymore," he whispers unevenly. "Listen to my voice instead, baby."

I shake my head, but he keeps talking anyway. He tells me about the first time he saw me and how unsure of myself I seemed in a room full of people. He says I looked like I was trapped in a glass box, and everyone else on the outside was observing me like a zoo animal. Then, he talks about the first time I confronted him. How I ran out of my door screaming like a banshee, fire in my eyes and spewing venom from my tongue. He recalls how utterly stunned he was by my courage, and how deeply he fell in that single moment.

"I've seen the woman who could hardly stand to be in her own skin, and the woman comfortable in a gothic mansion, at home with herself and the ghosts that haunt her. I loved both versions of you, and I love who you are now—someone full of both strength and vulnerability. Yet still, you carry fire in your heart, and that will never fucking change. They will never take that from you, Adeline."

His words only make me cry harder, but just as he promised, it slowly chases away the voices.

An indescribable amount of time passes before I finally calm down enough to string together a sentence.

"Sometimes, I don't know if I'll ever be able to fully tolerate your touch," I confess in a broken whisper.

"Are you okay with that?" he counters. "Is that how you want to live your life? Fearing the touch of a man—of *me*."

Do I? Part of me wants to retreat in on myself and not let another man lay his hands on me for the rest of my life. I don't want to see the images flash through my mind every time I feel skin slide against mine.

But then there's another part of me that rages and lashes against that notion. The same part that allowed me to use his hand and that knife handle as a release. I don't want those men to take more from me than they already have.

Because if I do, they'll never stop. I'll continue to hand over every piece of myself until there's nothing left but a chalk outline.

"I don't know how to... be okay with it."

"Not even with your own hand?" he rasps. He pulls away, gently setting me on the floor.

"You took back the power with that knife. Now you can take it back when it comes to physical touch. Let me show you."

My brows furrow as I stare up at him through puffy eyes with confusion.

His glistening stare picks apart my face, and I don't need a mirror to know that my skin is flushed red and dried tears mar my cheeks.

Reaching over me, he grabs a rose on the nightstand, twirling the stem in his fingers. The thorns slice through his skin and tiny pinpricks of blood sprout.

"You didn't clip the thorns," I whisper.

"I've been protecting you from getting hurt, but sometimes embracing the pain is the only way to overcome it. Take off your dress," he orders quietly. I blink and open my mouth, but he cuts me off, "Just trust me, Adeline. I'm not going to do anything you don't want me to."

I only stare at him, my heart picking up speed as his spoken expectations linger between us.

Swallowing thickly, I reach behind me and blindly unzip my dress, letting the top half drop down my arms. Quickly, I shuffle the material down my body before I can think about what I'm doing. What he's making me do.

"Good girl," he breathes. "Your bra, too, Addie. Take it all off."

I shake my head, the remnants of their voices starting to rise again.

"Don't think right now. Just do as I say."

Biting my lip, I snap my strapless bra off and throw that to the side.

"Good girl," he praises. His eyes stay firmly locked on mine. I wait for them to drop, but they resist.

Such a pretty diamond, look at—

"Don't think, Adeline."

I pinch my eyes shut, shaking the thoughts from my head.

My chest is too tight, and panic is starting to set in again.

"Zade—"

"Shh," he hushes. He sits on the ground, leaning against the bed frame and spreading his legs. My muscles tighten until I'm vibrating with the need to get away.

"Sit here," he says firmly, patting the ground between his legs.

Hesitating, it takes a few seconds to gain the courage to listen and crawl toward him. I look anywhere but at his face. If I see him, I might back out.

"Turn away from me."

There's no stopping the look of relief before I twist around and settle between his thick thighs.

I'm still strung tight, but I can breathe a little easier this way.

"I'm going to lean you back into me," he warns. Biting my lip, I nod my head, allowing his hand to come around my body and press on my chest, guiding me to lean back.

It feels like trying to bend a metal spoon. It takes effort, but eventually, I rest against his chest. His heat soaks into my skin, like the sun shining on your face on the first warm day of spring after a long, cold winter.

"That's it, baby. Relax."

It takes several swallows before the lump forming in my throat dissipates.

"Breathe," he whispers.

I do. I try to, at least.

The oxygen stutters out of me like an old engine. With every intake, it feels like I'm breathing in chemicals. Everything burns. Everything is too tight.

"Take this," he directs, holding the rose in his bandaged hand. Tiny trails of blood slide down his wrist, and something about that is calming, just like when he cut his hand open on the knife to bring me pleasure.

Watching someone else bleed doesn't make me feel quite so alone.

I take the rose, a thorn immediately pricking my skin, but I hardly feel it. Not with all of my attention on the heat of his body pressing into my back.

"Can I touch your thighs, baby?" he asks, his tone hushed and deep. Another nod of my head, and his large hands are slowly spreading my thighs. All of my focus zeroes in on the movement, and the terror is becoming too much. Tingles blossom in the tips of my fingers, and I know pretty soon, they'll travel up my limbs until I can no longer feel them.

"Relax," he soothes. "I'm going to ask you a question, and I want you to think about it really hard, okay?"

Sucking in a deep breath, I hold it for a few seconds before releasing it. And then I nod, working to calm myself.

"What makes you feel powerful, Addie? Was it holding that gun in your hand? Holding it to my head and knowing that you could take my life?"

Tears rise, followed by a touch of guilt.

"I'm so—"

"I don't want your apologies or guilt, Adeline. I want you to tell me the truth. What did holding a gun to my head make you feel?"

Tightening my lips, I quiet the shame and look past that. What did it make me feel?

It made me feel... in control. I was holding someone else's life in my hands, and it was my decision and only mine if I pulled that trigger. I held something precious. Something irreversible. And it was all... *mine.*

"It made me feel powerful," I admit.

"And what does power feel like?" he asks, his voice deepening as one of his hands trail up to my neck, avoiding my breasts. His touch is sensual but... safe.

"Let me feel you here."

His hand slowly slides up the column of my throat, giving me time to reject him. When I say nothing, he clutches the underside of my jaw, forcing my chin up as he pulls my head back against his chest. My gaze locks on the white ceiling as anxiety crawls through my body.

"Focus, Adeline. What does power feel like?"

I release another shaky breath and speak before I can think too deeply about it. "It makes me feel good."

"Good," he murmurs. "I want you to think about that feeling. In your mind, hold that gun to whoever you wish. To me. To any of the men that hurt you. Whatever makes you feel good."

I close my eyes, and the first person that comes to mind is Xavier. He's kneeling before me, begging for his life. I can still feel the heavy metal in my hand, but unlike just minutes before, my hand is perfectly still. No violent tremors rack my body as I hold Xavier's life in my hands.

I press the gun to his head, relishing in the pleas spilling from his lips. And I pull that fucking trigger.

"Now feel between your legs," Zade whispers, sensing how my breath has escalated for an entirely different reason.

Slowly, my hand reaches down, swiping between my legs. Moisture gathers on my fingers, and I'm surprised enough by the revelation that I completely forget about everything else. For just a moment, I bask in the fact that I'm aroused.

My breath falters, and shame filters in, but Zade senses that, too. With my throat still seized in his hand, he turns his head until his lips brush against the shell of my ear.

Warm breath skates across the side of my face as he whispers roughly, "Do you know how hard my cock gets when I think about all the ways I'm going to slowly torture the men that hurt you?"

I open my mouth, but no sound escapes. They evaporate on my tongue when Zade rolls his hips into my back, the evidence of his words digging into my lower spine.

It should repulse me. But it doesn't. And I clutch ahold of that feeling while it's there. I don't care if it's fucked up, it feels so much better than the constant agony.

I close my mouth and nod, acquiescing to the thoughts as the shame recedes.

"I'm going to touch your hand now," he whispers.

He keeps my throat in his grip while his free hand reaches up and wraps around mine, the rose still clenched in my fist. He squeezes tight, forcing the sharp thorns to spear my hand.

I inhale sharply, hissing between my teeth before gritting them against the pain. And then he guides our hands down until the soft petals brush against my pussy.

My eyes shutter as he glides the petals up and down, coating the rose in my arousal. I feel the blood rising to my cheeks as he lifts it again and presents the dripping flower to me.

"Zade…"

Blood trails down my arm as he releases my throat to grab my other hand and bring it to the rose, guiding my fingers across the petals.

"Do you feel how soft and wet these petals are?" he whispers. Licking my lips, I nod my head slowly. "This is what I feel every time I'm inside you."

Fuck, you feel like hea—

"Hold on to that feeling of power, baby. Don't let go of it."

I've tensed up again; my muscles strung tight. Shuddering, I shove out the intrusive voice and replace it with the image of pointing a gun to their head. Steady, and calmly as I pull the trigger.

I relax as he pushes my middle and ring fingers into the center of the rose, just like he would if it were my pussy.

The pain needling throughout my hand fades as a deep-seated pleasure takes hold. For the first time in so long, I feel sensuality and eroticism as I continue to push my fingers in and out of the rose, Zade's own fingers held over mine.

I feel the pressure building in my core, desperate for some type of release. Different faces flash through my mind like a movie reel, all of them meeting the same demise. The pressure between my legs grows and grows until I'm sure just one touch of my fingers would send me over the edge.

"Zade," I plead, though I don't know what I'm asking for.

"Tell me what you need," he says, continuing our movements with the rose.

"I... Touch me."

"Don't stop feeling this rose," he orders softly. I nod, my stomach clenching when he reaches between my legs.

The softest brush of his fingers nearly makes my eyes cross. I plunge in and out of the rose as his middle finger presses into my clit and starts circling the swollen bud.

My back arches and I can't stop the high-pitched moan that escapes as raw bliss rolls through me.

I force myself to feel Zade—to feel that a man is touching me. Making me feel good. And that I'm enjoying every second of it. And then I push those other men from my mind and think only of the one wrapped around me.

I don't want to come with the images of the depraved monsters that stole from me, even if I'm blowing their heads off. I only want to see the man that's given me everything. A beast who has bent my will to succumb to him yet has shown me the true meaning of love and devotion.

"Zade," I mewl as the orgasm crests. I hear him hiss through his teeth as he circles my clit faster. He still has his other hand wrapped around mine, the stem clenched in my grip. He flexes his fist, forcing the sharp thorns deeper into my flesh. The pain swirls with the heady pleasure and a hoarse shout rings out.

Rivulets of blood continue to trail down my arm, dripping off my elbow and onto my stomach. I look down, watching the streams of red aim towards where Zade touches me.

My mouth parts, the euphoria spiking as I watch him. His hand is fucking massive, with long fingers, thick veins laced throughout, seeming to pulse as he rubs my clit.

It's so erotic that I can't hold on any longer. I cry out as I finally let go, the orgasm crashing into me so hard that I nearly come off the floor from the power of it.

Zade growls, cupping my pussy as I ride the waves, my hips rolling against his hand while his name fills the air around us.

I feel him tensing beneath me, but I'm too lost to care. I'm too desperate for this feeling to never end.

We both drop the rose simultaneously, and I don't stop to consider what I'm doing when I reach back, grab ahold of Zade's face with both hands, and guide his lips down onto mine.

A deep rumble vibrates through his chest, and he once more seizes the underside of my jaw, granting us both a better angle as he devours me.

His tongue lashes against my own, tasting me until my lips are bruised and raw, and the orgasm has long since faded.

Yet the bliss remains. For the first time in months, those wicked men didn't plague my thoughts. I didn't hear their voices. Their laughter, and their cruel jokes.

And my body feels so much lighter because of it.

Finally, he pulls away, and all I can do is stare up at him in wonder— the person responsible for chasing away the monsters in my head.

They'll come back, but Zade isn't going anywhere either.

"Thank you," I whisper.

He closes his eyes and brushes his lips against mine softly.

"You'll always be safe with me, little mouse. Always."

Feeling invigorated, I twist in his arms and tear at his blazer, the buttons flying as his heated eyes lift to meet mine, his tongue slowly swiping across his bottom lip. Red is smeared across his cheek from my bloody hand, and the sight has my eyes nearly rolling.

He looks so goddamn savage, and I think my ovaries are exploding. He's going to get me pregnant just from this image alone.

"You sure you want to go there?" he asks, his voice dripping with sin.

"It's what I want," I say softly, albeit shakily.

He lifts up and the material slides down his arms. Then, I gather his button-up shirt until his abs are exposed, along with the dark tattoos inked into his flesh. Flattening my hands on his hard stomach, blood smearing across his skin, I push it farther up, but he stops me.

"Don't push yourself too hard. This wasn't about me."

When he goes to lean forward, I plant my hand on his chest and push him back firmly. His mismatched eyes round at the edges in surprise.

"Let me try, Zade. I'm not going to fuck you yet. I just want to touch you."

Chapter Thirty Three
The Diamond

I've never seen Zade indecisive before. Not until now, while he picks apart every iota of my expression to determine if he should let me touch him.

Then, like a monster tearing through flesh, his beast takes over. He seizes me by the jaw, bringing my face close to his.

"You think you're ready for me? Let's see how far you're willing to go to please me."

He lifts me off him, setting me to the side, then stands, pausing to look down at me with an unreadable expression. His face is smoothed into cold marble.

Turning away, he walks to a black chair a few feet in front of me. He sits there some nights if he can't sleep, waiting and watching for a nightmare to arise—always watching me.

Next to the chair is a little table where a glass and a canter of whiskey sits. He pours himself three fingers and then sits back in the chair, widening his knees with his arm hanging over the side, the glass held by the tips of his fingers.

He eyes me, taking a sip of his whiskey before resuming his position.

"Crawl to me," he orders, his voice as rough as lava rock, yet as enticing as the spiced whiskey he swallowed. "Show me how pretty you are begging on your knees for my cock."

My stomach tightens with heat, and I feel my thighs growing slicker.

I make a split-second decision and grab the rose, and place it between my teeth, reveling in the small stings on my lips from the thorns.

Copper blooms on my tongue as I heed his orders, crawling on my hands and knees with his precious rose in my mouth, hips and breasts swaying sensually.

His eyes light up, and his nostrils flare. The cool demeanor slips, and raw desire bleeds through the cracks.

When I reach him, I kneel and set the rose on my lap.

"Was that pretty enough for you?"

He chuckles and finishes off his whiskey, setting the glass down on the table.

"You're so fucking beautiful; I want to cut the eyes from those who get the privilege to look at you," he rasps, licking his lips predatorily.

He sits up enough to pull the shirt over his head, baring himself completely. My mouth waters at the sight of him and I feel my skin flush all over again from how sinfully delicious he looks.

Something about tanned skin covered in black tattoos… Jesus Christ, thank you, She-Devil for inventing a man like Zade.

My eyes linger on the scar cutting through his abs, and I decide that

I want to be as strong as Zade. A man who has faced death with a smile on his face countless times, only for him to turn around and do it again. Over and over.

Gently, I drift my fingers across the crimson handprint streaked across his stomach, intoxicated by the sight of him twitching beneath me. The tension condenses until it feels like I'm wading through lava.

My jaw is in his hand again within seconds, his thumb smearing the dots of blood along my lips.

"I want to see this blood all over my cock," he murmurs. "Take off my belt."

Heeding his command, the metal clings as my fingers deftly undo the buckle, and memories surface of him wrapping this belt around my neck as he fucked my mouth.

I want that again, but I know I'm not quite ready for it yet.

He releases my jaw as I make quick work of his button and zipper, delighting in the sound of metal teeth breaking apart for me. His cock bursts free before I finish unzipping, and this time, my mouth dries.

Somehow, I've forgotten how intimidating his size is.

Licking my lips, I grab the rose, spread my knees, and glide the soft petals through my slit again, once more soaking them with my arousal.

He watches me closely as I sit up, and drag the stem across his hip slowly, the sharp thorns biting into his sensitive flesh. He hisses between his teeth, his eyes flashing viciously.

Trapping my bloody lip between my teeth, I trail the petals alongside the ridge of his cock, delighting in the way his stomach clenches. Veins protrude from his length, and I follow them up to the tip with the flower, coating him in my wetness.

"Addie," he warns when I slide it down to his balls, causing him to tense. My lips curl mischievously as I lean forward and place a soft kiss on his cock, staring up at him beneath my lashes with a sultry look.

He growls, and his patience snaps. He's fisting my hair and leaning forward, his sharp words rumbling in my ear, "Do you want to trade places and make me beg on my knees? I've waited so long to feel your mouth wrapped around my cock, little mouse, and I would do terrible things for you if that's what it takes."

"Patience, baby," I whisper, my pussy throbbing when he groans. He becomes so malleable from a simple endearment, and once more, that sense of power flares.

Flattening my palm on his chest, I push him back, his body strung tight. Keeping our gazes locked, I dart my tongue out and lick around the tip of his cock, watching his lips pull into a snarl and his eyes blaze. He never looks human when he's inside of me.

I focus on him, blocking out the voices before they can truly enter, and holding on to the sight of Zade melting like ice beneath me. That vision gives me the control I so desperately need, and I realize it's so much easier to stay in the present when I have something to savor: Zade at my mercy.

I take him deeper into my mouth, sliding my tongue along the ridge and pulling a mixture of a groan and a growl from him.

His fingers drift into my hair, weaving through the strands and holding tight. Moans fall past his lips, spurring me on. I hollow out my cheeks, sucking him deeper until the tip hits the back of my throat. Even then, I don't let up, holding back a gag until tears leak from my eyes.

For a few moments, I hold on until I can't anymore, gagging a little and retreating until he pops free, a trail of red-tinted saliva clinging to my bottom lip.

Just like he wanted, the blood from my mouth is smeared down his length, and a sick thought flashes in my mind.

I understand why Xavier liked it so much.

"Keep sucking," he hisses, pulling me out of my head. Breathing in deep, I hold my breath as I swallow him once more, tears welling in my eyes from the sheer size of him.

His hand grabs the nape of my neck to keep me still while he pumps his hips, a growl rumbling from deep in his chest.

My pussy throbs in response, and embarrassingly enough, I almost want to cry. I was convinced I'd always be broken, never being able to touch or be touched. But giving Zade pleasure doesn't make me feel weak and helpless like I thought it would. To see him lose himself in my mouth makes me feel like a queen sitting upon her throne.

He needs me so fucking bad in this moment and knowing I can take it away… my thighs clench to abate the ache growing between them.

He fucks my mouth savagely, saliva spilling past my lips in which I use my hand to spread up and down his length, his teeth gnashing in response.

I come up for air, trails of spit connecting his dick to my mouth.

"Stick out that tongue for me, baby."

I do as he says without regard, peering at him through my wet lashes.

"Such a good fucking girl," he rasps. He grabs the base of his cock and slaps it on my tongue a few times, his brows pinched, and mouth parted.

A beast and a god twisted together, forming something wholly unnatural.

And I realize, I never needed to be afraid of his touch. It was *men* that defiled me, and Zade was never a man.

I tug against his hold in my hair, but he resists, fisting the strands tighter. He lifts his other hand and drags his thumbs roughly over the underside of my eyes, smearing mascara down my cheeks.

His chest rumbles, and his voice is guttural when he says, "You look like such a pretty whore for me."

A flash of anger ignites inside of me, and he only smiles in response. He jerks my head closer to him. The tip of his cock brushes against my breasts, and his eyes fall, a spark flaring in his gaze. By the time he drags his eyes up to me, I know exactly what he's thinking.

"You were never a whore for those men, little mouse. You know why?"

"Why?" I whisper.

"Because they never owned any part of you. They took what they did not possess. That doesn't make you a whore; that makes you a survivor."

A sheen of tears wells over my eyes. I drop them to conceal the weakness, but he jerks my head up, refusing to let me hide.

A devilish grin quirks his lips up. "But you are *my* whore. You're my everything, and you become so much more with each passing day. I possess every fucking part of you, Adeline. Even when you screamed and cried that you didn't want me, you could never let me go. All those nights you stood at your window, letting me watch you. Confronting me instead of running and instigating me knowing what would happen. And when you did run, you only ever used your mouth to try and get away. You gravitated towards me, just as I did you. And that is something no other man will ever have."

He's right. I never did act appropriately to him stalking me.

There's no denying how contradicting it is to assault and stalk a woman when you're trying to save others from the same thing. Nor is there denying how despite these things, there's a twisted part of me that has always liked it. It was never about my body succumbing to him, but my soul, too.

Xavier wanted from me what only Zade could accomplish. He wanted my body to reveal a hidden truth and show him that our connection ran deeper than flesh on flesh. And when the only truth he found was that I would never want him, he grew angry and desperate.

That was a truth only Zade could uncover.

Like attracted to like—his darkness to mine. I was running from it while he was forcing me to see who I really am.

Zade and I—we don't make sense to the outside world. Barely even in my own head. Yet I'm finding it hard to care anymore. I won't ever justify what Zade has done to me, but I do forgive him. Not only that, but I accept him.

He told me before that he wanted me to fall in love with the darkest parts of him, and I have.

Every fucked-up piece of him.

Sensing the resolve, he jerks my head again. "Spit on my cock, baby. Get it nice and wet for me."

Keeping my eyes locked on his, I stick out my tongue, letting the saliva pool before dripping off the tip and right onto his cock.

"Can never be too wet, can you, kitty cat?" I say coyly, echoing his words back to him from our first encounter.

He grins, the act damning to my soul. Lifting his hand, he thumbs my bottom lip harshly.

"Keep it up, little mouse. This sharp tongue isn't the only thing capable of getting me wet. I could come just thinking about my cock covered in your blood."

I bite my lip, a shot of fear pulsing through my system from his dangerous tone. A shiver rolls down my spine, hitting each vertebra on the way down.

It feels fucking glorious.

I rub my spit up and down his length, the noises crude. His eyes droop, his mouth opens as he stares at me like he's praying I defy him.

"Good girl," he drawls. "Now lean forward and put my dick between those beautiful tits of yours."

Biting my lip, I do as he asks, looking up at him seductively. He may be spitting his demands, but he's still under my mercy. Proven by the way his head tips back, a groan working through his throat, his Adam's apple bobbing.

He succumbs to me like the Titanic did the ocean. Indestructible—unsinkable—to everyone but me. I'm the raging sea that conquered him and sunk him to his very knees, and he was helpless to stop me.

He pistons his hips upward, and I squeeze him tighter between my breasts, tipping my chin down to let another trail of spit fall from my tongue.

The sight of his cock driving up between them has my pussy clenching, arousal spreading down my thighs. A moan of my own slips out, pulling his eyes back down to me.

"Is this making your pussy wet?" he grinds out past his teeth, punctuating it with a harsh thrust. "Moaning like a whore while watching me fuck your tits. Does it make you wish it was your pussy instead?"

"Yes," I confess, riveted by the fierce look on his face. My heart ramps up, but I trust Zade. I trust that he knows how far to push me.

"Rub your clit, I want you to come when I do," he orders, knocking away my hands from my breasts and replacing them with his own, squeezing them tightly around his length.

Reaching down, I swirl my finger across my clit, shuddering and grinding my hips against my hand harder.

My head begins to tip back, eyes rolling as I circle faster. Zade's hand sharply slaps the side of my breast, and I snap my head back down in response with a yelp.

"Eyes on me, little mouse."

He thrusts his hips in quick, short thrusts, and I can only stare, intoxicated by the sight of a god coming undone.

"Fuck, Addie. These tits are going to be covered in my cum. You ready for me, baby?"

I nod my head frantically, my voice trapped beneath the moans spilling from my mouth.

His grip becomes bruising, but it's hardly noticeable when my stomach is tightening, and I'm so close to falling over the edge for the second time tonight.

His hips stutter and then he's shouting, cursing my name as streams of his seed paint my skin. I erupt in the same moment, shuddering violently and rocking against my hand riotously.

Deeper and deeper, I fall into the depths of his depravity, and I find that I never want to come out.

It takes several moments for my vision to focus and the bliss to recede. I'm breathless and flushed by the time I come down. He reaches forward, grabbing me beneath my arms and lifting me up on his lap.

Then, he reaches over and grabs his shirt from the floor and cleans me up.

A satisfied look relaxes his face, drawing out a small smile. Until I glance down at his chest, seeing something I hadn't noticed before.

"What is that?" I ask, my voice strangled with shock. He balls up the shirt and tosses it to the side, then locks his gaze onto mine.

"A reminder," he answers simply.

I try to swallow, words getting stuck in my throat like dry bread.

"What did you do?" I croak. It burns my fingertips as I brush them across his most recent scar, as if he branded himself and the flesh is still sizzling.

Glaring at me is a macabre rose marring the skin directly over his heart, cutting into the old scar. A fucking rose. He carved a symbol of his love for me into his chest.

"Why?"

His gaze sears into me with so many different emotions swirling in the mismatched pools. Regret. Shame. Guilt. Fury. All prevalent as he stares up at me like I'm a fading mirage, and he doesn't know how to let me go.

"I told you I don't hide from my failures," he says softly. "What happened to you was my failure. And this serves as a reminder every day."

I shake my head, at a loss for words. Several times, I open my mouth, but nothing comes out.

"Zade," I finally choke out. "It wasn't your fault."

"Maybe not directly, but that doesn't exempt me from blame. Max sold you out because of the bad blood between us and I should've killed him when he first started giving you trouble. That was my first mistake, and because of that, you were kidnapped."

His fists clench and the muscle in his jaw thrums against his skin. Any second now, it just might burst.

"And that was my second mistake," he rasps. "My protection wasn't good enough. I can't always be by your side, we both know that, but it was too easy for them to take you. I won't make that mistake again."

His hand drifts through the tendrils of my hair before brushing softly against the back of my neck.

"I don't care if I need to set this world on fire until there's no one left but you and me. The world will burn around us, and I'll gladly live in chaos with you as long as the only person that is a danger to you is me."

Clenching my teeth, I dig my nail into the rose. He hisses but doesn't stop me.

"Stop taking the blame for other people being fucked in the head. *You* didn't put a target on my head. *You* didn't sell me out in the name of revenge and money. And *you* didn't kidnap me and sell me off into the sex trade. What you did was find me and save me."

I dig my nail in harder, a bloody crescent moon forming over the rose.

"You rescued me, and I will never forget that. And the only way I can repay you is by saving myself. Getting stronger and not letting what those sick fucks did to me control my life. I may have cracked, but they did not shatter me. My rose still has fucking thorns, Zade. Do you understand me?"

Before he can respond, I lean forward and collect the beads of blood on my tongue. Then, I slowly lick my lips, smearing the crimson around my mouth like lipstick.

His eyes zero in on the movement, his chest heaving.

"I wanted to know what it tasted like when someone else bleeds for me," I whisper.

He works his jaw. "I'll always bleed for you," he whispers before gripping my jaw in his hand and connecting his lips softly with mine, licking his blood from my lips.

"You're still my helpless little mouse, but only when it comes to my irresistible prowess," he says when he pulls away, gracing me with a shit-eating grin.

I close my eyes, a laugh bursting from my mouth. A single tear slips out, emotions rising up my throat. The happy vapors are back, and I hope to God they stick around for a little while this time.

"You're such a prick."

"No, baby, I'm just the masochist that can't get enough of your beauty, even when you draw blood." He glances down at the tiny droplets sprouting from where I dug my nail into his skin.

I purse my lips. "I guess I'm the prick then."

June 2nd, 2022

The first time I saw a rose with clipped thorns sitting next to an empty whiskey glass, I'm ashamed to admit that I cried. He always leaves them around, even still.

It was melancholic, and a part of me wished we could go back to that time so badly, where I was just a normal girl, and the worst thing to ever happen to me was gaining the attention of an ~~evil~~ enigmatic shadow.

The new Addie would roll her eyes at the old Addie, scoffing at her complaints over a stalker when the worst was yet to come.

There were many times when I was laying in that lumpy bed in Francesca's house, crying my eyes out because I knew my problems would never be so simple anymore. Crying because I lost that girl who took naked pictures of herself because she loved her body. The girl who laughed freely, wrote words that moved people, and walked through life never checking over her shoulder.

I want her back.

Because now, I can hardly look at myself in the mirror.

It's hard to laugh anymore.

I haven't written a damn word since I've been home. Not for a book anyway.

And I'm scared. So scared that this freedom will be snatched away as easily as it was the first time.

Chapter Thirty Four

The Diamond

"Ring around the rosies, pocket full of posies," Sibby sings loudly, skipping around the three wriggling bodies strapped to their chairs. "Ashes, ashes, we all fall DOWN!" she screams, kicking the back of Rocco's chair on the last word. She shouts it so loudly, even I jump.

I let out a long-suffering sigh. She's been singing all damn day, taunting them to the point that Francesca has officially soiled herself.

I'll admit—that was pretty fucking funny.

Zade let her have her fun and get as much information out of the three as possible—*after* she pinky swore and crossed her heart and hoped to die not to kill them. Unsurprisingly, Sibby has proven to be just as skilled with psychological torture as she is with physical. She made them want to die without even having to touch them.

I have a feeling it's partly because of her atrocious singing, but I'm not about to tell her that.

For the past week, she's been getting names of people who attend the Culling every year—whether they come as spectators or participants— the other traffickers who bought girls, and of course, any information Francesca and Xavier have on Claire.

"Rio Sanchez," Sibby sings. "Still not going to tell me where he is?"

Francesca rolls her eyes, feigning an attitude to conceal just how frightened she is of a girl circling her like a hungry shark.

It's not working.

Sibby is scary.

"I told you this already, I don't know where he is. He helped *her* escape, and then he fled. That's all I know, and frankly, I would gladly hand him over to you because I want him dead, too!" she says, her voice ending in a frustrated screech. She's flushed bright red and panting. Anger, pain, and frustration all etched into the harsh lines in her face. Old makeup is cracked and smudging, aging her ten years.

She is *so* going to die with acne all over her face and I find poetic justice in that.

I roll my lips, attempting to ignore the sharp pain stabbing in the center of my chest. Anytime I think of Rio and what will happen when Zade eventually gets his hands on him... I kind of want to cry.

My feelings towards him are complicated, and I'm not sure I'll ever truly understand them. Even more so now that I've met his sister and learned that the evil bitch before me was forcing him to do a lot more for her than I initially thought.

I said I wouldn't feel guilty when Zade got ahold of him. But then he saved me. And now, I can't say that I'll stop Zade... but I can't say I'll feel nothing either.

"Do you want him dead because he helped the diamond escape, or because he betrayed you and put a crack in that icy little heart?" I ask.

Her eyes spit fire while she glowers at me.

"He was nothing more than a good fuck," she seethes.

I bend at the waist, thinning my eyes. "Did you have to threaten to kill his sister every time you wanted him to fuck you?"

Rocco snorts, and Francesca's head whips to him in offense. He's pale, sweaty, and seemingly tired, but the malice in his eyes is unmistakable. "She stopped threatening that after the first two years—and I think it's just because he got tired of hearing it."

"Shut the *fuck up*!" she screeches, her face turning a ghastly shade of purple. Doesn't suit her complexion very well.

"No! We're in this fucking situation because of *you*!" he shouts back. "Because you couldn't keep a handle on that stupid little bitch and refused to get rid of her. And now look!"

Francesca's bottom lip trembles. "Sydney was worth—"

"She wasn't worth shit!" he roars.

"She was!"

"Or she was keeping your secrets," I cut in dryly. Francesca's head snaps to me so quick, she nearly does herself a favor and breaks it.

"What did she tell you?" she demands, her voice cracking and eyes wild.

I shrug nonchalantly, giving nothing away. Sydney didn't tell me shit, but Francesca doesn't need to know that.

"Sydney knew?" Rocco asks with rage.

Francesca's eyes widen, and she turns to Rocco with desperation.

"She found out... I-I don't know how. But she threatened to tell Claire if I allowed her to be auctioned. She acted out because it was the only thing keeping her in the house and our secret safe."

My brows knit, trying to decipher what exactly Sydney knew.

"Why didn't you just kill her?" Rocco growls through gritted teeth.

"Claire wouldn't allow me to! She forced me to deal with it as a punishment for failing to get Sydney under control," Francesca cries, nearly pleading with her brother.

Rocco looks away, "Is that why you stopped letting people fuck them?"

Now I really am confused. Sibby and I glance at each other, and she must note my expression because she comes around and gets in Francesca's face.

"Tell me what you were doing," she demands. "I don't like being left out."

Francesca snarls but quickly cowers when Sibby raises the pink knife to her eye and threatens, "I'll cut it out and make you chew it."

Gross.

"We were making money under the table. People would pay us for a night with one of the girls. We were making good money, too, but then Sydney found out and used it against me."

My brows shoot up, surprised by their gall to profit off of the girls behind Claire's back, yet not at all because—well, it's fucking Francesca and Rocco.

Even Xavier whistles and looks at them with a lopsided grin. He's just as exhausted as the other two.

"Brave thing to do. Claire would've murdered you slowly if she found out."

Rocco scoffs. "Should've just saved us all the fucking headache and let her tell," he spits. "She was already crazy from that fucking cult. Did you think Claire was going to actually believe her?" He ends his question with a patronizing laugh. Xavier shrugs in a *you got me there* way while Francesca just gapes at him.

None of them notice the frozen girl standing before them, her spine ramrod straight and shock painted on her face.

"What cult?" Sibby finally cuts in.

Francesca's mouth opens, then closes. "I don't know," she sneers. "All I know is some girl killed the leader, and the entire cult disbanded after that. Wandered aimlessly 'cause they knew fuck all of what to do with themselves."

My eyes widen gradually as she speaks.

There's no way.

"How did Sydney get to Washington?" I ask.

"How else? She was homeless and picked up off the streets from a trafficker and shipped to me to be groomed," she answers, her tone dipped in venom. "I'm one of the best in the *world*, and she was a tough case. I was working on her." She spits the last part to Rocco, flickering a scornful glare his way.

"Sibby, did you know her?"

She turns to me, a frown tugging down her lips.

"What did she look like?"

"Blonde hair, brown eyes. Two front teeth were crooked. She had a beauty mark on the corner of her mouth, too."

She works to swallow, but eventually nods her head. "Yeah, I knew her. She was my sister. I mean, all the children were my siblings. Daddy was the only one allowed to get anyone pregnant..." she trails off, seemingly dumbfounded.

That... actually makes a lot of sense—Sibby and Sydney coming from the same cult. Now that I think about it, their mannerisms are very similar. Bizarre, creepy, and their maturity stunted. They're both murderous psychos, but at least Sibby has a heart of fucking gold, whereas Sydney's was ashen.

Her expression drops, and she looks at me with all the seriousness in the world. "She tried to kill you? She was the one that kept hurting you?"

Thinning my lips, I nod.

"I'm sorry, Addie. It's my fault she ever ended up there."

Frowning, I say, "Sibby, it wasn't your fault."

"It was," she insists. "She had nowhere to go because I killed Daddy. All of them were left alone. She would've never—"

I grab her hand, squeezing it tightly. "Sibby, you couldn't have known any of that would happen. You did everyone a favor by killing that man. He was a demon, remember?"

Her lip trembles, but she nods. "Sydney was, too, and she probably smelled like a rotten egg. I'm glad you killed her."

I peck her cheek, hoping to rid her of any lingering guilt. "Go on upstairs. You did great, and we got everything we needed. I just have one more question to ask."

She smiles and skips up the stairs, sadness forgotten.

I train my gaze on Francesca. "What happened to Molly?"

Her brows pinch with confusion, so I clarify, "She was a captive back in 2008. She wrote in the journal, and I found it inside the floorboards in my room. I started writing in it, too. It's actually why Sydney was going to kill me. I was planning to escape, and she found out by reading that journal."

Her expression sours, and I can almost see the memories flicking across her gaze.

"She escaped. The first and last girl to get away… until you," she says, muttering the last part with indigence.

A smile curls my lips, and pride fills my veins.

For Molly and for myself.

"Thank you." Clapping my hands, causing the three of them to startle, I offer them a huge smile. "It's time."

Francesca's golden-brown eyes round with confusion and fear. Not so long ago, we stood in opposite shoes. Drowning in helplessness and sorrow, wondering how this could be happening to me. There she stood, staring down at me with the same expression that I now wear.

She showed me no mercy. And I will return that favor tenfold.

Maybe she did care, but not enough to save me from herself.

"Time?" she echoes, her voice breaking.

My grin widens further, not bothering to hide just how vindictive I feel.

"For the Culling," I supply, my voice dipped in honey and sugar. "And you, my dear, are the prey."

Imposters syndrome—something many authors deal with from time to time. When we accomplish something we never thought possible, things we only ever dreamed of, those are oftentimes the most difficult moments to grapple with.

Do I deserve this?

It's similar to what Francesca, Xavier, and Rocco look like now— staring at the tree line before Parsons Manor, feeling like an imposter in their own life.

Instead of the inability to accept their accomplishments, they're unable to accept their fate.

Am I really so vile—so evil—that I deserve to be hunted like a fucking animal?

I could answer that, but I'd rather show them.

Zade and Sibby stand on either side of me, a crossbow hanging loosely in their hands, the cold, gleaming metal identical to mine. The heavy weight feels familiar. I've been practicing for this very moment.

My heartbeat pulsates in my ears, drowning out Francesca's incessant sniveling. We're standing behind them, the brisk air saturated with anticipation.

"You know," I say loudly, causing her to flinch. "You would've beat the shit out of me if I had cried."

She shakes her head, refusing to answer. Her head is tipped down, a mop of stringy hair falling over her shoulders and revealing how badly she's deteriorating. Her spine is protruding from her skin, poking through the threadbare t-shirt she wears.

Xavier and Rocco stand beside her with stone in their shoulders, holding tightly on to the façade that they're strong and brave.

Such manly men, they are.

I'd like to see if that ideology holds firm when they're running for their lives or if they'll die in a puddle of piss and regret.

"You three are luckier than I was. There's no maze or traps in here for you. Just the sharp tip of our arrows."

"And if you can't find us? Then we get away, and you're fucked," Xavier retorts pompously. He must feel so smart right now.

I smile. "You won't get away."

He tips up his chin, eager to prove me wrong.

"You placed several rules on me, but I'm only giving you one. You can't escape out of the driveway. There are several armed guards stationed all the way down. If you want out, you go all the way through and find the road."

He stiffens, and my smile grows. Xavier thought he could cut left, run twenty feet, come out to my driveway, and escape that way. If they were going to make it hard on me, the least I can do is return the favor.

"Which one do you think is tastiest?" Sibby asks, bouncing on her toes with excitement and restlessness.

I curl my lip in disgust, wrinkling my nose. "Don't be gross. We're not cannibals."

Sibby scoffs. "I would never taint my body with demon meat. *We* won't be eating them, but the vultures will."

"She's got a way with words," Zade says dryly, a tinge of amusement in his tone.

That she does.

"Remember, Sibby, *don't* shoot to kill. Find and bring her to one of us when she's down," I remind.

She grumbles in response but doesn't argue. I want to experience all of their deaths, so just like the Culling, we'll kill them together.

"Ready?" I call out. Francesca's shoulders shake with sobs, but I pay her no mind.

Xavier and Rocco don't verbally answer, but their bodies tighten.

"Run," Zade commands, laughing when Francesca takes off and then immediately stumbles over her feet, nearly face-planting the dirt ground.

Sibby giggles, her bouncing increasing. She will be hunting Francesca, Zade will be after Rocco, and Xavier... is mine.

Zade wanted to line them up and test if he could shoot an arrow through all three of their heads at once, but I wanted them to swallow the same pill they forced down my throat. I wanted them to suffer as I did. To choke on the bitterness of having your life in someone else's hands, just to have it thrown to the ground and fucking stomped on.

Only a monster can create another monster. And that's exactly who

I've become.

Sibby takes off after Francesca, a nursery rhyme echoing across the forest. Zade takes a step forward, then pauses to glance back at me, only the scar slashing through his white eye and the side of his mouth visible beneath the black hood.

"You look absolutely divine dressed in wolves' clothing, but don't think I won't tear them from your body the second he's dead. Enjoy your hunt, little mouse. You won't be the only predator on the loose."

Warmth spreads throughout my stomach, dropping low just as his eyes do, giving me one last heated look before turning and taking off after Rocco.

I've told him some of the things Francesca's lovely brother has done to me. By the time the last breath leaves his body, he won't have a drop of blood left inside him. And for the first time, I'm not ashamed that I find pleasure out of another's death.

Biting my lip, I head into the forest. The temperature drops as I silently make my way through, foliage crunching beneath my feet. A sharp thrill is zinging throughout my body, yet I keep my pace quick but steady.

Xavier is confident he'll get away, but with how deep these woods are, we're confident none of them will find their way out before we catch up to them.

The wind blowing through leaves, birds chirping, and the critters rustling in the brush fade as my focus sharpens on what I do need to hear—branches snapping, the crunch of leaves beneath footsteps, and heavy breathing.

There's a clear impression of his boot to my left, so I turn and follow after his prints.

About fifteen tense minutes pass, and I alternate between a steady jog and walking. There are no maze walls keeping them confined in one area, so it'll be easy for them to get lost.

Xavier believes he can find his way out, but it would take him hours, and that's without getting turned around.

A sudden, loud screech startles me, sending birds tearing through the branches, followed by evil cackling. Sounds like Francesca's scream, and if she's not already hit, she came very close to it.

I exhale shakily, my heart racing and sweat gathering at the base of my spine.

Another scream from Francesca, the tail end cutting off abruptly—presumably from Sibby silencing her somehow. In that single moment, meant to be hidden beneath her scream, was a twig cracking.

My head snaps in the direction, off to my left, where I see a flash of a hand before it disappears behind a tree trunk. He's about thirty feet ahead of me.

Clenching my jaw, I raise my crossbow and take aim. The second he steps out from that tree, no matter which direction he heads, I'll have a perfect shot.

Does he feel like a fly caught in the spider's web? Trapped where he stands while the black widow stalks from afar.

It's exhilarating. The heady feeling pulsating between my thighs, causing my cheeks to flush and my lids to droop.

My focus sharpens until Xavier's fear is all I can see, smell, and taste. How helpless he must feel, knowing his end is nearing.

"How does it feel?" I ask, just loud enough for him to hear.

Far off in the distance, another shout rings out, this time from Rocco. But they're so far away, it barely penetrates the shroud wrapped around him and me.

He doesn't answer, possibly holding on to hope that I don't know exactly where he is. As if every breath he takes can't be felt through the strings of my web.

"Does it make you sick with fear?" I persist, taking another silent step. A sliver of his elbow peeks out, and I smile. "Is your heart pounding so hard, it feels like it's going to come out of your throat?"

The wind picks up, lashing through my hair and creating crooked branches out of the cinnamon strands.

When it dies, I inhale deeply.

"Smell that, Xavier?"

He shifts, his elbow disappearing and a few leaves crunching under his feet.

"Smells like death."

A stillness settles over us. So thick, even the birds quieten. And then he's jumping out from the tree. My finger is milliseconds from pressing the trigger when he abruptly pivots, heading the opposite direction, attempting to get me to fire the arrow prematurely.

While it didn't work in that regard, it did throw me off my equilibrium, and it takes me a second too long to catch up before he's darting behind another tree.

I launch the arrow just as he disappears, a startled shout piercing my ears. I don't stop to see if I've hit him. Immediately, I grab an arrow from the quiver on my back and begin to reload. Heart racing, I keep my hands steady as he takes off again.

Don't rush, Addie. Keep steady.

The second my crossbow is reloaded, I rush after him, finding a blood trail dotted in his footprints.

Desperation clouds his judgment, and he limps out from one tree toward another with a massive trunk, his leg dragging. My arrow is jutting out from his calf, blood bubbling from the wound as he runs. Taking aim once more, I breathe in deep and then release, pressing the trigger as I do.

The arrow slices through the warm, summer air and lodges in the center of his back. A piercing yelp, and he's falling flat on his face.

My blood heats and my heart sings from his agonized groans. Nails digging into the dirt ground, he drags himself forward, attempting to escape… to where? There's nowhere for him to go except to Hell.

"Somebody help!" he shouts from the top of his lungs, his voice breaking at the end.

"Goddamn, that's embarrassing," I say, approaching him. I kick his injured leg when I near, grinning when he curses at me, blood tainting his spit.

Crouching beside him, I cock my head, taking in his pitiful state. His blond hair is soaked with sweat, the beads of perspiration trailing down his red face. And those bright baby blue eyes—the very ones that watched me cry and bleed beneath him—are so full of rage and pain, they're nearly black.

"Silly rabbit, I told you that you couldn't escape me."

I hear leaves crunching in the distance along with what sounds like someone cursing and struggling, slowly getting closer as Xavier spits more curses at me that would send my mother to an early grave. The insults roll off my back, despite how hard he tries to hurt me. He's already done his worst when I was the one helpless and powerless.

Now, he's nothing.

A deep growl sounds from behind me, drawing my attention away. Zade approaches us, dragging a spitting mad Rocco by his collar, splattered with blood from head to toe. With his black hood drawn, chin tipped low, and his yin-yang eyes locked on me, I lose all cognitive function.

A dark god that embodies destruction and death, yet I've never felt more in love.

Rocco is no small man, yet Zade drags him as if he weighs absolutely nothing. He drops him on the ground, earning a few nasty words, which he dutifully ignores.

"Can he run?"

"Arrow in the spine," he clips.

My mouth dries as he nears, incapable of doing anything else but watching him bend down, seize me by the throat and crush his mouth into mine.

Milliseconds.

That's how insignificant of a moment it takes for me to respond. He pries my lips apart with his tongue, tasting me thoroughly and drawing an embarrassing moan from my throat.

He rips himself away, only to fist my hair and yank my head back until I have no choice but to look him in the eye.

"A good man would be sorry that he corrupted something so pure."

"You've never been a good man," I whisper, reiterating the exact words he's told me so many times before.

"No," he agrees. "But I have always been yours."

Swallowing, I open my mouth to reply but Zade's hand is releasing my neck and snapping to the side before I can blink. Gasping, I turn to find Zade holding the tip of an arrow inches from my face, blood leaking down his arm.

Xavier struggles to push the arrow further toward me to no avail. My mouth opens with shock, slow to process what the hell just happened.

While I was distracted, Xavier had ripped the arrow out of his calf and attempted to stab me with it. Zade saw it coming, despite that his gaze never left mine.

"Jesus, fuck," I breathe. "So uncool, dude."

If Xavier would've killed me before I killed him, I would gladly accept death. And if Zade tried to resuscitate me, I'd put my foot down and refuse to come back. How could I look myself in the eye after that epic of a failure?

Zade rips the arrow out of Xavier's grasp, black fury emanating from him. His hand is going to be nothing but shredded meat and bone if this keeps up. It's still healing from the knife, yet he shows no indication he's in pain.

Xavier's teeth are bared from both agony and frustration, and I can see he's ready to pounce again.

I grab the arrow from Zade's hold, and using the sharp pointed tip, I notch it under Xavier's chin, forcing him to look at me.

"Look at all that blood," I muse, echoing his own words with a sardonic smile.

Zade readjusts, crouching behind me, his knees on either side as he presses into my back. Xavier's eyes drift over my shoulder, hatred swirling in his eyes.

My breath hitches, shivering from the feel of Zade's hand sliding across my midriff, then lower, the tips of his fingers breaching the waistband of my leggings.

Xavier tracks the movement, his face reddening the lower Zade's hand drifts.

"What are you doing?" I whisper, though the answer is obvious. This is so fucking wrong, yet my pussy throbs when his fingers brush over my clit.

"When you stole from her, did you know the only one she thought of was me?" he asks, ignoring my question. I bite my lip, arousal flooding between my thighs as he continues to softly play.

Xavier snarls but doesn't deign him an answer.

"I want to show you why," Zade whispers, his deep voice dark and sinful.

His touch becomes firmer, and a low moan slips free. I close my eyes, embarrassed by that, even though Xavier can't see anything but the outline of Zade's hand.

"Don't be shy," Zade murmurs in my ear. "Show him why he never stood a chance against me."

I exhale a shuddering breath, unable to contain the breathless moan, my eyes opening then fluttering shut again from the pleasure taking hold of my body. He expertly rubs my clit, and soon my head is dropping back on his shoulder.

"Zade," I moan, my thighs beginning to tremble.

"Stop it," Xavier barks, his voice pained for more reasons than the arrow piercing his spine.

"Are you angry because she never moaned your name?" Zade challenges. He's right—I never did, despite how hard Xavier tried.

"Did she cry out for God?" he pushes.

"Yes," Xavier spits, and *fuck,* I'm falling apart. I thrust against Zade's hand, rolling my hips mindlessly, the bliss eroding my entire being.

"Good," he says, a grin in his voice. "That means she was crying out for *me.*"

"Oh my God, Zade," I sob, the orgasm building, forming into a sharp point right where his fingers are rubbing.

"That's it, baby," he purrs. "Show him who you're really praying to."

"Zade!" I cry out, splintering into millions of pieces while my soul breaks free, shooting far into the heavens. It's then I realize I don't belong there, not when my dark god is pulling me down into a world of sin and pleasure, making me come while holding an arrow to my rapist's throat.

We're all fucking damned anyway, forced to live outside of heaven's gates. I find I like it better living in the darkness next to my shadow.

Zade slips his hand from my leggings, cupping my pussy over the fabric while I ride out the rolling waves of euphoria.

Slowly, I come down, my vision spotty as clarity gradually resurfaces.

Panting, I look down to find Xavier seething, his eyes glassy as he glares at me.

Why does he look so betrayed when he's never owned anything more than my nightmares?

"You're a whore," he spits angrily. Zade stands, his presence looming, seconds away from taking the wheel and sending Xavier into the afterlife. I reposition the arrowhead against his neck, a droplet of blood forming beneath the tip.

"And what makes you think your opinion of me means anything at all?" I wonder.

Before he can answer, a loud screech cuts in, full of pain and frustration.

"Fucking psycho *bitch!*"

That would be Francesca.

On shaking legs, I stand and turn to find Sibby dragging Francesca's flailing body toward us, her red, sweaty face twisted with annoyance. Zade starts to head to her but pauses and points at Xavier.

"I hear you call her any names one more time, I'm cutting out your fucking tongue. Believe me when I say you wouldn't be the first."

My brows pinch. "Who was the first?"

Zade just grins, then jogs over to Sibby and takes over, relieving her of Francesca's weight and carrying the screeching woman the rest of the way, an arrow protruding from her ass cheek.

I'm still a little hung up on the tongue thing, but I decide that I don't really want to know anyway. Ignorance is bliss and shit.

"Where are your henchmen?" I call out, raising my voice above Francesca's screaming. From the sour look on Sibby's face, I'm assuming she wasn't imagining one of them as the one dragging Francesca.

"I told them to stay behind. They've been arguing with each other all day, and it's driving me *nuts*. I needed a break from those morons."

Zade drops Francesca next to Rocco, her scream heightening when she lands on the arrow. The stem breaks, though the arrowhead is still lodged deeply in muscle and bone.

Then, Zade approaches Xavier, the injured man's eyes widening with fear.

"Don't be shy, come lay with your friends," Zade says, grabbing Xavier by the front of his shirt and dragging him to lay on the other side of Rocco.

Their agonized moans, curses, and insults blend together, and Jesus Christ, is that annoying.

I approach them, staring down at the pathetic trio of rapists. A part of me wishes Rio were here so he could watch Francesca die alongside me. Who knows how deeply he's suffered at her hands? Like Sydney, his pain doesn't justify the pain he's inflicted on others, but I do know that it wasn't any less significant than mine.

"Embarrassing," I spit, revulsion thickening in the pit of my stomach. "How many girls were in your place now while you celebrated and got off on their torment?"

"Fuck you!" Francesca screams, spittle flying from her mouth. "You think you're better than us? I'll see you in fucking Hell, and when I do—"

"You'll what?" I cut in, laughing when she glares at me. I crouch down, putting my face in hers. "Torture me there, too? You will never be stronger than me, Francesca, and you want to know why? I survived you, but you won't fucking survive *me*."

I pull a special gift I had burning in the back of my pocket and present it to her. A heel I broke off from one of her shoes.

"Fucking choke on it, bitch."

She opens her mouth to curse, scream—do whatever—and I take advantage, shoving the heel down her throat, smiling when her eyes pop out of her head. She convulses, choking on it, but I'm already standing and moving onto Xavier.

"Have fun, Sibby."

Sibby grins while lowering onto her knees, and then crawls on Francesca's body. Raising her pink knife above her head, she plunges it down into the slowly dying woman's chest.

"No, no, no, wait, wait, it was all her—" Rocco begins, then abruptly ends when Zade plunges his knife directly through the side of his mouth. In through one cheek and out the other, the blade caught between his teeth.

Rocco screams, blood quickly pouring from his open mouth. I smile and turn my attention to Xavier. He looks on the verge of passing out, though I can't tell if it's from his injuries or because he's a pussy facing the consequences of his own actions.

Probably the latter.

"Just… kill me already," he whines. "I will beg you if I must."

"You want me to grant you mercy? Was that what that was, every time you sliced me open? Did you have mercy on me when you raped me? Paid money and tried to buy me like I'm a fucking object so you could torment me for the rest of my miserable fucking life?"

He stutters, sweat pouring down his face, growing more desperate and panicked. Especially as Sibby begins to remove limbs, and Zade starts to pluck out Rocco's eyes.

"I-I'm so sorr—"

"I don't want your apologies, Xavier. I want your suffering."

Before he can open his mouth and spew more useless pleas, I grab two extra blades from my thigh strap, and one at a time, force each hand flat and plunge a knife completely through, pinning them into the dirt.

Eyes wide, his screams mix with Rocco's, and now that… that's a beautiful sound.

I don't bother removing his pants. I just raise my knife and stab it into his pelvis, crimson instantly staining his soiled khakis. I keep stabbing until his entire groin area is ravaged, and I'm panting.

Now, he really is seconds away from blacking out, so I grab him by the hair, force his eyes onto mine, and shove my blade straight through his throat.

His eyes widen in disbelief as he begins to choke, crimson pouring from the wound and down the front of his shirt.

I lean in, as close to his face as possible, ensuring I'm the last fucking thing he sees.

June 4th, 2022

The first time Xavier gave me an orgasm, I moaned Zade's name. He hit me so hard, I thought I went blind. I cried while I came because I felt like I was betraying Zade, even though it was him I was imagining between my legs. Didn't change the fact that it wasn't. So I cried. Then cried some more when Xavier hit me.

I felt so fucking weak in that moment.

So. <u>Fucking</u>. <u>Weak</u>.

I never want to feel that again.

Is it shameful to admit that I enjoyed killing him? It sounds fucking terrible to say.

I should be ashamed of that, shouldn't I? But I'm not. Zade has truly corrupted me, and I'm not even sorry about it. I feel so much stronger now. So much more capable.

Now that I've committed the worst sin in the world, it actually made me feel more confident. Like maybe I don't need to check over my shoulder so much.

Because if I find someone standing behind me, then I can kill them. And that... that feels good.

Really fucking good.

Chapter Thirty Five
The Hunter

Usually, when I finish murdering someone, I feel all the tension release from my body. It can be an aphrodisiac sometimes. It's so rare not to be strung tight that when my muscles are loose and languid, it's fucking orgasmic. Another reason why I'm addicted to Addie and all the ways I melt beneath her fingertips.

But this time, I'm just fucking annoyed. Sibby did what she always does and took shit a step too far. She decided it would be fun to play fucking frisbee with body parts or some shit, so we spent an hour alone trying to locate every piece of Francesca so we could bury them.

By the time I picked up all ten of her fingers, I didn't fucking care anymore. Didn't help that Sibby decided to have an imaginary orgy directly after, forcing Addie and I to leave until she finished. Literally.

And of course, during the two hours it took to dig and bury the bodies, she felt inclined to tell me every sordid detail of what her henchmen did to her. Or rather, what she did to herself.

I let her talk and tuned out the parts I didn't care to hear. Sibby's never had real friends before, and despite how badly I don't want to hear how she got railed up the ass, I refuse to set an example of friendship by silencing her.

Sighing, I tiredly make my way up the steps, my movements heavy and lethargic. I'm covered in dirt and blood, and probably a few other things I don't care to know.

When I trudge into Addie's bedroom, I find steam spilling from the depths of her bathroom. I roll my head back, immediately overcome with images of her standing beneath the shower head, water sluicing down her naked curves. My cock hardens instantly, the tension in my muscles bracketing my muscles into stone.

Pushing the door open gently, I'm surprised to see her standing in front of the vanity mirror, eyes tracing her bare skin. There's a frown pulling down her lips, and she stares at her reflection with a mixture of abhorrence and curiosity.

She tenses, hearing my intrusion, yet she doesn't take her eyes off of herself. She's completely naked, and the sight nearly sends me to my knees.

Both in worship and sorrow.

Two long, jagged scars slice across her back. The sight of them makes me viscerally angry, and it reignites my desire to kill the man who caused them. I vividly remember watching Dr. Garrison stitch those wounds through the camera footage.

Learning to accept my own scars was a process, and one I faced alone. But Addie will never face anything alone again. Soon, I'll trace my tongue across each one and show her that she's still beautiful with or without them.

Scars only serve as reminders of what we've survived, not what killed us.

Blood and dirt coat her pale skin, flaking from her body and onto the heated rock floor. She runs her hand across her flat stomach, drawing my eyes to her fingers. Slowly, I move closer until what she's doing becomes clearer. Like plucking a string on a guitar, her nails claw at a tiny white scar.

"I had hoped these would fade," she murmurs, keeping her voice low in an attempt to hide the wobble. "They're more tragic when it's another carving sorrowful memories into your skin."

She flicks her gaze to me. "I hate them."

I grit my teeth, fury building in my chest. I would've loved to have killed Xavier myself. Take my time with him as I did with Max. But it wasn't my revenge to take. Though the satisfaction of getting her off before him is something I'll cherish.

"Every time I look at them, I think of him," she continues in a hushed tone. "I don't want to look at my body and see anyone else but me and you."

I stay silent and pull my hoodie and t-shirt over my head in one go. She doesn't even glance my way, too lost in the memories that gave her those scars.

"Do they still hurt, baby?" I ask, unfastening my belt and jeans before removing those, too.

By the time she answers, I've completely undressed.

"Sometimes," she whispers. "Sometimes they burn. As if the blade never stopped cutting through my skin."

I hum in response, the anger continuing to rise in my chest. Just like water boiling in a pot, it'll bubble over until everything I touch burns with me.

"Sometimes," she starts again, her voice raspy. "I wonder how you could still possibly want me."

I meet her stare through the mirror as I approach her from behind. That plump bottom lip finds its way between her teeth, and fear flashes in her caramel eyes.

It reminds me of those moments when I was a stranger, and she was an obsession I only knew from afar. So many times, that same look crossed her eyes. When she saw my roses or when I stood outside her window. Even more so when she was wriggling beneath my hands, arching into my touch while begging me to go.

It satisfied the dark part inside me reserved only for the woman standing in front of a mirror, wondering how strong she really is.

I craved her beyond good intentions, morals, and doing what's right. I wanted her so badly, I threw away those things to make her mine.

And if she thinks a dark mind and scars marring her flesh would deter me, she still doesn't grasp how deeply I long for her.

I press into her back, the heat of our bodies transferring into one another. She feels like a slice of heaven I'll never have the honor of seeing, but I've always preferred to find paradise in the depths of Addie's body.

My hand slides up the column of her throat, encouraging her to tip her head back against my shoulder, mouth parted.

"I've followed you through lifetimes, Adeline. My soul needs you so badly that I've become a shadow, destined to hunt you for eternity."

Her eyes flutter, and a little moan slips free, nearly writhing from the promise of haunting her soul.

She was fucking *made* for me.

"If you think scars are going to turn me away, then you haven't seen just how cruel I can be," I rasp.

Her breath hitches, and those caramel orbs round, flashing with trepidation as they focus on me. Her pulse thrums wildly beneath my hand, and I want to sink my fucking teeth into it so I can taste how much I scare her.

I snarl, letting the blackness in my soul bleed out and pour onto her skin, staining any innocence she had left. Those men took that from me, and I'll be damned if I let them have any more of her.

With my free hand, I knock away hers and trace the scar she was picking at, earning a little gasp from her throat.

"These will become mine, too. I will put a blade to every single one and claim them as my own. The only thing you'll see when you look at them is me," I growl, my hand flexing around her throat.

"You wouldn't," she breathes, challenge sparking in her irises.

I grin wickedly, delighting in the sight of her fear deepening. Just as her nipples tighten, and her arousal permeates the steamy air.

"That's it," I whisper, right before I tighten my hold until her air supply cuts off. "Fear *me*, little mouse. Not the sick fucks who have no right over any part of you."

Then, my other fist flies out, cracking the mirror. She flinches in my grasp, her nails scoring into my flesh as I pick a piece of glass out and present it to her.

Relaxing my grip, she greedily sucks in oxygen while keeping her eyes pinned to the shard of glass. She's trembling, and I roll my hips into her pert ass, groaning when she only shakes harder.

"Point me to the first one," I order.

I'm giving her a choice. I may be scaring her blind, but she knows how to get out of my hold. She knows how to turn the weapon on me instead.

She knows how to fucking fight me.

Sucking in an uneven breath, she points her finger to her stomach.

Deliberately, I move my hand to the spot, watching her closely through the broken mirror. Her gaze is locked on the glass, inhaling sharply when I press it into her skin, directly over the scar.

I pause, giving her one last chance to back down, but she turns her lips to my neck, her hot breath fanning across my skin.

So, I press the shard into her old scar, snarling when she opens her mouth and clamps her teeth onto my throat, biting down without restraint.

It's over as soon as it began, and she releases me instantly, chest heaving. It's not deep—just enough to draw blood.

Blackness licks at the edges of my vision as I succumb to the beast inside me.

"Next one." I hardly recognize my own voice, but it's one she trusts because she peeks through the mirror and points to another on her hip.

Again, I slice while she bites. Over and over until her front side is covered in cuts, and she's shaking. Then, I spin her around and lift her on the sink, cradling her to my chest while I slice over scars on her back until she's stained with blood, and my neck and shoulders are imprinted with bite marks.

We're both breathing heavily, brimming with lust, agony, and a restlessness that puts us both on edge.

She's trembling beneath my hands, and her eyes are like glazed caramel apples, high off the endorphins rushing through her system. I drop the glass, rubbing each thumb over a wound, intoxicated by the sharp hiss from between her teeth.

"Does anything about the way I love you feel tragic?" I ask, brushing my lips across her jaw.

"Yes," she whimpers. "But only because one day it will end."

A growl rips from my throat, and I fist her hair, tipping her head back and forcing her to see the truth.

"You and I will never end, little mouse. Even when we're six feet under, and our bones are dust, I will haunt your soul until it aches to be free of me. And then, I will hold you tighter."

Her lip trembles, fighting against my grip on her hair in order to press herself against me, her hardened nipples brushing against my chest.

"I don't ever want to be free of you, Zade. Not in this lifetime, and not in all the ones that come after."

She grabs either side of my face and crushes her lips onto mine, her nails scraping against the stubble on my cheeks.

She holds on to me like she's falling, but I have no interest in catching her. I will always fall with her, chasing after her even in death.

Her legs lock around my hips, so I pick her up, my hands sliding against her slick skin, and carry her to the clawfoot tub. She pulls away just an inch, her teeth chattering and drawing out a grin from me. She's grinding her pussy against my length, slipping and sliding from how fucking soaked she is.

Carefully, I step into the tub and lower us in it, crimson dyeing the porcelain with smeared fingerprints and fresh droplets.

Baring my teeth, I groan when she undulates against my cock, threatening to tear my sanity out of my head like a monster does a heart in a cheesy horror film.

Before I completely lose it, I reach forward and grab the handheld shower head that rests by the faucet. Then, I turn the hot water on full blast, playing with the temperature until it's comfortable.

"Zade," she pleads, lost in delirium. Addie was only ever shown pain with a knife, and now she's experiencing just how cataclysmic it can be when done right.

From now on, the only knife she'll ever fall prey to is mine, and she'll fucking beg me for it.

I switch the water to the shower head, before leaning back and spraying it over her body. She hisses, tipping her head back and continuing to move her hips in slow movements.

Her husky moans fill the space, bouncing off stone and porcelain, and sticking to me like hot wax. Red-tinted blood streams over her curves before swirling down the drain.

I turn the water to myself next and rid myself of the blood and grime from today's activity. By the time I finish, I find her staring down at me, a heat in her eyes that robs me of breath.

"Look at your new scars," I demand sharply. It takes a few beats before she drags her gaze from mine and down to her body. The wounds are still bleeding, the hot water not allowing the blood to clot. "What do you see?"

Sliding a hand across that same scar on her stomach, she exhales shakily. "You."

I lean up, curling my finger beneath her chin and raising her eyes back to mine. "Someday soon, little mouse, you will not be able to see anything else. I will be the only villain in your story, and the only one who has the power to make you scream."

The moment the last word leaves my tongue, I turn the shower head towards her pussy, the powerful spray directly on her clit.

She jolts, a gasp quickly transforming into a cry. Her hands grasp either side of the tub, and once more, her head falls back. But this time, she screams, just as I said she would.

"That's it, baby. You're so fucking beautiful when you cry for me," I bite out, gritting my teeth as she uncontrollably bucks against me. I lean up and curl an arm around her waist, pleasure building in the base of my spine too quickly. I lift her off of me just an inch, but she hardly notices.

"Oh my God, Zade," she cries. I capture her nipple in my mouth, swirling my tongue over the peak before biting down. Her moans grow sharper, and her claws score across my shoulders.

Blood continues to stream from her wounds, painting her body in red. An angel of death is what she is, kneeling above me with blood on her hands that will never wash away.

She's absolute perfection, and I will never get tired of showing her just how much I fucking worship her.

"I'm going to—" I move the shower head away, and this time when she screams, it's from frustration. Her nails bite into my skin, creating angry crescent moons. I grit my teeth, the pain morphing into intense pleasure.

"How do you get what you want, Adeline?" I snap. "Pray to God, and only then will I let you come all over my cock."

"Please, Zade, please," she begs desperately. Breathlessly.

I shake my head, denying her. "Please, what, baby? I can't answer your prayers if I don't know what they are."

"Let me come," she breathes. "Please, let me come."

"Such a good girl," I murmur, moving the spray back to her clit. Her eyes roll, and within moments, she's collapsing against me, grinding on my cock, and exploding all over me while I continue to batter her clit with the spray. She chants my name like it's a Hail Mary, and the only way she'll be forgiven.

She pushes my hand away when it becomes too much, relieving herself of the water. I lean forward and tap the lever, so it switches back to the faucet. Dropping the shower head, I sit back again, not bothering to plug the drain.

She's panting still, the aftershocks rolling through her and causing her to twitch over me like a malfunctioning robot.

Her pussy is hovering mere inches above my cock, and I'm nearly blind with the need to sink myself so deep inside her, I come out the other end. I could do it so fucking easily, especially while she's still recovering.

The urge to hurt. To damage and cause pain, to bend, and break—it's always going to be there. I will always want to rip Addie to shreds for my own sick enjoyment, but that doesn't negate my need to protect her. To treasure and hold on to her like she's the plastic rose my mother gave me.

I'm so fucking in love with her, and while my love is brutal and ruthless, it's also nurturing. Choosing when to be kind and when to let go will always be an uphill fucking battle.

And this is one of those moments where I need to tame the beast. As much as it makes my dick want to fall off from pain.

Addie turns her eyes to me, peeking at me almost shyly beneath her thick lashes. The ends of her damp hair are plastered to her wet body, molding around her round tits and over her ribs. Water droplets slowly trail down every part of her, and I can't decide which one to lick first.

Fuck. I really, really don't want to be kind right now. I want to put the devil to shame.

"Turn around," I tell her, voice tight and hoarse. She slowly shakes her head, then lowers herself on the ridge of my cock, forcing it to lie flat against my stomach. Then, she begins to slide up and down my length, enveloping me in her wet heat.

A growl rips from my throat, and my hips jerk up as a threat.

"Don't fucking test me, Adeline."

"You won't fuck me," she drawls, her pink lips curling into a smile.

"Don't be so sure of that. I can do a lot of things, but resisting your sweet little pussy is hardly one of them."

"You know I wouldn't forgive you," she says, a wicked glint in her eye.

Snarling, I seize her by the throat and bring her in close. "Your hatred has always tasted like heaven, little mouse. If I have to spend the rest of my life on my knees, then I will use my mouth for more than just begging for your forgiveness." I grin sinisterly, and her breath hitches. "By the time I'm done, you'll be kneeling beside me."

She shakes her head, refusing to back down. The little wench rolls her hips, gliding her pussy up to the tip, then down to the base again, drawing my balls up tight. Her eyes flutter as she rubs her clit against me, uncaring how precariously her life hangs over the knife.

"Just stay like this," she whispers, repeating the motion again and again until I'm close to snapping her neck like a goddamn toothpick.

My nerve endings ignite, and my body goes numb with pleasure. I'm no more conscious of how tightly I'm squeezing her neck than I am of life outside of the girl grinding against me. I'll die if she stops, but there's every chance she'll die before I can finish.

It's taking everything in me to keep my hips still. Her little hand wraps around my wrist, and it's then I notice that every vein in my body is protruding from my skin.

Forcefully, she pushes my shoulders back until I'm slamming into the back of the porcelain tub, ripping my hand from her throat. She sucks in a deep breath but doesn't stop gyrating against me.

My hands move to her round hips, and there's no stopping me from jerking her further against me, taking over her grinding and setting a pace of my own.

Pleasure is pooling in the base of my spine, and I feel every muscle in my body tighten as I draw closer to release.

It's when I'm lost to pleasure that I'm overpowered easily. She lifts up on her knees, away from my pulsating cock, and just when I was getting ready to explode.

Instantly, I'm overcome with frustration I've never felt in my life.

"I swear to fucking *God*, Adeline, if you don't sit back down *right fucking now*—" She slaps her hand over my mouth, and she might as well have stuck a lightning rod up my ass—I'm so goddamn shocked.

"Shh, baby," she whispers, a slight grin curling her lips.

Fuck. Her.

She wins.

And she already knows this, moving to wrap her hand around the base of my dick and point it upward. All words die on my tongue, completely forgotten as she gently lowers herself until the tip is breaching her entrance.

Her voice shakes as she says, "I'm in control, Zade. Not you. Me."

She drops her hand, her eyes pinned to me, a raging fire so hot, they look like liquid pools of whiskey.

My fucking favorite.

I clench my teeth, the fragile bones in my gums threatening to crumble as she lowers herself further until her tight heat consumes the tip of my cock. The side of my fist cracks into the tub, nearly unhinged from how incredible she feels.

"*Fuck,* Addie—"

Leaning forward, she plants both hands low on my hips, pressing down firmly. Her arms push her breasts together, and if I weren't so close to erupting, I'd have them between my teeth.

"Don't move," she sighs, breathless and raspy with desire.

I can feel the flames shooting from my eyes as I glare at her. I'm hardened steel and could shatter diamonds across my dick, but my control has always been nonexistent with her.

This is the worst torture a man can endure, yet I will gladly suffer through it if it means getting even an inch of her wrapped around me.

"Don't let that control slip from your fingers because if it does, I *will* be responsible for every one of my actions. I'll fuck you so deeply, you'll be crying for me to stop, and I won't, Adeline. You'll have to fucking kill me before that happens, and I will die without a shred of remorse."

They always say eyes are windows to the soul, and fuck if it isn't true because I can see the fear invading her body. Yet she still gets off on it just as much as she used to when I was only a shadow in the night.

Her pussy clenches, and I feel her arousal leaking down my length, drawing out a deep, guttural growl from my chest.

Hot water pools mid-level to my thighs, sloshing when she readjusts to balance herself better.

I hiss when she circles her hips, her nails biting into my sides.

"Harder," I bark. I need the pain to ground me. I need it to keep me sane. If I feel nothing else but her, I'll lose it completely. "Dig your nails harder."

She listens, and I shudder from the sharp pin pricks. It's just enough to keep me from spilling inside her.

Ever so slightly, she bounces her ass, her movements scarce and hardly allowing her pussy to swallow more than an inch of me. Yet it sends my eyes rolling.

One of her hands moves to wrap around the base of my cock, but I stop her. If she touches me, I'm done for.

I circle my finger and thumb around the base to stabilize it, and then use my other hand to rub her clit in tight circles. She's not taking nearly enough of me to get off on. Even then, she needs stimulation most of the time.

A long, uneven moan fans across my chest.

"Fuck, I need to feel this pussy. I need to feel it wrapped around all of me. Every part of you is mine, little mouse, and you will never feel whole again without me inside you."

"This is… this is as far as I can go right now, Zade. I can't do more," she says, nearly pleading for me to understand.

"Take as much as you can handle, baby. Give me all your pain."

With her hand back on my hip alongside the other, she digs her nails in again. I groan through gritted teeth, bliss clouding my vision. There's still so much of me left, but I won't force her to take more.

"You're doing so good, baby. And you look so fucking pretty. I can't wait to see how you'll look when you take all of me."

Her teeth chatter again, a moan slipping free.

"So fucking proud of you," I mutter, intoxicated by the sight of her sweet pussy suspended above me, even when she's allowing so little of me inside her.

"Zade," she pleads, voice hoarse.

"I've missed watching you soak my cock," I rasp, biting my lip to hold back another moan. She shudders from my words, rivulets of her arousal trailing down to my fingers wrapped around my dick. I circle her clit faster, eliciting a bone-rattling shiver from her.

"I've missed how tightly your pussy clenches around me. How you mold so easily around me."

She nods her head, lost to the pleasure as I am. Her eyes drift shut while her rhythm becomes choppy, shifting her focus to grinding against my hand.

"It's not enough, is it?" I breathe, watching her brows pinch. She bites her lip, and even with her eyes shut, I know she's struggling with herself. Fighting the instinct to seat herself completely down.

She wants to. Fuck, I can see how much she wants to. Still, she resists.

"You need more of me, but you won't let yourself have it. So, you'll have to settle for my cum filling you up instead."

Her mouth parts, a husky moan rolling off her tongue and down my spine. I can feel her right on the edge, desperate to throw herself off.

"You have five seconds, Adeline, or I will fuck you anyway."

That spark of fear is enough to send her diving off the cliff. She breaks, her thighs shuddering and eyes squeezing shut. A hoarse shout echoes throughout the bathroom, but I couldn't say who it belongs to.

I quickly follow her over the edge, lightning shooting down my spine and robbing me of all sense. She clamps around me so tightly, it nearly hinders the ropes of cum overflowing from my dick.

If this is what heaven feels like, I'm only sorry I've done nothing to deserve it.

An impossible amount of time passes before we both collapse, out of breath and ridden with electric currents.

Her cheek rests against my chest, wet strands of hair draping across my skin like drizzled chocolate, and I just know she can feel my racing heartbeat ricocheting between her teeth.

My fingers dive through her tangled tresses, and I wrap my other arm tightly around her. For several minutes, we just lay like this, catching our breaths and losing it all over again with every touch.

Eventually, I coax her to turn around. She hugs her knees while I squeeze shampoo in my hands and meticulously wash her hair, soothing any lingering tension in her muscles.

I tell her about the first person I killed, and she tells me about hers. A girl named Phoebe, who helped save Addie's life, only to be forced to take hers in return. She cries while speaking of the girl with flaming orange hair, and the fear she carried in her bones except when it really mattered. In the end, she embodied the flames that hung around her shoulders.

I rinse the soap out, her tears following the suds down the drain while she mourns, her head bowed with grief.

Then, I carry her out of the tub and set her on the counter, holding her mouth open as I brush her teeth. I kiss away every tear and remind her that she will always carry Phoebe with her, and those flames are now hers, too.

Chapter Thirty Six
The Diamond

"**X**avier's disappearance made national news," Daya tells me over the phone.

"Do they have any idea who did it?" I ask, massaging the muscle in my shoulder. My entire body aches from the training session with Sibby, and I'm damn near ready to collapse on the floor and just stay there forever.

I'd make a good fertilizer, and vines of roses could grow from my rib cage while I become one with the earth again.

Zade would probably call me dramatic for thinking that.

"All they have to go off of is the debacle at *Supple*. Of course, your faces were hidden, which helps."

"I was wearing a wig, too," I say.

"They won't be able to identify you. At least, the public won't, but

I'm sure Claire will know it was you two."

"But they can't prove it."

"They don't need to. She controls the entire government and all the worker bees that run it. Including the police force, feds—all of them."

I chew on my lip, digging at the spot on my shoulder harder. "So what, do you think Zade's face is going to end up on the evening news?"

She's quiet for a beat. "Or yours."

My heart drops, thudding heavily in the pit of my stomach. Claire pinning the murder on me would actually be convenient. It will absolutely destroy any reputation I have as an author, but that wouldn't be the worst of it. They could press charges, fabricate evidence against me, and convict me. And I wouldn't be going to jail, but right back into Claire's hands.

Fuck. Me.

"Zade isn't going to let anything happen to you, Addie," Daya assures. "Don't panic. We'll figure it out, and I'm sure this is something he would've planned for."

Though she can't see me, I nod my head. It does little to calm my racing heart.

"Maybe I shouldn't have—"

"Addie, don't be one of those where you're only sorry you got caught. Be sorry because it doesn't sit right in your soul, if that's truly how you feel. If I'm being honest, I feel nothing about ending Luke's life, so I guess we're both on God's shitlist or whatever. Regardless, what we're doing with Claire? It's huge. Bigger than you or me. And it's going to save a lot of lives."

I nod my head again, squeezing my eyes shut tightly.

"I know, you're right. I'm not sorry for what I did." I blow out a heavy breath. "I just don't know what's going to happen, and I'm scared."

"We're going to be okay. Remember who you have on your side."

On cue, I feel a touch brush away my hand from my shoulder before replacing it with his own, digging his thumb into that persistent knot.

My hand drops, and a mix of pain and pleasure erupt from where his skilled fingers work my muscles.

"I remember," I murmur, trapping a moan in my throat when he hits a particularly painful spot. "Thank you, Daya. I'll call you later, okay?"

The second we hang up, I let loose a groan. I figured if Daya heard that, it might disturb her. His other hand joins the assault, drawing out more sounds of pleasure. It hurts so fucking good.

"Daya break the news?" he asks quietly in a deep timbre.

"Yeah," I answer with a cracked voice.

"Nothing—"

"Is going to happen to me, I know," I cut in. "But sometimes things don't go to plan."

He directs me around, and I turn with a tired sigh. His scar crinkles from his amused grin, noting the sassy look on my face.

"You're going to want to tune into the news at eight o'clock then."

My brows knit, and a frown curls my lips down. "What did you do?"

"I haven't done it yet, but I'm going to." He flicks my nose, and I sputter in response, slapping away his hand. His smile grows, taking over his scarred face and brightening his yin-yang eyes.

Jesus, his smile is fucking dangerous. It easily stops my heart.

"Eight o'clock, little mouse. It'll hurt my feelings if you miss it."

"You can't sit there, Addie! You'll be sitting right in Baine's lap. And he's awfully bony, so he won't be very comfortable."

My ass is popped out mid-air, suspended over my leather couch when she stops me.

"Uhm, okay," I sigh, a smidge tired of avoiding my own damn furniture because Sibby's imaginary friends are sitting all over it. Can't they stand? It's not like their invisible legs are going to get tired.

I straighten and Sibby gasps loudly, causing me to jump and almost drop my wine.

"What?" I ask, alarmed, searching the couch for a spider or something. They don't scare me, but Sibby tends to morph into an even smaller child when bugs come out.

"I am so sorry, Addie. Baine grabbed your ass. Baine, don't *do* that! Zade is going to kill you, ya know? He gets his balls in a knot when people touch her."

"Balls in a knot?" I mutter, both confused and utterly fucking frazzled. I hike a thumb over my shoulder awkwardly when she continues to berate Baine.

"I'm gonna go over here," I mumble, just a little disturbed. I turn on the TV and flip to Channel 8. They're droning on about Xavier again, and I immediately break out into a sweat, waiting for my picture to pop up as a person of interest.

I think if I were, the police would have already come knocking, but my anxiety gets away from me anyway.

Taking a large gulp of wine, I glance at the time on my phone and note that it's 7:59 PM. If I know Zade, whatever he's about to pull, he'll be on time. Eight on the dot, to the very second.

I take another sip, rolling my eyes when Sibby's hand slides up her thigh, pushing up her black polka-dot dress, and then proceeds to slap at her own hand, yelling at Mortis for trying to hit on her in front of me.

She's getting better about keeping the sexual activities to herself.

My heart trips over itself when the image of the reporter on TV begins to skip and then turns to static before cutting out. I gasp when a picture of a man replaces the reporter, his black hood drawn over his head and face covered with a familiar black mask with a dramatic frown, and a slash through the eye.

No fucking way.

Slowly, I stand, my mouth open as I near the TV.

"*Greetings, fellow Americans,*" Zade starts, my brows jumping when I hear how abnormally deep his voice is. He altered it. "*In light of the disappearance of oil tycoon, Xavier Delano, this is a message for the police force, all government officials, and as always, the people of this country.*"

Zade crosses his black-gloved hands, seeming to get comfortable.

"*Xavier Delano was buying young women as sex slaves from human traffickers, then murdering them when he grew bored. I have released all evidence of this online. Pictured above are several women who he bought, tortured, raped, and killed. Remember their names. I have. In honor of all the women who lost their lives to this man, I took matters into my own hands. Xavier Delano is not missing. He's dead.*"

Zade leans forward and cocks his head. An eeriness pulses through the radio waves emitting from the screen. Raw danger radiates throughout my bones when I look into the bottomless holes where his eyes are hidden. I shiver, delighting in the feel of it.

"*He is not the first to suffer the consequences of his actions, and he will not be the last. I am Z, and I am watching. No one is safe. Especially not those who have betrayed me.*"

His video disappears, cutting back to the news reporter's pale, slackened face.

A loud crunch snaps me out of the hypnotizing effect I'd gotten lost in. I whip my head toward Sibby to see her shoving a handful of popcorn in her mouth. She must feel my stare because she stops mid-chew, her cheeks puffed out, and looks at me with wide innocent eyes.

"What?"

"He took responsibility for it all," I say, dazed.

Sibby blinks, appearing confused. "Well, of course he did. I mean, he wasn't entirely lying, but Zade would do anything to protect you." She cocks her head. "Did you honestly doubt him?"

My mouth parts. "I guess I just wasn't expecting… that."

Sibby shrugs, scarcely swallowing the first mouthful before she's stuffing her face again. "It was smart."

It was. No one is going to believe a city girl, who is also a popular and well-respected author, murdered Xavier over Z. They would look stupid if they tried to blame me still. Plus, everyone knows I'm a victim of sex trafficking. They could try to spin it that I sought revenge, but then they'd have to deal with the added stress of Zade leading an absolute riot over a survivor being wrongfully convicted. Not to mention that Zade would quite literally never let them just cart me away to jail. He'd put me into hiding and take the blame for that, too. And once again, the people would be rooting for Zade over the government, which is the last thing Claire wants.

Shit. Zade really did fuck up any plans Claire might've had, and all to protect me.

"Oh!" Sibby shouts, causing me to jump again. "You should write a book about it. Your readers would swoon over the big, scary guy coming to your rescue and then murdering your abuser."

She's not wrong. Even *I'm* swooning.

But I've been too mentally drained to write. I scrounge up the energy to post little updates every so often before dipping out again, too exhausted to even read the comments. My personal assistant has been intercepting all messages and questions until I'm ready to get back into my career again. I don't think I'll be able to truly focus on writing until Claire is dead.

"Did it bother you that he took the credit?" Sibby asks, misinterpreting my silence.

I laugh. "I don't care about the glory."

"Then why are you so tense?"

Because my blood has turned into liquid lava. God help me if Sibby is in the vicinity when I see Zade because I'm not sure I'll be able to stop myself from tackling him, and lord knows the weird little doll wouldn't willingly leave the room.

A plethora of emotions are running rampant in my body, and at the very forefront of it all is my need to thank him. And there are so many fucking ways I want to thank him.

Seeing him on screen, with his deep voice and black mask, putting himself under fire to protect me—all I could think about was how much I love him. And how badly I need to show him that. How badly I need to *tell* him that.

Zade will suffer little to no consequences for killing Xavier, at least not from the public. He doesn't need the support of the people to keep doing what he's doing. It's just something Z has always had regardless. And whether people choose to shift their alliances because he took a predator off the streets, it won't matter.

In the grand scheme of sacrifices Zade has made for me, it wasn't really much of one. Yet, it means the world to me anyway.

What we're doing is so much bigger than writing books, but it still would've devastated me to lose a career I love so much. It would've felt like losing yet another piece of myself, and I already have so little to spare.

"Oh…" Sibby says softly, realization dawning. "You want to fuck him. I understand now."

My cheeks burn, but I don't deny it. Because she's right. My thighs are clenched tight, and that familiar heady feeling is swirling deep in my stomach.

I won't lie and say that watching him just now didn't turn me on. My blood is on fire, and I'm nearly vibrating with desire. It was… well, it was fucking hot. What else can I say?

Sibby groans, sitting up with a pouty look. "Why do you guys get to have loud sex, and *I* can't?"

I turn to her, eyes wide and an expression that says, *are you shitting me right now?*

"Because you try to do it in front of everyone, Sibby."

She slams her back into the couch with a huff, shoving a sorrowful handful of popcorn into her mouth. "Not my fault you guys are boring."

I roll my eyes. Zade and I are many things, but boring is *not* one of them.

June 5th, 2022

I've never told a man that I love them. Never. Because I hate fucking doing it. Never mind that I've never actually been in love with anyone before Zade. But even in high school when that puppy love stage hits with boyfriends. You know, where you think you love them but you don't even know what love is? Something always held me back.

I still don't want to say it, but only because I'm scared.

There's this, I don't know, build up I guess? And I don't even know why. I know how Zade feels about me. I've known how he felt about me since the first note he left me.

Yet I'm sweating like a goddamn gym rat anyway.

Maybe it's because I don't know **HOW** to say it. Fuck, that's so it. Do I just pop out with it when he walks through the door? Or kiss him first? Do I give him a speech?

Fuck. That.

Fuck this.

I'm just gonna say it when he's least expecting it.

Then run the **fuck** away.

Chapter
Thirty Seven
The Diamond

I'm a ball of nervous energy by the time Zade walks through my bedroom door. Between the footsteps trekking back and forth down the hallway, and my anticipation to see Zade, I haven't been able to sleep.

It's well after midnight now, and I've been lying in bed in nothing but a black nightie, gearing myself up for his arrival.

Rolling over, I watch him gently shut the door and begin to shuffle towards the bathroom, sulfur, blood, and smoke permeating the air. My balcony doors are cracked open, allowing in the cool breeze and webs of moonlight.

I sit up and flip on the sconces hanging above my bed, feeling like one of those women sitting in a pitch-black room, clicking on a single lamp when their cheating husband sneaks through the door.

The thought of Zade cheating is laughable, though. That will always be one thing I'd never have to concern myself with.

He pauses, tipping his chin over his shoulder at me.

"Is this where we act like a married couple, and I ask where you've been and why you're home so late?" I tease lightly.

The lights radiate a soft yellow glow, creating a moody effect as he reaches his hand over his shoulder and tugs his hoodie over his head by the neck, pulling his white t-shirt with it.

I bite my lip, my eyes eating up his muscled, tattooed back and massive arms.

"Sure, baby," he says quietly. "But we both know my cock belongs only to you."

"Good, then you know I can remove it from your body if I want. Since it's mine and all that."

He turns with a grin, not the least bit concerned.

I cross my arms. That's just insulting. I'm pretty much a badass now.

"I got held up because the guy I was after was in the middle of an airport attempting to get on a flight to another country."

"How'd you get him out without anyone noticing?"

"Ambushed him while he was taking a piss. Then had to empty out a suitcase to stuff his body into."

I blink. That sounds... interesting.

Before, I'd call him disturbed. Sick. Psychotic. I mean, he *is* still all of those things. But it no longer repulses me like it used to. Or maybe it never did, and I was lying to myself.

I do that a lot.

"Who was it?" I ask.

"Some man that Jillian asked me to kill. Used to be her step-dad and abused her as a child," he explains, toeing off his boots and setting them neatly in the corner of the room.

I wasn't surprised to find that Zade lives meticulously. He doesn't seem like the type to leave his dirty underwear lying in the middle of the room for a week, or crusty dishes in the sink.

"Good," I murmur, happy that he could do that for her. "Is he the only one you killed tonight?"

"Yes," he responds simply, arching a brow.

I nod and lick my dry lips, nervous about broaching this subject. "So, Rio is still evading you?"

Zade glances at me. "I know where he is, Addie," he answers, approaching me, wearing nothing but his black jeans and belt.

My heart drops, but I work to keep my face blank.

"You don't want him dead," he states plainly, sitting on the edge of the chair beside the bed. I'm pretty sure we'll have to clean that—he's absolutely covered in blood.

"Why would you thi—"

"Don't lie to me," he cuts in sternly, facing straight ahead. His white eye flits towards me before returning to the black wall.

"I see your face anytime his impending death is brought up, yet you always keep your pretty mouth shut. I've known his location for a while, but I've decided that I'll wait to kill him until you open your mouth and tell me what you really want."

I'm nervous. Almost like he's caught me cheating, and I have to confess. It's nothing like that, yet I feel like I've been bad anyway.

"I don't know what I feel," I admit, pressing my back into the cool stone. "He hurt me. Often. But not in the ways you think."

"He didn't rape you," Zade supplies.

"No… he didn't. But he witnessed it happen from the other men and didn't stop it. But then… he couldn't have."

"Sure he could," Zade argues. "You think I'd stand by and watch?"

"Even if—"

"No. The answer is no, regardless of the scenario. If I were weaponless and had five guns trained on me, I still wouldn't stand by and watch you— or any of those other girls—go through what you did. And I get that his sister was used as collateral, but he could've asked for my help."

I frown. I hadn't really thought of that. Rio was very aware of who he was going up against from the beginning. So why didn't he betray those who were holding his sister hostage, and get Z to help him instead?

"You're right," I acquiesce softly. "Regardless of his choices, it's still hard to forget how much he helped me. When Sydney was trying to frame me, there were times he took the blame instead, and Rocco would beat the shit out of him for it. He may not have been able to step in every time, but he did what he could in a situation he felt trapped in."

Zade stays quiet, so I continue. "Francesca made him take care of my injuries from the car accident since they were his fault. But then I started getting injuries from the men, and then eventually Xavier, and he took care of those, too. I… don't know how to explain it. But he kind of became my friend. He was a little cruel in the beginning with Dr. Garrison, but he never looked at me like… He was the only man in that house that didn't sexualize me, and I guess in the end, he was my safe place. He did hurt me, Zade, but he protected me, too."

The muscle in his jaw pops, but I can't tell what's on his mind. It takes him a few moments, but eventually, he turns his head to me with an empty expression.

"Do you want me to spare his life?" he asks, voice monotone.

I open my mouth, but no words make it out.

"I don't know," I answer honestly. "I really don't know."

"What did we talk about before? Decide what you can and cannot live with. Can you live with knowing that I killed Rio, or can you not?"

I frown, looking down at my hands while I contemplate that. I've been picking at a hangnail without even realizing, a dot of blood on the side of my thumb.

"Would you do it?" I question, looking up at him. "If I asked, would you spare his life?"

"Yes," he responds. "I would kill for you—I *have* killed for you—but I would also put down a gun and never pick it up again if you asked it of me. The lengths I would go to for you are terrifying, little mouse. So easily, you could destroy me, and I would lie down and take it. I don't care if I live or die—as long as it's all for you."

"Don't say that," I whisper.

"I don't lie, Adeline, and I'm not going to start now. So, tell me. Do you want me to spare his life?"

"Yes," I answer after a few beats. "I want Rio to live with his own choices. Whether he regrets the decisions he made or not, I want him to live with it. And I don't want either of us to be responsible for taking away Katerina's brother."

Zade drops his head, but he nods. And the love that was nearly bursting from my tongue when I saw him on TV is back again, though it never really left.

I crawl from the bed and kneel between his spread thighs, grabbing his face in my palms and kissing his lips softly.

"Thank you," I say. "Not just for this, but for earlier, too. Taking the blame for Xavier's death."

"Didn't I say I'd do anything for you?" he asks, turning his head to kiss my palm before slipping from my fingers and standing up.

"I need to shower. Sleep, baby."

I open my mouth, but he's closing the bathroom door behind him before I can process his exit, leaving me kneeling on the floor and feeling a little dejected.

My heart sinks, guilt gnawing at my insides for asking him to spare Rio. I wonder if I should rescind my decision. Though if I'm being honest with myself, I think I'd mourn his death. And I'd never be able to look Katerina in the eye again, despite what her brother has put me through.

I'm sitting up in bed, mind racing over what to do when Zade emerges, steam rolling from the depths of the bathroom from behind him. He dons nothing but a black towel, loosely tucked around his waist and on the verge of slipping off.

My mouth waters at the sight, and I grow so heated, my blood boils until I'm left with nothing but vapors.

There will never be another that looks like him—never another that will be anything like him. And there's a small part of me terrified to see the day Zade dies. Though I'll have a lot to fucking say if he croaks before he turns ninety.

Asshole jumped through hoops to get me, now he has to suffer through a long life of having me.

I'll never understand how humans fear death when time is far scarier. It ultimately leads us to death because it's the only thing that truly makes us mortal. We're locked in the illusion with no way out.

Fuck, I really want out.

When he spots me, he pauses just briefly before sighing. "You're still up."

"And you're hiding from me," I retort.

He chuckles humorlessly. "I'm a stalker, baby. I've always hidden from you."

"Stop it," I snap.

"What do you want, Adeline?" he asks sharply, his frustration mounting.

"Dammit, Zade, I want *you*. I'm sorry that Rio gets to live, okay? Jesus, it's one of the very few things you've let me have power over, and you're making me feel guilty…" My voice trails off when he storms over to me, fear clogging my throat.

In seconds, he's standing before me, gripping my jaw in his hand, and pulling me up until my knees barely touch the bed. I squeal, clawing at his arm, but he doesn't relent.

"You love to pretend you're so fucking helpless, just like a little mouse caught in a trap. If that's what you want to be, I can show you what it truly means to be powerless. I can show you what it means to be *me*."

My eyes widen with bafflement, my nails digging deeper. "You?!" I echo, aghast from his implication.

"Yes, me!" he shouts. "I have no goddamn control when it comes to you. I lost it when I saw you in that bookstore and never got it back. You think me stalking you was control? Drinking from your body despite your cries? Do you think I have it right fucking now?" he growls, shaking my head to emphasize his point.

His eyes are blazing, dilated with both fury and something so potent, it burns me alive.

"You've said it yourself, I could use your body for my own pleasure, but what's one thing I could never take from you? What's the one thing I wanted the most from you, Adeline?"

"My love," I cry, tears welling and spilling over.

"That's right. Your love. The only thing I've ever needed from you.

You are the one with the power, you've just never known what the fuck to do with it."

It takes several moments, but slowly, it dawns on me. His words finally fucking process through the thick skull God cursed me with.

Zade gave in to every one of his darkest instincts because he never possessed the control to stop himself. He took, and took, and took because it was the only thing he *could* take. But that never made him powerful—it made him helpless.

Until now, I could never make sense of that when he's always done what he wanted. Stalked me, touched me, *fucked* me whenever he wanted. No matter how many protests fell from my lips, or how many times I fought him.

He chased me when I ran, pulled me back when I pushed him away, yet would worship me at my feet if I asked him to.

And I finally understand why. One cannot wield power if one does not have control over it.

"Glad to see you finally take over the throne," he murmurs, frustration radiating from his mismatched eyes.

I shake my head, retracting my nails from his arm and gently prying his fingers away from my jaw. He releases me, brimming with energy.

"I'm not taking over the throne, Zade. You *are* the throne. You've always been my pillar of strength, and I'm sorry it took so long to see it."

His gaze searches mine desperately, hunting for any hint of a lie. It would be like finding an active bomb. The second he discovered it, it'd tear him to pieces.

Slowly, I stand from the bed, backing him away from me until I'm on both of my feet. He doesn't give me much room, but I don't want it.

My heart pounds, and I drop my eyes, watching my hand rise to meet his heated flesh. He nearly burns to the touch, and I've never wanted to be consumed by fire more.

The pads of my fingertips brush across his defined muscles, beautiful tattoos, and the white scars slashing across several parts of his torso. My knees weaken while I focus primarily on the dragon running up his chest.

God, if that creature doesn't embody the man standing before me, I don't know what does. A fire breathing dragon capable of sending me fucking soaring.

Flattening my palm on his stomach, I push him away, almost fascinated by the way he relents without resistance.

"Take that off," I order, glancing at his towel, my voice trembling with desire. He stares at me, his silence loud and chaotic as he heeds my command.

I work to swallow as he slowly and methodically unravels the towel, taunting me while keeping his yin-yang eyes pinned on me.

It feels as if an entire galaxy is swirling in my stomach. There's a black hole, devouring all sense and reason. A sun sending solar flares lashing throughout my body, heating me from the inside out and sinking lower to the apex of my thighs, and a supernova, on the precipice of exploding.

He releases the knot, the towel dropping to the floor with a quiet *thunk*.

Fuck me sideways.

His cock is hard, the tip reddened and the veins prominent, and it nearly sends me to my knees with a prayer on my tongue. He's fucking glorious, and my heart wrenches with the reminder that this man—no, this *God*—is mine.

He straightens, and I try to tell myself to drink him in slowly.

Small sips, Addie. Savor him.

But I can't keep my greedy eyes from eating up the expanse of his physique, lingering specifically below his waist.

I haven't forgotten how terrifying Zade's cock is. Yet every time, it feels like a punch in the chest to see it in the flesh, knowing he has to fit that inside of me.

My mouth salivates when I recall the burn from him stretching me and how he'd have to work himself inside of me. Fuck, it's just like being addicted to the pain of getting a tattoo. Every bite of the needle you want to run away, but you stay because the outcome is pure fucking bliss.

Giving me a loaded look, he walks to the dresser and digs something out of the drawer. Jesus, his backside is almost as mouth-watering as the front. My lungs close, and I'm no longer breathing.

The sound of metal is what finally pulls my attention away from his body. He's advancing toward me, holding black handcuffs, and the sight sends my heart skipping like a rock across the surface of a lake.

I take a big step back. Most men would pause when they see hesitation, but Zade doesn't falter as he approaches me.

"What are you doing with those?" I ask, alarm building in my chest.

"Don't worry, baby, these are for me."

Meeting his stare, I'm instantly soothed. A range of emotions swirl in his black and white pools. Desire, love, and wicked intent. But he's so damn calm, and that's what makes me feel calm.

Furrowing my brow, I watch him hold out the handcuffs and key to me, but I don't take them yet.

"What are you planning?" I ask, looking up at him.

"Didn't I tell you before that you don't need a cop to get me in handcuffs? I said I'd let you do anything you want to me, and that's what I'm doing."

I'm not sure why I'm so surprised to hear that. He's made it clear I hold the power but seeing him physically hand it to me is still jarring.

Licking my lips, I hesitantly grab them and place the key on the nightstand. The second I do, he turns around once more, showing me the massive octopus tattooed across his back, the tentacles unfurling up to his shoulders and neck.

Some nights, I trace each line while he sleeps, familiarizing myself with the feel of his skin when he's not demanding it of me.

Just like those late nights, I brush my fingers over the fine details in the octopus, marveling over the talent that went into this piece.

The muscles in his back ripple from my touch, and I can't help but feel invigorated by the effect I have on him.

Enjoying his reaction, I tease him. Trailing the pads of my fingers lightly down his back, his arms, and to his hands. Goosebumps rise on his skin, and I bite back a smile. I don't think I've ever seen this man get something as trivial as *goosebumps*. It's a normal human reaction, but when has Zade ever acted like anything less than a deity?

I tighten the handcuffs around his wrists, inhaling sharply when he turns again and stands before me. Persephone imprisoning Hades—it's too sweet not to salivate over.

"You'll let me do anything I want to you?" I reiterate, hesitant to believe it. Seeing him so… defenseless—my brain can't quite process it.

His eyes darken, and his grin slips. "You've always been an atheist to my word. You're incapable of believing in something you can't see and lack faith because you're blind to what's right in front of you. I'm yours to command—I always have been. You just need to see it to finally believe it."

Clearing my throat, I whisper, "Sit on the bed."

Without hesitation, he steps back and slowly sits down, keeping his legs spread. My eyes gravitate between them again, and my heart flutters like a hummingbird's wings, equally transfixed and intimidated.

Forcing myself to focus, I grip the bottom of my nightie and pull it over my head, keeping my pace slow and torturous. Zade hums his approval deep in his chest, and it gives me a boost of courage. Enough to slip my panties down my thighs and step out of them.

There's never a sexy way to do it, but the way Zade's eyes hungrily eat up my body, it feels like I just performed a highly skilled trick on a stripper pole. In reality, I'd break my neck attempting that.

"Get on the bed and kneel," I tell him, tipping my chin up to direct him. He grins but does as I say, climbing on the bed with a panther's grace. He sits back on his heels with his knees spread, and more than anything, I want to take a picture of him so I can look back at it when we're old and gray and neither of us are even capable of sex anymore.

Strips of moonlight and the soft glow from the sconces accentuate the hard planes of his chest and abs, highlighting each muscle straining against his skin.

Only the devil can wield the shadows around his body with such divinity. A devil and a God—two opposing forces that make up one contradicting being.

Licking my lips with anticipation, I crawl onto the bed and then onto his lap, keeping my pussy suspended over the tip of his cock.

His lips whisper up the column of my neck, and I put my hands on his shoulders to not only balance myself but to keep him controlled.

My core throbs when a deep rumble vibrates throughout my hands, building as I deliberately brush my hardened nipples against his face. Right when he goes to bite down, I pull away, increasing the tremors shaking his body.

His head tips back until our eyes clash. I shiver from the uncaged lust spearing from his gaze. He looks at me like he's only biding his time.

Doing my bidding for now until the second I unlock those handcuffs.

In the blink of an eye, he'll snap, striking like a viper. My throat in his hands and my heart between his teeth.

I feel the fear pulsating in my clit, heightening my heart rate to dangerous levels.

"You think you're broken now, Adeline? Wait until you free me from these confines," he threatens, the deep timbre of his voice lined with sharp glass. "I'll fuck you until every single one of your bones breaks beneath me. Helpless little mouse, for me to mold and manipulate."

He's deliberately trying to scare me, knowing how much my body sings for the terror he instills in me.

Instinctively, I want to run from his terrifying promises and the creeping trepidation that he's going to do just that. I also want to challenge him so he can make good on them.

My heart thrashes against my rib cage, but I don't break his stare. Biting my lip, I reach between us and grab ahold of his length, delighting in the way his top lip curls into a snarl.

And then, ever so slowly, I slide the tip along my slit, wetting him before lowering myself increment by minuscule increment, until there's no discerning which of us is trembling.

I lean forward and wrap my arms around his neck, molding my soft curves into his harsh lines, and slowly work him inside me. It feels just as I remembered—the burning as he stretched me wide, but the insatiable bliss that accompanies it.

My demons are tickling the back of my brain, begging to be let in to wreak havoc on my sanity. Drag me from this precious moment where I reclaim something that was stolen from me. So, I focus every ounce of my attention on the man beneath me.

His thinning breath, the building earthquake racking his body, and the veins pulsing in his neck as he fights to keep still.

I nudge my lips against the shell of his ear, that heady sense of power arising up through my throat and off my tongue.

"Do you want to see how easily I can break you?" I murmur coyly.

He grunts as I drop lower again, more than half of his cock buried inside me. It feels like too much and not enough. It's never enough. Even when I'm filled to the brim, I want more.

I don't wait for him to answer, nerves eating me alive even though this feels right. So fucking right.

"I love you, Zade. Sometimes I can't fucking stand it," I say, my voice raspy and uneven. "But it was the only thing that kept me alive. You saved me. Even when we were apart, you saved me. And I hope to God you never stop hunting me."

His head rolls back, eyes to the ceiling, and he stills beneath me, as solid as the stone walls in Parsons Manor.

"Let me go, Adeline," he says tightly. I hardly recognize his voice.

I sink the rest of the way down, seating myself completely on his length. The stone cracks, and his chest ripples with a sharp inhale.

"Let me fucking go," he bites out again. I shake my head, though he's not looking at me. His Adam's apple bobs as he swallows.

I know what he's asking. Release the handcuffs. He could get out of them if he wanted to. And the fact that he's waiting until I do it myself speaks volumes.

I have a strong feeling that despite what Zade thinks, he's had more control than he gives himself credit for. But the second the metal falls from his wrists, it will dissipate. Now that I've given him everything, I will experience Zade truly at his most unhinged.

There was never a question that he would strike the moment they were off, but now he's a starved animal with fresh meat right outside its cage.

"I'm not going to do that."

Fuck it, I might as well take advantage while I'm still in one piece.

My mouth parts as I rock against him, allowing my eyes to drift and my head to tip back as euphoria builds where we're connected.

Low, uneven moans fill the air, so lost in riding his cock and how good it feels to use his body for my own pleasure that when his hot breath fans across my neck, it feels like waking up from a fever dream and not remembering where I am.

"I hope you enjoy this, baby," he rumbles into my ear. "I hope you revel in the feeling of your pretty cunt intact and your skin pristine."

My breath hitches, his tone darker than a black hole swallowing up the stars in the sky. No light escapes—not in them, nor in Zade.

I grind against him harder, gritting my teeth as his biting words eat at my bravery. Sweat coats both of our bodies for entirely different reasons. It takes effort to contain his beast, while mine is loose and out of control.

"You don't scare me," I lie, shivering when I roll my hips just right, the tip of his cock hitting that perfect spot.

"Shame," he murmurs, nipping at the sensitive flesh in the juncture of my collarbone, making my body quake once more. "I love it when you're a scared little mouse, thrashing beneath my paw and desperate to get away."

"Does it make you feel powerful?" I ask through gritted teeth, repeating a question he asked me not too long ago. An orgasm is building low in my belly, shredding my control as my movements become choppy.

"Of course, it does," he murmurs, his deep voice dark and wicked, our moans entwining when I roll my hips. "When you're in the palm of my hands, it's the only time I feel like this world is worth saving."

Panting, I rock faster, chasing the orgasm just within my reach.

"You like to use my cock to make you come, don't you, baby? Remember that whenever you think you don't need me. Nothing will make your little pussy feel better than I can. And look, I don't even have to fucking try."

My vision blurs, and I reach down between us, thrumming my clit while slamming down on his cock just right until I finally reach that pinnacle.

It feels like my soul is ripped to shreds in a matter of seconds. A scream tears from my throat, even though I can't hear it. Not when different pieces of my being are scattered in hundreds of thousands of different dimensions.

There's no sense of time or space, just colors and a feeling of completion. Like I was put together wrong before, and now that I've shattered, those pieces were stitched back together the correct way.

It's fucking addicting, and by the time I come down, Parsons Manor reappearing, I want to go back. Wherever I went, I want to go back.

Zade's chin is tucked low, seeming defeated in a way. It unnerves me so much that I twist at the hips and grab the key lying on the nightstand. Right when I go to lift off of him, he lifts his head just an inch.

"Don't," he warns.

Unsure of where his head is at, I listen and reach around him, fumbling to find the keyhole. Finally, the key slips in, but I hesitate to turn it.

There's a looming sense of foreboding. I know he's going to attack, but… it's not knowing exactly what he's going to do that unnerves me.

"Zade…"

"What's wrong, Adeline?" he taunts darkly, eyes still cast downward.

"Turn the key," he whispers.

Fuck, that's terrifying.

"I don't know if I want to," I admit.

"Would you rather I break free myself? You either choose this, or I make the decision for you."

So, what he's saying is I only have the illusion of a choice. What a fucking gentleman.

Working to swallow, I hold my breath and twist the key. The metal clicks, and the next second, his hand is wrapped around the underside of my jaw, lifting me up off his dick and into the air.

I cry out when I'm slammed onto the bed, stiff fingers digging into my neck as he fits himself between my legs and hikes one high on his hip. Without further warning, he drives himself inside of me until there's nothing left of him to give.

"Say it again," he demands. "I want you to look me in my fucking eyes and say it again."

He slams into me once more, wringing a sob from my throat.

My throat dries, the words coming up like dry bread. But I stare into his wild eyes, finding an entire universe within, and say, "I love you. And you've taken everything from me."

His head drops low between his shoulders, gliding his stare down my body all the way to where he stretches me, contemplating my words. And then he looks up at me beneath thick brows, a wicked glint in his stare. As if taking everything from me is all he's ever wanted.

He looks… God, he looks fucking terrifying. Like a man starved for revenge, and he's finally getting it.

A shuddering breath trickles from my throat as he plunges deep inside me again, a direct threat to destroy all that's left of me.

"You've taken my entire heart and soul and my ability to love another. Sometimes I hate you for that," I tell him, my voice quaking. He tips his chin up, now staring down his nose at me, a grin stretching across his face, crinkling the scar on his cheek.

I forge on, heart pounding as he grinds against me, enjoying watching me struggle to get the words out. "Sometimes, I wish I'd never met you. Because now that I have, now that I'm in love with you, I'll never be able to carve you out. You said I'd bleed out before that'd ever happen, and you were right. And I hate you for that."

Zade hums, licking his lips as if he ate something delicious. His hand drifts up to my cheek, swiping my bottom lip with his thumb.

"I'll never get tired of hearing you say you love me, and if you ever stop, I'll put strings in your fucking lips and make you say it."

Then, he leans down closer until his breath fans across my cheeks, and whispers, "But I don't believe you."

My mouth drops, and my brows furrow. "Are you fuck—"

He shuts me up with his cock, driving into me again with one thrust of his hips. "I've lost sight of my faith. I need to see it."

I thin my eyes, contemplating what more he could possibly want from me.

He rubs my lip harder. "You say so many things you don't mean, baby. The truth lies in your fingertips and in the soft curves of your body. In the tears you cry so pretty for me, and how hard you come for me. Show me the truth."

For several beats, I'm at a loss of how to do that. Then, it dawns on me, and he must see the realization in my eyes because he grins again, staring down at me with amusement.

The look angers me as if he thinks I'm going to merely get on my knees for him and recite poetry or some shit. The challenge burns in my chest as my eyes drift over to my nightstand.

Following my stare, he cocks a brow and turns back to me, picking up on my thoughts without having to say anything.

I've bled for Zade, but only to replace the marks of another man.

Soon after I was taken, he carved a rose over his heart. And now… I want him to do the same to me.

He leans over and grabs the knife from the nightstand.

"This what you want?" he asks, twirling the knife until the light glints off of it.

"Yes," I say, though I don't sound the least bit confident.

"And what do you want me to do with this? Slice you open again?"

I shake my head, reaching up to brush the pads of my fingers across the jagged rose on his chest.

"I want this," I admit. Grabbing his wrist, I guide his hand, holding the knife right above my breast. The previous amusement shutters from his eyes, replaced by something dark and treacherous.

"I want one just like yours," I say, rolling my hips to remind him that this is real.

He tenses, the veins roping up his arm and neck pulsating. He's studying me closely, and I'm beginning to lose my nerve.

"Please, Zade," I plead quietly.

Closing his eyes, he takes a deep breath, and by the time he's opening them, his beast has taken over.

"Rub your clit, baby," he directs. I do as he says, reaching between us and finding the sensitive little bud and start circling it lightly. My lids flutter, acute pleasure rising and stealing my breath. I feel my pussy clench around him, throbbing with desire as my touch grows firmer.

He growls, rolling his hips so I can feel how full I am of him.

One of his hands slides beneath me, cupping the back of my neck firmly while he leans in close, poising the tip of the knife right above my heart.

He's looking up at me beneath his lashes, waiting for my reaction. I only give him a husky moan as a response, grinding against him. I've been at the mercy of Zade's pain before, and it was one of the most euphoric experiences in my life.

"I'm not going to stop," he warns me.

"I'm not scared of you," I bite, moaning again as an orgasm builds.

"So many lies," he whispers, right before he presses the blade in and starts to cut.

I suck in a sharp breath, burning pain flaring in my chest. Slowly and methodically, he begins to thrust in and out of me, keeping his movements gentle so he can slice cleanly.

This isn't short little cuts like last time, but one long, continuous drag. It's nearly blinding, so I rub my clit harder, moaning from the cornucopia of pleasure and agony ravaging my body.

It feels as if a gasoline-lined rose is seeping into my skin, and it's steadily catching fire beneath his touch.

"I will carve a garden of scars into your flesh, little mouse. Only my pain will bring them to life." I tip my head back, groaning from the sharp bite of his knife. "They'll only ever grow beneath my touch."

I squeeze my eyes shut, and his voice cuts in sharply. "Look at me, Adeline. I want you to watch me brand you as mine."

Though it's a struggle, I force my eyes open, trading between the macabre rose being engraved into my skin, and his glimmering mismatched eyes.

"You're doing such a good job, baby," he whispers, sparing me a quick glance. Sweat forms along my hairline as the two different sensations battle in my nerve endings.

"You take it so fucking good," he groans, biting his lip as blood bubbles and pours from the wound, pooling in the divot in my throat and the sheets beneath me.

My breath hitches as his cock hits that spot inside of me, sending my eyes rolling to the back of my head. I arch into the knife and twirl my fingers faster, uncaring how grotesque the rose will look.

Nothing about our love is pretty. It's full of jagged lines, chipped pieces, and sharp edges. It hurts like fucking hell, but it's not a masterpiece if it didn't make you bleed for it.

He curses, the blade slicing through my skin faster.

"Don't you dare fucking come yet, Adeline. Not until I tell you to."

I don't listen, continuing to chase after it despite his warning. Nothing else matters right now except coming all over his cock with his knife in my chest.

He growls, the hand around the back of my neck sliding up and fisting my hair so tightly, I cry out. After a few more moments, he pulls the knife away, the agony still lancing throughout the bloodied rose.

I'm so close. Right on the precipice.

But then he jerks my head back farther, forcing me to bow off the bed. Seconds later, the sharp edge of the knife is pressing into my jugular, and Zade's dangerously soft voice is filling my ear.

"I can slit your throat so fucking easy. And the harder you come, the faster your blood will drain from your body," he drawls.

My fingers still, a different type of agony stealing my breath as I force the orgasm back down.

"You don't fucking come until I tell you to," he repeats, his voice biting and as rough as sandpaper. Despite his threat, he fucks me harder, pressing his chest into mine and earning a pained cry in response.

His breathing escalates, the sharp edge biting into the sensitive flesh on my neck. With every thrust, he jerks my body and causes it to scrape against my skin.

"Zade, please," I cry. "You feel so fucking good. I need it so bad."

He inhales sharply, and then he's flinging the knife across the room, the sound of it cracking against my vanity mirror swallowed by my sharp cries.

His hand comes around my throat, mouth still pressed into my ear.

"Say it again," he demands, quickening his pace.

I bite my lip until I taste copper, struggling to hold on—to keep from exploding around him. I'm in a losing battle, and I *am* a fucking liar. I'm terrified of what Zade will do—enough to keep grappling at that control. Yet I know if I let go, I'll welcome his punishment as chaotically as I did the tip of his knife.

"I love you," I choke out, the words scarcely leaving my tongue before his hand is clamping down, arresting the oxygen in my lungs.

"Such a good girl. I want you to soak these sheets with your cum as deeply as your blood, do you understand me?"

My mouth opens, but no sound escapes. He's gripping my throat too tightly to allow a single decibel to slip through.

Blackness licks at the edges of my vision, taunting me as it creeps in slowly. The pressure in my head heightens, and I feel how bright red my face is. Panic unfurls in my stomach, into the whirlpool of bliss and agony. It's a battle of needing him to stop and preferring he snap my neck if he does.

I'm clawing at his arm, and when my eyes begin to roll, he releases my throat right as a tidal wave crashes through me.

The combination of the blood draining from my head at a dizzying speed and the earth-shattering orgasm reduces me to delirium. My pussy clenches around him so tightly, I feel him strain to sink into me.

"Zade!" I scream through a ravaged throat, hoarse and cracked, my arms looping around his neck, desperate to hold on to something, and needing it to ground me as I'm shredded into pieces.

My ears ring as my body bows completely off the bed, the euphoria clawing at my insides too intense for me to process.

He refuses to stop, fucking me harder even as I thrash in his hold. His hands clutch my hips with a bruising force, and if I could see past the image of God staring in my eyes, asking me if I'm ready to come home, I'd find an unhinged man on his knees asking if he can come, too.

Tears spring to my eyes, and my face contorts with a helpless cry as my body is ravaged. All of the sensations—it's too much.

"Oh my God, please, I can't anymore!"

I feel his fist slam into the mattress beside my head with a guttural growl, and his tongue slides along my cheekbone, lapping up the teardrops.

"Eyes on me when you're praying to me," he snaps. I shake my head, more tears spilling over. "Fuck, you're so beautiful when you cry for me. Do you think I'll ever stop now? I want to drink your fucking tears like they're the blood of Christ."

I shake my head again, a silent plea for him to stop. But he refuses, and I wonder how much longer I can take it before I black out.

"Am I your salvation, too?" I choke out, barely getting the words out before a sob breaks free.

"You were always going to be the one that saved me, little mouse." He shudders, and I feel his body tightening as he nears his end. It's coming for me, too, and I'm scared what will become of me once it hits.

He fucks me faster, slipping his hand between our bodies and sliding his fingers against my clit, and this time, I don't see anything at all. My mouth opens on a near-silent scream, and he roars, supplying the sound of us breaking apart, adrift in our own decimation.

He stills, but my hips have a mind of their own, rolling against him as we're both reduced to ash.

You are dust, and unto dust you shall return.

Time ceases to exist, and by the time we both regain clarity, we're panting and trembling with aftershocks. My cheeks are wet with tears, still leaking from my eyes as I attempt to catch my breath. But I can't. Not with the sobs racking my bruised throat.

Zade loops his arm around my neck, holding me to him tightly as we both try to come back down from… whatever the fuck that was.

"I love you, too," he rasps.

Every day, we come a little closer to death—our bodies deteriorating just a little more. And if this is what dying feels like, then I never want to feel anything else.

Chapter Thirty Eight
The Hunter

I t's quiet.

Too quiet.

The clock ticks in the background, and a methodic pair of footsteps creaks above me. Back and forth.

Tick, tick, tick, tick.

Yet, it's silent. *Claire* is silent.

She took precautions after my television appearance four days ago and crashed all her devices the same night.

I knew it was a possibility that Claire would take my threat to that level—it was a variable I would be stupid not to consider. But if it meant keeping Addie from being charged with murder, which could've led to another kidnapping attempt once in police custody, it was a risk I was willing to take. I could've taken her somewhere no one would find her, but that would be ripping her away from any semblance of a normal life. Not that she has much of one now, but at least we have a chance at getting it back once Claire is taken care of.

I had hoped the red-headed bitch would be too prideful to consider disposing of her devices, but I suppose Claire wouldn't be where she is if she was an idiot.

We tripled down on security around Parsons, ensuring not a goddamn bird gets past the perimeters without me knowing about it. In the meantime, we're working on getting a signal back on Claire. Now that we know exactly where she is, I can have one of my men get as close to her island as possible. Then, we'll fly out a drone that can send a viral EMP to her location. That'll send a virus to any technology within her area, and then we can decipher which devices are valuable from there. It will take a couple of days to get someone out there and within range, and there's plenty she can cook up in the time that she's off-grid.

Tick, tick, tick, tick.

I roll my neck, the muscles popping and groaning.

She hasn't made any moves yet. But that's not fucking right. The bitch is reactive. Her head is the size of this manor, and just as dark as the inside of it.

The footsteps halt, as if hearing my thoughts and offended by the notion. I take a sip of my whiskey, daring the asshole to try me. I'm on edge enough to fight air, and I'll fucking win, too.

After a few moments, the footsteps resume, and I huff out a humorless laugh.

Whichever ghost it is, it's as restless as the bones in my body. Maybe it's a direct reflection of how I feel. A manifestation or some shit. Parsons Manor is full of energy, and I wouldn't be surprised if it could be so easily manipulated.

I gulp down the rest of the contents in my glass, hissing at the burn. The clock continues to tick, drawing near the three AM mark.

I got home a few hours ago from taking down a ring. This one has victims as young as newborns, and I haven't been able to sleep yet. I'm too full of rage and with the knowledge that Claire has something planned.

Phantom fingers of dread are inching up my spine like a spider, tightening my shoulders with each jab. Whatever it is, it's going to piss me the hell off. Call me fucking psychic, I guess.

Tick, tick, tick, tick.

Pulling out my phone, I dial Jay, bouncing my leg as it rings.

"You hate me," is his groggy answer.

"Something is wrong," I say, digging in my pocket to pull out my cigarettes.

"What happened?" he asks, sounding more alert. I shake my head, struggling to put it into words.

"I don't know yet. It's quiet around Parsons. No sign of anyone. But that's too obvious."

Jay's silent for a moment. "I assume this is about Claire. What could she possibly do?"

"Who fucking knows," I grumble, irritated with myself, and angrily sticking the tip between my lips. "The cunt will think of something creative, I'm sure."

He yawns. "Did you talk to Addie about it? You couldn't have woken her to talk about your feelings and then call me when you know something is actually wrong?"

Shithead.

"She's sleeping."

"*I* was sleeping."

"She also went to bed angry because she got in an argument with her mom about getting on medication or some shit. I didn't want to disturb her."

I'm pretty sure her mom was trying to convince Addie to get *me* on medication. Antipsychotics, to be exact. I laughed, and Addie then promptly agreed with her mother.

In response, I rolled her onto my face and ate her pussy until she was riding my tongue into oblivion. The little liar loves me just the way I am.

He sighs. "You're lucky I understand the wrath of a scorned woman." He pauses. "And a man, if I'm being totally transparent."

I roll my eyes. Idiot. He understands it so well because his booty calls are just that, and they don't like it. But does he stop fucking them? Of course not.

"I'm sure they'll both get over it," Jay placates. "From what I've heard, they love each other. They just have a funky way of showing it. Or acknowledging it."

I flick the lighter, about to light my damn cigarette, and just as the flame ignites, so does the proverbial light bulb in my head. My heart drops.

"Shit, Jay, check Addie's parents' house," I clip, finally singeing the tip and inhaling deeply.

He pauses. "You don't think Claire would try something with them, do you?"

"Who else would she go after? I have no family, but Addie does, and it wouldn't be hard to find out that her mother has been visiting frequently."

I hear bed sheets rustling and then the whir of his computer turning on. That dread now has me in a chokehold, and I feel with every fiber of my being that something will be amiss.

Where's my fucking laptop?

Not anywhere close to me.

"Jay," I prompt, growing impatient as I take another drag, my knee bouncing restlessly.

"I'm looking," he mumbles. A few seconds later, he curses, "Shit, they have a Nest camera. Someone busted in about thirty minutes ago."

Fuck. I fly off the stool, nearly sending it toppling to the checkered floor.

"Her parents don't have cameras inside the house, so I can't see what's happening," he says, voice tight.

I've already stubbed out my cigarette in the sink, and am rushing toward the stairs, mouthing a few choice words on the way.

"Send a drone out to keep an eye on the outside. I'm on my way there," I direct, swinging around the railing and taking the steps two at a time.

"Sending one now."

"Thank you," I say, clicking off the call as I fly down the hallway and through Addie's bedroom door. She's facing away, curled in a ball, and sleeping soundly. The balcony doors are cracked open, allowing in a cool breeze. She tends to get overheated from her nightmares, so those doors are always open.

I rush to her, not bothering to stay silent.

"Addie," I call, nudging her softly. I hate to wake her when she seems to be getting a moment's peace while sleeping—but she'd murder me if she discovered something was wrong with her parents, and I left to handle it without telling her.

Her eyes crack open, brows knitting as she comes to.

"What?" she croaks, gearing up to throw the sheets over her head. I grab her wrist, squeezing tightly so she understands the severity.

She freezes, her eyes now flying open to stare up at me.

"What happened?" she asks, panicked as she sits up.

Fuck. She's completely naked, and the fact that it hardly distracts me is how strongly my inner alarm bells are blaring.

"Get dressed. We're going to your parents'," I order, stepping away from her and heading toward her dresser.

"What? Why? What's going on?"

I shake my head. "I had a bad feeling Claire was up to something, so I had Jay check their house. Someone broke in about a half-hour ago."

She's scrambling from the bed and beside me in seconds, slapping away my hands and grabbing the clothes she needs.

"Why would she go after my parents?" she asks, frantically pulling on clothes.

"Because outside of myself and Daya, it's the only other way to get to you. There's been no communication, which means they might not have done anything drastic yet."

She shakes her head, panic pulling her brows into a tight knot. "I don't get it. I don't understand why she's after me like this."

I grab one of my guns from her dresser, check the clip, and tuck it into the back of my jeans. The knife I gave her for her birthday is downstairs, but I'll be grabbing extra guns for her.

"At this point, it's just personal, baby. I'm the biggest threat to her organization, and you're the biggest payday she'll ever see in her lifetime. You will simultaneously make her richer than any human has a right to be and bring me to my knees."

"Xavier already paid for me, and now he's dead. So she's trying to make double the money on me," she snipes.

She rushes over to her sneakers lying haphazardly at the foot of her bed. "She can't possibly think this will work. Does she think I'm that fucking stupid to run into the same situation twice?"

"It's not about how smart you are, it's about how desperate you are. And if she gets ahold of your parents and uses them as collateral, you will be desperate enough to do anything."

Addie huffs, stomping her foot to get the shoe past her heel.

"I'll be damned if I become like Rio," she mutters under her breath.

I'll sooner make it into heaven before that happens.

"What the hell is she going to do anyway?" she asks aloud, though it sounds rhetorical. She turns to me, her light brown eyes sharp. "The stupid bitch is going to try to get me to trade my life for theirs, am I right?"

"Most likely," I concede, following her out of her bedroom door. The moment we step out, it feels as if the walls open their eyes, watching us rush through the dark hallway. Addie cuts through the shadow figures creeping across the floor, paying them no mind.

"Should we wake Sibby?"

I open my mouth, but then as if conjured straight out of a Rob Zombie film, she steps out of her bedroom door near the staircase, covering her mouth as she yawns. Her pigtails are skewed, and her purple nightgown hangs off one shoulder.

She squints her eyes, staring at us with confusion. Addie stops short, gives Sibby one look, and then clips, "Get dressed quickly. You may get to have some fun tonight."

Whatever fatigue was clinging onto her wisps away in a matter of seconds. Her eyes widen with excitement.

"Can my henchmen come, too?"

I sigh. "Only two can fit, and only if they don't get in the way." They're imaginary, yet the assholes somehow still cause problems. She takes off back into the room, squealing.

"Give us two seconds!" she shouts from the depths, but Addie is already tapping her little feet down the stairs like a roadrunner on crack.

"Don't forget your knives and guns, mouse," I call after her. "And, Sibby… limit your knives and guns."

I hear a dramatic sigh from the room, but I ignore her, sticking my Bluetooth in my ear.

Within two minutes, we're piled into my car and taking off towards her parents' house. It's an hour away, but I'm determined to get there in half the time.

Ten minutes into the drive, the men were dragging Addie's parents out of the house. Jay made a split-second decision and gunned down their truck. The drone he's using is special grade, equipped with bullets, and highly illegal.

The men took her parents right back inside and will be waiting for our arrival. There's a slight risk that they'll kill her parents before we get there, but that would be entirely stupid.

If her parents are dead, there's no leverage. And if they tried to escape, Jay would shoot them down. Either way, they lose.

"They know we're here," I remind Addie as I pull into the driveway.

Despite Serena's disapproval of Parsons Manor, living in a secluded house is in her blood. She doesn't live in the burbs like I'd imagine, but a beautiful home behind a thicket of trees, and far from the road. It isn't removed from civilization like the manor is, but it's not easy to find, either.

"You don't think they killed them, do you?"

"No, baby," I tell her truthfully. "If they did, they know that if I don't kill them, Claire sure as hell would. She'd lose her leverage."

Addie rolls her bottom lip between her teeth as I come to a stop. The house is dark, and the surrounding trees sway in the wind, the branches casting crooked shadows across the home, exuding an ominous feel. It's a large white three-story house with a massive window on the top center, showcasing the silhouette of a chandelier.

I call Jay, and he answers immediately.

"Keep an eye on the house and make sure no one else comes in," I order.

"Already on it, boss man," he says, the tapping of his keyboard following his confirmation.

I turn to Addie and ask, "You ready?"

She spares me a single glance before opening the door and stepping out, silently answering my question. Sibby scrambles out after her while I shut the car off and follow after them.

Addie's hips sway angrily as she half-runs toward the front door.

I eat up the distance in a few long strides, grabbing her arm and hauling her back. Her neck nearly cracks from how hard she whips her head to glare at me.

"Don't go charging in mindlessly."

Ripping her arm from my grip, she scoffs at me.

"I'm not an idiot," she snaps. I smirk and raise my hands in surrender. If this weren't her mother in danger, I'd bend her over and fuck her until she does go stupid.

"Sorry, baby. Proceed."

Leaving me behind, she charges up to the entrance, then as if hitting slow motion on a movie, her movements become gradual and smooth as she reaches for the front door.

Turning the knob, she quietly opens the door, the darkness bleeding out from the depths of the foyer while her other hand grips the knife strapped to her thigh, readying for someone to jump out and attack. No one does, the silence deafening. Stepping farther inside, her eyes scan every direction. When it's deemed clear, she nods Sibby and me in after her.

I bite my lip, fucking relishing the sight of her in charge. My girl is strong and capable, and I'll gladly follow her lead.

The blackness swallows us whole as I soundlessly shut the door behind me. It's so quiet, you could hear a mouse fart. Addie disappears into the darkness as she moves deeper into the house. I can't see much, but I can feel everything.

The chill coercing the goosebumps across my flesh to rise, the heat moving throughout the pipes, and the eyes watching my every move. They come from all directions and nowhere at all. Yet, they're as real as the ghostly fingers I feel brushing across my skin in Parsons Manor.

Thankfully, Sibby understands the situation perfectly and contains her giddiness. She's used to creeping through houses, but she always had the protection of the walls. In Satan's Affair, *she* was the creeping eyes.

Maybe now she'll understand that gut feeling of knowing someone is watching you that wants to cause you harm but never knowing where they are until they're right in your face.

We travel down a long hallway, passing portraits of Addie gradually aging until she was a teenager. Normally, I'd stop and stare at her childhood pictures, fantasizing about the kid versions of myself falling in love with her had I seen her then. Something tells me that I'd be enraptured by her no matter how young we were.

Now, it's so eerie in here that those smiling eyes in the pictures appear sinister. As if the different versions of Addie are laughing at us because they know the danger awaiting us. I want to laugh right back because *I* was the danger awaiting her.

We emerge into a kitchen, finding the expansive area clear. She starts to head to the left, but a slight shuffling sound arises from our right. She freezes and glances back at me. I nod towards the noise. As much as she wants to find her mom, we can't leave dangerous men behind.

Nodding, she turns and veers toward the noise.

"Watch your step," Addie whispers a moment later. Keeping an eye on Sibby's feet, I see her step down, her boots sinking into the soft carpet.

It's a large living room, with a massive TV screen mounted on the wall to our right and plush couches surrounding it, along with a recliner. I imagine that's where her dad sits, yelling at whatever football team plays on the screen.

His image fades as a different person replaces it, a body emerging from the darkness like a demon called forth by its master.

Addie and Sibby spot him the same time I do, their bodies briefly bristling from the creepiness before we all spring into action. Addie rushes toward the dude, but I feel another person creeping behind me, and I glimpse metal right before I grab Sibby by one of her pigtails and yank, jerking her out of the way of a flying knife that was centimeters from impaling her in the head.

A breath of hot air fans across the back of my neck a mere second before I turn around, sliding my gun from the back of my jeans and taking aim at the culprit who threw the knife. I fire off a shot, hitting the person in the throat and scarcely dodging another knife to the face, catching his wrist right before it could connect. My scars get Addie hot and bothered, so I wouldn't have minded if he succeeded.

The silencer attachment produces the smallest of sounds, quieter than the man now convulsing on the floor, choking on his own blood. Whipping back around, I find Addie scuffling with the first person. Just as I step in to help, she uppercuts the guy, her blade plunging up through his mouth and into his brain.

After she rips the knife from his head, he flops to the ground, dead before he hits the ruined carpet.

Fuck, that's my good girl.

Sibby peers around, and from what I can see, she's pouting. Her lips are pursed, disappointed she didn't get to partake in the action.

"There will be more," I assure quietly, my heart pounding from the adrenaline in my system. It's like morphine pumping through my veins, giving me a high that drugs could never emulate.

Addie faces me with rounded eyes and her hand dripping with blood. Her chest heaves, and from here, I can smell her excitement.

An animalistic urge is beginning to take over. I want to take her to the ground and fuck her in the pool of blood. But her mother is somewhere in this house, most likely hurt and being held hostage.

Stepping back, I dip my chin in approval, feeling just how feral my stare is. She works to swallow, turning and scanning the room to distract herself from the energy thickening between us.

Pulling myself away from my murderous little mouse, I walk ahead and check every corner of the room, finding a small staircase in the back corner. I peer up the steps, seeing nothing but endless black.

"That's my room," she whispers from behind me. Turning my head, I peek at her over my shoulder.

"I think I'll stay out of it for now," I answer, my voice hoarse. "Go check to make sure no one is up there. Quickly."

"We need to find—"

"Addie," I growl. "If we don't clear the house, they could be lying in wait until you're distracted and kill you. So please just check the fucking room, baby."

Snapping her mouth shut, she does as I say, keeping a wide berth as she walks past me. It takes her only a minute before she's making her way back down the stairs.

"Clear," she breathes. "Let's check their room now, please. It's on the other side of the kitchen."

"After you," I drawl. She rushes past me, leading us back through the bloody living room, then towards the stairs on the backside of the kitchen, right before the dining room.

Light on her feet, she quickly climbs the steps, Sibby and I close behind. They're all aware of our presence but stomping around like elephants will only help conceal where they're hiding.

The upper floor is a large circle surrounding the stairs, the monstrous chandelier hanging directly above. The diamonds hanging from the gaudy fixture glint in the moonlight spearing through the massive window.

The air is thicker up here, weighing heavily on my shoulders like God himself is trying to hold me down.

Someone is up here, but they're not visible. Not yet, at least. An ominous feeling races through my bones, enough for me to step forward and push Addie behind me. I'll slap duct tape over her mouth if she tries to argue. I don't care how capable she is, I'll always protect her.

But she doesn't argue, indicating she feels it, too. My chest tightens as I look around, waiting for the other shoe to drop.

It only takes a few more seconds. A bright red laser spears through the window, landing directly on my chest.

"Zade, get down!" Jay shouts through my earpiece.

"Shit," I curse before I dive directly into Addie and Sibby, tackling them both to the ground and nearly sending us right back down the stairs.

The window shatters, and I feel the heat of the bullet slide past my arm, taking a chunk out of my bicep with it.

Sharp glass rains down on us, little slices stinging my cheeks and hands. Addie and Sibby cover their heads, attempting to protect themselves from the barrage of tiny knives.

"Fuck, is everyone okay?" I ask through gritted teeth.

"All's good," Addie groans, followed by Sibby's irate confirmation.

"The motherfucker was shielding his body with something, wasn't picking up on the infrared sensors in the drone until he repositioned," Jay explains hurriedly, then muttering under his breath, "Probably used fucking Styrofoam."

Before I can tell him to, a blast of fire lights up the sky, then quickly fizzles out.

Sniper dude just got sniped.

"He's dead," he announces in my ear, breathing out a sigh, but then immediately starts panicking again, "Please tell me everyone is alive. You're all alive, right?" he asks repeatedly.

"We're all good. But there could be more," I say. "We'll stay away from windows as best as we can. Keep me updated on any more movement."

Another sigh of relief. "Will do."

Sibby growls, wiggling beneath Addie, who is gripping my injured arm and looking over it, her fingers coated in my blood. I quickly check it over. It's superficial.

"You okay, baby?" she asks quietly, her voice shaky. It'd take nothing short of an incinerator to melt me, except when it comes to Addie. Then I'm fucking slush.

I place a kiss on her forehead. "I'm fine, mouse. Let's get moving," I say.

"I really want to stab someone right now," Sibby snips, finally sliding out from beneath Addie. Glass has to be cutting into her, but she doesn't seem to notice when she's too busy yelling at herself.

"Mortis, *move!* Quit clinging to me like a leech, I'm fine. Zade's the one that took the bullet, stupid." In her attempt to detach herself from her imaginary friend, she ends up kicking me in the head.

See? The assholes always cause problems.

"Sibby," I hiss through gritted teeth.

"What? It's not my fault," she sasses, not the least bit sorry.

Groaning, I roll off of Addie and sit up.

"Get up. We need to get away from the window." I stand and help the girls up, one of them now in a seriously foul mood. Her temper is only going to continue to rise until she stabs someone, and my headache is only going to worsen until that happens.

They gently brush the glass from their bodies, and with the moonlight spilling into the room, I note tiny cuts all over their faces.

"Which one is your mom's room?" I ask, keeping my voice low and swiping a few shards from Addie's backside that she missed. Sibby is sticking out her ass and wiping her butt off, but in her head, one of her henchmen is helping her.

"First door on the left," she responds.

"Sibby, I want you to go and check the other rooms," I tell her. Surprisingly, she doesn't complain and takes off, probably praying for someone to try her. *I'm* praying for someone to try her.

Glass crunches beneath my boots as I hug the wall, sliding along it until I reach the door with Addie following my lead.

I crack open the door, tucking myself back around the corner in case more bullets come flying.

"Stay here for now," I order, not giving her time to argue. Holding my gun up, I slip into the room. It's pitch-black in here, and I wish I had thought to bring my night vision goggles.

Straining my ears, I listen for any noise, but I don't hear anything. Not even the sound of breathing.

As my eyes adjust, the bed becomes clearer. Empty, save for the rumpled bed sheets and skewed pillows. A lamp is knocked off the end table, upside down with the cord ripped from the wall. There must've been a struggle getting them out of bed.

I let out a slow breath, continuing to scan my eyes over every inch of the room, trying to pick out any figures standing in the shadows or lying on the ground.

"They're not in here," I call out quietly.

Addie sneaks into the room behind me, her footfalls light and her body poised for threat. She's come so far from the girl who ran headfirst into situations without properly thinking it through. She's a trained killer now, and fuck if it doesn't make my chest tight with pride.

I never wanted to change Addie. Despite how dangerous her impulsiveness and stupidly brave tendencies were, it's what made her so fascinating. But her circumstances took that out of my hands, and while I still needed my brave girl, there wasn't any room for thoughtless actions anymore.

There's nothing thoughtless about how Addie moves now, and my fascination with her has only amplified. All those idle threats she used to make about killing or hurting me—she could make those come true now.

Fuck. Yes.

"Where do you think they could be?" she whispers, bringing me back to the situation at hand. I'd berate myself for getting distracted by her if I knew it would change anything, but it won't. Dying with Addie on my mind is the only way I want to go out anyway.

I shake my head. "I don't know. But if there are people in the house, that means they're most likely still in the house, too."

Addie walks to the bed, pressing her hand into the sheets. "It's cold, so they've been gone for a minute." Turning to me, she decides with resignation and dread, "I think we need to check the basement." Her body is stiff, and her shoulders tense.

"What's wrong with the basement?"

She shrugs a shoulder. "It's creepy down there?" she says, though it sounds like a question.

"You like creepy."

She seems to pause on that thought, and then relaxes, nodding her head. "Yeah, you're right. I do like creepy. Let's go."

Sibby emerges from one of the rooms just as we exit her parents' bedroom, appearing more frustrated.

"No one is up here. I busted in every room," she says with disappointment.

"Basement," I clip. "They might be down there."

Addie leads us back down the stairs and towards the basement door in the dining room.

"If they are down there, they'll hear our footsteps and know we're coming," I murmur, once more pushing Addie behind me. It's better if I'm the one getting shot at so she can handle her parents.

The door creaks open, and it's like looking into a massive black hole in the ground.

"How big is the basement?"

"Pretty big. It's not finished," she answers on a whisper. "There are rooms down there, too."

Slowly, I descend the stairs, and my sight is completely robbed.

There's a cold chill and another heavy weight of dread down here, like an evil goddess beckoning me into her lair. Such a warm fucking welcome.

In the far back corner of the basement, a tiny sliver of light shines from the depths of what looks to be a hallway.

That pit of dread yawns, consuming my insides until all I feel is doom.

Addie and Sibby flank either side of me, and though I can't see their faces, I can feel their restlessness.

"We're in the family room, down that hallway is the unfinished side," Addie informs me, her voice barely above a whisper.

Just as I take a step, the glow extinguishes as if they cut the lights out. I freeze, my eyes beginning to adjust.

They didn't cut the lights out. Someone is standing at the entrance of the hallway. They're unmoving, but I feel their eyes boring into where we stand. My hand tightens around my gun, and I slowly raise it, preparing for them to attack. Then, they slowly step back and disappear down the hallway again, the glow taking their place once more.

My heart pumps wildly in my chest. Shit, that's freaky. Even I can admit that.

Sibby scoffs. "I spent too much time in haunted houses—no one is creepier than me. Let me go first."

I shrug, deciding Sibby fucking with them wouldn't hurt.

"Have fun," I mumble, dropping my weapon an inch, though I refuse to relax. There could be more lurking around down here.

She giggles loudly, the sound sinister, before she softly sings a lullaby as she heads for the hallway. I can't be sure, but if I know Sibby, then I'm positive she's skipping there.

I grab Addie's hand, leading her to where the little doll now stands in the entrance, her tiny body highlighted by the light.

Her pink knife is in her hand, and she stabs the tip into the wall beside her. Then, with her lullaby growing louder, she slowly walks down the hallway, dragging her knife as she goes.

Addie cringes, but I can't tell if it's because Serena is going to be pissed about that or if it's because Sibby is just as creepy as she promised.

Both are daunting.

Voices arise from the room they're in, sounding nervous and slightly angry.

"Don't come any closer," a deep voice barks. Sibby pauses, abruptly cutting off her lullaby, and cocks her head.

"That's not very nice," she whispers, her childlike tone sending chills down my spine. "I just want to play."

"I will blow your fucking head off, bitch," he spits. A large man fills the doorway at the end of the hallway, and I quickly usher Addie out of sight before he spots us at the mouth. I flatten myself against the wall and peek around the corner.

If he tries anything, I'll be the one blowing heads off.

He's burly and tall, with a bald head, black tattoos covering his pale skin, and a bushy beard surrounding his thinned lips. A gun is in his hand, aimed directly at Sibby. But she doesn't seem the least bit frightened.

Muffled whimpers emit from the room, both masculine and feminine, and the sounds relax me a bit. They may be hurt, and definitely scared, but they're also alive. That's all that matters right now.

"My henchmen won't let that happen," she says. I've no idea where she imagines her harem to be, but the only one intimidating the armed man right now is her.

Which is admirable when she's five foot nothing.

"Drop the knife," he orders her. Sighing, Sibby listens, her knife clanging down the wall.

"You might as well tell me to undress next if you're going to strip me of things," she pouts. Gripping the bottom of her shirt, she starts to pull it up, doing just that.

The man's eyes widen, and his gun drops as he watches Sibby take off her shirt. Thank fuck she's wearing a bra.

I shake my head. Her methods are really fucking weird but still effective. She throws her shirt at the man, causing him to flinch back. Within that small increment of time, she grabs another knife strapped to her thigh and whips it at the man, the tip of the knife lodging in his eye straight through.

The whimpers rise to full-fledged screams of horror as the man tips face first, dropping like a bag of sand. His weight lands on the knife, driving it completely through his skull.

Quickly grabbing her knife and shirt from the floor, she pulls it on and skips the rest of the way into the room, stepping over her convulsing victim.

"Let's go," I say, grabbing Addie's hand and rushing into the room behind Sibby, attempting to avoid the mess.

Serena and her husband, William, are bound to two chairs in the center of the room, duct tape slapped over their mouths. A single light bulb dangles above them, illuminating the two men on either side, each holding a gun to their head.

The intruders are tense, on edge now that Sibby flung a knife into their very dead partner's eye.

"Mom... Dad...," Addie breathes, and I feel her body bristling with the need to run to them.

Serena's eyes are wet and bloodshot, smudged with black mascara. Her blonde hair is mussed, and her silk pajamas are torn at the collar.

William squirms beside her, profusely sweating. His graying hair is matted to his head, and his white t-shirt is soaked. A cut mars his cheekbone, and a bruise is already beginning to form around his eye.

"You got here quicker than I expected after your friend fucked with our truck," the intruder to my left says, his gun digging into Serena's temple. He has deep black hair that hangs down around his ears, tangled and greasy, and a massive, hooked nose with a scar cutting across it. The other is a short, blond man with a baby face, who appears to be way out of his element.

"I was looking forward to having fun with them just a little bit longer. Maybe see if Mommy has a golden pussy too." His finger curls around a strand of Serena's hair, and she jerks away with a muffled scream.

"Don't fucking touch her," Addie snaps. The man only smiles.

"I wanted to turn them into a nice display for you, too," he continues, ignoring her. He shrugs a shoulder, attempting to appear nonchalant. "I suppose you'd make a better exhibit. Z hanging out of that big window in the front of the house, just like you did with the doctor. How poetic that'd be."

"I'd love to play arts and crafts with you," I murmur, drawing my switchblade from my hoodie and opening it, the zip of metal lost in Serena's suppressed cries.

The man cocks the gun in response, his threat clear.

"You kill her, you kill the only thing keeping my bullet out of your brain," I warn.

"Oh, Mommy's the favorite, I see. Well, then we can do without the father, can't we?"

His gun pivots to Addie's father, who now has two guns pressed against his head. The man's intentions are clear: killing one will only cement Addie's need to trade herself to save the only living parent she has left.

"You do that, then there will be no diamond at all." My gaze snaps to Addie, my heart coming to a screeching halt when I see her holding her knife to her own throat.

Oh, hell no.

Chapter
Thirty Nine
The Diamond

I dig the blade into my skin until I feel a sharp pinch, blood slowly trailing from the wound. Zade's eyes track it, his eyes alight with fury.

The greasy-haired man returns his gun to my mother, a smart-ass grin on his face.

"Touché, diamond." He tips his chin up to his partner, who's still holding his weapon to my father. "Grab her."

Then, he addresses Zade and Sibby, "Both of you drop all those weapons, and kick them away."

The guy with the baby face approaches me, and I take a big step back. "You don't get to touch me. Not until I know you won't hurt any of them."

His eyes narrow, but then they flit over my shoulder, and a moment later, I feel the danger behind me.

"Fuck, Addie, move!" Zade barks, but it's too late.

A gun presses into the back of my head, distracting me long enough for his arm to come around and grab ahold of my knife, flinging it to the side.

Concrete fills my bones, my body turning to stone as he wraps his arm around my neck and pulls me back into him, moving his gun to my temple.

"You forgot to check the attic," the new intruder whispers in my ear. He drops his arm from around my throat and slides his hand across my tailbone and down my thighs, checking for any weapons, and then throwing them to the floor when he locates them. He squeezes my ass for extra measure, and I can't contain the snarl from slipping free.

Oh, yeah. He's going to die.

Tension radiates from Zade, his murderous gaze tracking the man's wandering hand. I bet he's imagining all the ways he could remove it from his body, just like he did Arch's. Sibby is still, her eyes bouncing in every direction, probably calculating how quickly she can kill one of them before their gun goes off.

"Better be careful," Zade murmurs, his eyes boring into the man holding me. "That diamond has sharp edges."

Baby face turns his weapon on Zade, "Shut the hell up. Both of you get against the wall."

Zade smirks, raising his hands in mock surrender, but the look in his eyes is deadly.

Sibby refuses to budge, though, so the man storms toward her and grabs her by the arm, attempting to haul her there himself. She goes wild, scratching at him and causing a massive scuffle.

Hooked on the inside of my sleeve is a pen gun—a handy little weapon Zade got me. I put it there for a situation exactly like this, deliberately keeping it out of any apparent spots to hide a weapon. It only has a single bullet, but it'll be enough.

The chaos distracts all the men enough to slide out the pen gun from my sleeve without any of them noticing.

Sweat beads across my hairline, and though adrenaline is running rampant in my system, calmness overtakes me.

Hurriedly, I take aim on the greasy-haired man and click the button on the pen, the bullet ripping from the small weapon and through the man's brain, killing him immediately.

The utter surprise is enough time for me to knock away the gun from my head, my captor's reflexes delayed as he fires off a shot at my feet, scarcely missing my toes. The bullet ricochets, and I think I hear someone gasp, but I've already turned around and am sending my fist flying into his face.

My father is shouting through the tape on his mouth, but I can't look now. My opponent slides a knife from his pocket and swings it at my face.

Rearing back just in time, the blade slices through the air within an inch of my nose. Grabbing ahold of his hand wrapped around the handle, I snap it back, his wrist breaking from the force.

He cries out, dropping the knife. Before I can land another punch, this one to his throat, his head kicks back, a hole now in the center of his forehead.

I turn with wide eyes, finding Zade tucking away his weapon.

"Sorry, baby. He touched your ass, therefore, I needed to kill him."

A piercing scream distracts me, drawing my eyes to Sibby happily stabbing away at the man beneath her, while my dad squirms like a worm on a hook. His stare pinballs back and forth from the psychotic girl at his feet to his wife.

My eyes widen when I get a good look at my mother. Her head is drooping, chin tucked into her chest and blood soaking through her shirt.

"Oh my God," I cry, rushing over to her. Zade reaches her first, pressing his fingers against her throat to feel for a pulse.

"She's alive," he breathes. "But her pulse is faint. She needs a doctor now."

Tears immediately well in my eyes, and panic turns my brain to mush. I open my mouth, limbs frozen, and wide eyes locked onto my dying mother.

"Adeline," Zade barks, and my eyes snap to him. "Focus, baby. I need you to come here and put pressure on the wound."

Finally unlocking my muscles, I do as he says and press both hands against her chest. Crimson bubbles through my fingers, coating my skin within seconds.

Distinctly, I see Zade untying her bonds and then my dad's. There's a sharp command telling Sibby to stop grinding on the dead man beneath her, then Zade talking to Jay through his earpiece, but everything is drowned out after that.

There's too much blood rushing in my ears. Too much anxiety eating me alive from the inside out.

"Mom," I say shakily. Dad's arms come around her, gently lifting her head and calling out her name. Tears are streaming down his ruddy cheeks, and it's then I realize my own face is wet.

"Serena, hey honey, look at me," Dad coaxes, but her eyes stay firmly closed.

"I need to lift her," Zade says.

"Don't you touch her!" Dad shouts, going to slap Zade's arms away. "We need to call an ambulance."

"Dad!" I exclaim, pulling a hand away to stop him. "Stop, he's trying to help."

"I will be faster than an ambulance, I promise you," Zade assures, staring firmly in my father's eyes. Dad is a rule follower. He goes by the book. And even in his mania, he understands that Zade isn't taking her to the hospital only because he's faster, but because we've all committed a crime, and he doesn't want them to know.

Which means we're not going to a real hospital, either.

Gritting his teeth, Dad releases Zade and lets him pick up my mom, her head flopping onto his chest as he stands.

"Everyone get in the car. Let's go, *now*, Sibby."

We climb the basement steps, tear through the house, and pile into Zade's car—all of it a blur. I let Dad sit in the passenger seat while my mom is draped across mine and Sibby's lap. I continue to put pressure on her chest, whispering to her softly to stay alive.

Zade must still have Jay on the line because he says, "Call Teddy and let him know we're on our way. Gunshot wound to the chest."

"Let me guess, there's some made-up story you have, huh?" Dad snaps from the front seat while Zade tears out of the driveway and onto the road. He handles the car with ease, despite the unnerving speed we're traveling.

"Well, no, not really," Zade answers, not the least bit perturbed by my dad's anger. "We're not going to the police. And we're going to a surgeon, with real experience—"

"We're not going to the hospital?!" my father booms, his voice deafening. I flinch, heart pounding. I've told Zade before that my dad wasn't an integral part of my life. He always lingered in the background, there but not really—kind of like Gigi's ghost in Parsons Manor.

But there were a few times in my childhood where he raised his voice, and each time, it sent birds scattering off their branches and my back hunching in attempt to make myself smaller.

He's a simple man, but he can also be scary.

"No, sir," Zade responds casually. Nothing intimidates him, and if I haven't had a close look, I'd think he has balls of fucking steel hanging between his legs.

"I don't care who the fuck you are, you better turn this car around and take us to the GODDAMN HOSPITAL!" he yells, his face growing increasingly red, even in the dark of the car.

"Raise your voice to me one more fucking time," Zade threatens, his voice deepening. "I guarantee you that I can knock your ass out without even swerving this car." My dad rears back, eyes bugging with shock

"Dad," I cut in before my other parent ends up getting shot, my voice soft but stern. "I would never let her die, and you know that. Please just trust us."

His glare sears through me, but I don't look away, my entire body beginning to shake from the mix of adrenaline, shock, and panic.

Scoffing, he turns away, muttering under his breath, "I can't fucking believe this shit. Adeline, what the fuck have you gotten involved in?"

I frown. "I didn't even do anything, Dad."

He turns back to me with incredulity. "You think I didn't see the three of you kill those men in cold blood? The little crazy one—"

"Don't call me crazy!" Sibby screeches from beside me, causing me to flinch, the pitch hurting my ears. I pause, noting how manic she looks right now. Her chest is pumping, and her brown eyes are wild, like she's a tiger cornered in a small cage.

Dad must see it, too, because he trains his glare onto me. "Don't sit here and act like you're the daughter I raised," he barks. "You just murdered someone."

"He was going to kill Mom," I defend, in disbelief he's lecturing me right now. He's in shock and angry, and taking it out on me.

He clenches his teeth, baring them at me as he spits, "If she dies, this will be all your fault. That bullet hit her because of you!"

His words feel like a bullet of their own, hitting me right in the chest and punching the air out of my lungs.

"What?" I choke out.

"When you were fighting with that guy, and the gun went off," he barks, his face reddening. He stares at me like... like I'm a monster. "The bullet ricocheted and hit your mother."

My mouth opens, speechless. I remember it ricocheting but never saw where it hit, distracted by the man I was fighting with.

Wave after wave of guilt slams into me, and fuck... this *is* my fault. I blink, my vision blurring with a fresh wave of tears. It feels as if my chest is cracking wide open, my heart spilling out right alongside my mother's.

"She's not the one that pulled the trigger," Zade barks, defending me.

Huffing, he turns around and stares out his window, vibrating with fury.

"This is your fault, too," he accuses snidely, directing it toward Zade. "The both of you. None of this would've happened if it wasn't for your criminal boyfriend, Adeline."

Zade turns his head to my father, the leather steering wheel groaning beneath his tightened fists, and for a moment, I'm convinced he's going to completely snap it in half.

"I think it's best you shut your fucking mouth from now on, or else I will do it for you. As you've made clear, I'm not a good man, and I care very much about how you talk to Addie. That man was holding a goddamn gun to *your* daughter's head. This is nobody's fault but the people who broke into your home."

Dad meets his stare, words on the tip of his tongue. In the end, he shakes his head and turns to look out the window again, content with where his fingers are pointing.

The car falls into a weighted silence, the four of us conflicted for different reasons.

I look down at my mom, a sob working up my throat as I stare down at her pale face. My tears drip onto her cheeks, but I don't dare remove my hands from the wound to wipe them away.

"I'm so sorry, Mom. I don't want to do this life without you, so stay with me, okay?"

Try as I might, my PTSD is beginning to resurface as Zade whips us into a driveway within twenty minutes, driving up to a wooden cabin with a warm yellow glow emitting from the windows. I recognize this cabin—barely.

Zade brought me here right after he found me, and I hardly remember a thing about this place or Teddy, just that both the house and the doctor were warm and inviting. Opposite to the memories of a different doctor that are currently sending my blood pressure through the roof.

"This is Teddy's house?" I ask, my hands numb.

Flashbacks of waking up in a make-shift hospital, an old man with pale blue eyes and a deranged smile beneath his bushy mustache leaning over me, asking me to come with him. My heart pumps wildly, and it feels like it's cracking my rib cage from the force.

The second the car comes to a stop, Sibby is scrambling out of the car as if she was stuck underwater with no air. She storms off somewhere, muttering about having to leave her henchmen behind. None of us have the mental capacity to worry about her in this second.

"Yes. I know you might not remember much, but his name is Teddy Angler, and his son is Tanner. They're good friends of mine," he answers, shutting the car off and hurrying to the back door.

"Keep the pressure on her chest," Zade instructs. Quickly and carefully, he slides Mom out of my lap, cradling her against his chest while I keep my hands firmly planted on the wound. Together, we rush up to the front door just as it opens.

Two men usher us in, Dad close behind. The warmth and comfort of the house are familiar, yet still shocking to my system.

I recognize both men. The elder one is Teddy, and the younger one—though still in his forties at least—is Tanner.

They lead us down the hallway straight ahead and into a room with a hospital bed, IV pole, and several other machines.

Panic resurfaces, and I'm no longer standing in Teddy Angler's hospital room but Dr. Garrison's. He's standing before me, pleading with me to come with him, a crazed look in his milky blue eyes. Half of his head is gone, blown off from Rio's bullet, and his shredded brains exposed.

No, no, *no*. I don't want to go. I don't want to—

"*Adeline*," Zade calls roughly, shaking me until Dr. Garrison fades, replaced by concerned yin-yang eyes. "You're here with me, little mouse. No one is going to take you from me."

I blink, vision blurred, and chest tight with panic.

"I'm sorry," I whisper, frustration beginning to filter in alongside the million other fucking emotions I can hardly contain.

"Don't be, baby. Come sit down, and let them operate. Your mom is going to make it, okay?"

"Is that what Teddy said?" I ask, peeking around Zade's shoulder, but I can't see much behind Teddy's larger stature and Tanner on the other side.

Dad sits in the corner of the room, staring at Mom with a pinched expression.

"He hasn't said much, which is a good thing. If he's operating, then there's a chance."

Nodding my head, I let him lead me back out into a small living room filled with green and navy blue plaid couches, a bearskin rug, and a deer head mounted above the brown fireplace, a fire raging within. The floor, walls, and furniture are made up of burnished wood, giving the house a homey, relaxed feel.

I collapse onto the couch and start to drop my head in my hands but immediately jerk away, reminded that they're covered in dried blood. I glance around, hoping that I'm not ruining Teddy's couch, and sit on the floor instead.

Then, I remember Sibby is still absent, and my head is swiveling all around.

"Where did Sibby go?" I question, wiping the snot leaking from my nose. Honestly, of all things, embarrassment is low on the list of things I should be feeling. And something tells me Zade has seen me in far more ridiculous situations while stalking me, so snot bubbles are the least of my concern.

Zade sits next to me, pulling me into his chest and cocooning me in his arms. As nice as it feels, I'm incapable of relaxing. Thousands of bugs are crawling beneath the surface of my skin, filling my skull with the buzz of their wings.

"I'll check on her in a bit. There wasn't room in the car for her henchmen, and they stayed behind. I think it's freaking her out. They weren't there when she was taken to the mental facility, and she probably has some sort of separation anxiety now."

I nod my head. Her henchmen are as real to her as Zade is sitting next to me. It's not as easy as just making them go *poof* or conjuring them before her whenever she wants. She sees them as real people, so she has to make sense of it when they do appear.

Eventually, they'll come back to her, and she'll probably see two men dressed as monsters walking up the driveway toward her.

"He was right," I whisper. "It was my fault she was shot."

"You didn't fire off the gun, nor did you personally aim that bullet at your mother. It was not your fault."

I remove myself from his arms, feeling uncomfortable in my own skin. It doesn't matter that I didn't pull the trigger, I still caused it when I pushed his arm down.

Sensing my inner turmoil, Zade rolls his neck, cracking the muscles. Sitting forward, he rests his elbows on his spread knees and links his hands together.

My eyes lock onto them, tracing the veins running through them. Those hands have killed so many and have protected many, too. How does he compartmentalize his sins from his good deeds?

"If you were me, would you feel guilty?" I question, my voice hoarse from the tears.

He casts his stare down, contemplating that. "You've seen me shoulder responsibility for a death I didn't cause. When I took down a ring, and that little girl was shot and killed right before I got into the building. Or when you were kidnapped when I was supposed to be protecting you... it's hard not to take it fucking personally. Feeling that weight is what makes you human. But there's a difference between feeling another's pain and blaming yourself because someone else hurt them."

He lifts his gaze, the intensity burning his eyes searing me from the inside out.

"The rose carved into my chest is proof that it's never that simple.

Sometimes I cling to that guilt because I don't feel so far gone. But that doesn't mean I won't remind you every day that the blame you shoulder isn't worthy of you."

I close my eyes, a weak attempt to hold back another wave of tears. A sob works its way out of my throat, and I cover my mouth to contain it, but that's not any more effective.

"She was trying to build a relationship with me," I blither. "And I… I was being difficult about it."

Zade grabs my hand and pulls me into him, and though I feel undeserving of the comfort, I take it anyway, allowing it to soak into my bones while I cry into his chest.

I've taken pleasure in killing before, but that doesn't mean I live without a heart. And all I can think right now is how peaceful it must feel to be empty.

"Addie, wake up."

A hand softly jerks my arm, tugging me out of a restless sleep. I crack open my bleary eyes, dry and irritated from the tears.

"Is she okay?" I ask instantly, not even fully awake yet, looking around to see my tired father sitting on the other couch, his face set in a frown.

Zade, Teddy, and Tanner stand before me, and I feel a tad like they're evaluating a patient with the way they're staring at me.

Teddy and his son look nearly identical. Both with soft green eyes, laugh lines, and square jawlines. The only difference is that Teddy has significantly grayer hair, and more wrinkles. Unlike Dr. Garrison, his presence is soothing, despite the words coming from his mouth.

"She's not out of the woods yet," Teddy answers gently. "The bullet just barely missed her heart, but thankfully, it went clean through and missed vital organs. She lost a lot of blood, and she's still in danger of infection. She's going to be out for some time, but I want you all to know you're more than welcome to stay here," he explains, casting a look at Dad.

I nod, though I find little relief. She's alive, but that could easily change.

"Do I need to give her blood or something?" I rasp, my throat just as dry as my eyes.

"That's okay, sweetheart. Your father is a match and kindly provided some, and I also have some bags of O negative stored if I should need it."

Nodding again, I stand. "Can I see her?"

"Of course," he acquiesces softly, lifting his arm to direct me forward.

"I'm going to check on Sibby," Zade says, pointing over his shoulder.

Frowning, I ask, "How long has it been?" I don't remember how long I cried for until I eventually fell asleep in Zade's arms.

"Only about three hours. She's still sitting outside on the doorstep waiting for her henchmen."

Nodding, I turn and head for the room, heart in my throat. And when I open the door and see her lying there so still and pale, I nearly choke on it.

The machine next to her beeps, her heart rate steady for now. There's a chair beside her already, assumingly where my dad was sitting. He stayed in the room with her the entire time, and I feel a little guilty for that, too. I should've stayed with them.

But even now, being in here is threatening to send me back into that place with Dr. Garrison. I slide my hands through my hair, gripping the strands tightly in an effort to ground me. To keep me present.

I'm safe. Zade is right outside. And there isn't an evil doctor trying to kidnap me.

Blowing out a breath, I sit in the recliner, and grab my mother's hand. It's cool to the touch, but she feels… alive. Not cold and stiff like a corpse, which brings me a small amount of comfort.

"You want to know what really fucking sucks?" I begin softly. "When I came home, there were a few times you had asked me to talk about what I went through, and I could never find the words to describe the terror of waking up to men holding you hostage, threatening to kill you. The unknown if you're going to live or die. I told you that you wouldn't understand. But I suppose you know what that feels like now, huh?

"And then, you'd try to explain to me the terror *you* felt when I was gone and not knowing whether I would live or die. And you said I'd never understand that, either… But that's also not true anymore, is it?"

My eyes begin to burn again, and I release her hand to rub at them with the heels of my palms, silently threatening myself to keep it together. I'm tired of crying. It's fucking exhausting.

Once I feel like I have it somewhat together, I drop them and grab her hand again.

"I'm holding your hand, but you're still gone. And I don't know whether you're ever going to wake up. So I feel it now. And that… that just really fucking sucks."

I sniff, rubbing the pad of my thumb against her hand, not sure if I'm comforting her or myself at this point.

"Dad hates me now, too. So there's that," I whisper. "I've shacked up with a criminal."

I sputter out a weak laugh. "*I'm* a criminal. And I suppose that might be the one thing Zade is responsible for. Turning me into a trained killer. But you know what? I like it. I like being able to protect myself now. And I like that I don't feel so weak anymore. Does that make me a bad person?"

I pause, frowning. "Don't answer that. You're going to ask me to stop. And you're going to tell me you want the old Addie back. But she's gone, Mom. And I know Dad disapproves of the new version of me, but I hope one day, you both will relearn to love who I've become."

A single tear breaks free, and I curse the drop for betraying me. I quickly wipe it away, sniffling again.

"I'll understand if you can't. Sometimes I struggle with loving myself, too. But you know the one person who will? Who will always love me unconditionally? It's my criminal boyfriend. And don't you think that's just fucking admirable?"

I smile without humor. "I think it's only fair if we try, though. You decided that when I came home, I was worth loving as a broken shell of a person. I think you can learn to love me as someone who is fierce and strong, right? So now, I want you to come home, and whatever version of yourself you wake up to be, and whatever version you grow into—I'll love you, too."

June 28th, 2022

I've always been pretty indifferent toward my dad. Growing up, he didn't play with me, or even really talk to me. My mom made all the decisions when it came to how to parent me. He never really seemed bothered by me, but not interested either.

I think I stopped giving a shit by the time I was five or so.

The last thing I feel now is indifference. If I'm being honest, I think I kind of hate him. Zade had teased me before about having daddy issues, and I never really felt that applied to me. But I suppose it does now. Because I fucking **hate** him right now.

He won't let me see Mom.

He gave **ZERO** shits about me my entire life, but now he suddenly cares what I'm doing with my life. Now, he cares that I'm not on the straight and narrow, and has the nerve to act like *he* didn't raise me that way. He didn't fucking raise me AT ALL.

Calling wasn't working so I went to their house today, and was promptly locked out.

It was also the first time I drove since my car accident, and I cried the entire way home. I'm surprised I didn't get in another. That would've sucked considering I stole Zade's car.

I wasn't ready to get in mine yet and see that ketchup stain missing,

Chapter Forty
The Diamond

"Let me talk to her," I demand through the phone, plunging my trembling hand through my hair.

"Addie, I'm tired of having this conversation. It's best you give your mother some space for now," Dad answers, sounding exhausted.

"Then let's stop having it!" I shout.

We've only been talking for one fucking minute, and it's his own fault when he won't give the phone to my mother. I've tried every day since she's been home, and he won't give in. I even went as far as driving there, but he wouldn't let me in.

Teddy kept her for over a week, monitoring her and slowly nursing her back to health.

She was out cold nearly the entire time. And the few times she did wake, I don't think she has much recollection of. She was mainly confused and disoriented, and in a lot of pain.

Dad, Zade, and I stayed by her side the entire week, while Sibby went home with her henchmen. It took them four hours to reappear, and the second they did, she was back to her old self. I'm sure they had lots of orgies while we were gone.

Once Teddy felt Mom was stable and could recover at home, Zade drove us back to their house. His team took care of the bodies and even went as far as restoring the house to its former state. I think Dad was shaken when he walked in, and it looked as if nothing ever happened.

He let Zade and I help get Mom settled in their bed and then promptly kicked us out. That was five days ago, and he still won't let me see or talk to her.

My only reprieve is he'll let Daya in, thinking she's removed from my felon life or something. But now I'm unsure if he'll even allow that anymore.

"Why? Did she say that herself, or is that a decision *you're* making?"

"I know what's best for my fucking wife," he snaps, his anger rising. But I don't shrink away like I normally would've. I told Mom that version of myself was gone, and it was the truth.

"So, what you're saying is that I'm not good for her," I conclude, my voice shaking with anger. My fist curls, and the urge to send it flying into the wall nearly overcomes me.

"You and that boyfriend of yours," Dad corrects. "I've agreed not to go to the police about this entire situation. But that doesn't mean I will allow you both to be in her life if this is what will happen. If you want to fuck off and become a criminal, fine, but don't involve us in it."

The phone clicks off a second later, and I erupt. Letting out a frustrated scream, I send my phone flying across the room, right as Zade steps through the door.

He stills, eyes tracking the phone as it crashes into the stone wall and crumples to the floor in pieces.

"Do you want me to go kidnap her?" he offers.

I snap my head to him, my rage deepening.

"He's not letting me see her because we're criminals. And your solution is to… commit another crime?"

"Well, when you put it like that."

Growling, I whip away from him and storm towards the balcony, needing to get away.

The warm wind whips through my hair the second I step out, sending the strands flying around my face. It only embodies how I feel, like Medusa with a crown of angry snakes.

It's not fair, but it's becoming harder and harder to look at Zade and not blame him, too. I'm beginning to revert back to that bitter, hateful part of myself that was convinced my life wouldn't be such a goddamn shitshow if Zade didn't come barreling into it.

And like Medusa, because I'm wrongly being punished, I want to punish everyone else in retaliation.

I feel Zade behind me before I hear him. Always so silent—always sneaking up on me.

"Your dad is being an asshole, Addie, but she's going to recover, and he won't be able to keep her from you," Zade assures quietly.

What if he gets into her head by then? Convinces her I'm bad for her, and then she decides that I'm not worth loving after all.

And they will always feel that way while I'm with Zade. They will always see him as a bad choice, and as long as I'm with him, they won't allow me into their lives.

Just when I get the chance to have a real relationship with my mom, it's ripped away from me. It kind of feels like condensing my entire childhood into one day and making me relive it.

"Maybe you should leave," I mutter.

A beat passes before he drawls, "You want to repeat that for me, little mouse?"

Clenching my teeth, I bark, "You need to leave."

I told my mother that Zade would always love me unconditionally, but that love is what almost got her killed. He said it himself—Claire wants me so goddamn badly because of him. Because of how much I mean to him.

Accepting his love was hard, but I learned to be okay with it when I was the only one in danger. Now, I don't know if that's the case anymore. My parents may be assholes, but are their lives worth sacrificing for this shit?

I keep my eyes pinned to the water sparkling in the afternoon glow, but his silence is so powerful, it invades all five of my senses. All six of them, if I'm being honest. Because I can feel how enraged he is.

"You think that's going to solve all your problems, don't you?" he chuckles.

I whip around. "Maybe it would. You can kill Claire and all her minions, and I will finally be able to live in peace."

He cocks a brow, and his eyes have never suited him better until this moment. One so ice-cold, and the other so full of darkness—two dangerous parts of him reflecting onto me.

"This is getting old, Adeline."

I rear back. "Why, are you mad that you can't make me obsess over you to the point where I need you by my side every fucking second of the day? Or because you can't—"

"What, baby? I can't what? Make you love me? Care about me? Or is it that I make you feel all those things when you don't want to?"

He gets in my face, anger tightening his scars and amplifying the icy darkness in those yin-yang eyes.

Have you ever come face-to-face with a pissed off bear? Looked into the eyes of the beast as it seethes? Most don't live to talk about it.

"You think I'm going to believe your little lies? As if I possess an ounce of insecurity." He ends that last statement with a laugh, and it grinds against my nerves. I feel my face brighten while my eyes darken.

He's laughing at me, and I want to hurt him. Not with my fists, but with my words. I want him to hate me so he will understand what it feels like to hate someone so much, yet still crave them.

For once, I want him to feel what *I* fucking felt when he forced his way into my life.

"No, but it will bother you when you find that all your efforts have been wasted." His smile slips, and I feel my first dose of victory. I take a step into him, enjoying the way he stiffens. "All that time spent, using my body against me in the name of love, only to never make me love you at all."

This time when he smiles, there isn't an ounce of amusement. It's fierce and speaks of a man held with a rope around his neck, faced with the decision to hang himself and save his loved one from the same fate or throw her to the gallows instead.

Is he going to hurt me back in order to protect himself? Or is he going to stand here and take it?

"Oh?" he challenges. "Professing your love and begging me to carve a rose in your chest was for fun?"

He bares his teeth, and my lungs constrict. "Did you get so good at writing books that you don't know the difference between reality and your imagination anymore?"

I narrow my eyes. "Stockholm syndrome is real. A human reaction to someone constantly threatened. It makes sense to trick our brains into thinking we love the person. If only it makes it easier to tolerate them."

He cocks a brow, unimpressed. And that act is still just as heart-stopping as it's always been.

"Does this feel good? Does it feel good to punish me for something your father is doing?" he asks, his deep voice merely a whisper. That small dose of victory turns into a pool, and then a flood as pain lances across his eyes.

Does he hate me yet? Does he feel what real love feels like?

You can't truly love someone if you've never hated them. Two sides to a double-edged sword, and they both cut fucking deep.

"It feels like I'm finally setting myself free," I spit.

He nods slowly, his piercing gaze assessing.

"And you said you didn't have daddy issues," he muses, stepping away from me. It makes my heart skip, seeing him pull away.

The flood of victory has made its wave through my body, and now the tide is pulling it back, and I'm beginning to feel the ramifications.

He takes another step away and angles his body towards the doors. A crater has formed, filling with an ocean that divides us. It's funny how this is the furthest I've felt from him, even when hundreds of miles separated us.

A seed of panic sprouts, but maybe that's just adrenaline. Because the way Zade peers at me now, it looks as if he's going to choose himself. He's going to lash out, and I will be the one left hanging.

"Please, baby, run free then. Show me how far you get before you realize you're only running from yourself. How long will you last when I possess everything that gives you life?"

My chest tightens, but I laugh, mocking him as he mocks me. "You possess nothing but a demon in your body."

He ignores me. "Your heart, your soul, and your very breath. Run, little mouse. This time, no one will be chasing you."

His last words choke me, and then he walks through my room and out of the door, softly closing it behind him.

Shit. I suck in a breath but only wheeze when my lungs refuse to work. *Shit, shit, shit.*

I turn, and work to keep breathing but it feels as if I'm tightening my lungs further, reducing them to tiny metal wires that slice through my insides with every inhale.

Stop it, Addie. This is the right decision.

Is it, though?

You're protecting your family.

Then why does it feel like I've alienated my very soul from my body? Pushed it out as if it didn't belong there.

You don't need him to survive, Addie.

No, I don't. I've proven that to be true during the months where I was forced to do nothing *but* survive. I can live without Zade.

But that doesn't mean it won't fucking hurt. That doesn't mean I won't live without a large piece of myself missing. Like losing a limb, I'd always feel him even when he's no longer a part of me. Does that make me weak? Dependent?

Or just someone madly in love.

Shit.

I pace the balcony, panic forcing my body into a malfunctioning state. Back and forth, screaming at myself to run after him, and fear turning my body right back around.

He could reject me. I was callous, and a complete asshole when he's shredded the world apart to get back to me. And what do I do? Push him away.

Fuck. I went from blaming myself, to blaming the one person who's done everything for me.

I freeze for a beat, and then drop into a crouch, feeling like a bulldozer just ran through me.

"Addie, you fucking *idiot*," I growl to myself.

My parents would've been kidnapped and possibly tortured if it wasn't for him. He knew Claire was going to pull something, checked on them to make sure they were safe, and got us up and over there before they could take them. Who knows what Claire would've done to them? I don't believe for a second that they wouldn't have been left unharmed.

Fuck, he saved them, just like he's done for me, and for hundreds of others.

Such an idiot.

Finally, my gears shift into autopilot, and I race towards the door. It'll be like those cheesy romance movies, I assure myself. I'll swing open the door, and he'll be standing on the other side, waiting for me because he knew damn well that I was bluffing.

But when I open the door, heart on my sleeve and an apology on my tongue, I find that he's not waiting for me at all. He's gone.

I deflate, and my hope fizzles like helium out of a tired balloon.

No, fuck this. The last thing Zade and I are in is a Hallmark movie.

I storm out of the room, down the hallway, and head towards the steps. My feet carry me down too quickly, and in my rush, I nearly faceplant the checkered tiling, the handrail scarcely saving me. I came two inches from having to confront Zade with my front teeth chipped, and that would have been entirely embarrassing.

Like instant karma shit that only God would hex me with.

The front door obnoxiously bangs against the stopper, and before I can get wiped out by rebounding wood that probably weighs more than I do, I take off down the porch.

There. Just a hint of Zade's back remains before he completely disappears in the thicket of trees.

"Hey!" I shout, hurrying after him. I get close enough to see his chin tip over his shoulder, only a moment before he takes off into a sprint.

I gasp, affronted by the pure audacity of this man. "Oh, you *asshole.*"

You deserved that.

"Shut up," I mutter to myself. I take off after him, and I just know he's getting a sick enjoyment out of reversing the roles and making me chase after him.

He's giving me a spoonful of my own medicine, and it tastes like ass.

I've gotten faster with all the running I've done in the past several months, and my endurance has strengthened. But I'm still no match for Zade. His long legs eat up the dirt ground faster than mine, and I become frustrated as the distance between us grows.

Soon, he disappears altogether, and I slow to a stop, panting heavily and on the verge of tears.

I spin in circles but quickly put a stop to that when I only serve to make myself dizzy. For several minutes, I wallow in my misery while I catch my breath. Tears line the edges of my eyes, and the only person I have to blame is myself.

I may be a little broken right now, but that doesn't excuse my behavior toward Zade.

Just as I turn to find my way back to Parsons Manor, a twig cracks from behind me.

An ominous feeling rises the hairs on the back of my neck, and my stomach drops. Whirling around, a startled yelp rips from my throat when Zade is right there.

Shock paralyzes me, and before I can muster a word, he's gripping me by the throat, lifting me, and slamming me into a tree right beside me.

I cry out, disoriented and now breathless as he leeches the oxygen from my lungs, squeezing until I'm sure he's going to snap my neck. Despite my nails clawing at his hand, he doesn't relent. Instead, he lifts me higher, and out of desperation, I kick up my legs and curl them around his waist, bowing my back to alleviate some of the pressure.

My body nearly goes through the movements to dislodge his hand from my throat, but I stop myself. Whatever he has to say, whatever he plans to do—I deserve it.

Frankly, I don't *want* to escape him.

He's breathing heavily, and even in the throes of panic, I know it's purely from excitement. His mouth strays only an inch from mine, his minty toothpaste mingling with leather, spice, and a hint of smoke, the intoxicating aromas clouding my senses. Gradually, his hand tightens, and instinct begins to take over. I thrash against him, but he only presses deeper into me.

"What's wrong, baby? Didn't get enough the first time and came back for more?"

I slap at him, my vision beginning to blacken, and I don't need a mirror to see that my face is tomato red and seconds away from turning purple. Finally, his grip loosens, and I greedily suck in air, though he doesn't remove his hand.

"Fucking *dickhead*," I choke out, and *yes*, I see the hypocrisy, but fuck him anyway.

He scarcely gives me a moment to breathe, then he's threatening to rob me of air once more. His grip isn't as tight, leaving a kernel of space in my windpipe that allows me to inhale.

"Come on, little mouse, you know I only answer to two names," he taunts. "Let me hear you say my name. It sounds so much sweeter when you can't breathe."

"Zade," I growl, but he shakes his head.

"Uh-uh," he tsks, voice dipped in sweet venom. "I want you to call me by my other name, Adeline."

Tears of frustration pool in my eyes, one breaking free and slipping past my lashes. He tracks the droplet, a savage grin ghosting across his lips before the tip of his tongue darts out and licks the salty water from my face.

I clench my teeth, pride rising, fueled by anger for this insufferable man. When Zade and I are happy, it's easy to forget how much he enjoys seeing me suffer. And I wonder if this is why I lash out thoughtlessly. Maybe a part of me likes the way he makes me suffer, too.

He drifts the tip of his tongue over the side of my cheek and to my ear, leaving a wet trail in his wake before dark whispers warm my skin instead.

"If you make me tell you again, I will strap you to this tree until the birds are ready to eat."

"*God*," I bite out, my voice hoarse from the strain. "Are you happy now?"

He bares his teeth, and I realize that the fear he instills in me will likely eat me alive before the birds ever could.

"Not even fucking close," he hisses. "I think I quite like the idea of tying you to this tree—the birds feasting on the helpless little mouse."

Terror glides down my constricted throat and low into my stomach, morphing into an inebriating feeling that burns and burns until my eyes droop into a half-lidded state.

"Punish me then. I deserve it," I hiss.

I *want* him to.

As long as he's here, touching me, hurting me—it's better than him being another ghost haunting Parsons Manor.

"Or is the kitty cat too scared of the mouse?"

He tips his head back, a laugh working its way from his throat and sending chills down my spine. Evil. It was an evil laugh, and my excitement ramps up.

He suddenly drops me, and steps away, barely giving me time to catch myself. Just as I straighten, he tips up his chin.

"Have you come here to ask for forgiveness?"

"Yes," I whisper. "I'm—"

"Undress," he orders, cutting off my apology.

Biting back a retort, I listen, and tear the articles of clothing from my body until I'm naked. It's hot outside, yet I shiver beneath his blazing eyes.

My nipples harden beneath his wandering gaze, causing his nostrils to flare. Suppressing the urge to cover myself, I lean back against the tree, another shiver racking my body from the rough bark.

Licking his lips, he gazes at me like a hawk would a mouse. Predatory and full of intention. Slowly, his long fingers undo the buckle on his belt, before jerking it out from the loops of his black jeans.

A rock forms in my throat, but I don't bother swallowing it down because I know it'll come right back up. Especially as he strides towards me, and then behind the tree. The trunk isn't large by any means, so just as I go to turn my head, his hand comes up from behind me and grips my jaw, forcing it straight.

"Face forward, Adeline," he orders, his deep voice full of warning.

His hand retreats, and my heart pounds erratically, causing my breathing to hiccup. The weight of anticipation is suffocating, and when I finally see his belt come into view, I can't help but flinch away.

It loops across my throat and around the trunk before it tightens, the leather groaning from the force. My eyes bulge, my precious air supply cutting off for the third time as he refastens the buckle. The fucker used his belt to pin me to the tree.

He comes out from behind me and faces me once more, his devilish gaze taking in his masterpiece.

"You're fucked in the head," I tell him, and then cough as the leather digs into my skin.

He hums at me. "You use pretty words as sharp knives, and I think you've become attached to seeing me scarred. Do they make your pussy wet, baby?"

I raise my chin, deciding to take a different route and go with the truth for once.

"Yes," I admit, as firmly as I can manage.

He stares at me, his mismatched pools as intense as the cold wind ravaging my body. The pale scar cutting through his white eye stands out proudly amongst the otherwise smooth flesh.

It hurts to look at him.

His gaze thins, and he approaches me until I can feel the blissful heat radiating from his body.

"I didn't mean what I said," I whisper before he can say whatever words are resting on his tongue. "I'm sorry."

He pauses, and my discomfort grows as his gaze intensifies.

"I've given you nothing but honesty, and you continue to give me lies. Is this another attempt to bring me back in just to kick me out again?"

I swallow, my throat drier than the bark digging into my back.

"No," I rasp, and my lip trembles from the shame burning the backs of my eyes. "You're right. I… There's no excuse for what I said. I don't want you to leave. And I do love you."

"So you've said," he murmurs. He cocks his head and muses aloud, "Yet you tried to take it back. You gave me something precious and then tried to rip it away."

I shake my head, desperation clogging my throat.

"I won't do that ever again," I swear, another tear burning a trail down my cold cheek. It snags his attention, and I watch his eyes zero in on it, tracking it until it drips from my chin.

When he looks at me once more, it hits me that this isn't just a punishment. This will be a test to prove my love. To prove that I mean it when I say it.

"You cut me because you know I'll gladly bleed for you. So now I want to see you bleed for me."

I open my mouth, prepared to tell him that I already have, but before I can, he bends and grabs a long, gnarled twig off the ground, fisting it in his hand. Whatever I was going to say somersaults right back down my throat, and my heart stalls in my chest.

"What are you going to do?" I ask hesitantly, eyeing the branch like he's holding a gun.

Scratch that, give me the gun. I've survived that before.

He responds to my question by rearing his arm back and slapping me across the thigh with it. For a blissful second, I'm too shocked to feel anything, but then the sharp, piercing pain comes racing in, and all I can do is let out a strangled scream. I look down at my thigh in disbelief, an angry red welt already protruding from my skin.

My chest heaves, watching a line of blood bead from the wound before trailing down my thigh.

I look up at him, mouth parted, eyes wide, and utter bewilderment on my face.

"You fucking whipped me," I gasp, incapable of saying anything other than the obvious.

He crouches down, looking closely at the tiny trickles of blood staining my thigh. Lifting his hand, his fingers feather across the wound, and I hiss in response.

He looks up at me through thick, black lashes, and if I weren't strapped to a tree, I'd collapse from the raw intensity on his face. "Are you not willing to bleed for me?"

I bite my trembling lip. I cut him deep, an invisible wound that will scar him as permanently as the marks on his body. Some days, when I'm lost in my own head, I forget how intensely Zade loves.

"Giving my heart to you was something I prayed I'd never do," I whisper. "But you've always been a God, and I didn't realize my pleas were going straight into your hands. Yet they always went unanswered."

Seeing him now, kneeling before me, I understand why. The day I handed over my love to him was the first time a God fell to his knees, bowed his head, and prayed. He prayed because I gave him the one thing he could never control, and he never wanted to lose it.

My vision blurs, and I struggle to keep the tears at bay. "I'll bleed for you, Zade. I'll always bleed for you."

His eyes shutter, and he drops his gaze before I can decipher the emotion in them.

Slowly, he stands, and by the time he raises his lids, I see nothing but my own reflection. I brace myself, but it does little to prepare for the lightning searing across my flesh when the twig lands on my stomach.

Breathing through the pain, I plead, "Let me see your scars."

Surprisingly, he grants me that small favor and removes his hoodie from his head.

I soak in his naked torso and release a shaky exhale. Where he hit me is almost precisely the same place as the scar on his stomach. Through blurred vision, I watch him whip out his arm, landing another strike to mirror his chest wound, reopening the unhealed rose over my heart.

I told him to carve that rose into my skin because I wanted to bear the pain we endured together. When he lashes out again, replicating yet another mark, I realize he's giving his pain to me—sharing it with me.

Steadily, the burn from each wound transcends until I feel every beat of agony in the apex of my thighs. Blood covers my body, painting my flesh in a mosaic of pain and pleasure. With each strike, my clit throbs, and I grow wetter and hotter. I'm panting by the time he drops the twig, my legs trembling and threatening to give beneath me.

His own chest heaves and his low-slung jeans only define how hard he is.

A deep, rumble sounds from his throat as his gaze eats up the art piece he's created on my body. My skin is the canvas to release his pain on, and I'm happy to accept each angry stroke.

"I've only ever wanted to love you. But I think hating you tastes just as bittersweet."

"Please," I whisper, incapable of uttering anything else.

I'm in his arms a moment later, the belt around my throat seizing my breath. But I don't care—hardly notice—when all I can feel is the slide of his skin against mine. He grabs the belt and lifts me higher in his arms, raising the leather strap with me to accommodate my new position. My legs wrap tightly around his waist, and I roll my hips, shuddering from the feel of his hard length sliding against my pussy, the roughness of his jeans only heightening the pleasure.

His hands skate over the marks, eliciting a sharp hiss. A sound quickly swallowed by his lips. My back arches, bliss racing up my spine as he devours me, his tongue tracing the seam of my lips before plunging through, exploring my mouth as his hands do my body.

Every touch aches, though it feeds the growing wildfire raging beneath my skin. Desperately, I tear at his jeans, the zipper barely releasing before his cock tears from the confines.

My hand wraps around his length, drawing a shudder from him that has nothing to do with the wind still ravaging Seattle. He's hot to the touch and so fucking hard that I feel a pinch of uneasiness.

But the dark God doesn't care if I falter. He grabs the backs of my knees and forces my legs apart, freeing him from my hold. Kneeling before me, he slings each of my legs over his shoulders and drags his mouth against my inner thigh.

I suck in a breath when his lips skate close to a welt, the pain flaring brightly as his teeth sink into my flesh. Blood drops down between his teeth, and I cry out as the agony begins to overwhelm me.

Finally, he releases me, a perfect bite mark imprinted next to the welt, dotted with saliva.

"I think I could eat you alive, Adeline. Consume every bit of you while you scream beneath me. And even in death, you would still torture me. I would die of starvation because nothing else would compare to you."

"You will never be able to live without me, Zade," I breathe. "If you're my death, then I'm your fucking lifeline."

He grins humorously, the tilt of his lips dangerous as he drags them up my thigh and towards my aching pussy. I'm drenched, and the slightest touch of his tongue will send me soaring.

"You are," he agrees. "You're the only thing I need to survive. I will follow you into the afterlife, little mouse. And then how will you escape me? There's nowhere to run after you've been dragged to Hell."

His mouth closes over my clit before I can think to respond. My head kicks back from the explosive pleasure that erupts beneath his skilled tongue.

I cry out, my eyes rolling as he works me with such precision; it's as if I'm nothing more than a violin that sings for him when he strokes me just like that.

The way I scream for him could be nothing short of art.

Just as he promised, he devours me. Biting and sucking until I'm pleading for mercy, then licking me until no other words exist but his name on my tongue.

My thighs clench around his head while I mindlessly buck against him. I'm climbing a mountain, and the higher I get, the harder it is to breathe. What a dirty little trick—to fool me into danger. By the time I reach the peak, there will be no air left, and that climb will have only been for heaven.

His hands brush against my battered thighs, smearing crimson into my skin and reawakening the sharp pain.

It slams into me, sending my body plummeting off that mountain and my soul into paradise. A scream tears through my constricted throat, hoarse and strained as I grind against him, trapping him between my thighs and robbing him of oxygen.

Prying my legs apart, he grips me under my knees and lifts me a little higher as he stands, relieving some of the pressure on my throat. I place my hands on his broad shoulders, balancing myself.

My arousal glosses his wide lips, chin, and down the column of his neck. Slowly, he swipes out his tongue, collecting it like a poor man tasting a delicacy for the first time.

He hums, pleased by the taste of me. My stomach tightens in response to the near-crazed look in his eyes.

Molding his warm body against me, I shudder from the feel of his skin pressed into mine. I could never deny how good Zade feels, even when I was desperate to.

"Wrap your legs around me," he orders roughly, his tone hushed. He removes his arms from beneath my thighs and I circle them tightly around his waist.

One hand glides up the outside of my thigh, while he anchors the other on the tree beside my head, supporting our weight. His head is bent down, nose gliding along the column of my neck.

"I'm too addicted to you to ever let you go," he murmurs. My eyes flutter closed, another dose of relief hitting me straight in the heart.

"But I don't know how to make you stay," he continues, his tone darkening. My brows pinch, feeling a sense of looming danger on the horizon.

"I will—"

His chin tips up until his mouth is right by my ear. "I don't believe you," he whispers, cutting me off.

He said the same thing to me only a couple of weeks ago, and I had asked him to carve a rose into my chest to prove my love. But then I tried to take it away, and I don't know how I'm going to prove myself again.

My heart pounds, and I scramble for a way to convince him. I don't exactly have a great track record—I know that. Pushing Zade away and running from him has always come so easy to me.

Too easy, if I'm being honest. But letting him slip through my fingers—that's something I've never been able to accomplish.

"I knew you were going to do this to me, little mouse. I've always known it was going to come to this," he says softly.

I'm a mass of confusion and heart-pounding dread.

"What are you—"

Before I can finish, he tilts my hips up just enough to slam me down on his cock, driving himself inside me at the same moment. Despite how turned on I am, it's never enough to prepare for his size.

My back bows, the leather belt holding my throat hostage just as a strangled cry releases, quickly carried away with the wind.

Zade tips his head back, a deep growl building in his chest. He presses me deep into the tree, grasping my hip in a bruising hold, steadily sinking his cock deeper and deeper until I'm unable to take any more of him.

I let out another choked cry, sensations unfurling from where we connect and throughout my entire being. The rough bark digs into my skin, but I hardly notice when he's invading my body so thoroughly.

The hand holding my hip slides up to my stomach, his fingers digging into my skin.

"Would this being swollen with my child make you stay?" he asks darkly, then groaning as if overcome with bliss from the thought.

My mouth parts, my attention split between his almost threatening words and the way he's moving inside of me.

"Uhh." Somewhat of a response but it sounded more like a moan. "Maybe one day?" I squeak out, almost coughing when the belt constricts against my windpipe.

He withdraws to the tip, then seats himself completely inside me, his pelvis grinding into mine. I choke, and my eyes nearly roll from how full I am.

Hot breath fans across my ear, and it feels like a warning. "I wasn't asking permission, baby. Would you stay, or would you run off with my child?"

I'm so disoriented by his line of questioning; it takes me a moment to catch up. My heart drops, and I gasp both from his implication and from him grinding against me again, his pelvis stimulating my clit just the right way.

"You… I have the IUD," I say. It would be difficult to tamper with that. Not unless he physically pulled it from my body.

"Do you?" he murmurs, his deep voice low and challenging. He poses the question in a way that suggests he knows the answer to that question better than I do.

My nails dig into his shoulders, and when realization begins to set in, I push at him. Of course, he resists against me, a steel fortress that even a nuclear bomb couldn't crumble.

"You didn't," I snap.

"You sleep so heavily sometimes," he responds, pressing deeper into me as I try to shove him back. He slides out again before slamming into me once more, drawing a mix between a moan and an enraged gasp.

"Zade," I warn, voice shaking.

He groans against me, now steadily fucking me.

"Will it make you stay?" he questions again. I turn my head toward him, training my glare on him, despite the cyclone of pleasure swirling deep in my stomach. Taking in my expression, the fucker has the audacity to smile.

"You're not asking if a baby will make me stay. You're asking if I'd stay if you forced a pregnancy on me," I bite out.

The hand supporting our weight against the tree slides down until it's leaning on the belt strap, causing it to tighten and cut off my air supply.

I choke, but he doesn't let up. His eyes are wild, and it's now, I wonder how my words could affect him so deeply.

He does the worst things sometimes, and yet here I am, wrapped around him even as he threatens me.

"Am I still worth loving, little mouse?" he asks through gritted teeth.

I attempt to swallow, but it gets stuck in my throat.

Fuck, the asshole really brings out the worst in himself. And he does it without any remorse, baring all those dark parts on a silver platter, challenging me on if I'm going to accept it or not.

Darkness licks at the edges of my vision, but I give him the truth. I nod my head, answering both of his questions. He is worth loving. And I would stay.

He relents on the belt, and I cough, sucking in air desperately, though it's useless. Any oxygen I collected in my lungs is punched out of me when he increases his pace, the hand on my stomach gliding down until his thumb reaches my clit, circling the bud until my eyes roll.

I'm not ready to have children. I've never been ready for anything Zade throws my way. Yet, it doesn't stop me from meeting his thrusts, an orgasm forming low in my belly.

"You'll never escape me, little mouse. Do you think anyone could ever make your pussy cry the way I do?"

He angles his hips, hitting that spot inside of me that has me clenching around him. I shake my head, incapable of speech. The only thing I can do is claw at him, scraping my nails across his back and gouging deep, red cuts into his skin as he has done mine.

Growling deep in his chest, he gnashes his teeth,

"I dare you, Adeline. Deny that my name isn't carved into every star you see when I make you come, and I will show you that a God can create them just as easily as he can destroy them."

The knot in my stomach tightens to its breaking point, and my moans turn into hoarse screams as he brutally fucks me against the tree, continuing to circle my clit with his thumb. The belt around my throat digs into my skin, confining my windpipe just enough to send blood rushing to my face.

"Only you," I mumble, the words lost inside the sounds of pleasure tearing past my lips.

"That's it, Adeline. Now take my cum like a good little girl."

My back bows, and I erupt, crying out from the sheer force of the orgasm tearing through me. I feel myself clench around him, his cock spearing through my tightening pussy with a force that rivals the pleasure consuming me.

My vision snuffs out like the sun behind a moon during a solar eclipse. His darkness devours my light, and I decide I'm content living in the shadows.

His palm slams next to my head, and with one final thrust, he explodes with a deep growl. Grinding his hips against mine, he empties himself inside me, cursing beneath his breath until the last drop is wrung out of him.

Several minutes pass, and both of us slowly come back down and catch our breaths. Well, *he's* catching his breath. I'm still struggling for mine due to the belt around my throat.

He grins when he notes how red my face is—I can feel it burning beneath his stare. Reaching around, he unclasps the buckle, and the belt drops a second later.

My rib cage protrudes from how deeply I inhale, feeling like I'm taking the first breath after drowning for so long.

That was how I once described what Zade's love felt like, and it's never felt truer until now.

As I'm still drinking in the precious oxygen, he grips my jaw between his fingers and forces my gaze to his.

"Never again, Adeline. I could take you pushing me away when you were still discovering how you felt for me. But not anymore. That was your last time. Understand?"

I nod, shame reigniting. "Yes, never again. I'm sorry," I croak, wrapping my arms tightly around his neck. "But I hope you know I'm always going to run from you. I like the way you chase me."

He bites his lip, the heat in his eyes flaring. Leaning forward, I kiss him softly, praying he can feel just how much I mean it.

His hand dives into my hair, amplifying the sweetness to something more savage. But too soon, he's pulling away. I chase after him, stealing one more before he sets me down, supporting me while my legs grow accustomed to holding my weight again. They shake fiercely, and I just know the dickhead's ego is ballooning again.

"Need a wheelchair, baby?"

I sniff and mutter, "No," affronted by his big-ass head. "They're just tired from you making me run."

He chuckles, knowing damn well how untrue that is. But I smile back, and I realize that I like the way Zade laughs as much as I like the way he punishes me.

"How are they going to feel when you're nine months pregnant and I'm chasing after you?"

I tighten my lips, but then smile with victory when I realize I'm not even ovulating. When I tell him so, he only smirks.

"I didn't take out your IUD," he says, bending to gather our clothes.

My mouth drops open. "Then what the fuck was all that?"

He shrugs, still grinning as he pulls on his jeans and glances at his phone before tucking it away again.

"I mean, don't get me wrong, I'm fucking relieved. But what the shit, Zade?"

"I needed to be sure you're one hundred percent in this with me. A baby is the only thing that could permanently tie your life to mine. Legally, at least. Ethically… well, I will always be in your life, whether you know I am or not."

Shaking my head, I tug my jeans up my body, the coarse fabric rubbing painfully against the welts on my legs. My shirt doesn't feel much better.

"Yeah, whatever," I mumble. "You're a dick."

He laughs again, accepting that statement without even a hint of shame. He pivots to walk back toward Parsons Manor, but I grab his hand, turning him back to me.

"No more lies," I say. "From either of us."

"Baby, I never lied. I never actually said that I took out your IUD."

"You still made me believe that you did," I argue.

He grins wickedly at me, one side of his lips tipping up.

"When I do get you pregnant, you will know about it," he promises, though it sounds like another threat. "You will watch me pull the IUD from your body myself."

That… oddly makes me feel better.

And I need therapy.

I sigh, "You're always going to be a creep, aren't you?"

"And my being a creep is always going to make your pussy wet. Let's get back. Jay tried calling and it might have something to do with Claire."

Chapter Forty One
The Hunter

I'm surprised to find Jay sitting on the couch next to Daya, both tapping away on their computers. He jumped about ten feet when we walked in, still clearly spooked by the manor.

"Which ghost fucked with you?" I ask, smirking.

"Dude, I swear to God, I was taking a piss, and something *breathed* down my *neck*. I was just waiting for it to try to give me a reach-around."

Daya looks at me, a droll expression on her face. "I told him to come talk to me when he goes in the attic. I'm still mad at Addie for that one."

Addie's eyes widen. "It was *one time!*" she defends. "And nothing happened to you," she finishes on a mutter, plopping down on the couch across from her. I take a seat next to Addie while Sibby growls and slams a drawer in the kitchen, mad about something. Again.

"I lost my peace of mind. That's what happened to me," Daya

retorts. "That demon could've gotten attached to me, and then I would've brought it home and lived in torment for the rest of my life."

"Could you blame it? You're the whole package," Addie says, grinning when Daya narrows her eyes.

"Flattering me only works sometimes."

"Is it working now?"

"A little."

"Have you guys seen my pink knife?" Sibby screeches from the kitchen, frantically opening and closing drawers and cupboards.

I've grown to care for Sibby deeply, like an irritating, psychotic kid sister. But fuck, I'm going to have to find a home and job for her. Give her a purpose in life outside of annoying the ever-loving fuck out of me.

"Did you ask Jackal?" I ask, arching a brow when she looks at me with narrowed eyes. She knows damn well I'm referring to the time she felt the need to share with the class that Jackal fucked her ass with her knife. As if anyone wanted to know that.

"He only used it on me that *one* time, and I think I'd remember getting a knife shoved up my—"

"Maybe you dropped it somewhere in your room," Addie cuts in urgently.

She huffs. "I already checked there, but I'll look again," she mutters, trudging towards the stairs with a frown. The only other thing capable of sending her into a tailspin outside of losing her henchmen is losing that knife.

Jay clears his throat, cheeks red as his gaze flickers to Sibby, partially intrigued and partially disturbed.

"I think I know who Claire's partners are now, finally," Jay announces, bringing the topic away from ghosts and getting fucked with knives by imaginary people.

My brows jump in surprise. "Yeah?"

We've concluded that if we can get to her partners, it'll be much easier to draw Claire off her comfy little island.

I'm ready to say fuck it and bomb it. I could get ahold of the resources, but it'd take too long. And as tempted as I am to gather as many people as I can in the Z organization and invade her island, she has a small army there, and I'm not willing to sacrifice so many valuable lives for the bitch.

Not when I can sacrifice the lives of her partners instead.

"As you know, she's been communicating with two sources, but their IP addresses were untraceable, and the identities hidden. But sending the drone out was successful, and I just got intel that she booked a flight for those same two people to visit her. Their names were on the flight log," he tells me, pulling up the information and twirling his laptop to show me.

Gary Lawson and Jeffrey Shelton.

"They're both lobbyists," Daya chips in.

"Fitting," I murmur, looking over the pictures of the two men on Jay's screen.

Typical, creepy-looking old men who get hard-ons for little children and making Americans as miserable as possible while living lavishly.

"When are the flights?"

Jay grins, his hazel eyes blazing with excitement.

"Tomorrow. They're departing from a private airport in Los Angeles."

I turn to Addie and notice a tiny twig sticking from her hair, along with pieces of bark, dirt, and a small leaf. There are also small blood spots that are beginning to soak through her blue t-shirt, though she's trying her best to conceal them. Worst of all, there's already a deep bruise forming around her throat, and I'd be a goddamn liar if I said that didn't make my dick hard all over again.

It takes effort to bite back my smile. She looks thoroughly ravaged, and she's attempting to appear as if she hadn't been.

Glancing at me, she shoots me a look that says, *shut up, or else.* The grin begins to slip through.

Such a scary little mouse.

But just this once, I'll listen.

Which is really hard to do when Daya is staring at her, too, brows raised. Addie just thins her lips, and I have a feeling they'll be discussing in detail just how intimate she became with what nature has to offer.

"That gives us just enough time to intercept their flight."

Addie cocks her head to the side, curious. "What are you planning on doing exactly?"

Now, I let the grin loose, the savagery bleeding through.

"I know exactly how we're going to make her come to us."

Her brows knit in curiosity. "Which is how exactly?"

I train my gaze on Jay, and though he looks just as curious, he also looks wary. Shithead never approves of my plans. Which is stupid. They're awesome.

"Gary Lawson and Jeffrey Shelton are going to get in a confrontation with Z. And guess who loses?"

"Them," Addie guesses confidently.

"No, baby. *Me.*"

Addie bounces on her toes, nervous energy radiating from her in waves. She's been restless since we had arrived at the airport a couple of hours ago. We flew to L.A. as quickly as we could, just to give us time to plan and prepare. Now, we're waiting in the private jet on the airstrip, and she's started morphing into the Tasmanian Devil from Looney Tunes.

"Why don't you take a seat? They're comfortable as fuck," I suggest.

To emphasize my point, I kick my feet up on the little brown wooden table in front of me and recline back.

"How can you be so relaxed right now?" she asks, but she's looking at the seat like maybe it wouldn't hurt if her ass sat in it for just a second.

"This is the least exciting thing I've ever done while on the job."

She arches a brow, and if I didn't know any better, I'd think she was offended.

"Well, that's fucking rude," she says dryly. Definitely offended. I grin.

"Would you like to go up to the front seat and fuck next to the dead pilot?" I query, very interested in what her answer will be.

She always surprises me.

Right as she opens her mouth, distant voices arise, distracting her like a dog spotting a cat.

Damn. I'll have to pull that answer out of her later.

The voices draw nearer, and she instantly stands, rolling her shoulders to release the tension lining them. She hasn't gotten accustomed to going on missions yet, and her anxiety persists, despite her being able to fight. There are some days she gets through my defenses even and knocks me on my ass. But the way she looks right now, it's as if she's about to appear before a judge and get sentenced to life or some shit.

"Don't underestimate yourself, Adeline," I draw lazily, my muscles languid and relaxed. They usually are when blood is about to spill all over my hands.

"I'm not," she defends. "They're old, saggy men. Their security guards—"

"Are my men," I finish. Addie's mouth forms an O.

"You sneaky dog," she whispers, a smile tipping up her plump lips. Those caramel orbs stare at me with an amused glint.

We both quiet as the two men and their respective guards approach the steps and start climbing, the metal ringing beneath their weight.

"She's going to have to come back to the states eventually," one of them mutters, sounding irritated.

The first person that breaches the entryway is Michael, and I almost laugh when he slides his gun from his holster and points it at me.

Jeff and Gary follow behind, with another one of my men, Baron, taking up the back.

"What is going on here?" Gary exclaims, the two old men pausing and backing up the moment they spot us.

I lift a hand in a hello gesture. "I've come to turn myself in, Gary. Why else would I be here?"

"Turn yours—what on earth are you talking about? Who are you?"

"Ah, terribly sorry," I say, grinning. I reach over to the seat beside me, grab my mask, and hold it over my face. "How about now?"

It's comical how quickly they pale, and their eyes widen, recognizing my mask from my television appearance.

Tossing it to the side, I tease, "Did you like my presentation? I was really nervous."

Gary sputters, unsure how to respond. I stand, and they immediately back away, two bumbling idiots that bump into Baron in an attempt to create distance, but the mercenary is like a brick wall.

Jeff turns to Michael, his face now beginning to redden. "Why aren't you shooting him? Shoot him!"

Michael just stares at him blankly, causing his face to purple. Then, he drops his gun, smiling when Jeff begins to sputter incoherently.

"I see you've gotten comfortable behind the smokescreen," I observe. "Content in shouting demands, and secure with no one ever knowing who you are."

"Laziness," Addie tacks on. Her body is relaxed now, and in place of her anxiety-ridden stance, she's a suave feline, her claws extended and ready to slice some throats open.

The prey becomes the predator.

She's the most beautiful creature I ever did see.

Gary trains his glare on her, lasers shooting from his eyes, but if he expects that to intimidate her, he's sadly mistaken.

"And who the hell are you?"

She turns to me, a silly smile on her face. "I really wanted to say something cheesy right there. Your worst nightmare," she mocks, eyes widened comically as she faces Gary again.

He snarls at her, clearly unamused. I, on the other hand, am smiling like an idiot.

She waves a hand casually. "No, really, I'm the diamond you all are so fond of. I'm kind of offended that you don't recognize me. Especially because you guys are on my ass so damn much."

Jeff's face drops, clarity surfacing now that he realizes who she is.

"Obviously it was Claire's brilliant idea to go after my parents, but did either of you have anything to do with that, too?" Addie asks, a darkness slithering over her features. Gone is the lighthearted humor.

Gary can't even hide the sick triumph on his face. Addie catches the look immediately, and without saying anything further, she raises her gun and shoots him directly in the kneecap, face blank.

The old man's eyes pop, and he instantly collapses in a fit of screams and blood. Jeff bumps into Baron again, sweat gleaming from his receding hairline as he stares down at his partner with an ashen complexion.

"You fucking bitch!" Gary exclaims. Anger licks at my nerves, so I shoot his other knee, eliciting another pained scream from his throat. Michael and Baron shake their heads, staring at the pair like they're the dumbest people alive.

I'd have to agree.

"Now we're going to have to carry you out, Gary. You're such an inconvenience. So, here's how it's going to go. You're going to come with us, and we're going back to Seattle and to a nice, secluded location where I am going to be tied up and gagged. Maybe I'll let my girl get a few punches in on me, too. Addie here will be tied up as well, but no one is touching her."

Even in his state, Gary looks up at me with incredulity.

"Then, you're going to call Claire and let her know that you've captured Z and the diamond. Tell her to come to you instead now that we've been apprehended."

"Why on earth would we do that?" Jeff asks, his face twitching from a mix of emotions.

"I think it's time Claire comes out to play, don't you? She's been hiding long enough."

Jeff and Gary glance at each other, the latter sweating rivers down his flaming red face from the agony.

"I don't want any part of your scheme," Jeff starts, but I raise a hand, cutting off whatever useless shit was about to pour from his mouth.

"That's the thing, Jeffrey. You don't have a fucking choice."

Jeffrey still thinks he has a choice.

The entire flight and drive to the location in Seattle, he pleads his case. It was all Claire's idea. They just endorse her business ventures and help her with logistics and money.

Blah, blah, blah.

It isn't until Addie crawls from the passenger seat to the back and presses her gun into his knee that he finally shuts the fuck up, clicking his dentures so tightly together, they just might become permanent.

Michael drives us to an abandoned wine distillery corroded from nature. It reminds me of Parsons Manor, almost. Scrawling with overgrown vines, threading up the side of the gray stone walls. And a lone building in a field of grapes and tall green grass.

The van jostles from the uneven dirt path, nearly swallowed by the plant life surrounding it. Gary is on the floor, cradling his bloody knees, growing paler with each bump. Baron wrapped them up to stem the bleeding, but he looks on the verge of passing out. Once that happens, he won't live much longer.

If he dies, he dies. We only need one of them anyway.

Michael parks the van outside the building and jumps out, going ahead of us to break down the boarded doors, while Baron helps me carry Gary's useless body out of the van.

The inside of the distillery is just as haunting as the outside. The vines have infected the interior walls as well. Weeds poke through the cracked foundation, their own stems stretching across the floor.

It's a massive open space, some of the machinery left over, rusted and pockmarked. Exposed pipes are threaded through the ceiling, and a few of them are beginning to break and droop.

I drag Gary off to the side and position him directly under a hanging pipe, letting Jesus decide if he wants to send that heavy piece of metal crashing down on his head. If he pisses me off enough, I might even shoot it down myself. I drop him unkindly, ignoring his curses while Baron escorts Jeff inside, having him stand beside his crippled partner.

Addie's carrying three metal chairs in with several ropes wrapped around her arms. I'd offer to help, but she'd have my balls for it. I'd gladly hand them over anyway.

She's grown into her strength and independence so much since she survived trafficking, and there are times my chest physically aches from both pride and the need to fuck her.

She glances at me, a carnal smile on her face as she sets the chairs down and opens them up. I stalk toward her, delighting in the way her little body tightens with need. A black and blue ring stains her throat, and every time I see it, the beast trapped in my rib cage thrashes.

"If I didn't know any better, I'd think you're excited to hurt me," I murmur, desire flaring as I watch her round hips sway.

"You'll be the helpless little kitty cat," she coos, grinning wider when I give her a dark look.

"Will you still think so when you're trapped between my teeth?" I grab her by the throat and bring her in close, her caramel eyes dilating with lust. I brush my lips across the side of her mouth, drawing out a shuddered exhale.

"I was only ever helpless when I fell in love with you. And you may hold all the power over me, little mouse, but I've never been defenseless. Don't mistake my lack of control for weakness. All the ways I've hurt you have always been intentional."

She bites back a smile right before her fist rears back and lands directly in the side of my cheek. My vision blackens for a brief moment, and then my equilibrium teeters as she spins me around and pushes me back into the metal chair.

My weight nearly sends it crashing backward, but her foot catches on the chair between my legs, stopping me from falling but coming *very* fucking close to crushing my dick.

It feels like my bones are cracking from the monster inside me, fighting to get out, and a growl works past my lips. Just as I go to charge back at her, she's grabbing me by the throat, pushing me back down, and climbing on top of me, straddling my waist with her thick thighs.

My hands land on her hips and squeeze while she leans forward.

"Don't mistake my submission for weakness, baby," she breathes into my ear, voice husky with desire. "All the ways I'm going to hurt you will be intentional."

Before I can begin to form the threats rising up my throat, her lips are crashing into mine, not only silencing my dark promises, but completely ripping them to pieces.

Her mouth moves over mine savagely, and I'm lost to the way she commands me. I could flip her so effortlessly, but I fucking love bowing to the dark little goddess.

Grabbing my hands, she forces them behind the chair, clamping them together.

A sharp pain pierces my bottom lip, her teeth sinking into the tender flesh and drawing blood. Before I can snap back, she pulls away and looks over my face with pride.

It's only then I notice the rope is tightly secured around my wrists. If I wasn't seconds away from ripping her throat out and fucking her blind, I'd be impressed.

"Black eye and a bloody lip. I think that's enough kicking your ass for now." She firmly slaps my cheek in a *good job, sport* type of way before lifting off of me and settling in the chair beside me.

All I can do is stare at her and fantasize about the ways I'm going to punish her for that later. But just as well, my cock is harder than granite because that was probably one of the hottest things I've ever experienced in my life. Every time I think I've never been harder, she goes and proves me wrong.

Sensing my insidious thoughts, she rolls her shoulders, feigning boredom.

Addie has always been a runner—especially from the truth.

"If you're done with your foreplay, let's finish this, yeah?" Michael says, standing next to a red-faced Jeff with his arms crossed and a bored look on his face as well. The punk is also a liar and probably adjusted himself while I was distracted.

Gary is still groaning on the floor, and Jeff shifts uncomfortably next to him, eyes bouncing everywhere else, avoiding my stare.

Taking a deep breath, I try to focus back on the situation. "Doesn't look like we hit the femoral arteries, so he's going to have a very slow death. We'll let him suffer there in the corner for now."

Michael nods and grabs Jeff by the arm and hauls him in front of us.

"Tie me up, Baron," Addie says to my mercenary, who's been leaning against the wall to my right. She's smirking because she knows damn well how suggestive that sounded.

"Are you trying to get me killed?" Baron asks, his deep baritone voice pitching higher.

Addie rolls her eyes. "I won't let him kill you."

She shouldn't be so sure about that. But I keep my mouth shut and my stare sharp when he gives in, knowing that him or Michael are the only options to tie her up, considering she already bound my hands.

Baron makes quick work of the rope, stepping away before I can find a reason to cut his hands off. Who am I kidding? I don't need a reason.

Michael turns to Jeff. "Give me your phone," he demands, then rudely snatches the device from the old man's hand the second he pulls it from his pocket.

"All right, kids, look like your asses just got kicked by two old men that throw their backs out just from lifting their small dicks to piss."

He could've just said, *say cheese* and had the same outcome.

I glare at him, and Addie turns her head away, squeezing her eyes shut like she's too ashamed to have her picture taken.

"Make it a little shaky with a shitty angle, and voila, a typical picture taken by a degenerate," Michael says, smiling in victory after he snaps the photo. Then he turns the phone to Jeff.

"What would you typically say if you took a picture like that?"

Jeff glances at the image. "That we wasted money on all the other stupid fucks and should've done it ourselves from the start," he spits. Once he realizes that he helped Michael's message appear authentic by literally taking the words out of his mouth, his eyes darken with rage.

Michael's fingers fly over the keyboard, mouthing the words aloud as he types them just to piss Jeff off. Then he pauses and looks to the old man with a shit-eating grin.

"Hey, how do you spell 'stupid'?"

A vein pulses on Jeff's forehead, giving Michael an, *are you fucking kidding me?* look. Michael just stares, intent on making him spell the word. Snarling, he spits each letter through gritted teeth.

When finished typing, Michael slaps him on the back of the shoulder roughly and says, "Thanks, man. Would be lost without you."

Addie snickers, and now I'm going to have to cut Michael, too, just for making my girl laugh.

"Z has officially been captured," he announces, clicking the Send button with triumph. "And now… we wait."

"I hope you're not stupid enough to tell Claire they kicked our asses," I tell Michael, nodding towards Jeff.

He waves a hand. "Don't worry, princess, she'll know it took the entire military to bring down the big bad wolf. Your reputation won't be tarnished."

"I'm not worried about my rep. It's simply just not *believable*."

Chapter Forty Two
The Diamond

My equilibrium teeters as my feet dangle over the cliff. I'm sitting on the very edge and I'm just waiting for the earth to give beneath me and send me crashing into the rocks below.

I'm balancing on the edge of life and death, and the thrill it gives me is undeniable. My heart is in my stomach, and even though it'd take putting my head between my legs for me to fall over the ledge, it feels like one inch forward, and my life is done for.

I love it.

The sun begins to dip in the cotton candy sky, a beautiful array of colors stretching toward me. I'm not sure if it's the beauty before me or my precarious game with death that makes me feel alive.

Though both have the power to make me feel insignificant.

"So I see today is the day we both die," Zade announces from behind me, causing me to jump.

"Why would we both die?"

Stupid question. I know what he's going to say the moment the last word leaves my mouth.

"Because if you fall, I'll follow after you."

"Claire would be happy about that," I say, kicking my feet against the rock. "Your death would be the best thing to ever happen to her."

To no one's surprise, she asked a million questions before she believed that Jeff and Gary actually captured Zade and me. He had to explain how he found Z. On their way to L.A., they received intel that Zade would come after an auction house in Washington, so they quickly set up a coup and captured him. Of course, I came running when I found out he was being held hostage, and voila. Z and the diamond have been captured.

When she wanted to do a FaceTime call, we could see the intent in Jeff's eyes from a mile away. The second she got on the call with him, he planned to expose us. But Zade had already anticipated that. It's not hard to assume the old fart would try to pull one over on us. He's as predictable as he is stupid.

Everyone has a weakness. A soft spot like on the back of a baby's head. Hit that spot hard enough, and they're done for.

Of all people—his wife, kids, and mistress—his mother was the catalyst. Funny that he's a momma's boy when women are the number one thing he doesn't respect.

Bernadette Shelton is nearly on her deathbed anyway, but after one of Zade's mercenaries took a heart-warming picture of her lying in bed on oxygen, and his gun poised on the tank, Jeff decided to act right. He doesn't know that Zade nearly kicked his employee's ass for it and forced him to leave her an edible arrangement for the scare, but the threat worked regardless.

Zade coached Jeff on the story, he then answered Claire's questions, and she decided it was legitimate enough to come off her cozy island.

Mission accomplished.

Her flight is sixteen hours, so we went back to Parsons to catch up on sleep while Zade is having a team watch over Jeff at the distillery. Gary… well, he died. He was useless with his blown-out kneecaps, so Michael finally put him out of his misery.

"Baby, if you want me dead, I'll hand you the knife to stick in my chest. Sending us both over the cliff would be a little overkill."

"And I thought my mom was the dramatic one," I mutter.

My back is still to him, but I swear I can hear the fucker grinning. "You're right, *you're* the sensible one."

Shithead.

"You want to tell me why you're out here?"

"Couldn't sleep. Was hearing the footsteps again," I admit.

"Seems like they're manifesting your fears," he says. His presence closes in on me, and I feel him crouch down beside me. If the ground beneath me wasn't being tested before, it definitely is with his weight.

"What do the footsteps remind you of?" he questions softly, his voice whispering across the shell of my ear.

"My lack of freedom," I say, staring out at the Bay. "They remind me of how trapped I was. Every time I'd hear her heels coming toward me, something terrible always followed, and there was never any escaping it. There was one time I heard them, and I tried prying all the nails out of the window so I could throw myself out of it. Didn't even care if it killed me. All I accomplished was breaking *my* nails instead."

His hands land on my hips, and he's pulling me back, pressing me into his hard chest.

"So sitting on the edge of this cliff makes you feel free?"

"Yes," I say, turning my head to look up at him. His eyes glitter in the sunlight, and I can't tell which is more dangerous: the edge of this cliff or the way Zade looks at me. "And it makes me feel alive."

His hand comes up around my throat, tilting my chin further back. His full lips brush across mine, eliciting sharp tingles throughout my body.

"Is it the promise of death that makes you feel alive, little mouse?"

"Yes," I whisper, electricity dancing between our mouths.

"Then we will both taste heaven together," he murmurs.

He kisses me softly and slowly, and I feel every second of it in my soul. Pulling away, he directs, "Face me, baby."

Biting my lip, I spin and lean back on my hands, bending my knees and spreading them apart.

His eyes drop, traveling across the curves of my body, sending chills down my spine. He looks at me as if he wants to rip me apart with his teeth, and I don't think I would stop him if he tried.

My breath hitches as his hand slips beneath my t-shirt, and I shiver from the feel of his skin on mine. Slowly, he lifts the fabric up until I'm forced to lean forward so he can remove it altogether.

I shiver again, the breeze whispering across my heated flesh.

"Do you trust me?" he asks.

"Yes," I answer without hesitation.

He plants a hand on my chest and roughly pushes me. I gasp, convinced that I'm about to fall off the cliff, but he catches me. I'm flat on my back, and only my head dangles clear over the edge, but it doesn't calm the absolute panic circulating throughout my system.

I lift my head, staring at him with wide eyes, my heart racing.

"Jesus," I breathe. He smirks, reaches beneath me, and unclasps my bra, my nipples hardening immediately beneath the cool breeze.

Then, he hovers over me, his warmth seeping into my flesh as he trails his lips over my jaw and down my neck.

"He's not the one you should be praying to," he murmurs darkly, sending shivers rolling down my spine. "Only I will be your salvation."

His fingers grab the waistband of my leggings and tug them down, removing my panties with them. It's warm and muggy outside, but a whole week of rain has put a cool mist in the air, causing my skin to break out in goosebumps.

"Head back," he orders.

Swallowing nervously, I do as he says, and I'm overwhelmed by both vertigo and fear. The adrenaline in my system becomes more potent, and my heart pounds erratically.

His lips whisper across my chest, over the swells of my breasts, and to my nipples. His tongue darts out, flicking one of the hardened peaks before his warm mouth closes over it and sucks harshly.

I moan and arch into him, the movement causing my head to slide farther down, and I nearly jump out of my skin. He chuckles darkly, releasing my nipple then traveling down my body.

My heart is nearly coming out of my throat, yet I can feel my thighs growing slick from the thrill. Especially as he slowly parts them, nipping at my sensitive skin as he descends toward my center.

By the time his hot breath fans across my pussy, my legs are trembling and smarting from the bite of his sharp teeth.

He places a soft kiss on my clit, and I jump again when his fingers swipe up my slit, collecting my arousal on his fingers.

"Come here," he orders. I lift my head, dizzy from seeing the world right-side up again. He pries my mouth open and places his fingers on my tongue. Instinctively, I suck, and Zade's nostrils flare.

"That's what freedom tastes like. I want you to have that on your tongue while you watch night fall, and I show you how absolute your life is."

His fingers retreat, and he bumps my chin, indicating for me to drop my head again. I do, my vision blurring.

Emotion clogs my throat, trapping the flavor in my mouth as he returns to my pussy. I tremble as his tongue slowly slides up my slit, licking me thoroughly and groaning as he does.

"Fucking nirvana," he purrs, dipping his tongue inside me before ascending to my clit.

I gasp when he sucks hard, the sunset blurring and my eyelids fluttering as he begins to stroke the sensitive bud. My back arches again, though this time, I'm prepared for the small drop and the way it steals my breath.

My hands curl, grasping at the grass and pulling roughly when he hits a spot that has a sharp moan exploding from my throat.

"Zade," I plead.

His fingers rejoin his mouth, two of them plunging inside me and curling, and I roll my hips into his face so roughly, I feel my body inch down the edge of the cliff further. Another sound bursts from my throat, crowing at the sharp thrill that makes my heart feel like it's going to combust.

His free hand lands on my hip, holding me in place while he devours my pussy, lapping up everything I have to offer like he's a prisoner on death row, and this is his final taste of liberation.

There's a smile pulling at the corners of my lips, tears in my eyes, and moans falling off the tip of my tongue while I stare at the sunset, finding what I've been searching for. An orgasm settles low in my stomach, sharpening from the feel of my perilous existence hanging by a thread.

His tongue flicks at my clit skillfully, and it takes little effort to send me barreling over. My eyes roll, and a scream ricochets down the jagged rocks and into the water. It feels like I'm close behind, tumbling over the sharp points and into the depths of an ocean I'd gladly drown in.

It seems like hours before my body comes down, and right as I do, he's dragging me toward him and flipping me onto my stomach. Disoriented, I'm unable to resist when he pulls me up by my hips, settling me on my knees with my head still lowered and peeking over the cliff.

Gasping, I clutch tightly onto the edge, my fingers digging into dirt and rock as he comes down on me, pushing my chin clear past it. My thighs strain from the effort to keep from pitching forward.

His bare cock slides between the crevice of my ass, yet it feels like he's taunting me with a candy-coated bullet. Beneath the delicious illusion is a threatening vow capable of destroying me.

Fisting my hair, he tilts my head back the slightest bit, giving me a full view of the scenery, "Have you found absolution yet, baby? Or do you need my cock to give it to you?"

His dark words send a chill down my spine, and I shiver from how exquisite it feels.

"Life could never be complete without you," I moan.

A deep, rumbling growl reaches my ears before he pulls his hips back and sinks himself inside me, only getting a few inches in before it becomes too much. I yelp, the burn from his size causing me to screw my eyes shut.

Fucking hell, he needs goddamn dick reduction surgery.

I feel his answering grin as if hearing my thoughts, and I'm seconds away from throwing us both over the cliff just to spite him.

"You take it so fucking good, Adeline," he purrs in my ear, his tone devilish. "I will never get tired of the feel of your pussy succumbing to me, and how you cry so fucking pretty when it does."

On cue, a sharp moan releases from my throat as he inches himself in farther, my body succumbing to him just as he said.

"Keep watching," he says sinfully. Forcing my eyes open, I watch as the sun begins to crest the water, casting the world in a deep red glow.

He works himself inside me, pumping in and out slowly until he's seated completely to the hilt, confirming my own words.

I'm so full of him, and I've never felt more complete.

"You're searching for life inside that sunset, yet I seek death between your thighs," he rasps, his deep voice husky with desire.

Withdrawing to the tip, he thrusts inside me forcefully, and I cry out both from the bliss and the terror of being pushed over the edge.

But he doesn't relent and continues to fuck me, testing the strength of the earth beneath us with every stroke. He keeps his hand tightly curled in my hair, bringing me back every time his hips push me forward.

I trade between staring out at the water and looking down into the unforgiving rocks that seem to come closer and closer.

My vision blackens from the acute pleasure radiating between my thighs, and the sounds that release from my throat are uncontrollable.

"Oh my God," I sob, and he drives inside me so hard, my teeth clack from the force.

"You won't find God in the sun when he's already inside you," he growls, reaching beneath me to find my clit and strum it expertly while hitting that perfect spot inside me, abusing it relentlessly until I erupt, my body going limp from how powerfully I come for him.

"Zade!" I scream, and I no longer care if I live, as long as this feeling never dies.

He gnashes his teeth, savagely fucking me until he meets the demise he sought after. A roar tears from his throat and he drives inside me so deeply, the both of us nearly meet our end at the bottom of the cliff.

We'd haunt Parsons Manor together, and it's undeniable how much I love the sound of that.

"You have a spectacular forehead, my friend," Zade says, a cloud of smoke swirling from the depths of his mouth. Jeff is strapped to a metal chair, and Zade is sitting across from him, puffing on a cigarette with one hand, and bouncing a little bouncy ball off his forehead with the other.

"Where the hell did you even get the ball from?" I ask, shaking my head as it rebounds off Jeff's very red face again and back into Zade's awaiting hand.

Our captive is not a happy camper. He's seething at Zade, his entire body shaking from how heated he is.

He shrugs noncommittally. "I found it."

Okay. Whatever.

The sound of tires crunching through dirt and blades of grass distracts me, and my heart drops with both adrenaline and anticipation.

"Claire's here," I announce. Zade only bounces the ball again in response, his posture relaxed as always.

There are at least fifty men surrounding the area, all hidden from sight. If shit goes awry, we have plenty of backup.

"Jay, she got a battalion with her?" Zade asks him, the Bluetooth chip in his ear as always. He'll probably die with it in there. "…Three?

Someone's a nervous Nelly," he murmurs.

"Three cars?" I clarify, my anxiety worsening. Sweat forms on my hairline, and I can't tell if I'm nervous there's going to be a full-blown shoot-out or if I'm nervous to see Claire.

The lead-up to the confrontation is what sends my nerves into a tailspin. The anticipation of what's going to happen. Who's going to get hurt or die. Yet, in the midst of the chaos, I find peace, as if I'm standing in the eye of a hurricane.

I just hate the calm before the storm.

"Did you think she'd come alone?" Jeff snips, staring at me like I'm stupid. I narrow my eyes, tempted to rip that ball from Zade's hands and bounce it off his forehead myself. Then who'd look stupid?

Sensing my train of thought, Zade vaults the ball off his face without looking away from me, landing back into his hand perfectly, his grin deepening.

"Thank you." I look at Jeff. "Next time, it'll be a bullet."

Smartly, he keeps his mouth shut. I was so hoping he wouldn't.

Zade and I stand when car doors slam shut, the green ball dropping from his hand and rolling off into the distance, replaced by a gun. My own weapon is in my hand, my heart pounding heavily as we wait for Claire to enter.

Several nerve-racking moments later, the huge doors open, an entourage entering first, guns raised. Of course, when they spot us, they freeze, awaiting orders from the red-headed devil in the back, slowly breaking through her guards.

"Just as expected, Jeffrey. Did you really think you were convincing?" Claire's musical voice rings out, finally making her way out of the group. They crowd around her, uncomfortable with her being exposed in any capacity.

Just like she apparently wasn't stupid enough to believe Jeff actually captured us, she also wouldn't believe that we don't have the place surrounded by our own men.

It'll be a battle of whose bullet flies the quickest. Or whose aim is the truest.

My shoulders are tight with tension as I look over the evil bitch who's responsible for so many lost and broken souls. Her bright red hair is perfectly curled around her head, with matching lipstick and black liner smeared over her lids. She dons an all-white pantsuit, which is a message in itself. She expects to walk out of this building with her clothing just as pristine as when she walked in. No blood to be shed— at least not hers.

As fucking if.

A murderous rage arises—not because she had me kidnapped and nearly sold off to a wicked man, but because she went after my mother.

I guess I should thank her for the free therapy for my mommy issues. I'm not sure where we stand right now, but what I do know is there is a desire to fix our relationship that wasn't there before Claire turned my world over and fucked it sideways.

"Lovely to see you both again," she remarks, her tone posh, as if we're going on a stroll in a garden, holding our little teacups and biscuits.

Pious bitch. There's nothing classy about her nor the way she does business.

"Why did you come if you knew it was a trap?" I ask.

"This isn't going to end in bloodshed, my dear. I think it's time we settle this. Z has proven to be resourceful, as have I. Instead of... fighting each other, I think we can come to an agreement instead."

I train my gaze on Zade, who has his brow arched, but an otherwise blank expression.

Facing Claire again, I wonder if this is an attempt to get a target from one of the world's most dangerous men off her back. She's right—she *is* resourceful. The hag has an entire government at her disposal. But she is as weak as the shield she hides behind. Forced to use others to protect herself because she's incapable of doing it herself.

She only has the brains behind the operation, but not the strength. Whereas Zade... Zade has both brawn *and* brains.

Claire knows she can't hide on that island forever, not any longer than she can evade Zade's wrath. She's backed into a corner and knows that Zade would be hard to kill. She's met her match, and the only way out is with a bargain.

"Let's sit, shall we?"

"Let's," Zade murmurs, turning his back to grab the back of the chair Jeff is sitting in, literally dump him out of it, and motion for me to sit in it as if he's pulling out my seat in a fine-dining restaurant. Claire takes the one across from me, Jeffrey's bound body between us.

His face has turned a concerning shade of purple from both anger and embarrassment. Claire hardly glances his way, flicking her eyes to one of her men and ordering, "Dispose of him."

Seconds later, a bullet is sluicing through Jeff's brain and out the other side. He's dead before his head hits the floor.

Mine and Zade's gazes clash, an amused glint in his mismatched eyes as he grabs the third chair, twists it, and straddles it backwards, turning his intense gaze to Claire.

Her pulse thrums in her neck, and she works to swallow. I snort softly. If I didn't know any better, it seems that her lady bits are no more impervious to Zade than any other red-blooded woman. Given the chance, she would gladly fuck Zade before she put a knife in his throat.

"Before we start, how about we establish a mutual trust? All of my men are tucked away out of sight, not a single barrel down your throat, so how about you send your cronies to the door? They can stay if they must and will have a perfect shot at me, but they need to back the fuck off, yeah?"

Thinning her gaze, she considers Zade's request for a moment before acquiescing. Reluctantly, her guards spread out across the front entrance, ensuring they all have a perfect view of us.

"Lay it on me, Claire. What's your proposition?" Zade asks but then holds up a hand to stop her when she opens her mouth. "Make sure it's good, too. You had my girl kidnapped, raped, and tortured, and her mother nearly killed."

Her red-stained lips tighten into a firm line, seeming not to appreciate the reminder of all her wrong-doings. Makes me wonder how the fuck she sleeps at night. Or maybe she's secretly a reptile and doesn't need to. That's honestly more believable at this point.

"I will help you eliminate trafficking," Claire says. When Zade and I stay silent, processing her offer, she continues, "While the skin trade is vastly profitable, there is something more that I desire."

"And what is that?" Zade prompts, voice deep and low.

"Absolute control over the human population, of course. Right now, people are too self-aware of their useless existence. I want full power—us *both* to have full power."

My brow pinches, a nasty look on my face.

"To do what with?" he asks. "What exactly do you intend to do with this power?"

"Create a whole new era, of course. We can do anything we want. We could make their lives useful, give them a real purpose."

"And what would that purpose be?" I cut in. "To be mindless robots that would serve you?"

"Suffering would end," she snaps, turning her glacial green eyes to me. There really is no soul in there. "And this planet would thrive. If humans had real law and order, we could do so many things. End world hunger, close the gap between the poor and the rich, and lessen poverty and homelessness."

I shake my head. "You're trying to make taking away people's free will sound virtuous."

"It is," she retorts.

I blink, absolutely confounded. "Are we in a movie? There's no way you're serious." Turning to Zade, I find him staring at Claire, absently rubbing his fingers together, his brain churning. "She's serious, isn't she?"

He cocks a brow. "It would appear so."

More than anything, I'd love to know what he's thinking. This is something you only see in theaters or books. Some new world order shit that seems so far outside the realm of possibility, people turn it into fiction for entertainment. I've literally written books like this myself.

"You're exchanging one form of slavery for another," he says finally.

"I'm exchanging human suffering for a new, better world," she argues. "The technology you could create would advance us into an entirely new era." She turns her attention to me, and I realize she *is* a fucking reptile. She's a goddamn snake. "No one would ever suffer through what you have ever again. No more children sacrificed. No more women sold. I would dismantle it all."

"What's stopping you from doing this now?" I argue. "What's stopping you from trying to take over?"

"Zade," she answers simply, turning to address him. "You've been a thorn in my side since you created your organization and have set out to destroy everything I've worked hard for. And I'll admit, you're quite good at it, which is why I want to form an alliance where we're working together, not against each other. I will give you what you want so badly, and in return, you help me with what I want."

"Talk to me like I'm stupid, Claire," Zade says dryly. "You want me to stop exposing the government? No, you want more than that. You want me to create some type of technology to implant in people's brains and make them actual robots? Make it to where they have no fight?"

She raises her brows, a smile forming. "Now there's an idea. I can create a new world with laws and consequences for breaking them. Your technology could advance us and make it easier to enforce these laws. We could force people to walk in a straight line, wherever we draw it. But taking away their ability to think for themselves? My God, that'd be wonderful."

Her eyes alight with excitement. "Could you do that?"

I can only gape at her, utterly speechless. Does ending human trafficking sound like a dream? Absolutely. But in exchange for some fantastical idea to rip away people's free will and turn them into zombies.

I'm not even sure what exactly she'd do with them all, but I don't care to know. I want the same thing Zade has always wanted. To eradicate the skin trade. But that desire has never come with unrealistic expectations.

"Technology can do anything. Its only limitation is its creator," Zade says.

She grins, and I see something twinkle in her eye that she's stolen from so many. From me.

Hope.

But it doesn't belong to *her*—it belongs to the souls she's responsible for breaking.

"You see? We can do anything," she breathes. "I believe you have no limitations."

Zade's stare darkens, and the tightness in my chest eases.

"You're right, Claire. I don't."

She completely misinterprets his meaning because her smile only widens, too blinded by the possibilities to see what's lying in wait.

"You already have power," I remind her. "You're a shadow government that controls the entire country. More so now with your partners dead. That's not enough for you? Now you want world domination?"

She leans forward, baring her teeth as she hisses, "Maybe your puny brain isn—"

"You know what your problem is?" Zade cuts in. "You don't know the first fucking thing about forming an alliance. Do you really think insulting her is going to get you anywhere?" Zade stands, and though I can see Claire fighting with herself, she forces her spine straight. Her bodyguards take aim, but Zade moves as if he's encased in bulletproof armor.

My heart picks up speed, adrenaline surfacing because the bozo does *not*, in fact, have on bulletproof armor, and if one bullet comes anywhere near him, I'm going to fucking lose it.

"Belittling those who support you isn't smart. Haven't you read the history books? Using fear to demand respect is a fragile construct. It doesn't last because no one can trust you, and the first opportunity they have to betray you, they take. Z isn't built on fear, Claire. It's built on the mutual desire to kill people like you. And you know what? My organization trusts me to do that."

Her eyes widen, sensing the incoming doom before it happens. A line of bombs is planted along the front of the distillery, right below where Claire's men are standing. In seconds, the explosives detonate, creating a deafening blast.

The force of the explosion sends us back a step or two, and I cover my face as debris flies around us. We made sure the bomb wasn't so powerful that it'd send the building crashing down around us, but enough to blow someone—or *someones*—to pieces.

A few of her guards who were standing on the outskirts wriggle, missing limbs but still alive and set on going out in a blaze of glory. They're shot dead before they can lift their guns towards Zade and me, his team behind us and hiding in the depths of the distillery.

Zade seizes Claire by the throat and lifts her in the air, a snarl overtaking his face. Her eyes bulge as fire rages behind her, washing her in the very glow her soul will forever be consumed in.

"You sent my world crashing down around me just like this, remember? Setting off bombs and then taking Addie from me. How does it feel, Claire? To have come so close to succeeding, only for your soul to be ripped away instead?"

She kicks her legs desperately, trying and failing to gain some type of footing to relieve the chokehold Zade has her in. Clawing his skin, she leaves trails as red as the paint on her nails.

"Would you like to do the honors, baby?" he asks, looking over his shoulder at me with eyes as bright as the fire before us. Something deep and carnal flickers in my stomach, and I can't deny the excitement thrumming in my bloodstream any more than Zade can.

"Yes," I smile, approaching the pair. He readjusts, gripping Claire by the nape and holding her in place, despite her desperate efforts to get away. Clutching my black and purple knife tightly, I lift it to her throat, pressing until blood sprouts beneath the blade.

This woman is responsible for every one of my demons. I was fairly normal before the Society laid eyes on me. And while fear and adrenaline always did something inexplicable to me, the thought of murdering someone was repulsive. It was something I rallied against when Zade came into my life, and even when I fell in love with him, it was something that I hadn't fully accepted yet.

And now look—she's faced with her own creation, an angel of death with a knife to her throat and intoxicated by the sight of her blood.

"Please!" she begs shrilly. "We can work something out!"

"You reap what you sow, Claire," I say, then slowly slice the knife across her throat, cutting through sinew and muscle. Blood splatters across my face, but I rejoice in the feel of it. I stop right before the jugular, wanting her death to be a slow and painful one.

Will it be her own life flashing before her eyes or all the ones that she stole?

I hope they come down from paradise and personally drag her to fucking Hell.

Slowly suffocating on her blood, Zade drags her over to the raging fire in the front of the distillery, her men's dead bodies scattered.

Claire's fight increases, and even amid death, she can feel when it's only going to get worse. Pausing before a fire, Zade grips her bloody throat in his fist and lifts her, staring into her wide, desperate eyes.

"Fucking burn, bitch," he growls, then vaults her into it, her body instantly consumed in flames.

Choked screaming arises, but the sounds can hardly make it through. Her form convulses and thrashes, and I wrinkle my nose at the rancid stench that follows.

She walked into this place firmly believing she could conquer the world if only she gave Zade the one thing he's been working so hard for.

Doesn't she know?

Zade is a God.

And the only one who will conquer this world is him.

Chapter Forty Three
The Diamond

Sibby dances in the living room, her polka-dot covered feet swirling across the checkered tile, rejoicing in our long-awaited success, while Zade is on the television, interrupting another broadcast.

He exposed the shadow government and their control over human trafficking, stealing children and women, and selling them off for sick people. In the ten minutes he's been speaking, he gave the world hope that the sex trade will slowly begin to die.

"Claire Williams is not the first to contribute to the sickness that infects our world, nor is she the last. One by one, I will disinfect the pests from society, and only then will we find peace. I am Z, and I am watching."

He cuts out, once more replaced by a wide-eyed reporter, a nervous laugh tinkling from her throat.

"Who's going to take over Claire's spot?" Daya asks from beside me, shoving a handful of popcorn into her mouth.

I arch a brow. "You think there should still be a shadow government?" I ask curiously, grabbing my own handful and stuffing it in my face.

Daya shrugs, swallowing before answering. "Sure. I think the government should definitely be controlled by somebody, just not a person that is only interested in fixing things in this world for their own gain. We need someone who cares about the environment and advancing science and medicine without inhumane experimentation and quite literally using us as slaves. I think we've had enough of that shit in our history. This planet needs to be cleansed badly, and the people in charge right now? They're not going to be the ones to do it."

I purse my lips. "I think you're right. I just don't know who would do it."

"You don't think Zade would?"

Shaking my head, I chew on a few half-popped kernels. They're my favorite part of eating popcorn.

"It's hard to say for sure, but I think Zade enjoys what he does now too much. Regardless of who's in power, it's going to take a very long time for human trafficking to actually end. I can't see him being content sitting behind a desk making decisions rather than being on the field and physically taking them down."

Daya nods, her sage green eyes drifting back to the screen, the reporters still attempting to regain their footing after Zade's interruption. Media is controlled by the government, which means everything they spew to the public is sanctioned by the very people Zade is threatening to destroy. It's no wonder they're uncomfortable when they're quite literally the mouths that feed us the government's brainwashing bullshit.

"I'll do it," Sibby chirps, topping off her announcement with a ballerina spin.

Daya and I glance at each other.

"You would want to rule the government? You're mentally unstable, Sibby," I say bluntly.

She stops spinning and narrows her eyes at me. I've sparred with her far too much to legitimately be scared of her anymore.

"I care about the world and cleansing it of demons. Can you imagine?" A wide, dreamy smile spreads across her face. "Living in a world of flowers? One big garden, just like the planet should be."

"See? Unstable."

She growls at me and stomps her foot. "I could do it, Addie. I know I have a temper, and that I'd need help. But I could fix this world," she tells me vehemently.

Cocking my head, I actually consider what she's saying. Sibby's methods would need to be controlled, but… she's admittedly the most fanatical person I've ever met when it comes to ridding the world of evil. Is that actually possible? Of course not. But maybe having someone who believes it is, wouldn't be so bad. And with her knack for smelling the ones who are rotten, she could have a team of people helping her who have good intentions.

"What would you do?" I wonder.

"Wait, you actually think she could do it?" Daya cuts in incredulously, her eyes bouncing between Sibby and me.

Grinning, I shrug a shoulder. "She would be better than Claire. And she wouldn't do it alone. Her entire purpose in life is to better this world, is it not?"

Daya's lips part, floundering for an objection but coming up with none. Really, anyone put in that position of power could be argued against. There's no perfect person out there. Sibby isn't without sin, but her intentions are pure.

Oddly, she'd be the least likely to go on a power trip or be negatively influenced.

She's too… passionate.

A light knock on the door pulls my attention away from training with Sibby. Of course, her fist is powering into my cheek a second later, nearly sending me toppling over.

Ears ringing, I grab the side of my face and glare at her. She smiles wildly at me, and she doesn't even need to open her stupid mouth for me to know what she's going to say.

Never look away from your opponent.

I point at her. "Never sleep with two eyes closed, how about that?"

She giggles, and heads towards the steps while I make my way to the front door, sweating profusely and my head now pounding. It pisses me off enough that I whip open the door without bothering to look who's outside first.

My eyes widen when I find a strange man I've never seen before standing next to my mother.

I gape at them, too blindsided to do much else. As always, her blonde hair is perfectly coifed with a layer of light pink lipstick brightening her lips. And she's staring at me, waiting for me to speak, but I'm incapable.

"Hey, honey," Mom says, smiling weakly at me.

Finally shaking myself out of the stupor, my body moves on autopilot.

Leaning forward, I wrap her in the world's most gentle hug, wary of her wound but so fucking glad to see her. Tears spring to my eyes, blurring my vision as my sinuses burn from the effort to keep them at bay.

She pats my back. "Sweetheart, you stink."

"Sorry," I say, but I'm not the least bit sorry at all. Blinking back the tears, I step away.

Normally, she'd turn her nose up at me, but it stays firmly in its place. It's relieving when I haven't seen or talked to her since the day we brought her home over a month ago. I've stopped calling my father, deciding that hearing his insults wouldn't be healing for any of us.

"Why are you here? Where's Dad? And who are you?" I question, directing the last one towards the stranger standing next to her.

Now that I'm looking at him, I'm even more confused. Light brown hair, the top messy and unruly, pretty blue eyes, and a killer smile. Almost as killer as his body. He can't be any older than I am, yet he carries himself with refined confidence—something most men my age don't possess.

An odd feeling prickles at my senses, though I can't discern exactly what.

All I know is he's fucking hot. What the hell is my mother doing with him?

"Kraven," he answers with a smirk.

"Oh my God, is this your boyfriend?" I ask, eyes wide.

"Adeline Reilly, don't be inappropriate. Of course, he isn't. He's been helping take care of me while I recover. Now let me in, I have ten seconds before I fall at your doorstep and don't get up again."

Dramatic as ever, I see.

Kraven smiles, dimples appearing as he grabs my mother's arm and helps her into the house and toward the red leather couch. Dumbly, I watch them pass by, wondering how the hell she convinced my father to let someone else nurse her back to health. Especially someone who looks like... that.

And that may not be her boyfriend, but with the way her cheeks redden, she's definitely not unaffected by him. In all honesty, if my mother ended up with a younger man… good for her.

I'd be proud.

Snapping myself out of it, I close the front door and take a seat across from her. Sibby is probably upstairs showering, and Zade is currently tracking down a dark web user who has a knack for torturing children on a live video feed.

When I'm not training with Sibby, I'm working on my new story. I've missed writing, and it's served as an excellent escape now that Claire is finally dead. Pretty soon, I'll be done with my first book since being home again, and I wholeheartedly believe it's my best writing to date.

"How are you feeling?" I ask her, glancing at Kraven.

"Irritated," she huffs. "Your father is driving me nuts."

I tighten my lips, a stabbing pain in my chest with the reminder of him, but also oddly comforted that she finds him just as ridiculous as I do.

"Does he know you're here?" I ask.

"Would it change a damn thing if he did?" she retorts. There goes her nose—hiking up in the air with superiority. It brings a smile to my face.

"I tried to see you," I murmur.

She visibly softens. "I know you did, honey. I was too weak to do much, but I didn't agree with your father. Regardless of your horrible taste in men, you're my daughter and always will be."

I give her a droll look. "Clearly, I'm not the only one with horrible taste in men," I say pointedly.

She pauses, and then surprises me by chuckling. Now it feels like I'm the one with the gunshot wound. I mean, I'm funny, I know this. But my mother has never thought so.

"I suppose not," she concedes. "Where is your boyfriend, by the way? I'd like to thank him."

My brows jump in surprise, and now I wonder if Sibby hit me so hard that it sent me into an alternate universe.

"Don't you give me that look," she sasses. "He may be a bad influence, but he saved my life. So did that nice doctor of his."

"He's not here right now, but I'll let him know."

She nods stiffly, glancing at the ceiling when the floorboards above creak.

That may have been Sibby, but it also may not have been. Maybe it was Gigi—I haven't seen her in a while. But that's the fun in Parsons Manor. You just never really know.

Shifting uncomfortably, I open my mouth, readying for another apology, but she holds up a hand, silencing me.

"I know what you're going to say. Another thing your atrocious father was wrong about. It wasn't your fault I was shot, Adeline. I don't remember much about what happened, and I'm grateful for it. But what I do know is that man was holding a gun to your head. And if taking a bullet in the chest means that my daughter doesn't have one through her skull and is six feet under... then it was worth it."

My lip trembles, fresh tears lining my eyelids. I dip my chin, working to gather my composure before I'm reduced to a blubbering mess.

"Thank you," I whisper, my voice tight and raspy.

When I meet her gaze, it's soft and almost sad. It only makes my chest ache more.

Clearing my throat, I wipe beneath my tears, preparing to change the subject.

"So uh, Kraven, why'd your parents name you that?"

Mom sighs, shaking her head at my rudeness. Whatever.

It's a valid question.

He grins. "It's my father's name," he answers shortly. Vaguely.

"Okay, Kraven Jr., what company do you work for?"

"Addie," Mom snaps, but I ignore her. Also, a valid question.

"My mother is a traveling home health nurse, and with the patients' permission, I tag along to help sometimes." He shrugs a shoulder, glancing at my mother. "We all got along great, so when Serena needs assistance running errands or getting around, I give her a hand."

Mom smiles warmly. "His mother is an absolute angel, and Kraven has been a gem, too. Your dad has been working a lot again, so the extra hand has been a big help."

Relaxing, I nod my head, relieved that she's been taken care of so well.

I'm typically not a suspicious person, but my fighting skills haven't been the only thing I've fine-tuned over the months. My instincts are sharp, and though I don't necessarily get a bad vibe from Kraven, I do feel like he's not all he makes himself out to be.

Before I can get another word out, Sibby comes storming down the steps, hair wet from the shower, fresh-faced, and dressed in a royal blue t-shirt dress and big, pink bunny slippers on her feet.

Right when she goes to say something, she freezes, her entire body locking. As if in slow motion, her eyes slide to Kraven, widening when their gazes clash.

"What the hell are you doing here?" she snaps.

Goddammit. I knew there was something off about him.

Brows hiked, I turn to Mom's caretaker, finding him just as surprised as Sibby.

"I could ask you the same thing, Sibel."

Epilogue
The Hunter

"**S**till can't find her?" I ask Daya, glancing up at her as I pick at my salad. I knock my fork into a crouton, watching it tumble off my plate.

She twists her lips, a flash of guilt in her green eyes.

"No," she admits. "No wonder she got away with murder for so long. She really knows how to fucking disappear."

I nod my head, fighting to keep the frustration at bay. It's not Daya's, or Jay's, or even my fault that we can't find her. The little demon-slayer knows how to hide—she's been doing it for too long to make the mistake of getting caught a second time.

Three months ago, Sibby disappeared. We don't know where she is, but we do know that Kraven is with her.

Addie said that when Kraven came with Serena to visit, she knew something was different about him. And then, when Sibby saw him, it was like watching a ghost materialize right before her eyes.

They didn't say much, most likely because Addie and Serena were watching, but apparently, they said all they needed to silently.

That night, she left while Addie and I were asleep. And we haven't seen either of them since. Kraven disappeared without a word as well, and both his and Addie's mother have been worried sick.

"She's going to give me gray hair," I mutter, stabbing my fork into a leafy green.

Daya plays with the gold hoop in her nose, the corners of her eyes tight as she and Addie exchange a look.

While Sibby is good at hiding, the fact that my facial recognition program hasn't spotted her on a single fucking camera across the entire. Fucking. World for *three months*—the girls presume she's dead.

But I refuse to fucking believe that. Fuck that.

I know she's out there; I just wish I knew what the hell she's up to.

"She'll turn up," Addie chips in, though she doesn't sound confident. She picks at her salad and murmurs, "She always knows how to surprise us."

Tightening my lips, her words remind me of the little secret I have burning a hole in my back pocket. If I hide this from her, not only will I not be able to live with it, but she would also be hurt if she ever found out. And as much as I like to cause Addie pain, it's only pleasurable when it ends in her coming all over my face or cock.

Groaning internally, I bite the bullet and say, "Speaking of surprises."

Her caramel eyes lift with confusion, and I reach into my pocket, pull out the note and toss it to her. Brow furrowing, she picks it up and quickly reads it over, her eyes gradually widening as she registers what it says.

Slowly, her round stare drifts to me, and I arch a brow.

"It was in the mail. But I think I still need convincing, if you ask me," I tell her, referring to the note. Her mouth quirks up, and the surprise slowly fades into relief.

And I guess I can live with her being happy, even if it's a fucking dickhead that's causing it.

Addie thrashes violently, her hand coming within scant inches of my face as an agonized scream releases from her tongue, followed by what sounds like Xavier's name. My vision blackens, and I'm furious that the monsters polluting her nightmares aren't *me*.

I'm the only monster allowed to haunt her fucking dreams.

Gritting my teeth, I grab her flailing arm and roll her to her side, facing away from me. Tucking her arm into her chest, I pull her tightly against me.

Her naked flesh slides against mine, eliciting a carnal desire deep in my chest. It goes beyond claiming her. I want to possess her. Mark her. Embed myself so deeply inside her that there is no Adeline Reilly outside of me anymore.

I prop myself up on my elbow and release her arm to spit on my fingers and rub the wetness across my cock. Breathing in deep, I sink myself inside her, pinching my eyes shut from both the burn from the friction and how fucking good she feels.

She wakes with a startled yelp, her pulse thrumming in her neck and pussy clenching around my length. I bite back a groan, too enraptured by the panicked look in her eyes and her visible shaking.

"Zade?" she whispers, voice hoarse from her screaming.

I thrust my hips once, eliciting a sharp gasp from her plump lips. She tenses, then relaxes, molding the curve of her ass deeper into me.

"Do you feel me, baby?" I whisper, gliding my hand up her stomach, through the valley between her breasts, and to her delicate throat. Her pulse thrashes against her flesh, and I can feel every heartbeat through the column of her neck.

Still heavily panting, she wets her lips before breathing out, "Yes. I feel you."

I hum. "Who owns this pussy, Adeline?" I ask darkly.

"You," she whispers, the answer automatic.

"Good girl," I murmur. "The man in your head isn't the monster, little mouse. I am. Every time you scream out another's name, I will replace it with my own. And I don't care how much it fucking hurts."

I roll my hips into her, and she shudders against me, whimpers falling from her lips.

The moonlight spears through the balcony doors, painting our bodies in a soft aura only heaven can create. My eyes trace the curves of our bodies, soft lines that separate her soul from mine.

Two beings, scarred and desecrated, yet we look like fucking art. A masterpiece even da Vinci couldn't do justice. I want to pin her to the wall and show her what art looks like when it's fueled by passion.

"When you're scared and can hardly breathe, this is where I'll be. Deep inside of you. Whether I'm with you physically, or in your heart, I'm always going to be there."

She shivers, and I withdraw my hips before driving deep inside her, pulling out a husky moan from her throat.

My control slips, and I let myself break for a moment, my head falling back, eyes rolling, and a groan escaping from the feel of her perfect cunt wrapped around me.

Goddamn nirvana.

Dropping my chin, I trace the curve of her thrumming neck with my lips, then bite down right over her pulse like a man possessed. Her fear tastes so much better than I imagined.

She inhales sharply, and I slide my mouth up to her ear, enamored by the way she shivers beneath me.

"I will chase away your demons, Adeline, and they will run and hide because I'm fucking scarier."

I thrust inside of her deeply to emphasize my point, earning a sharp gasp. Her hand slaps down on my hip, sliding back until her claws dig into my ass.

"Zade," she whispers, arching her back and grinding into me.

Biting back another groan, I lift her leg and hook my arm beneath her knee, keeping my thrusts short and hard and hitting that sweet spot inside of her that makes her pussy weep. Addie's eyes roll, sleep-addled moans filling the room and inside my chest, spurring me to fuck her harder and faster.

I anchor her leg higher by sliding my hand up to her throat and squeezing tightly, eliciting higher-pitched moans with the new angle. I clench my teeth, overcome with a rainfall of emotions. Rage. Love. Need. *Obsession.*

As they swell and magnify, my hand ascends up her neck and to the underside of her jaw.

"Look at me while I ruin you, Adeline."

Grip harsh, I jerk her face towards mine, capturing her wide caramel pools with my own.

"You will always be mine," I growl. "Even in your fucking nightmares."

A cry rolls past her lips, but she doesn't shy away. No, she meets each and every one of my thrusts with a force of her own.

Pleasure races down my spine, gathering at the base and nearly blinding me with ecstasy.

"Oh my God, Zade, please," she pleads breathlessly.

Releasing her jaw, I slide my hand down the planes of her stomach to her drenched pussy, the tips of my fingers teasing her clit.

"You pray so pretty, little mouse," I murmur. "But I want to hear you screaming for mercy."

I pull out of her, my dick protesting loudly, and it's almost painful to roll away from her to dig through the nightstand.

"What are you doing?" she groans, and I just know her pussy is clenching, searching for me.

Grabbing what I need, I tuck her back into my arms. Her chin rests on her shoulder as she tries to figure out what I'm up to. She looks fucking divine slathered in the moonlight, and it almost distracts me.

Uncapping the lube, I soak my dick in the liquid, gritting my teeth as I spread it down my length. Still reeling from the loss of her pussy, my hips thrust into my hand involuntarily like a savage with no restraint.

It's like I've always told her—I have no fucking control with her.

"Zade," she draws out, alarm bells ringing in the tone of her voice.

Before tossing the bottle over my shoulder, I squirt a generous dollop of lube onto my fingers, then slide them down through the crevice of her ass. She inhales sharply as I coat her backside, and whimpers as I plunge a finger inside, then another, stretching her and preparing her for what's to come. She shudders, and whether it's from surprise or fear, she's incapable of doing anything else but gasp for breath.

I take my time stretching her, nipping along her shoulders, and leaving love bites while wringing little mewls from her throat. By the time I withdraw, she's panting, and her muscles are loose. I slide my hand beneath her thigh and lift it up once more.

"Wait," she breathes. "You are way too big. I don't know if I can handle it."

"Your body was fucking made for me. So you're going to be a good girl and fucking take it."

I just know fear is trickling through her bloodstream now, and her pussy is fucking soaked in response. She's nervous, yet she keeps those little white teeth glued shut.

Smart girl.

"Do you trust me?" I ask, amused when her eyes snap to mine, sharp knives shooting from them.

"I trust you with my life. But do I trust you not to rip me in half? Absolutely not."

I grin, baring my teeth in a savage smile. "You get off on my pain, don't you, Addie?"

Before she can protest, I position the head of my cock at her tight entrance and gently push in. Her eyes pop open, the pain registering as I slowly stretch her. My fingers are working her clit immediately, balancing the agony with pleasure.

"Zade," she breathes, a war raging within her. Her nails are digging into my outer thigh again as I breach past the tight ring and slowly sink myself inside her.

Groaning, I bite her shoulder, nearly vibrating with the need to both draw blood and fuck her ass until she's sobbing.

Somehow, I refrain from both. As much as I love to hurt her, I have no desire to do so without bringing her pleasure, too.

Methodically, I work myself inside her until there's nothing more of me to give.

"Fuck, baby, you take it so fucking good," I praise. "That's it, good girl, open up for me."

She fists the sheets, and like a flower blooming beneath the sunlight, her entire body relaxes, accepting me inside her as if it's the only thing that gives her life.

We're both trembling, on the precipice of shattering from how tightly we're fitted together. I give her thirty seconds—a small increment of time to adjust. It's all the control I possess.

Releasing a deep breath right when I hit that mark in my head, I withdraw to the tip before driving back inside of her. She yelps, and I circle her clit harder, earning a sexy little whimper that has me tensing with need.

"I own every part of you, Adeline. And I will make you feel me for fucking days when I'm done with you." I set a steady pace, her body like soft clay beneath my insistent hands, and I mold her into me until the two of us become one.

"God," she moans, her voice choked with pleasure.

"That's it, keep moaning my name. I'll take us home to paradise if you pray hard enough," I taunt, fucking her harder.

"Oh, God, like that," she gasps, her head kicking back. "Right there, Zade."

I growl, pleasure pooling in the base of my spine, the sounds of our flesh smacking arising.

"Look at you, taking my cock like a good little whore," I rasp. "You're squeezing me so tight, it's like you can't stand to lose me."

"Yes," she mewls, her voice husky and cracking with desire.

"Yeah? You want it deeper?"

She pants, nodding her head eagerly, and it's all I can do to not spill inside of her.

I flip her onto her stomach and roll on top of her, then lift her hips until she's on her knees. Her gasp turns sharp when I slide back inside her tight ass, the angle allowing me to fuck her deeper.

"Oh, fuck," she breathes, ending it in a high-pitched cry. She jerks forward, almost as if to pull away, but I tighten my hold on her hips, refusing to let her escape.

"Can you take it, little mouse?" I challenge. "I know how much you love to run, but I want to see what it looks like when you stay."

Panting, she slams back into me, causing my head to kickback from the utter bliss. It takes a few seconds to gather my wits, on the precipice of losing it altogether.

"There's my good little whore," I murmur, then I begin to move, gradually quickening my pace, making sure to not injure her.

"Zade…" she moans, long and loud while I fuck her faster, spurred on by the way she arches her back, nearly begging for more.

Soon, she's meeting my thrusts again, and the pleasure that settled in the base of my spine swells. I crowd over her, one hand fisting cinnamon strands and bending her head back until our mouths touch, while my other slips beneath her and finds her swollen clit again, delighting in the way she begins to sob.

Sweat coats our skin, and the vulgar sounds deriving from where I fuck her battle with the sharp noises from flesh hitting flesh. Yet, her screams rise above it all, filling the room and entwining with my own moans, a crescendo of pleasure echoing throughout Parsons Manor.

I trade between kissing and nipping her lips and hovering above them, swallowing every fucking syllable she produces.

She tenses, and her tight ass clenches around my cock as she nears her climax. I rub her clit faster, desperately chasing her toward it so I can send us both flying.

Her eyes roll, and she shudders as if a demon is being exorcised from her body. And then she breaks. A scream releases from her throat, the tortured sound bleeding into my name.

"*Fuck,* Addie!"

My head kicks back, and an orgasm rocks through me, stealing my breath and vision. I'm blind from how deeply it crashes through me, ropes of cum filling her so thoroughly, it leaks past her entrance and pools beneath us.

The sounds that burst from my throat are unrestrained, my voice hoarse with all-consuming ecstasy.

It takes several minutes for my sight to return, and when it does, I find Addie on her stomach, heaving for breath and appearing on the verge of blacking out.

Struggling to catch my own breath, I gently pull out of her and flop onto my back, my head still swimming.

But I refuse to leave her like that, so I force myself up and into the bathroom where I grab a small cloth and wet it with warm water.

When I return to her, I gently clean her up, making sure there's no blood from any tearing. I'll have to get some ointment for her anyway since she'll be sore.

"Next time," she mumbles into the bed. "I'm running from you."

I grin, reaching over to grab a rose from the nightstand and then tuck it in her ear, whispering, "You know how much I love to chase you, baby."

"You're a menace," she grumbles, grabbing the rose from her hair and twirling the smooth stem in her fingers. She gasps when a ring falls from it and rolls onto the bed.

As if it's a spider, she hesitantly picks it up, spinning it to get a good look. It's a white gold band shaped in a vine with tiny white jewels encrusted into it. The band forms into a rose made up of bright red rubies.

"There aren't any diamonds in it," I murmur.

She swallows, and croaks, "Are you proposing because you're in love with me or because I gave you anal?"

I tip my head back, a laugh working from my throat. And when I drop my head down again, a smile still on my face, she's sliding the ring onto her finger.

"Don't answer that. You'll make me change my mind if you say it's because you're in love with me. I want to be rewarded for the anal."

My grin widens, and I roll her over to me, kissing her bare shoulder. "I do love you, you know?"

"I know," she whispers. "And I'll marry you anyway because I love you, too."

I'll never get tired of hearing her say that.

"Hey, Zade?"

"Yeah, baby?"

"Thank you for bringing me the happy vapors."

I bite my lip, feeling my chest crack from how fucking addicted I am to this girl.

I was wrong.

Heaven isn't a place you go to when you die, it's inside the person that's worth dying for.

"Addie?"

"Yeah?"

I bring my mouth close to her ear, delighting in the way she shivers. I'm already hard for her again, my obsession limitless.

"Run, little mouse."

I don't know what you did to convince
him and I don't really want to know.

Thank you for saving Katerina and keeping
her safe. But fuck you for sparing my life.
Especially cause I think you did it to fucking
spite me, and I can't even blame you for that.

Stay safe, princesa

If you enjoyed the Cat and Mouse Duet, then you will love my enemies
to lovers standalone, Does It Hurt?
Scan below to buy!

Want sneak peaks, exclusive offers, and giveaways?
Join my Facebook group H. D. Carlton's Warriors!

MORE BOOKS BY H. D. CARLTON

ACKNOWLEDGMENT

I have a lot of people to thank, but I always start with my readers. You all are the light of my life, and I am so very grateful for each and every one of you. Thank you for continuing to support me, even when I have trouble understanding why.

To my alphas—May, Amanda, and Tasha—you three are probably sick of me by now. I complain a lot, and gripe about how badly I suck and how awful these books are, and y'all just continue to shoulder it. But seriously, I don't know what I'd do without any of you. Probably have even shittier books. I think I'd actually die without you guys, and I will never ever find the words in the dictionary to express how much I love you guys. Don't ever leave me.

A special thanks to Autumn for getting this book on track. You helped me with this book more than you know, and I will forever be grateful for you. And to my other betas, thank you for putting up with such a shoddy version of these books and help making them better.

Angie—I don't know why the hell you put up with me, either, but I'm greedy and will forever keep you anyway. Thank you for sticking by me and always being so damn reliable, warm, and just a fantastic friend. I love you.

Rumi—you're stuck with me, too. Thank you for doing such an incredible job cleaning this hunky-monkey up and making it purdy.

Of course, a special thanks to Cat for these BEAUTIFUL covers, and to Chelsea for making the guts look pretty.

Last not but not least, thank you to Victor, who pretty much manages my brain and keeps this author thing from crashing and failing, then exploding. I love you.

ABOUT THE AUTHOR

H. D. Carlton is an International and USA Today Bestselling author. She lives in Ohio with her partner, two dogs, and cat. When she's not bathing in the tears of her readers, she's watching paranormal shows and wishing she was a mermaid. Her favorite characters are of the morally gray variety and believes that everyone should check their sanity at the door before diving into her stories.

Learn more about H. D. Carlton on hdcarlton.com.
Join her newsletter to receive updates, teasers, giveaways, and special deals here.

Facebook
Twitter
Instagram
Goodreads

Printed in Great Britain
by Amazon

27483847R00370